Praise for Thirty Days

'This wry Belgian writer takes a sharp, very human look at how lives meander and collide. For all the serious issues it explores, it is also very funny and astute: a fearless exposé of the world we live in'
The Irish Times

'*Thirty Days* is a novel about goodness and compassion. The book finds the perfect balance between sensitivity and humor, hopefulness and criticism, cheer and despair'
Flanders Literature

'*Thirty Days* is a slice of life so compelling and warm that I stayed up far too late to finish it'
KATE MACDONALD, author of *Anne of Green Gables Cookbook*

'A dialogue for our tough and fickle times. Read it slowly. Put it aside. Read it again'
DAVID VAN REYBROUCK, author of *Congo*

'Annelies Verbeke is a literary phenomenon'
EDINBURGH BOOK FESTIVAL

'A superb narrative. This is a Verbeke that should not be missed'
De Volkskrant

'A courageous, inspiring, and poignant book'
De Standaard

'A novel that for all its lightness of touch is profound, funny, serious, absurdist, and engaged'
De Groene Amsterdammer

'Every novel by Annelies Verbeke is an adventure, but with the surprising and stunningly beautiful *Thirty Days* she sums up all the limitations of human existence magnificently. A masterpiece'
Feeling

'Verbeke has a wonderful knack of bringing characters vividly to life in a few expertly chosen evocative words, through gesture, knowing looks and clever metaphors'
The Big Issue

'Verbeke has pulled out all the stops to paint a lively story. *Thirty Days* is a polygonal star whose points are expertly connected'
Literair Nederland

ANNELIES VERBEKE is a writer of novels, short stories and plays. She made her literary debut in 2003 with the much-lauded novel *Slaap!* ('Sleep!'), which sold over 75,000 copies and was published in 22 countries. Verbeke's books have received numerous awards and nominations: *Thirty Days* was chosen as best Dutch novel of 2015 by readers of a leading Dutch newspaper, awarded the F. Bordewijk Award and Opzij Literature prize for best novel, and nominated for the ECI Literature Prize. Two years later her short story collection *Halleluja* was also on the shortlist of the ECI Literature Prize and won the J.M.A. Biesheuvel Prize for the best short story collection of the year. Her work has been compared to that of Katherine Mansfield. She lives in Ghent, Belgium.

After finishing her studies at the University of Manchester, LIZ WATERS (UK) worked for some years with English-language texts and at a literary agency in Amsterdam before becoming a full-time translator of literary fiction and non-fiction. Authors whose books she has translated include Linda Polman, Fik Meijer, Paul Scheffer, Lieve Joris, Jaap Scholten, Luuk van Middelaar, and Douwe Draaisma. Recently published are her translations of *A Foolish Virgin* by Ida Simons and *The Many Lives of Jan Six* by Geert Mak.

Thirty Days

Annelies Verbeke

Thirty Days

Translated from the Dutch
by Liz Waters

WORLD EDITIONS
New York, London, Amsterdam

Published in the USA in 2018 by World Editions LLC, New York
Published in the UK in 2016 by World Editions Ltd., London

World Editions
New York/London/Amsterdam

Printed by Sheridan, Chelsea, MI, USA

This book is a work of fiction. Any resemblance to actual persons,
living or dead, or actual events is purely coincidental.

Library of Congress Cataloging in Publication Data is available.

ISBN 978-1-64286-005-4

First published as *Dertig Dagen* in the Netherlands in 2015 by
De Geus.

This project has been funded with support from the European
Commission. This publication reflects the views only of the author,
and the Commission cannot be held responsible for any use which
may be made of the information contained herein.

Co-funded by the
Creative Europe Program
of the European Union

The translation of this book is funded by the Flemish Literature Fund
(Vlaams Fonds voor de Letteren – www.flemishliterature.be)

Vlaams
Fonds
voor de
Letteren

Twitter: @WorldEdBooks
Facebook: WorldEditionsInternationalPublishing
www.worldeditions.org

How with this rage shall beauty hold a plea
Whose action is no stronger than a flower

WILLIAM SHAKESPEARE, *Sonnet LXV*

30

He drives through the hot, clear weather, through a landscape that remains foreign to him but that he's hesitantly starting to love. Sometimes he still misses the city, the colours, the sounds, the distractions. Here it's different, not worse. The blossom and buzz of spring turned into a promising summer that fled an excess of rain before coming back to confound the approaching autumn. The fields are still sodden. As if not growing dull and blotchy, the crowns of the trees nod with restrained bravura at the sky, incessantly: bring it on. Hop poles bear fat baubles, drunk on themselves, ready for harvest. Lonely dust whips up and catches in puddles. Roundabout art plumbs the depths. He's not sure whether all of this strengthens or stupefies him.

In a village shared by France and Belgium he sees two men with flat caps and baskets, of pigeons, perhaps. Apart from that, many ponies and a farmer, his glistening tractor circled by seagulls. The other people are hard to see. They're behind front walls, or, like him, in cars, between front walls.

Today he's expected in a nice neighbourhood. In this region the houses are fewer than in the other scraps and patches that make up this small country. With its liking for red brick it keeps things simple. Just the occasional Spanish hacienda among the mock farmhouses—he's yet to spot any pagodas from the Brussels Periphery. The cacophony of building styles, so frequently written off as tasteless, has always cheerily endeared him, the way the houses stand next to each other like twelve-year-olds on their first day at high school, thrown by pure chance into long-term togetherness, adrift in their desperation. It pleases him to see the two modern houses where he parks his van leap out of the monotony.

He lifts the tub of sponges, cloths, rollers, and brushes out of the back of the van and selects one of the pots of paint he's put ready. Pick Nick, from the Joie de Vivre collection, for the largest of the kitchen walls: his suggestion; their approval.

'Alphonse!' he hears as he crosses stone slabs in trimmed grass to the front door of one of the houses.

It's the woman who lives here, a beautiful woman with a confident voice. He met her the evening they chose the colours. Her sportswear looks new, the fabrics showing no trace of exertion, and the sweat has beaded only at her temples, in the margins of her hair, which is held in a ponytail. She gives an awkward wave. He puts down the paint pot to shake her cold hand.

'Not been here long, I hope?' she asks. 'My husband's taking our daughter to school and I thought I'd just have time for a run, but part of the route was under water and I missed a turning.'

'Only just got here,' he says.

He's come to repaint their kitchen and living room. He estimated three days, but now he suspects he'll have it done sooner; they've made meticulous preparations. The curtains and socket covers are off, the furniture is in the middle of the room, draped with sheets, and the long kitchen worktop is empty.

A black dog runs at him in ecstasy, skidding and

banging its head on a table leg before continuing with undiminished bounce on its original course.

'Björn!' the woman shouts.

'Hi Björn,' he says. Tail wagging, the dog snuffles at his outstretched hand, then farts and turns round to investigate, shocked.

The woman joins in his laughter, until Björn's frenzy reignites and she drags the animal by the collar to the neighbouring room, where she shuts him in. 'I think he's got a multiple personality!' she shouts above the distraught howling behind the door. 'And he misses the cat. Benny. Benny and Björn! As in ABBA?!'

The dog bears more resemblance to a late-1970s hard rocker, thinks Alphonse.

'They were inseparable. When dogs and cats grow up together they can get to be friends!'

'Cats mostly live longer than dogs!' he shouts back.

'She was murdered!' and because Björn ends his dirge while she's saying it, she repeats: 'Our cat was murdered.'

It's the denouement of a story she's eager to tell, a long story that smoulders behind her lips, but this is too soon—she swallows it on hearing her husband's car.

The husband too has an athletic build. A swimmer.

'Hey, the Fons!' he says, as if they've known each other for years, and raises both thumbs. His master's voice reactivates Björn.

He's forgotten their first names. He must look them up in a moment.

'Ready for the big job? I wish I could help, but there are plans that need finishing.'

He's an architect, Alphonse reminds himself. He works from home.

'I've shut him away,' the woman says as her husband strides over to the door behind which the howling and scratching increase.

'Shut away?' the husband asks in a childish voice. 'Is my very best buddy shut away?'

Wrenched back and forth between mixed but extreme emotions, Björn skitters across the floor, trembling with irresolution.

The man picks him up. 'He's a Portuguese Water Dog,' he says, while the dog attempts to insert its tongue between his moving lips. 'Our daughter's allergic to most other breeds.' He turns his attention and that piping voice back to the thrashing dog, setting it down on the floor: 'And who else has a Portuguese Water Dog? What am I saying, two?'

For an answer he looks at Alphonse, his hands making a graceful, proffering gesture that transmutes into two pointing fingers, two pistols. 'Obama!'

'Well, anyway,' mumbles the woman. She gives Alphonse's forearm a brief, feeble tap, announces she's off for a shower, and hurries out of the room.

The man tickles Björn's head, then kneels in front of the dog, lifts its front paws, looks deep into its round eyes and whines: 'You know I didn't mean anything wrong by that, don't you?'

'I'll get started,' says Alphonse.

Els and Dieter, they're called. It's written on the estimate. Els left after making him a cup of coffee and Dieter has been working upstairs for some hours now, in his study on the other side of the house. He makes frequent trips to the toilet.

In the absence of their inhabitants, houses often inform Alphonse about the kinds of stories they're going to tell. Or they mislead him. That happens too. A wastepaper basket with children's drawings torn into tiny pieces, or shrines, or holes in the plasterboard, recently kicked.

Els and Dieter's house gives little away. They've tidied their things into sleek fitted cupboards and drawers. On the walls are pictures of the family in the snow, the family in swimming gear on a slide; the series runs thematically through the four seasons.

One of the living-room walls is made up of large glass doors that look out onto the garden at the back of the house. In contrast to the orderly interior and the front garden's manicured lawn, it makes an unkempt impression. The ladder against the wooden fence reminds him he's forgotten his own. He can make do with a chair, removing his shoes to stand on one, but it's not easy working like that.

Björn keeps Alphonse company, silent but watching his every move. For a long time he believed the barking of dogs came down to one of two messages: 'Don't do that!' and 'Hey!' They had nothing else to say. Björn isn't the first dog to have caused him to doubt this, even yawning along with Alphonse as he stretches after applying the masking tape. Coincidence, he thinks, but it happens again.

He mentions it when Dieter comes down to check there's nothing he needs.

'That means he likes you,' says Dieter. 'Dogs have a lot of empathy. Just lately I read that they don't bark to communicate with each other. It's a language they've developed for talking with us.'

'I thought only humans found yawning contagious.'

'We don't know very many people who yawn when we yawn, do we, buddy?' Dieter pipes at the dog. No further explanation is forthcoming.

'I've forgotten my ladder,' says Alphonse. 'I could go home and fetch it, but I notice there's one in the garden.'

'Can you get it yourself?' Dieter heads off upstairs.

Outside it's even hotter now. Alphonse does his best to avoid stepping in dog mess as he crosses the garden. Isn't Björn ever walked? In attempting to remove the ladder he sees there's another on the other side of the garden wall. They're linked by a worn purple swimming board with M AND L FOR EVER written on it in felt-tip pen. It's a rickety structure, easy to dismantle. He props the board up against the garden wall and resolves to tie the whole lot together again more securely later.

As he cleans the living-room walls, the sound of the hard brush sends Björn to sleep. The ammonia Alphonse uses to tackle the greasier surfaces in the kitchen wakes him up again, though. He sneezes and slinks away to the hall with a look of alarm. Then claws tick on the stairs. Alphonse opens the glass sliding door to dispel the stench.

When his master comes down to make himself a sandwich, the dog isn't with him.

'Like anything?' Dieter asks, his thoughts clearly elsewhere.

Alphonse has his own sandwiches, but he accepts a cup of coffee.

Dieter looks past him, at the ladder, then out of the window. He walks over and slowly shuts the sliding door.

'Mila put that ladder there,' he says. 'Children.' He smiles apologetically, then signals his habit of eating at the computer.

Mila is about thirteen and resembles neither of her parents. With a dramatic sweep she throws off her backpack.

'Hello,' she says. Then, dismayed: 'What's my ladder doing here?'

'Perhaps you could say hello to Alphonse first?' Her mother has come in behind her.

'I just did. What's my ladder doing here?'

'I borrowed it for a bit, because I forgot mine. I'll put it back shortly. I'll tie the swimming board nice and tight. Promise.'

'But I need it now.'

'Homework first,' says Els.

'Haven't got any homework.'

'I don't believe that.'

Mila storms out of the room the moment her father comes in.

'Hello!' he says crossly. Without responding, she runs up the stairs.

'Puberty. We won't be spared,' Dieter chuckles. 'You don't think of that when you're in it yourself, how your own children will subject you to it eventually.'

'It's not that bad,' says Els.

She asks whether he has any children.

'I don't think so.'

They find that funny and something gleams in their eyes, a slight curiosity, slight suspicion. Alphonse resolves not to make that corny old joke any more.

He fetches the cable ties from the van. On the other side of the house he attaches both ladders to the swimming board.

'I'm calling on your neighbours shortly, by the way,' he says, back in the kitchen.

Els and Dieter stare at him as if he has a hatchet embedded in his skull. Why the neighbours? He explains that he's taking them some colour swatches, so they can choose a colour. As soon as he's done here, he'll make a start there.

Dieter wraps his arms around his head. Els slaps a painted wall with the flat of her hand. 'Damn,' she says, looking first at her Pick Nick-pink hand and then at the skeletal fingers on the wall. 'Sorry.'

Alphonse presses a cloth to the mouth of a bottle of turpentine and holds her hand in his to clean it. For a moment she stands there like a crestfallen child, her fingers wide open so that his resolute, fatherly strokes can find all the paint. Then her rage flares again. 'Really, what are they playing at?!'

He takes a small, new roller out of its packaging and skims it breezily over the handprint like a lightweight steamroller. It works.

'Everything we do, they copy,' Dieter explains. 'No idea what's going on in those people's heads. They see your van out front and before you know it, their kitchen's in need of a new colour too.'

'Their bedrooms.' They haven't heard him.

'It's been going on for years. We buy a house, they buy a house. We have a baby, they have a baby. We get a new car or travel across the United States and they do too.' Els glumly removes traces of paint from under her fingernails. 'What are we supposed to do? Move?'

'We're not moving.' It's Mila who's spoken. They didn't hear her coming downstairs and as she crosses the living room to slide open the glass door they stand motionless next to the granite worktop and stare at her.

Els waits till she's outside before going on: 'It's even got to the point where they've started interfering in our lives. They think they can make certain adjustments to our lives.'

Dieter wants to interrupt. His mouth points in her direction and his lips purse several times, backed by an index finger describing the path of a powerful insect.

'We don't know that,' he says eventually.

'I'll see you tomorrow,' says Alphonse.

They thank him, somewhat startled by the abrupt ending and slightly dismayed at how much they've divulged, but they haven't told him the whole story yet.

Before he steps into the hall, he sees them, floating on a flying carpet above the garden wall: two thirteen-year-old girls, flinging their smiling faces forward and back.

He catches another glimpse of the girls through the window in the rear wall of the neighbours' house before he's led to an armchair. His clients sit in two separate chairs to his left, each with one leg thrown over the other. They're slightly shorter and rounder than Els and Dieter. Between him and the couple, bubbles tinkle in the glass of tonic they've put on the coffee table for him. At his feet pants a small, attentive dog of an indeterminate breed. When Alphonse picks up the glass and puts it to his mouth, the animal seems to hold its breath.

'Where are you from?' the woman wants to know.

'From Brussels,' he says. 'I've been living here for almost nine months now.'

'Yes, yes,' the woman enunciates. 'But where are you really from?'

'From Brussels, he said, didn't he?' Her husband stands up nervously. 'Would you like an olive, Mr, er?' he asks. 'Cheese?'

'No, thank you. And just call me Alphonse.'

'We're Sieglinde and Ronny. I'll go and get some anyway,' says the woman after her husband has sat down again. She goes to the kitchen, which is walled off from the living room. It sounds as if she's emptying all the cupboards.

'How did you get on next door?' the man asks. He's

obviously trying to make the question sound neutral.

'I think I'll be finished there by tomorrow evening.'

'Didn't she say anything, Els, when she heard you were coming to see us?' Sieglinde lays out little bowls of olives and cheese, putting cocktail sticks and a napkin holder beside them.

Alphonse isn't immediately sure how to answer. 'It seemed to interest them,' he says.

Ronny sniffs. 'No doubt!' exclaims Sieglinde. 'She's crazy, Alfredo.'

They're more forthright than he was expecting.

'Alphonse,' Ronny corrects her before he can.

'Sorry. For years she's been telling anyone who'll listen that we're copying them. We could say the same about them, but we don't, because we're still in command of our faculties.'

'It all came out one evening, at a party,' Ronny goes on. 'A party right here in our house, actually. They were our guests. First they sulked in a corner for some reason or other ... '

'Well. *She* did.'

'Then they had too much to drink as usual and suddenly it was "another coincidence" that we had a dark-blue Peugeot. It's not even the same model! And over there, didn't that chandelier seem familiar to them, and that shrub at the bottom of the garden and I don't know what else.'

'Well, okay, but the idea that we brought Lana into the world purely because they'd just had a baby. Tell me, Albert, who would ever think that way?'

'Alphonse.'

'Pardon me. Who would think that way? I was in my late twenties. Everyone around us was having their first baby then. I was four months gone before I realized she was pregnant too. But no, we were copying them. How full of yourself do you have to be to think something like that is even within the bounds of possibility?'

While speaking, Sieglinde and Ronny have stood up to perform an angular dance that for Ronny now ends with a punch to his thigh and in Sieglinde's case is still ebbing away in one index finger, which taps the centre of her forehead like a woodpecker's beak.

Alphonse settles into the backrest of the chair. When a confession starts as energetically as this, it usually lasts a while.

'If it'd stopped there, well … But no, no, it gets even more absurd.' Sieglinde is now bending down onto the coffee table like a she-ape, weight on her fists, buttocks in the air, nostrils wide, like her eyes, magnified by her glasses. 'Did she say anything about her pussy?'

Alphonse has to give the question time to sink in. 'It's dead, I believe?'

'She said a bit more about it than that, I'll bet. Her story is that we killed their cat.'

'Yes, and the reason why is even more interesting. We killed it because our own cat was run over and because they think we think they did it—we, incidentally, don't ask ourselves who was responsible, we assume it was an accident—and that's why we, eye for an eye … '

'Cat for a cat!'

' … killed their pet—get this—by impaling it with a dart! A dart from a blowpipe! We shot a poisoned dart at it!'

'Because that's what we're like, Alphonse! That's the kind of thing we get up to!'

'Alphonse,' says Ronny.

'That's what I said.'

For the bedroom ceilings he recommends Balanced

Mood, from the Colores del Mundo collection. They agree that the pale bluish-green he slides out of the colour swatch will do perfectly.

On his way home Alphonse crosses wide fields on narrow roads. The low sun gilds the stalks of tall grain and an indefinable longing. No one else knows that in the mornings, still brittle and directionless after the embrace of sleep, he rarely listens to music because he finds the immediacy of it almost impossible to bear. Now he puts on the radio and when he looks up there's an oncoming vehicle, making no attempt to slow down. He drives right up to the edge of a maize field and stops the car to listen.

Duke Ellington's 'Caravan', in a version by Dizzy Gillespie. He knows every note. Camels trek through the desert, but the trumpet sets fountains playing. The water flows over his shoulders, down his back. That strange violin solo, too. When the track finishes, he turns off the radio.

He eats the remains of yesterday's pasta. Does it seem peaceful or merely quiet without Cat? He hopes the yoga retreat has given her what she expected from it, even if he doesn't quite know what that was.

She's not answering her phone. He needs to return Amadou's call. Why does he keep putting that off? His friend getting in touch again after all these years made him so happy he immediately invited him to come and stay for a short holiday, bringing his new girlfriend with him. In a large part of his memory, Amadou walks at his side. There's no reason to avoid him now.

Or he could start up Skype and see his mother. She's always there, in a full house, surrounded by people who need her advice or just want to be with her, some of them feeding on the fruits of her goodness.

He's tired and can't seem to shower away the fatigue. What he feels is getting harder and harder to name. He knows what it isn't. It's not anything that hurts. Not at all. But it's some kind of waiting.

The bleep of the phone, the landline this time, cuts through the water in his ears. He turns off the tap and wraps himself in a bathrobe. His guess is Dieter.

'Alphonse?' It's Sieglinde.

'Yes,' he says.

'I just wanted to call you. Because we got rather carried away today and because we're not proud of it. We'd also like to thank you for listening.'

'That's all right. Don't cry.'

'It's out of our control, know what I mean?'

'Yes.'

'Okay. Sorry to disturb you. Have a good night.'

'Sleep well.'

29

Next morning he finally gets hold of Cat. She seems cheerful.

'You're feeling good, then?' he asks.

'Yes,' she says, unhappy with the subject. 'But I have to go now.'

'Where to?'

'Well, to yoga. Another four days.'

'Have fun.'

'Bye, Alphonse.' She's never come up with a shorter form of his name, which is something he appreciates. Apart from her parents, everyone calls her Cat. Not very long ago she had a malignant tumour. They have to assume it won't come back.

'Fonzy!' Dieter calls out. He's wearing a dark-blue bathrobe, clearing away the breakfast things. 'Great that you also work on Saturdays,' he says in English. Sometimes people do that, suddenly address him in English, even after he's had conversations with them in Dutch and even though there are four languages he speaks more fluently.

Els, who let him in, has jogged out of the door, this time with Björn on the lead. In the garden, bent over their swimming board, wearing anoraks, the girls are sitting on the top rungs of their ladders writing something on a piece of paper or card. When they see him standing at the window they wave in the manner of ladies-in-waiting. In reply he imitates the pope driving past.

Dieter's gaze flutters out past his shoulder, a nervous moth that, despite the call of the light, quickly returns to the semi-darkness. He mumbles that he's going upstairs to get dressed, walks across the living room to the hall but stops when he hears Alphonse slide the door open. He's a father, Dieter is, and he's obliged to entertain some slight suspicion when an adult man, ultimately a stranger, wants to talk to his adolescent daughter and her friend without involving him, and without there being any clear reason for it. So he returns to keep watch, Dieter does, peering into the garden, which he's increasingly been avoiding, touched as ever by the harmonious relationship between the girls, a thing no longer talked about between these walls for fear of damaging it.

The children's faces become more undecided, more serious during their conversation with Alphonse. What is he asking them? Is it time to step in? Then there's some nodding. The girls nod, Alphonse nods, and they all turn in his direction, smiling feebly, it seems to him.

'Sit down for a moment,' says Alphonse, shutting the door behind him. In the background Mila and Lana bend down over their concerted scribblings once more.

Dieter does as he's asked, resting his hands on his thighs and looking at the floor, paler than before, the bathrobe now lending him a fragile serenity.

'Sieglinde and Ronny didn't kill the cat.' Alphonse stays on his feet as he talks.

'I thought not.' Dieter doesn't look up. 'How did it happen?'

'It was a friend of the girls. A local boy who's never dared come round since.'

'I know the one. I've never seen him here blowing darts.'

'It was an accident. The boy shouldn't be punished for it. And neither should your daughter or her friend.'

Dieter nods. And nods again.

After that the glue that seemed to fill the room during their conversation flows out. The silence is driven away by metallic noises: the extending legs of his own ladder, his screwdriver opening a lid. Upstairs, Dieter takes a bath.

For most of the day the three family members leave him to paint in peace. They steal past respectfully, or express their approval when he turns to look at them. The work progresses quickly. Wall after wall begins to shine.

Just before midday he hears Els and Dieter's voices intoning through the ceiling, Els getting agitated about something, then coming round. When they eat lunch at the kitchen table, they want him to sit with them. Once he's there, no one can think what to talk about. They put local cheeses on his plate, peeled fruit, straight from the tree, he simply must taste it. Björn too awaits his reaction.

As he's clearing up in the evening, they both grow restless.

'A beautiful job,' Els tells him. 'And so quick.'

'To think you've been here for barely two days,' says Dieter.

Alphonse taps on the window. Mila and Lana wave back. Then he shakes Els and Dieter's hands.

'I'm not far away,' he says. 'On Monday I start next door.'

They nod.

'There's more work here too.' Panic in their voices.

'The rooms upstairs could do with repainting this year.'

'You know where to find me.'

They walk with him along the hallway, catching his eye at every opportunity.

When he reaches the van and turns back toward them, Björn rushes at him full tilt. He picks up the floundering dog and carries him to the front door, where he lays him in Els's arms. For one second she looks at Alphonse as if he's just delivered their baby, then they laugh it off.

On the village square in Watou he orders a coffee on the empty terrace of a full bar. He has to admit the barman is right: it's summer at last and the weather seems odd. There are motorcyclists passing through, and two youngsters on slender horses. At the church, overlooking the square, a statue of Jesus stands with arms spread. In the middle of the square is a soldier, accompanied by a lion.

He finds himself in a strange, beautiful life. Does he demand too little? Does he receive too much?

After settling up, on his way to the van, he sees the front of the statue. The soldier is holding a revolver to his chest, barrel pointed away. The nearby figure of Christ, head bowed, now seems frozen in the act of raising his hands.

Some things continue to amaze him here. Like having to drive twenty minutes for a shawarma.

It's a new place, with a sign outside made of glittering sequins so that the letters Pita Merci move in the wind and reflect the weak evening sunlight. Inside it's clean and empty. Linoleum. With great precision the young man at the till is arranging a roll of tinfoil, some knives, and a large salt cellar. Next he concentrates on laying all the plastic forks in the holder the same way round, teeth toward him. His face is strikingly flawless.

'*Gardesh*,' he says happily when he sees Alphonse come in.

They don't know each other. It's a long time since anyone called him that and he likes it.

'Nice place.'

'Thanks. Expensive, though. Work, work, work.'

'No doubt. I'd like a large shawarma with all the veggies and samurai sauce, please.'

The young man laughs. 'Spicy then. Always.'

'Sorry?'

'You guys always want spicy sauces. And lots of chicken.'

Although Alphonse has now opted for the other rotating pillar of meat, it's true that he eats a lot of chicken. Like almost everyone he knows. And it's true that he has a preference for spicy sauces. He doesn't want to feel as if he's been caught out in some way. 'I thought my eating habits were my own. A personal thing.'

'Well they're not,' says the man and then—suddenly roguish, suddenly even younger—'With every shawarma: a free show!'

He puts the pita bread in the oven and leans down over his smartphone, which he's connected to a speaker. After a false start he finds the right track. There are swelling tones that then ebb away, like searchlights across a dark expanse. He performs stretching exercises of some kind with his fingers on the counter between him and Alphonse, arms extended, his head of thick, slicked-back hair slightly bowed. He fixes his customer with the gaze of a falcon. Alphonse wonders whether anything is expected of him. Then an electronic beat bursts forth, intertwined with a regularly repeated, orientally inspired motif. He walks over to a pillar of meat. Alphonse can't really see how he cuts slices from it, but time and again he swaps the two knives he's wielding, throwing them briskly behind his back, above his head. With a graceful bow he then whisks the bread out of the oven and, juggling with salad servers, fills it with tomato, onion, cucumber, and grated carrot. At one point the salt cellar, which he's not using, describes ellipses through the air. A tub of spices brings up the rear, leaving a red cloud with every twist. He keeps everything in motion, including the salad servers, not just with his hands but with taps from his elbows, shoulders, and left hip. When the salt cellar lands upright on his head, he moves it left and right like an Indian dancer while shaking red spices into the pita. Alphonse applauds. As two knives and a small cleaver are launched into the air he takes a step back. The way the young man transfers the meat—still sizzling a little on the hotplate beneath the rotating pillars—into the bread while knife-throwing remains a mystery. Impossible to miss, though, is the moment when he stiffens and the knives and cleaver clatter to the ground around him. With trembling lips and a heavily bleeding ring-finger stump he turns and looks at Alphonse.

Alphonse yanks a dozen napkins out of the holder and the shawarma man presses them to the wound. 'Where's the finger?' he asks.

They both simultaneously twist round to check the hotplate and when they can't see it there it comes almost as a relief to Alphonse—although relief of a kind that doesn't preclude goosebumps—to spot the body part under his shoe. He narrowly manages to prevent himself from switching his weight to that foot and lifts his leg as if stepping away from a landmine. The extreme helplessness of a severed extremity, the unreality of it. He picks it up off the floor with a paper napkin. It's the third time he's witnessed this. The other two involved fingers as well. He recalls an accident with a power saw at a building firm he worked for. That finger stood upright on the ground, as if someone on the floor below was pointing up through the ceiling. Longer ago there was a fingertip belonging to Aline, his sister, who'd been helping in the kitchen with a knife far too big for her.

The dull thud of the fainting man drives out those memories. He's lying in a strange, crooked position on the spattered tiles. All that's moving now is the blood pouring out of the wound. With one hand Alphonse lifts two heavy feet onto an upturned plastic bowl, then goes in search of a freezer. Most of the shelves are frozen shut. The first one that he manages to open, after some wrenching and tugging, is filled with the most detailed ice sculptures, figures the size of Playmobil characters, a Viking, a king, an oriental warrior, all with the same face. It must be the unusual face of the proprietor, the young man on the floor. Alphonse doesn't have time to look any further. He'd rather not use such finds to staunch a wound. In the next drawer up he comes upon normal ice cubes.

He divides them between two tea towels, laying the finger on one of the stuffed towels and placing the other on the young man's forehead. It's a while before consciousness returns. Alphonse is just about to call an ambulance when the victim looks up at him in alarm.

'Can you stand?'

The young man nods and allows himself to be helped to his feet.

His name is Duran. On the way to the hospital and in the casualty waiting area, his expression evolves from appalled confusion to resigned gloom. Every time his bandaged finger stump sinks dispiritedly to his lap, Alphonse urges him to bring it up to his ear again, which reduces the bleeding and raises the spirits.

'My father said, "Duran, you live too far away. What are you going to do in that hole? Your family can't help you run the shop and you can't do it alone, with your eyes." I tell him, "My eyes are good, that's all in the past." I used to have a lazy eye, a patch on my spectacles, difficult for a child. "You can't see the butterflies," my father said—he meant that test, with the butterflies and so on, hidden among blots, everyone saw them jump into view except me. "I don't need to see those butterflies," I tell him. Lots of arguments, but I made the move anyhow. I thought: just you wait, Father, there are blots everywhere, keep looking and eventually I'll jump out from them. You'll see me then.'

He holds the bandaged stump in front of him, horrified by it. Alphonse is just about to urge him yet again to keep his hand vertical when a round-chested doctor comes marching along the corridor. She must be in her late forties and she has orange brushed-up hair, as if her head is on fire.

'Lost a finger?' she asks.

'I've got it with me.' Alphonse points to a plastic bag on the seat next to them. The towel with the ice inside is soaked through.

'Can I have a look?' She can't wait, plainly. He hopes he's not about to disappoint her. He's wrapped the finger in a wad of cling film, fearing it might otherwise be damaged by the cold. Duran looks the other way, as nonchalantly as possible.

The doctor takes the wrapped finger and gently taps it on the arm of the seat. 'Good. Not frozen.' A delighted little laugh escapes her. 'Follow me!'

'But you have to look! How often do you get the chance to see the inside of your finger?' She's talking to Duran, who might perhaps have preferred to be given a general anaesthetic.

The doctor stops sewing briefly to turn her attention to Alphonse, who has gone to sit on a chair by the wall. 'You can come a bit closer if you like.' The fact that neither of them responds to her cheery invitations seems to disturb her. She's meticulously described and named everything she's done; surely a patient could expect no more of her than that?

'Will he be able to use the finger again?' Alphonse asks, sensing that her bemusement is subsiding into annoyance.

'If I'm the one putting it back on, that's just about guaranteed,' she says, with a hint of defensiveness but mainly with pride.

Duran's ring finger is encased in a tight bandage stiffened with a strip of metal. In the car he takes his hand out of the sling that was secured around his neck in the hospital.

'A ring finger is better than an index finger,' he says, determined to get back to work that evening. 'And I'm left-handed.' He looks askance at his driver.

Strange, thinks Duran, that this man is the only person ever to have seen him unconscious. He didn't leave him for one moment, not in the shop and not in casualty. He's struck by how normal that seemed.

'Thanks.'

Alphonse takes his eyes off the road and raises one corner of his mouth.

'No, I mean it. Is there anything I can do to thank you?'

'There is something, actually. Those little figures in the freezer—I'd like to take another look.'

Sometimes air can be displaced by a feeling. Suddenly the car is filled with embarrassment from floor to roof. Am I the only one who knows about the ice men? Alphonse wonders. 'They're beautiful. That's why I'd like to see them again.'

'It's a strange hobby, but then all I do the rest of the time is work. I work really hard. Often fourteen hours a day. And I go to the gym, too.'

Alphonse doesn't insist. He agrees to let Duran make him something to eat. He parks right in front of the shawarma shop. In this part of the country there's never any shortage of parking spots.

With the good fingers of his injured hand, Duran moves a teabag up and down in a cup of hot water. 'You can take a look,' he says. 'But over there if you don't mind.'

'Of course,' says Alphonse. 'Otherwise they'll melt.'

They place two chairs next to the open freezer and bend down over the drawer.

'They all look like you,' says Alphonse, at the risk of rekindling Duran's embarrassment.

'That's why they're all called Duran,' says Duran. 'This is Duran Khan, dressed like Genghis Khan, and this is Ataduran.'

Apple tea steams on a low table close to Alphonse's legs. The sweating pillars of meat have resumed their dervish dance and the floor is daubed with blood. Companionship comes in strange guises, he thinks merrily.

'Here,' says Duran. 'If you can guess his name you can

have him.' He shows Alphonse a Duran dressed in straw and feathers, with a loincloth, a spear, and a shield.

'Shaka Duran?'

'Yes. So he's yours. Never show him to anyone.'

At home Alphonse liberates the ice man from the freezer-block flat Duran has shut him into. He puts Shaka Duran in the smallest plastic box he can find and lays him to sleep between two packs of spinach in the freezer compartment at the top of the fridge. If Cat finds him, he'll have to explain it was a well-intended gift.

28

On Sunday it rains. In the early morning the wind hurls hard drops at the windows. The salvos continue till Alphonse lifts his head from the pillow.

He sits on the edge of the bed and realizes that in his dream the sound of the rain was the stutter of automatic weapons, fired by uniformed men at naked figures up against a wall. He was not among them.

With his first sip of coffee he wants to hear Cat, who answers out of breath. She has no time now, she's in the middle of a storm that broke just when all the mats, cushions, and blankets had been dragged deep into the woods. Now they're fetching everything indoors again. The atmosphere has hit rock bottom. The guest lecturer is as much of a disappointment as the weather.

Alphonse says he misses her. She misses him too.

She once taught him a headstand. Sirsasana is said to rejuvenate the brain cells, optimize the metabolism, and combat both grey hair and varicose veins. Could he still do it? Aware that no impulse is ever risk-free, he takes a folded blanket from the sofa and lays it on the floor. He puts his elbows at the edge, shoulder-width apart, slides his fingers together and presses the crown of his head to the blanket, nestling the back of his skull in his hands. The trick is to keep your shoulders low, he recalls, to avoid straining the neck. He takes small steps toward his face, straightens his back and stretches his legs. He's vertical. It's improbably pleasant, until the desire to stand like this for a long time is replaced by an awareness that he doesn't know how to stop without pain. When he bends his legs to begin the descent, it's as if he's about to snap, so he stretches them again.

Someone knocks on the front door, which only his neighbour, Willem, is in the habit of doing.

'Door's open!'

'Don't leave it open! This isn't Brussels, but all the same!' Willem shouts from the hall, and then, eye to eye with the sirsasana: 'Oops, how did that happen?'

'Could you just help me down?'

'What do I do?'

'Push back, that's all. Support me.'

'Hell's bells, man. I'm almost eighty.' With the seriousness of the elderly, Willem switches from a weightlifter's stance to one in which he's holding Alphonse's legs like the arms of a wheelbarrow. After it's all over he makes no attempt to conceal his pride: man in late seventies helps far younger person out of physical predicament. Successfully, too. He runs his fingers through his grey mop and flashes Alphonse a smile. Yes, he would like some coffee.

'Cat not awake yet?' he calls to the kitchen, where Alphonse is pouring him a cup.

'It's her yoga week.'

'So you thought: how about standing on my head for a while? I've always said it's dangerous. Cat ought to give it up as well. She's far too thin. Marie-Jeanne said the same. She had an eye for these things, that's why she baked all those cakes for you. To think I'll never eat them again.'

While Marie-Jeanne was alive, Willem mainly went

on about how irritating she was. Because her part in any conversation was usually confined to the question: 'That's not true, is it?' Or because she was unable to enjoy dining out and always started looking for her keys even before they'd paid the bill, only to find them later, at home, in places where they could only ever be located after a protracted search. He often complained of her lack of interest in the Great War library he was compiling, an indifference that verged on hostility. 'The First World War's over!' Alphonse heard Marie-Jeanne wail, distraught, a week before her death. She thought garages were for cars, not books, and conservatories for vegetables. Willem believed this had to do with a lack of schooling, a disparity that had driven a wedge between them on several occasions. But he thought such things about her only while she was still around. Her death had made the newspapers, as a consequence of the sequence of bad luck that led up to it. On the way to the fishmonger's she'd fallen victim to some geraniums that threw themselves at her along with their terracotta tank. She was taken to hospital with a fractured shoulder and toe, in an ambulance that spun out on a bend so that she had to be transferred to a second one along with two paramedics who argued and bled with equal intensity. After a gas canister explosion at the bedside of a smoking lung patient in the wing where her broken bones were set, followed by a fire and a chaotic evacuation, Marie-Jeanne Maes's undoubtedly stout heart stopped.

They'd been neighbours for just a few months when the tragedy occurred. After the funeral, Willem shut himself up in his house until Alphonse and Cat invited him to dinner. From then on he came round at least once a week. After he'd supplied them with a crate of old soap, a harlequin the size of a seven-year-old child, a device weighing a ton that could vacuum-pack sandwiches, a polished shell casing to serve as an umbrella stand, and the painted head of a sphinx, Cat gently relieved him of the notion that he had to bring them a gift every time.

On this occasion Willem has a book with him, Alphonse notices, but it doesn't look as if he intends it as a present.

'There's not one Hun, not even a doctor at the universities of Berlin or Munich, who can come close to the beauty and grandeur of a Senegalese!' Willem pontificated, one finger in the air like a dry twig and one eye cast askance at the book. Alphonse's raised eyebrows seem to please him. 'Premier Clemenceau. In 1914. You can say what you like about France, and the *tirailleurs sénégalais* were certainly cannon fodder, but at least the French regarded their African troops as human beings. That's one side of the story, anyhow.'

'At least they regarded their cannon fodder as human,' Alphonse grins.

Willem nods. Since the arrival of his new neighbour he's been concentrating specifically on the fate of the *tirailleurs sénégalais* in the First World War, and since the death of his wife they've become an obsession.

'To the Germans they were apes, a threat to white women, whose interest in them betokened a lack of historical awareness. That says something about attitudes to women, of course. Always a threat to the social order. They undoubtedly had a lower level of education, women in those days, but education and intelligence are two different things. Just look at Marie-Jeanne: she left school at fourteen, but think how much I learned from her.'

Alphonse leans back in the sofa. Willem has become the widower of a saint, and as such his ability to cope is increasing. His indignation at the treatment of Africans in the First World War seems to comfort him somehow, or at least to distract him from sorrows of his own. In the early weeks of mourning there were so many tears that Alphonse didn't know what to do. They were the answer to every question, the response to every joke. This is a great improvement. Anyhow, he likes listening to the polite, West-Flanders-accented Dutch of this elderly French teacher. He never has to strain to understand, as he does when conversing with some of his clients. Willem stresses every syllable, carefully articulates every consonant, even if it's a substitute for another.

'The Germans had every reason to dehumanize the African troops, of course. That way they could think of the French as fighting a war by impermissible means. For their part, the French had to keep repeating how brave, strong, and loyal the *tirailleurs* were. "Faithful children" is how they were seen. Certainly not the image many of those black soldiers had of themselves.'

'Would you like to join me for breakfast? I haven't had any yet. I've got raisin bread.'

'From which bakery?'

'Moeyersons.'

'In that case, yes. There's not enough salt in the bread from Gaudesaboos. And the image they had of their colonizers changed too, of course, as a result; they suddenly found themselves watching the French face a more powerful foe.' He peers past Alphonse, as if he can see it all happening right now on the fields beyond the curtains. 'All those young lads who'd known nothing but sun, who were then made to come and get their feet frozen off in a conflict that had nothing to do with them. I know I've asked you before, but wouldn't you like to take a trip with me to see the graves of the *tirailleurs sénégalais*? There are some on this side of the French border. If there's one thing I want to do before I'm called to another place, it's to make a full inventory of those graves, those names.'

'I'd like that,' says Alphonse. 'But not in this weather.'

He feels like staying indoors all day. He's moved many times, but only recently he walked through this rented house one morning and had the feeling it was a good house, handsome and sound, that without noticing he'd come home. Since then he's been enjoying the strength and solidity of the walls, the way they keep the warmth in, the rain out.

He turns on the computer and opens Skype. His mother is online and he calls her with the kind of happy nostalgia he always feels. The sound that accompanies the request for contact is cleverly chosen: first a few expectant tones ending in a question mark and then, when someone on another continent surfaces, something like expanding bubbles of air. There's Dakar. The inside of the ground-floor apartment where she lives now.

'Hello, son,' she says, in Jola, a language he speaks almost exclusively with her and his sister these days. 'You're getting fat.'

'Hello mother. These are muscles.'

He ought to fend off the things clients serve up to him, especially the cakes. Her red headscarf stays neatly in place as laughter tosses her head backward. There's a lot of noise around her, as ever.

'Everyone in need of you again?' he asks.

'Some are here to ask advice, others pretend to be but just walk from the back door to the front door because it's the quickest way from that street to this. As long as they knock first, it's fine by me.'

'How is everything?'

'Aunt Agnes died.'

Her younger sister. 'When did that happen?'

'Three days ago. We buried her the same day. She'd been ill for some time.'

'But you should have rung me!'

'What would you have done?'

'Sent money for medicines. Commiserated.' He has few memories of this particular aunt, who went to live in a village in Casamance and kept her distance from the rest of the family. Agnes' most striking characteristic was her ability to combine surliness with a huge appetite for life. The eccentricity harboured by most members of the family was wilder in her. She worked as a beekeeper, the only female beekeeper in Senegal, and the only lengthy conversation she ever had with him was entirely about propagating bees. She made him taste the honey they made. He must have been about sixteen. His aunt was younger then than he is now.

'Aunty hasn't gone. The atoms that held her body together are free now. They no longer have to collaborate to keep one person intact. It's like unravelling a sweater; stitch by stitch the shape it was trapped in dissolves. And all those billions of atoms get absorbed into something else: a snail's house, a mango blossom, and her own bees. She'll throw herself into a river and flow to the sea, become a smooth shell on the waves, the feathers of a rising osprey and the wind blowing through them. In that boundlessness she's happier now than she can ever have been as a person.'

His mother tells some beautiful stories. He finds it hard to move on to ask about Ebola, but he does nonetheless. There's no news. Senegal is surrounded by neighbouring countries with a growing number of cases but for now it's been spared. Sceptical voices whisper that this need not necessarily be the truth.

The hours that remain disappear in music. He takes the bass guitar in his hands, the familiar smooth wood, the thick strings that fit the grooves in his hard fingertips. He goes to stand at the window and plays the first thing that comes to him, a low song for the green and brown crops, the tracks of mud on the roads, the smouldering fringe of cloud, a bright spell. He presses the pedal with his foot, steers sounds in a loop that continues after he rests the bass in its frame and takes the rounded back of the kora into his lap. Against a hard crust of bass the kora tells a polyphonic story, about the *tirailleurs'* trench foot, the cakes Marie-Jeanne baked, the laughter of thirteen-year-old daughters, the sick and dying in Liberian streets, buzzing swarms of bees without his aunt. And through the window the fields, always the fields, the trees alongside them: out of the ground, into the sky; he watches it happen, time and again.

27

Only Sieglinde was still home when Alphonse arrived. She hastily led him through the bedrooms and announced she had to go to work, but an hour later she's still here. She walks from room to room, upstairs and down, the little dog in her arms. He passes them on the stairs and meets them in the kitchen where, lost in thought, she presses a pointy kiss to the tiny canine skull. The animal keeps its eyes fixed on Alphonse, who believes he can read 'say something' in them.

'Ça va?' he asks.

The eyes behind the lenses of her spectacles seem even bigger and bluer than before.

'Do you have a family?' she wants to know.

'A girlfriend. Partner.'

'No children?'

'No.'

She scrapes her lower lip with her upper teeth, knows it's a risky question but asks nonetheless: 'Why not?'

'That's the way life has gone,' he says.

'You still want them?'

He finds it strange that most people talk about hypothetical children in the plural, as if they usually present themselves as a class. 'It's something I'd welcome. It's not essential.'

'So it doesn't matter?' She makes no effort to hide her

incredulity. 'What does your partner think about that?'

'At the moment she'd rather not think about it.'

That could mean a lot of things. Sieglinde has now started licking her lips: one of many tics designed to prevent her curiosity from being transformed into words. Then her face hardens. 'She'd better. Yes. Think about it.'

'There's still time.'

That's not what she means. She speaks quickly and solemnly, as if performing a theatrical monologue she's known for years. 'A lot can change, in yourself, and not always for the better. All I'd heard about having your first child was that it's the best experience of your life, an unbeatable experience that connects you with everything. That it's only then that you really feel what love means, what it is to be human. That's what I was told. Of course I knew you could find the occasional degenerate woman wandering about who'd never be ready for it, a weak link that just wasn't intended to procreate. I turned out to be such a person. I didn't foresee that as soon as I fell pregnant I'd start going down. During the contractions I was sucked into a deep hole. It's because of the pain, I told myself. Soon they'll lay the child on your tummy and the euphoria will come. Then they laid the child on my tummy and all I could think was: get it off me! The next day was no different, nor the day after that. A year and a half passed before I could feel anything but loathing. Not just for the child. No one knew, other than my husband. If it wasn't for him I'd have ended it all. That's another thing I remember from all those months: it defies imagination, how much you can hide. I held the baby in my arms and chattered away with an endless succession of visitors, all the time hoping that if a meteorite landed it would hit our house. I think she's doing fine, my daughter, but I'm always afraid it's left its mark on her. Because it wasn't anything natural, what I had. Nature has its own cruelty, I'm fully aware of that, indifference too, certainly, but there was no sense in the way I was, it was pure devastation, and it took control of me without any trouble at all.'

The silence grows. She's finished for now, he thinks, but there is more.

'Lana's really nice.'

'Yes.' Shaken, she bends over the little dog in her arms and plants more kisses on the tiny scalp. 'When did you meet her?'

'She was with Mila, on their ladder. We had a brief conversation.'

She stares at him without blinking. 'They were here. Our neighbours. Yesterday they were suddenly at our door. We thought what now? But it was cake. Cake and a lot that was left unsaid, a lot of awkwardness. Made tea. Chatted for a bit about the children and the dogs. About you for a moment, too. Walking on eggshells. Within an hour they'd gone and Ronny and I didn't know what to say. All in all it wasn't too bad.'

She puts the dog on the floor. 'Anyhow, I have to go. I'm already late. And I'm keeping you from your work.'

'What's he called?' Alphonse asks.

'Who?' Again those blue flashing lights behind the glasses.

He looks down at the dog, which is lying on the floor with its head on the toe of his shoe.

'She's called Happy. A bitch. And she seems to be comfortable with you.'

He wobbles his foot. Happy raises her head and lies down somewhere else, allowing him to carry his things upstairs.

'Alphonse,' she says from the bottom of the stairs when he's almost at the top. 'Can you take a look in the bathroom? It's between the bedrooms.'

'You want me to paint that too?'

She hesitates. 'Not necessarily. Just say what you think about it. But not right now. See you this evening.'

She hurriedly puts on her coat. Happy yaps at the closing door.

There's nothing unusual about the bathroom, nothing to paint or repair. The walls are tiled from top to bottom, the ceiling coated with a damp-proof membrane. What does she want him to look at? Then he sees it, on the rectangular washbasin, between the tap and the hairbrush. He holds the white stick closer. The blue cap has been broken off. One short and one longer vertical stripe indicate a positive result, he believes. Not necessarily a favourable one.

He doesn't know what he should tell her and he racks his brain while taping the skirting board. What he certainly must make clear is that he's got no experience at all with post-natal depression.

In Brussels, in the many periods when he was unable to make a living from his music, he worked on and off for a building firm, sometimes as a painter and decorator. People used to tell him all sorts of things then too. As a musician it happened less often—it must have to do with interiors, with insides.

He was warned about the dour, taciturn character of people in the Westhoek, but in his experience they're no different from clients he's had in the past; after reluctantly presenting their problems, they make no secret of the needs that accompany them. Cat says his skin colour underlines the fact that he's an outsider to their lives, and that's why they allow him access. His colour is the clergyman's cassock, the psychiatrist's duty of confidentiality. He's not convinced by this theory; in Brussels he worked with other Africans, many of whom had a greater tendency to prompt suspicion, or at least reticence, even though he couldn't see that they gave any reason for it. The defensive looks that rested on them, with that willed blindness, seeking differences as confirmation, seeking an authorization for inequality, had sought him sometimes too, and found their mark. Yet clients started talking to him more and more frequently. They laid their secrets out before him with an eagerness he found overwhelming; it was as if they hoped he might rescue them from their lives. 'You're just ridiculously patient,' Cat has tossed at him more than once. She still feels quite a bit of annoyance at the amount of time he devotes to his clients. He's never really managed to explain to her exactly what happens when the unburdening begins, why he keeps responding to it. He can barely convert the experience into thoughts. Mutual hypnosis—that's how he's tried to express it to himself. According to Cat he's a magnet to the deranged, and colleagues and friends in the past have pointed to some such power of attraction. He can't convince himself of it. These are simply people who want to change the colour of their walls. They've spotted his number on the internet or under the rainbow logo on the side of his van. They're not marginal figures mumbling to themselves before noticing him across a crowded town square and sidling over to him. This isn't the exception, this is the norm behind closed doors.

What about him? If it's true that he has more patience than most and therefore, for whatever reason, evokes more trust and sparks more hope, is he the one who needs to adjust?

He's never found listening difficult. Giving advice is a different matter. He's sparing with it, although clients often seem to expect him to pronounce. When it comes to an escalating row like that between Dieter, Els, Sieglinde, and Ronny he ventures to be resolute, since the people involved—these four aren't the first he's encountered—will all stand and shout that it's the quarrel itself that's the real torment, patching it up the only remedy. They know this, but they can't act upon it. Then he happens along, and casually makes the whole thing drop away.

Happy has tiptoed shyly past the door on several occasions. This time she decides to mention something. With each bark her tiny white body slides a centimetre back.

'Pee-pee?' He sounds hoarse. His voice has been sleeping for several hours.

The dog races down the stairs ahead of him.

He opens the door to the garden and waits inside until the animal has finished and is flurrying around him again with nervous leaps. He strokes its head until it falls asleep on the living-room carpet.

This is something he can do. Listen, soothe, comfort. Sometimes confront. Encourage? Clients who want to change more than the colour of their interior decor have to do that for themselves, ultimately. Do you really have to rule out offering help, even when you're asked for it, for fear it might be true that the road to hell is paved with good intentions? If he'd come upon a single case in which his intervention had made things worse, he'd have found himself a different job. It's not abnormal to enjoy this, not wrong to be happy to leave for work in the mornings because people are waiting for you. It's not vanity. Not arrogance. It's something that happens to him and something he can do. He pushes the paint roller up and down, surrounding himself with Balanced Mood. He still has no idea what he's going to say to Sieglinde.

Happy barks when the door opens. He can hear from Sieglinde's footfall that it's her arriving home. She comes straight upstairs, two steps at a time.

First she looks around the room. 'Yes. Peaceful. Beautiful. Thanks.' Then she turns those enormous eyes to him: 'Well?'

'I don't know what to say.'

'It's a test from four months ago. I kept it. I'm five months gone now. It's too late to do anything about it.'

Is she five months pregnant? 'Some people find peace and a greater sense of freedom once the options are limited. Others don't, of course.'

'I kept the test because sometimes when I wake up in the morning I think it's not true. And I'm hardly putting on any weight.'

'Does your husband know?'

'Yes. He says it'll be different this time.'

'That's something at least.'

She looks at him. She still hasn't told the whole story. She doesn't seem to take offence at his inability to guess.

'Hey, I do hope you've had something to drink today.'

'I brought some water with me.'

'Just take what you need, all right? Shall I make tea?'

'Yes, please.'

She hurries back down. 'A Chocotoff?' she calls up from the bottom of the stairs.

Through the half-darkness he drives into Zoetemore, the village where they live now. He's hungry, he'll have to

49

call in at Duran's place shortly; he wants to know how he's doing, but he doesn't feel like eating shawarma this evening. He thinks of Duran's finger and the severed fingers he saw in earlier years. Life consists of an immense number of accumulations, most of which you're not even aware of: all those times you experience similar things, the actions you undertake—how often you fill a bucket, kiss a shoulder, sit on a swing, and how many times still remain to you. He thinks about this as he puts the key in the lock, then looks up in response to a knock on the glass. Willem waves at him from his first-floor window, gesturing to him to wait. He seems in a panic.

'Have you seen it yet?' his elderly neighbour asks, dashing out of his front door with a wallpaper scraper in his hand. He points past him to the concrete wall across the street, a monstrosity full of asbestos that the council has promised to remove before spring. Although the last elections were several months ago, a poster has been stuck up there of an extreme right-wing politician. Willem throws himself at it, scouring it off with his scraper. 'It's those sons of the newsagent's,' he says. 'Or the father. The mother, possibly. Both their families disgraced themselves in the war. That never washes out.'

Alphonse remembers the woman, who always struck him as an ungainly little girl grown old. In their fleeting moments of contact he felt sorry for her. Could she have done this? He doesn't know. Neither does Willem. Are there other people in this village who want him out? His legs feel weak as he walks over to his neighbour and stands next to him until the last bits of paper have gone.

'Voilà,' says Willem. 'Like a drink? Something strong?'

Alphonse shakes his head. 'Thanks all the same.'

At home he takes his things out of his backpack. His smartphone tells him Amadou has twice tried to call. He pours himself a glass of fruit juice and rings him.

'Ah, there you are.'

'Yes, at last, sorry. And man, ça va?'

They laugh for a moment, at the rapid Wolof larded with French that they're speaking, that they share, and to declare unimportant the times he didn't ring back.

'Everything all right?'

'Yes, yes. When are you coming?'

'Next week, if that's still okay?'

'Yes, fine.'

He hears a woman mumble something in the background. Amadou's girlfriend. He's never met her.

'Is your wife happy with that?' asks Amadou.

'Cat always likes having visitors. Only thing is, I have to work. I can't take any time off.'

'Yes, you've already said. If you'd prefer us to make it some other time, we will.'

'I'm looking forward to seeing you.'

'It's been ages.'

He dictates the address again. He can hear a pencil writing it down.

They won't try to reconstruct how it happened that two men who virtually lived together for years came to spend so long not seeing each other. If anyone should ask they'll put it down to the distance, to being busy. There was a more definitive breaking point, however, Alphonse recalls. Although he can't any longer bring to mind the precise details, he believes it happened in the underground passageways of a busy railway station, an ugly incident that would happily have remained as inconspicuous as it was banal. There in the station Amadou asked him for a loan, enough to cover lunch and a ticket, and he, Alphonse, refused, without explaining but convinced that it happened too often, that he kept lending people money when he didn't have any himself, suddenly bitter about the many times he hadn't got back what he gave. He was aware at once how much his refusal was resented, saw Amadou's thin body bend, and afterwards he realized that Amadou didn't belong in those statistics, that he'd made a mistake. After that day they still walked for a while at each other's side, but both with a sharp stone in one shoe. The distance and being busy were just convenient excuses.

He's glad that his friend has restored contact, and that he'll soon see him again. Whether he's missed him he can't say for sure. Still, there are people he can't simply dismiss as belonging to the past. Cat thinks that's nonsense. If you haven't seen someone for years, then it's clear, according to her, that you don't regard that person as important enough, either that or you're not important enough to them. In their telephone conversation later that evening she calls the upcoming visit of Amadou and his girlfriend 'strange'. She warns of disappointments, because it would be a fairly big coincidence if they'd 'changed in the same way'. Aside from that, she thinks it's a good idea.

That he thinks so too doesn't tally with his hesitation about ringing back and making firm arrangements with Amadou. Sometimes he wonders if he likes his job so much because the contacts are as fleeting as they are intense. He listens, allows people to share, then leaves, as if they'd met while travelling.

In search of frozen soup his eye falls on the box containing Shaka Duran. He opens it and looks in. When he stands the figure upright, it sucks his finger tight to its ice-cold lips for a moment.

As he spoons his soup, he reads the newspaper. Dyslexia means he has to haul the letters of every word, more slowly than he'd like, into their places. This time the exhaustion induced by the struggle is outweighed by his interest in the article. One of the leaders of the largest party calls herself fundamentally happy. That touches him. He's never felt any connection with the woman, but he has secretly called himself that too, not long ago either: fundamentally happy. Things in common, connections he's not seen before, are less a source of confusion than of summery hope. He had a similar feeling on reading an article about the love letters an extreme right-wing politician wrote to his late mistress. 'Soyons heureux, vivons cachés,' the man told her in one of them: 'Let's be happy, hidden away.' The French saying, which slipped out of a Flemish nationalist in a moment of passion, has often passed through Alphonse's mind. It would have different resonances for Cat. Now that they've been living here for almost a year it turns out the advantages of isolation escape her. In any case she'd find it a less than credible slogan for Alphonse, a man who devotes so much time and attention to complete strangers. In the context of the extreme right, that 'vivons cachés' carries a hint of a back turned, a slammed door followed by crossed arms, a 'not in my backyard!' and a fist shaken at whoever dares walk past the window. But inside that house are the man and his sweetheart. For a moment Alphonse clearly sees the connection, a brightening bundle of immaterial threads between the most diverse people who—perhaps only sporadically, perhaps only now—find their fundamental happiness in isolation: a child at play, Lego-brick imprints on its bottom, mouth slightly open; an elderly Russian lady murmuring in front of an icon in a St Petersburg church; the politician, dreaming during a powernap, alone and united with the woman he misses; a Chilean singer disappearing into her song, sitting on her bed, in front of a mirror; and he himself, here, moved, close to tears. Dozens, thousands of others are on the point of taking shape, of soaring up, when the feeling disappears into the background just as abruptly, giving way to embarrassment, a dry cough, the sound of the dishwasher, his new habit of looking through the window to the far side of the street to check that no fresh posters have gone up. He finishes his soup. Is fundamental happiness a conceit, an illusion? Can it be taken away?

26

Sieglinde is about to step into her car when he slams shut the door to his van. Lana is already in the passenger seat and she waves to him over her shoulder, her face friendly in the rear-view mirror. After a furtive glance at her daughter and the windows of her house, Sieglinde makes a quick telephoning gesture with her thumb and little finger. He assumes she'll call him. Five months, he thinks. Does her daughter know?

'Door's open,' she calls.

Inside he finds Ronny, over a bowl of swollen Honey Loops. He's reading a stapled wad of papers, which he slides into a leather briefcase when Alphonse walks into the room. His head jerks to one side a few times, a tic Alphonse hasn't noticed before.

'What's he eating now, you're thinking.' Ronny jabs his spoon at his breakfast. The question had not occurred to Alphonse. 'My daughter left them. I just hope it's not anorexia. And I can't throw anything away.' Again those little jerks of the head. Now he's put his hand over his ear like a shell and is moaning plaintively.

Don't ask, thinks Alphonse. It'll probably come of its own accord.

Which it does. 'Yesterday I was working in the garden and I think something flew into my ear. Or crawled.' He's started using his hand as a sink plunger. 'I've got to get it out.'

Insects in bodily orifices: a wasp sting in a classmate's mouth, thirty years ago, rushed to hospital; a fly in Cat's nose in a restaurant, making one eye fill with tears and he thinking it was emotion; a beetle in his own ear, on his last trip to Senegal.

'It's buzzing. Would you have a look?'

He consents, having expected to be asked.

Ronny goes over to stand by the window. 'In the light.'

Alphonse cautiously steps into the man's personal space, the territory of pores, hair roots, and vulnerability that deters him initially in anyone other than Cat, even though it somehow fascinates him at the same time. He concentrates on the surprisingly small, pink ear, pulling gently at the earlobe to get a slightly better view of the auditory canal.

'Can you see it?' asks Ronny, one alarmed eye up close, the iris in the corner.

The inside of the ear remains dark.

'I can't see anything, Mr ... '

'Oh, just call me Ronny. I've got a torch. Wait.'

Ronny leaves him behind at the window, rummages in one of the kitchen drawers and comes back with a tube-shaped lamp.

'I really can't see anything. It might be a hair or something.'

'But it's buzzing! And it's rubbing its legs together, listen!'

On Ronny's instructions, Alphonse lays an ear against his. 'Only the sea,' he says.

'You can't hear it?!' Ronny is surprised by the anger in his own voice.

'Perhaps you ought to see a doctor.'

'Yes. I don't know how I'm supposed to find the time, but I think I'll have to, it's driving me crazy.'

'Good luck.'

'Thanks. And sorry. Nice work, by the way. That colour is ... ' He thinks about it as he knots his tie. 'Calming. Thanks for that too. And once again, my apologies. I urgently have to leave now.' In his haste he bangs his hip on the corner of the marble tabletop. He manages to stifle the pain until he's out of the room.

By the time Sieglinde rings, work has absorbed Alphonse for several hours. He takes the call.

'Ronny's left, hasn't he?' is the first thing she asks.

He reassures her.

'I had a strange dream. I was about to give birth— something that in spite of everything I've never dreamed about before—and it wasn't too bad, all told, even though I had to do it inside some kind of crude timber structure; my husband decided to lodge a complaint against the doctor. I got my child, a son. It was different from last time. I felt confused, but there was no extra gravity, no crushing. I held him in my arms and the next moment Dieter was at my side.'

'The neighbour?'

'Yes. We slowly walked down a wide staircase to the main foyer of the hospital. Halfway down, the sunlight fell through a skylight onto the child's face. It was intense and unreal. I watched dust dancing in the sunbeam. "Look," Dieter said. "He's got a moustache." I could see it now too: golden-brown hairs on the baby's upper lip, smooth and full, like the curved little eyelashes of a doll, a vertical block of them. We laughed about it. "We'll call him Führer," said Dieter, "our little Führer." We looked again, and this time the child undeniably had the face of Adolf Hitler, elderly-looking the way newborns can sometimes be, and it had a moustache with that telltale shape.' Sieglinde pauses. 'What could a dream like that mean?'

'What were you feeling?'

'Dieter and I slowed down and shared our worries. Yes, my son did look very much like Adolf Hitler. Then I felt a sadness coming, a kind of despair, but I was resolutely determined to bring the child up as well as I could, to love it unconditionally.'

He erupts with laughter, finding it impossible to suppress. 'That's a funny dream, isn't it?'

'I had to laugh about it myself, at first. Although it moved me, too. It moves me enormously, to be honest.'

'Well if you feel you're prepared to be a loving mother to Hitler, then it's bound to work out this time.'

'Yes, that's what I mean,' she says, happy.

He's finished before they get home. Not wanting to leave without saying goodbye, he writes 'Done! Have a good evening' on a Post-it, with his name underneath.

At the wheel he rings Cat, who is back earlier than planned. She asks him to pick her up, so that they can do some shopping together in what she calls 'the real supermarket'. She's explained to him more than once why she's willing to drive so far to get to this particular shop but he keeps forgetting.

Cat jerks the door open just as he's about to put the key in the lock. She's not too thin, she's beautifully slim, and she looks healthy. Everything's going to be all right.

'Pussywuss,' he says.

'Don't call me that.' She presses a smile to his lips and they embrace.

He quickly showers and puts on different clothes, a hat on his head.

On the way out, Cat's arms struggle with her leather

jacket, the one he likes, as she's well aware. 'Can we go in mine?'

They walk over to her car and he opens the passenger door for her.

'How was yoga week?' He starts the engine.

'Oh yes. Yoga.'

'Too much of a good thing?'

'No, no. It's just that most yogi aren't terribly Zen. Every time I start to think: this is where I belong, it turns out that it's not after all. My fault, probably. I'm not a group person.'

'Fortunately I'm not a group.' He puts on his sweetest face and strokes her right breast like a toddler caressing a small mammal.

She glances down. 'You've finished early?'

'Yes, and I've kept tomorrow morning free. I'll go with you.'

'No, I'm going on my own.'

'But why?'

Her eyes remain fixed on the road. 'It's *my* check-up.' His strange woman.

It could have crushed them, getting those first test results. Ovarian cancer—cunt cancer; he didn't like her calling it that. Since the diagnosis she's been as brave as she was angry. The radiation and the surgery had the intended effect and recovery was gruelling but steady, although later tests showed that another, relatively minor operation was needed. Secondaries are almost out of the question, children not. Her hair grew back in valiant waves. A routine check-up, tomorrow. With good news. Good news. Good news.

They continue their journey wordlessly and park in silence.

He's always found commercials for the supermarket on supermarket radio perplexing: enticing people to where they already are. In this case it's a conversation between two highly charged ladies, Marlies and Suzanne. Marlies is giving a cheese and wine evening but has forgotten to buy the cheese and Suzanne plans to surprise her husband Bert with mussels and chips but she's forgotten the chips. When they've finished laughing, good fortune is all that remains: the supermarket is still open.

Cat puts it down to the drink. He chuckles.

She's in the act of feeling a mango when 'Águas de Março' drowns out the voices of Marlies and Suzanne. Elis Regina and Tom Jobim take over from them, their sticks, their stones, the end of the road—she loves this song too, he knows she does, and now she's feeling the mango rhythmically, picking up another one in her other hand, shaking them discreetly back and forth, her feet following. It's glass, it's sun, it's night and it's death, a snare and a hook, a small piece of bread. He stands behind her. She puts the mangos down. '*Matita-pereira ... mistério profundo.*' He doesn't speak Portuguese but he's often listened. Her hand seeks his, her back in his arm, steps across the floor that they share with a furtive audience. It's the wind and it's blowing, it's pride at a fall, it's the rain and it's raining, it's riverbank talk. He sings the final lines of the refrain, his mouth to her ear. ' ... É a promessa de vida no teu coração.' Good news, tomorrow. A thorn, a fish, the house's design, a body in bed, a little alone. She's becoming conscious of her surroundings, wants to turn to see who's looking. 'Just another moment,' he begs, which softens her. Continual fever, a light and a scratch, it's a bird in the sky, and one in the hedge. When Elis and Tom's whistling turns into a zazaziza of laughter he slowly lets her go.

An elderly lady, staring at them, enthralled, makes her escape as quickly as possible on being spotted. An athletic man and a small, chubby woman are striding behind a supermarket trolley to the racks of onions. The man places a bag amid the other shopping in their trolley. Then his hand, briefly, for less than half a second, touches the woman's bottom.

'What is it?' Cat asks.

'I know those people.'

Dieter sees him first. Noticing him stiffen, Sieglinde follows his gaze. There's no escaping. 'Alphonse!' Her voice trembles.

Dieter hesitates, wondering whether or not to bring the trolley, then leaves it behind. 'Hey, Fonzy,' he says, apparently unaware that he's moving his body back and forth as if at a wailing wall. 'Nice hat.'

'This is Cat,' Alphonse says. 'My partner.'

They shake hands. Dieter and Sieglinde laugh as if at a dirty joke.

'We thought ... ' she starts. But she seems to have no idea what they thought.

'We were ... ' says Dieter.

'By chance ... '

'Both suddenly all out of something!'

'And we ran into each other here! Ha ha ha!'

'Cheese!' shouts Dieter.

'He was all out! Ha ha ha!'

'So I said ... ' Dieter gestures with his elbow in the direction of his neighbour. 'Come on!'

'Let's go shopping!'

'Okay,' says Alphonse.

Five months, he thinks, but now he has to speak. They're still grinding their teeth with those forced grins. 'I've just finished the bedrooms. Hope you like the result.'

'Oh, sure to! Absolutely! Thanks!'

'Our place too! Very professional!'

'Well then, let's just carry on shopping,' says Alphonse.

'Yes!' they shout in chorus.

Once they've percolated far enough between shelves insulated by bags of crisps, Cat plants a finger on his forehead. 'Magnet.'

'They're neighbours. A few days ago they were still arguing like crazy,' he explains, as quietly as he can.

'And now they're groping each other.'

'You noticed?'

'The only thing missing was a sandwich board saying "Affair". They're taking a risk, aren't they? In a supermarket like this.'

'They live even further away from here than we do.'

'All the same! They were! Here! By chance!'

'Shh. We'll talk about it in the car.'

They spend the evening on a bed of harmonious gossip, casual affection, and shared vegetable-slicing. Cat is in the bath waiting for him when the telephone intrudes, the landline.

'Let it ring,' she says.

He picks up nevertheless and sits at the top of the stairs with the receiver to his ear.

'It's his,' is the first thing Sieglinde says.

'Dieter's?'

'Yes.'

'Who knows that?'

'You. Me.'

Why him? 'I thought you hated each other till the other day.'

'We did. But I always had more of a problem with Els. Dieter and I usually can't stand each other either, but there is an attraction.'

'Complicated.'

'Horrendous.'

He can hear Cat getting out of the bath.

'And Lana? Is she ... '

'God, no! No, no no. It hasn't been going on that long.' She hesitates for a moment. 'Haven't you ever been in love with someone you could barely stand?'

'No.' He's fairly confident of that answer.

'Sometimes I think nature makes me fall in love with people to prevent me from murdering them. If I hadn't been in love with them, I'd have murdered them, I mean.'

'Does Ronny suspect anything?'

'He's at the doctor's at the moment. With an insect in his ear.'

'It was bothering him this morning. He asked if I could see it.'

A sigh. 'There's no insect in his ear. It's psychosomatic. It always is with him.'

Cat walks past without touching or looking at him. She goes downstairs. He tries to grab the loose cord of her bathrobe but misses. Downstairs she turns on the television.

'He could hear it buzzing, he said.'

'Yes, yes,' says Sieglinde. 'He's got a flat opposite that Delhaize supermarket. Dieter, I mean. Of course it's not very clever to go shopping together. Business with pleasure, we thought. Since you caught us we've agreed that at the very least we'll always take two trolleys in future.'

That dream of hers, he thinks. He has to wrap this up.

'But about the baby, you're no longer so frightened?'

'I don't know.'

The television is on in the living room.

'I don't know what to say.'

'Nothing. I just wanted to explain.'

'Okay.'

'The rooms look splendid, by the way.'

'Thanks.'

They say their goodbyes. To explain. He fails to imagine anything specific about the attraction between Dieter and Sieglinde.

Cat has already fallen asleep on the sofa, nodded off in her bathrobe, her open laptop in her lap. On the coffee table is a bottle of white wine with only a centimetre left. She started it in the bath. He turns off the television and cautiously wakes her, aware that there's little she dislikes more than being woken in the first phase of sleep. This evening is no exception. After sitting upright with closed eyes for a while, she goes upstairs without saying anything. When he puts his arm around her under the down cover, she shakes him off.

'Your patients,' she mumbles. That's what she calls his clients sometimes.

25

The first thing he sees is a boat-shaped cloud. It sails between him and the sun, then onward, allowing more and more sunbeams to warm the window and stretch out toward the quilt, toward his arms, hands, and face. He lies there until the sun is fully visible, astonished by the emotion its embrace evokes in him. He's in the habit of sleeping with the curtains open because the light helps him to wake, and the endlessness of the sky is what he likes to see first. But this morning it shines at him more magnificently than usual, and at the same time more sweetly. As if this year the summer is refusing to yield.

He looks at Cat, who's still sleeping. Soon she'll be getting good news, he thinks. He carefully lowers the blinds; she sometimes complains about too much light too early. In the bathroom it's the smells that take him by surprise, those of his bowel movement as well as the shower gel, every particle intensely present, almost tangible. 'What's happening to me?' he wonders, but the smells are already fading into the background.

Dressed in his underpants and a T-shirt, he fills the kettle and rummages in the garage in search of a lighter pair of overalls. While lifting the straps onto his shoulders, he walks barefoot along the hall and picks up the newspaper from the floor.

It's the photo of a dead Palestinian child on the front page that recalls his dream of the night just past, if only a few horrible details of it: heart-rending close-ups, no story. There was a man with his brains dripping down out of his long hair, a woman's bleeding nipples, a child with ripped stumps for fingers, and none of them were dead, they screamed, stared at their wounds in panic, fully conscious, stumbling about aimlessly.

And then there was the sun and that cloud boat, warm light, a reaffirmation of the supreme happiness with which he woke. He wonders how he could possibly wake so happy after a dream like that. He searches his memory for similar experiences but finds none. Was it the realization of having been spared extreme suffering that struck him on waking? He used to take the assertion that things 'could be worse' as a threat, as if you were about to discover that your suffering could be far greater than it already was. Now it's different, now he sees the extraordinary magnificence of every day on which no fateful turn of events befalls him.

He hears Cat coming downstairs and takes a second cup out of the cupboard.

'I didn't get much sleep,' she says.

She's wearing his bathrobe, which would leave anyone else guessing as to her figure. She's far less pale than she has been.

When he puts the cup down for her she turns her face toward him and he kisses her on the lips. She pulls the paper closer by one corner, groans on seeing the burnt child and throws it down on a nearby chair.

'I had a strange dream,' he says. 'It was horrific. I saw mutilated people, but when I woke there was only light and I felt happy.'

She looks up at him, suspicious.

'Still do. Something strange is happening to me. Something's changed.'

He wants to explain it to her but he can't find the words, managing only to increase her mistrust. She uses a knife to break up a lump of sugar at the bottom of the cup in front of her; an industrious pixie, infuriated by a stone in the soil where it's trying to plant something. The corners of her mouth point down.

Cat studies the man she lives with. Sometimes he seems like a caricature of vitality, a man for yoghurt adverts. She loves him with an intensity that she begrudges him on occasions because she can't imagine it's reciprocated to the same degree. That he's chosen this morning to emphasize his zest for life is one illustration. He takes no account of her, really, and not because good news is coming. This morning she's going to refuse to be dizzied by his confidence.

'Let me go with you.'

It makes no difference that he's correctly interpreted her disgruntlement. She resolutely shakes her head.

'I can wait in the car.'

'Let me do this alone,' she says.

He wants her to call him as soon as she knows anything.

He's set aside half a day to go with her, so the appointment with his next client isn't until the afternoon. He reluctantly throws himself into his paperwork, putting his mobile phone where he can see it and checking the landline is working—it's working.

The folder of invoices is a catalogue of domestic problems. Although his memory usually lets him down when it comes to names and faces, he recalls the houses and the conversations he's had in them. Because those conversations are rerun repeatedly in his mind as he works, it often seems in retrospect as if he's left them behind on the walls, covered with a thin but impenetrable coating to protect them against time.

Today, however, the invoices and the reminders they bring fail to distract him. Cat's appointment was at 8.30. It can sometimes be busy in hospitals. He mustn't bother her, mustn't ring.

At ten o'clock he can't bear to wait any longer. She shuts off his call. She's face to face with the doctor, he tells himself. She's sitting there looking at the doctor. Last time the results were as good as they could be at that point; today she has to be declared completely cured. She seemed to assume the results would be given to her immediately.

For another half-hour he paces the floors and stairs of their house, faster and faster, then he calls again. And again when she fails to answer.

'Yes?' she says, her voice powerless.

Seagulls, he thinks. Is that the sea? 'Why didn't you ring?'

'I'm on the beach.' De Panne, perhaps, where her parents live. Did she want them to be the first to comfort her? He can't imagine so.

'What did the doctor say? Not good?'

'No.'

An ice-cold fish is tossed into his stomach cavity, where it thrashes for life.

He can guess which part of the beach she's walking on: the broadest, between the campsite, the dunes, and the sea. 'Stay there,' he says, deaf to her protests.

He curses this region of winding lanes now; if a ring road ran north from their house he'd be with her in fifteen minutes. It takes twice that long.

After he's parked the van, though, he finds her almost immediately. She's sitting cross-legged on the dry part of the beach. This is where they usually come for a breath of fresh air after visiting her parents.

The way she stands up—reserved, ill at ease—prompts a sympathy that softens him. He won't leave her side. Their raincoats fly up in a wild dance as they embrace.

'What exactly did the doctor say?'

With a dismissive gesture, she turns away from him and starts walking.

'The last test was fine, wasn't it? Is it back now? At the same place? How's that possible?'

She shrugs. He presses her to him again. You generally only believe there's a pit called tough luck after you fall into it. The unfairness that makes such a fall possible. His anger turns against him. He's forty—how can he still let himself be misled by a few months of joy and inner harmony? He'd secretly started to believe in an autobiographical success story. A light that shone inside him. Fundamental well-being. Were he to cling to a more clearly defined faith, he'd be convinced he was being punished now for managing to enjoy personal happiness in recent months. It's certainly a bitter warning.

Cat doesn't want to talk about it. Not now. Nor does she want to visit her parents, calling them the worst option after bad news, a view he can only endorse.

He doesn't understand why she wants to keep him out of this, so he asks her to explain. They've shared plenty of misery in the past. But she insists: no need to cancel his appointment with his new client, she'd like to stay here alone for a while in the wind and sea air. 'There's no way I'm going to do myself any harm,' she says finally, irritated.

Everything has a heaviness about it when he reaches the van. It doesn't feel right to drive off and leave her at this point. Being unwanted gnaws at him. THE LAST STRAW-BERRIES! he reads—a message chalked on a sign beside the road, a metaphor, the title of a song about this day on which things turned their back on him after all, completely unexpectedly. He mustn't have such melodramatic thoughts. He stops at the side of the road, close to a muddy ditch, to allow a monstrous agricultural vehicle to thunder past. Everyone is eager to share their distress with him except the woman he loves. It seems a reprehensible thought, but he's unable to shake it off.

The woman is transplanting a hydrangea in her front garden, between a small model windmill and a low holly hedge. She's about sixty and her head is down. The pinafore she's wearing makes her as timeless as this district, on the boundary between fairy tale and destitution. He loves the old houses, especially the small ones, slightly lopsided, with their postage-stamp gardens filled with kitsch and the glories of nature, every sundial so polished, every calyx so diligently propped that even the most cynical guardian of good taste couldn't help but be moved by it. The care this woman devotes to her little garden certainly moves Alphonse. Perhaps he's more receptive to it now that his mood has sunk so low.

Then she looks up at him and he's startled by his own sorrow, which he sees magnified and stretched like a reflection in a fairground mirror. She smiles, the woman, but inside her deep eye sockets lie heaps and heaps of something else.

He introduces himself, reminds her of the room he's agreed to take in hand. It's just one room and she's called Madeleine Claeys—it all comes back to him now.

'Yes, thank you,' she says, or rather sighs, in a hoarse monotone; she must be deeply tired. 'I'll show you the room.'

He walks inside behind her and up a narrow flight of stairs. Unlike the front garden, the house is badly neglected. The wallpaper in the stairwell cries out for replacement—it might well be older than he is—but he never makes suggestions.

Oh, so it's one of those stories, he thinks as she pushes the door open for him. The silenced child's room from another era, radiant with weekly cleansed disuse, the smooth patchwork quilt over the narrow mattress, washed every year, the ancient teddy bear and scary clown on the pillow gazing at the stains on the wallpaper, the only interruption to which is a black-and-white photo of a sweet little boy of about two years old. A beautiful child, it goes without saying. An old one, though, thinks Alphonse.

'My brother. He's dead.' The woman's rasping voice sounds decisive.

He nods, doesn't wait for any further information, not after this morning. 'Do you want it to look the way it does now or to be unrecognizable?'

'The latter,' she says. 'The walls, ceiling, floor, skirting board, door, and door frame. All of it. The furniture can go into the next room for now. If you see anything you can use, just take it with you.' She stiffly descends the stairs.

After he's emptied the room he calls Cat, who to his exasperation and sickening concern doesn't answer. Thirst plagues him. After the day's emotional start he forgot to bring a bottle of water. Since leaving him in the dead child's room, the woman has not shown her face.

His large feet diagonal on the narrow stairs, he cautiously goes down. He knocks on the door and opens it on receiving her feeble permission. She's sitting at a window looking out on the front garden, in a rattan chair with a tall back to it, smoking a cigarette. She glances round at him and waves at the cupboard above the sink when he asks for a glass of water. His thank-you doesn't seem to get through to her. She's staring at a blackbird on the window ledge, then she looks at her fingers, holding the burning stub of the cigarette, which she puts out amid the pile in the ashtray.

Still no one who feels like talking to me, he thinks. Perhaps it was something I used to have that's gone. The blackbird flaps wildly against the glass.

In the room he looks again at the portrait of the little brother.

Insufficient daylight comes into the room and the chandelier is feeble. His hands are clumsier than normal and the results messy. When he tries to check whether a skirting board is firmly fixed to the wall it breaks in two without the slightest resistance, emitting a rotten burp.

He looks at the piece still attached to the wall by clusters of bent nails and curses the generations of DIY enthusiasts who make his work more difficult, and not just in this house. They hide the pipes of a defective floor-heating system but forget to release the pressure. They concrete over television cables, saw through supporting beams, brick up drains. Here the floor isn't level, an imperfection that the unequal skirting boards are intended to resolve by means of an optical illusion but in fact only emphasize. And what have the weekend dabblers stuffed into the gap between wall and floor? Paper?

They're letters, or at least full envelopes. He pulls them

out of the groove one by one, all the way from the corner where two walls and the floor come together to a point where the skirting board is still clinging on. Perhaps there are more; he could wrench all the skirting loose. First he wants to see what's inside. If it's money, this may be a means of testing him, to see whether he'll pocket it. Something like that happened to him once, at a previous job.

When he opens a letter, the graph paper tears in half. There's a number at the top—'1972'—the year perhaps. Then writing, in an irregular hand, switching from blue to black ballpoint halfway. People who manage to overcome dyslexia develop their brains more thoroughly than people who don't suffer from the disorder, a teacher once impressed upon him. In his case the letters continue to jump over one another like playful lambs. Handwriting demands more effort than print, and Madeleine doesn't seem to care about punctuation. It's only when he reads the sentences for the fourth time that their meaning starts to come through.

'i still see him every day after school i have to mum not any better dad no news and hes older than i was then no one can ever get used to it my Moustaki record broken in two *dix-sept ans et vivre à chaque instant ses caprices d'enfant ses désirs exigeants* but i am seventeen that doesnt matter itll stay the way it is tough luck'

He opens a second envelope, also unmarked. On the paper, ruled this time, is a neat '1987' and the message: 'everything the same without that shouting it would be different try to enjoy nature'.

It must be her abbreviated diary. In 1990 she writes: 'he would have a deficiency something remarkable but it wouldnt show colour blindness for example i would always be the only one who could calm him the parents of his last girlfriend would have a riding school and after the relationship was over because she cheated on him i would say that i always thought she stank of the stables i would also inspect his clothes tennis hed have a talent for that but not enough ambition because he also benefitted from his youth and his trainer would have a hard time with that we would always like looking a lot at certain television programmes he and i but he less and less so we would slowly discuss less and less about them but talk a lot about the garden and sometimes about cooking and we wouldnt mind that'

His telephone fishes him out from among the letters. Cat. What is he reading, sitting here? He has to regain control, or at least hold chaos at bay. He puts the phone to his ear before he's had a chance to read the name of the caller.

It's not Cat, it's Duran. He knows straight away that he's talking to the young man of the finger but doesn't immediately understand what he wants.

'I got your number from the Yellow Pages,' Duran begins. 'It's only because I have a chance to go to Sapporo. With a group from Argentina.'

'Sorry?'

'I'm going to Japan. It's much bigger out there.'

'What is?'

'Ice sculpture. Sapporo, haven't you heard about it? They found me via internet, the Argentines. They were selected months ago. They rang me on an old number and mailed me. I saw it just in time. So I can still go.'

'Fantastic. I didn't know your sculptures were on the internet. I thought no one was allowed to see them.'

'I like to keep this separate from the shop,' he says seriously. 'Anyhow, I'm in the Argentine group. They're very good. They want Durans from all over the world. And Shaka Duran is one of them.'

'I can bring him round.'

'I don't like to ask. It was a present. I tried to make a new Shaka Duran but I can't with my bandaged hand. Otherwise I'd make them there, like the other participants, but in the circumstances I'll have to take them with me, see?'

'When do you need him?'

'As soon as possible. The moment I'm back from Japan he'll be yours again. Thanks.'

'I'll be round tomorrow morning early, all right?'

'That's really very good of you.'

He has to go to Cat, even though he's done far less work than he intended. It's a long time since he felt a sense of embarrassment steal over him. It permeates the general unease of the day. Not only has he done little work, he's breached this woman's confidentiality, although that didn't occur to him as he was reading. He decides it would be pathetic to stuff the envelopes back into the crack so he piles them up on the floor.

'I've found some letters,' he says as he walks into her living room.

She's still sitting in the same position, but now with a flowery shawl over her shoulders.

'Just take them with you,' she says, her expression shrouded in cigarette smoke.

'Ça va,' he says, in no fit state to think of a better answer.

He doesn't want to take the letters into the house so he leaves them on the passenger seat.

Cat has cooked. She talks about her parents, how she'll

go and see them this week after all, and about the translations she's working on: a sixteenth-century Spanish mystic and a folder for a timber company. She thinks it's absurd that she finds herself financially obliged to take on the latter sort of jobs. As he's aware.

He wants to ask her if she's scared, but despite her communicative mood, which makes him think of Madeleine's notes, she continues to avoid eye contact. In bed she falls asleep immediately. Several hours later he wakes aroused and confused with her lips around his member. She licks and glides, climbs him and rides him; he can't keep up with her, wants to slow down, to turn on the light to see her, but she's a whirlwind, a beast with a hundred tongues that gives him no chance and then suddenly escapes him again. He throws an arm around her warm stillness and hopes for a night without dreams.

24

With the morning light, he strokes her back. He needs to talk to her, soon, to penetrate the unfamiliar shield she's put up, but now she must sleep, for as long as she can.

Wash, dress, coffee and newspaper: acts you perform at fixed times fail to stimulate the memory sufficiently to be remembered, but on mornings like this, at the start of pleasant days, the rituals take a firmer lead.

He walks around as he eats his bread with chocolate spread, looking for his shoes. The sense of having forgotten something creeps over him. He walks to the van in the hope it's nothing important and drives out of the street more slowly than usual.

For the past three seasons a boy with some kind of intellectual disability has stood in front of the last house. He addresses Alphonse as 'scallywag'. He hasn't been there for several days. Cancer again, no doubt. He tries to shake the word out of his head. 'No. No,' he mumbles. It's a long time since he last talked to himself.

Then, just before the second road junction, he knows what it is he's forgotten: Shaka Duran. He turns the van and drives back by the same route, this time at walking pace, behind a combine harvester. Once again he'll get to his client later than intended. He squeezes the wheel, telling himself there's no sense in getting upset.

It's still quiet in the kitchen. When you visit your

house unexpectedly it sometimes feels like someone else's. He looks for the freezer box containing Shaka Duran and opens it carefully to check the sculpture is still intact—even the delicate spear is undamaged. With the box in a plastic bag between two freezer packs, he hurries out again.

'*Merci, merci!*' The owner of Pita Merci looks immensely tired. 'Watch out, it's slippery there.' The floor is wet and clean, and in the corner there's a bucket of water that smells of roses. Duran cautiously opens one corner of the lid. He nods his approval, closes the box again and carries it solemnly to the freezer.

'What about your finger? When do the stitches come out?' Alphonse asks his back.

'In five days. But I'll be in Japan then. They can do it anywhere, the doctor says.'

'Ha!' snorts a voice from behind the counter.

When Alphonse takes a step to one side and stretches his neck he sees a sullen sixty-something sitting on a low chair, head resting on an arm, the arm on a knee.

'This is my father,' says Duran.

'A pleasure,' says Alphonse.

The father gives a dour nod in response and tosses a few Turkish words in Duran's direction. Duran gives a reticent answer, then adds something placatory.

'My father doesn't think it's a good idea for me to go to Japan. We've been talking about it all night. He doesn't see the point. I'm grateful he's willing to keep the shop going while I'm away.'

The father stands up brusquely and shouts something at his son, gesturing toward Alphonse.

'He says I'm not Argentinian. He thinks ice sculptures are for children and he'd like to know your opinion.'

'I think they're beautiful,' says Alphonse. 'Cleverly done.'

Duran translates triumphantly. The father raises his hands to the ceiling and shouts again.

'"Another lunatic," says my father.'

With his next statement the father stands up and puts one finger up close to his son's nose.

'He's telling me to stop translating.'

'I have to go, anyhow. Good luck in Japan. Good day to you, sir.'

'*Merci*,' say father and son in unison, both slightly thrown by their audience's sudden departure.

Madeleine Claeys pretends to be lost in thought as the van comes up her drive, but behind the reflections in the window separating her from the front garden she keeps a careful watch on the driver. He's a man who doesn't like to arrive late. The fact that it's nevertheless happened for the second time must have to do with some disturbance to the peace that usually surrounds him. You can tell that just by looking: he's a person surrounded by peace. She wants to hear it from a person like this.

He's startled by how quickly she opens the door.

'Sorry,' he begins, but she interrupts him.

'Have you read them?'

Only then does he think back to the pile on the passenger seat. He can't remember seeing it there this morning.

'Only a few,' he says. 'These are strange days. Do you want me to read them?'

'I want you to read everything, then tell me about them. Before you do any more work.' Despite her slight stutter she says it with complete conviction.

He agrees and goes back to the van. The pile of letters is still there. He picks it up and arranges with Madeleine that he'll read them all in the room and then come and find her.

They are variations on a single theme.
'1993 when i sit next to him i draw little hearts on the ball of his thumb with my finger i casually say something about cowardly men and that the hands can go slowly but the years fast in the end and that i accept it can go even quicker but that i wont leave him alone i often say that i wont leave him alone i tell him about what ive seen that day or the night before its never much a swallows nest or once a procession a fanfare mostly i say nothing and wipe his mouth or look its no good really those eyes turn but real contact what is that i stroke him comb his hair usually with earplugs in because i feel i deserve routine and earplugs'

'2001 in the end it comes down to limiting damage done to others which is why i agreed to it my brothers vocal cords were cut last month neighbours at the day centre have been complaining about the shouting and screaming for years and in the end even the social workers spoke to me about it i dont blame anyone he did shout most of the day never a whole day not year in year out and i know that for them it wasnt mainly about decibels but about how he shouted because anyone who heard it thought he was in unbearable pain now you only see that and you have to come close.'

When he's read all of them he goes downstairs.
'Gin and tonic?' she asks. He nods and takes a cigarette from the pack she's holding out. He smokes just a few a year. He waits on the poof that belongs with the sofa near the window until she comes to sit next to him. She puts his glass on the side table and her own to her lips.

He tells her the story she knows, about her younger brother who was born normal but after a fall or an infection would have been better off dead. He tells her she never doubted it was her fault, that her mother convinced her of that, blaming her not just for her brother's condition but for her father's disappearance as well. She's never dared allow herself to see that there are a lot of things that guilt has nothing to do with, that a child can be inattentive and inattentiveness fatal. That events don't even require inattention in order to be fatal. She was the only one to go and visit him every day, out of love and to punish herself. Sometimes a partner threatened to come between them, but never for long. Anyone who didn't disappear of their own accord she chased away with double-glazed loneliness, her world of bedsores, severed vocal cords, and malicious fate, a sorrow so great and incontrovertible that everyone walked away from it. And that her brother then finally found peace and she went on living, he tells her that too. Now she must set the fire. He'll paint the room and she must fill the decades that remain to her with what she enjoys, everything she can still love.

He waits for the sobs to subside before wiping back the grey lock hanging over her face.

'Dropped, that's what,' she says.

'Come on.'

She nods.

Outside, in the long narrow garden at the back of the house, they gather wood. He lights it with thin twigs and one of the letters. It burns quickly in the dry air. Without any hesitation Madeleine throws the other letters on, one by one so as not to smother the fire, until she's finished and takes his hand. He doesn't let go until the last blackened fragments have turned to white ash.

The rest of the day he wets the wallpaper in the room. It seems to have been waiting for his paint scraper and it makes way without complaint for walls flayed smooth. He brushes flakes of paint from the ceiling, sands and repaints the parquet and the skirting boards. At the end of the day he finds himself inside a cube that's waiting, naked and buoyant, for a new coat.

He doesn't see Madeleine until he's clearing up. She called out to him earlier that she was going shopping. He leaves the house promising to be back the next day, while she puts a considerable quantity of pasta away in a cupboard and ice-cream cakes in an empty freezer.

'Hungry,' she says.

At home he finds Cat, also looking into an empty freezer compartment, but peering and groping. Her face is tear-stained. The packs of spinach, the bag of croquettes, and the leftovers of soup she's pulled out stand near her feet weeping too.

He wants to take her in his arms but the scene dissuades him, first because he finds it disturbing, then because of a suspicion that he can explain all this, although he doesn't yet know how.

'I'm going crazy,' she says.

'No you're not,' he says.

'I no longer know what I dreamed and what's real. Yesterday I went to get something out of the freezer and I saw a box at the back that seemed to have been hidden there.'

With secret pleasure he decides to let her tell the whole story.

'When I open it up there's a little guy made of ice inside, about as big as my forefinger, dressed in a loin-cloth and a pair of those straw legwarmers, with a shield and a spear. Beautifully made, I've never seen anything like it. All ice. No idea if it was supposed to be an African. Its face made it look white. I put it back in the box and thought: I'll have to ask Alphonse—the fact that I forgot isn't normal either!'

He sees her dismay—greater, crazier than he's used to in her—and wants to interrupt, but she rattles on.

'And now it isn't there, because of course it never was, I'm imagining things and that I imagine things is my own fault!' She ignores the placatory arms he holds out to her, his lips pouting to say something. 'Because I'm not sick, or only in my head. I'm not sick any longer, I lied.'

What is she saying?

He looks at the rising water in her eyes, watches it pour over the rims.

'The tests?' he begins.

'I'm cured.'

'But that's great, isn't it?' He doesn't know what he's feeling, doesn't know who this woman is or why she's allowed him to live in hell for the past two days. Before her sobbing intensifies, her expression mimics his own: a mouth that slips from smile to horror and back again.

'That's what you wanted more than anything, isn't it? To be healthy? It's what I wanted more than anything!' The tighter his embrace, the smaller and more angular her body becomes, until he lets go because he no longer recognizes it. 'Why?' He needs to know. After all the youth it cost her to defeat the enemy, why does she want to collaborate with it? Is this a version of the Stockholm syndrome? 'Why did you lie?'

'Before I got ill it always seemed as if I was going to lose you.'

He can't believe she's saying this.

'No. Don't go away now.' Sure enough, he's at the door, in the hall, covering the last metre to his van. 'It's better to talk about it straight away,' he hears her call through the half-darkness before the car door cuts off her voice. He thinks so too, in theory, but it seems his foot wants to press the accelerator and he has to flee any delay that could bring him to a halt.

He wonders how come the radio is tuned to a classical channel. 'Liszt,' says a voice by way of a starting shot. He knows little about classical music. Is it pure chance that even the music is suddenly different from anything he knows? He's no idea where he's driving to, but he does know that he has to drive and that a shaft of beauty is filling the car. The piano sounds so lovely at first, so orderly, to the point of pampering. Night falls over the endless rows of trees—what kind of trees? are they ash?—on both sides of the road, trees whose leaves are changing and then letting go because they've been sucked dry by the trees, which made them to store food, to eat from when winter comes, because trees know how to survive. He wants them to embrace what the music says, to pamper him, to make him turn round. But a small rodent has crept up to the highest piano keys and it's now multiplying and mice are hurrying in dense throngs up the neat stalks, out of the ground into the sky, and when they throw themselves from the branches they become descending bells, then bell-ringing that catches the sky unawares. The twilight dissolves into night.

He turns off the music and leaves the engine running. Was it true what she said, that she might have lost him at any moment before she got sick? It was true. He remembers the turmoil of times past, the thirst, recalls a firework competition he took part in with friends, coincidence really, not even their style, a random detail that strikes him as symbolic of those days: a firework competition. There were loud nights with lots of movement, with stages and audiences, for him, with crowds dancing on the spot, ogling at women, smiling, full of disbelief about how he met his girlfriend.

His mother worked for Cat's family—a diplomat couple—and he lived with her and Cat's father, in Dakar and later in Brussels. When he was twelve and the diplomat, no longer young, suddenly fell pregnant with Cat, his mother became a nanny, Cat's *m'bindan*, and moved to Mexico with the family. He saw little of his mother from then on and was brought up by his uncle in Brussels, and in arguments Cat sometimes accuses him of blaming her for that, although it's not true. He remembers the days of childhood dragging when he missed his mother, but also the contentment derived from an underlying conviction that she was with him, that she loved him, as she said she did, even when he couldn't touch her. He found comfort in that, the fact that love can persist without proximity. He saw Cat a number of times while she was growing up, paid less attention to her than, as she said later, she'd hoped. When she was eighteen she fell so much in love with him that she told everyone about it, her parents, his mother, eventually even him. He was thirty then, accustomed to the sweet sweat of parties and women, all carried by bass lines; he didn't know where to start with her, thought her beautiful but too young and, although he barely knew her, too close. He also wondered if it was history, their prehistory as well as the history of the peoples that had produced them, which needed to be set right by love, while she kept insisting, with rising despair, with rising urgency, that history had nothing to do with it, that it was him, his body and his soul, his voice and laugh and everything he could do, simply him. He talked about her with his mother and she approved: 'a good child' and 'good for him'. He couldn't do this for his mother, he kept thinking, and then, hesitantly, he did it for himself. Because he saw a lot he could love, how Cat's rattling bracelets betrayed her nervous way of moving, how she waved, her other, secret voice when she discreetly sang along to songs; there was so much he could love, if he were to become calmer, if he were to fall in love with her. And there were those who said that love doesn't work that way, that love is either there or not and has nothing to do with choices, and there were those who told him that, like it or not, one of the two always has a greater love, and the people who knew this were all people like him, people who avoided love because they desired too much and therefore anticipated only disappointments. So he carried on with her in those first few years, but he also carried on avoiding her, because he carried on fearing he'd made a mistake. Their relationship had pauses, or rather gaps, intermezzos full of sobs, blazing drama, and declarations of freedom. But she was there when the disappointments piled up, she was there without ever giving way. And there was always her body, too, which took him in like no other, a body he knew better and better, loved more and more until he loved it like no other, which ensured that after a few years he, surrounded by flirtatiousness and despite his greedy past, wanted no other body. She was wrong. His love for her didn't blossom when she got sick; it was several months before the diagnosis that he arrived at the disconcerting realization that he was madly in love with the woman he'd lived with for years, and only then did that love, through the slosh and foam of his fear of losing her now that he'd finally found her, pour over his lips. He could no longer love her in silence, no longer not. Has her lie changed that?

He turns off the engine.

It's not the first time he's spent the night in a car. He remembers stretching out comfortably on the back seat, at an age that still permits it, in Tonton Jah's car, surrounded by alcohol fumes and apnoea, longing for a blanket. He remembers a friend's car, the mutual hope that something would happen, and when it happened realizing it wasn't working, that for incomprehensible reasons it wasn't working, stopping and falling asleep in bewilderment, woken by her words: that she hadn't slept a wink. Or later, drunk himself, spending the night in a car loaded with instruments and musicians, woken by the engine that was still running, turning the engine off, then on again, leaving. Spending the night in a car after an argument with Cat, years ago. Seeing the full moon, as now.

23

When he wakes, from the cold and the pain in his neck, beside the road, he's looking out on a meadow with one cow. Perhaps there are more cows, but he can't see them through the dark and the fog. Although its colour is shrouded in gloom, he knows it's a brown cow, typical of the region. Their eyes meet. What does it see when it looks at me? he wonders.

Not a cow, thinks the cow.

His phone reveals that Cat has tried to ring him once. It's only 5.15, too soon to call on Madeleine. Other than he and the cow, no one seems to be awake. On this trip through the dark he can see hardly any lighted windows. The streets are empty—not even the occasional Harley rider or a bored child in a driveway.

To wake reality he turns on the radio. The newsreader seems drunk with sleep. Or is he actually drunk? The news doesn't get through to Alphonse, until the voice says that an Ebola sufferer from Guinea has travelled to Dakar and is now under observation in hospital. Rarefied air fills his body, his head. He can see it: the trip in small, overcrowded buses, the sweat, the unavoidable bodily contact.

At home he looks at her body on the sofa, goes to sit near it on the chair by the wall next to the window, through which more and more light falls. The chest moves almost imperceptibly up and down, soundlessly sleeping, the eyelashes long and still. Then the body tosses, shakes itself, the head too, bumping from back-rest to arm before curling around the chest, sinking further away.

And now understanding hits home, now it's capable of negating everything else. It thunders past his temples, becoming tender rain; it rains inside him. She might live a very long life. But you have to open your eyes, he thinks. If you open your eyes, it's fine to go on; we're not just two separate people if you just open your eyes, now.

She blinks against the air and the light, scrambles upright when she sees him sitting there, so poised that it makes her rub her eyes.

'I'm so sorry,' she says. 'That wasn't something to lie about.'

The living body entices him. He pulls off his sweater and nestles between her legs, feeling the warmth of her thighs and soft sex through the fabric of his overalls, warming her long, narrow feet in his hands, laying his face on her belly. She strokes his hair and presses him closer to her. Even understanding vanishes into the background and he forgets what this was all about; desire is all that remains.

It took him an effort to tear himself loose from Cat's body, but this morning he has managed to arrive at Madeleine Claeys' house on time. She greets him with Darjeeling and éclairs, amid furniture she's rearranged and carpets hanging out of windows, as if the house is a face with many tongues that droop panting from its many mouths, all exhaustion and relief.

Madeleine takes a bite of éclair and urges him to follow

her example. He says he'll get a paunch, which she tells him is nonsense.

She carries on cleaning after he goes to the room. There he paints the walls a very light pink, almost white, encouraged by the sun that projects its beams through the uncurtained window and brightens the expanding surface. This is the right colour for a new beginning, a colour without political overtones, too difficult to be commercial and too elusive for reproach.

'It's wonderful!' she exclaims, next to him in the room, a sugary waffle in her hand. Her next problem will have to do with insatiable hunger.

She doesn't want to stop at this room, the whole house must be reborn and he must see to it that it is. She's initially horrified that he can't start for another month, then she resigns herself.

'I'm a bit hyperkinetic, I think,' she says. 'It's just so strange. Still to be alive. Understand?'

'I think I do.'

'So strange and so good.' She plunges a spoon into the bowl of fruit salad she's made for herself and brings it to her mouth. Guessing what he's thinking, she says: 'Fruit isn't a problem.'

It's only four o'clock when he sets off for home. Once the fog lifted it was a golden Saturday. The first leaves on the plane trees are turning. Despite the morning sex, his muscles mainly recall the cramped position in which he spent the night. Like the weather, they urge him to go for a walk.

Before he knows whether or not Cat is home, he looks at the fridge, the freezer compartment; everything is as it used to be.

'I'm up here,' she calls.

Two steps at a time, he runs upstairs, to her desk. To judge by the page on the screen and the expression on her face, she's translating a poem, not an instruction booklet.

He goes to stand next to her. Seated, she puts her arms around him, bumping her forehead against his stomach. I'm sorry, is what it means. And that she's grateful for what's starting to look more and more like forgiveness.

'What are you translating?' he asks.

'Friar Luis de León. The sixteenth-century Spanish poet. For an anthology. When this is ready, we're rich.'

They laugh.

'A poet you'd probably like,' she goes on.

'Read it.'

'It's not finished.'

'I want to know now.'

'The poem is called "The Solitary Life" and it starts "How peaceful is the life / of those who shun the world's uproar / to follow the hidden path / of those few wise people / the world has brought forth." Or perhaps: "has known".

'Beautiful.' The words 'the hidden path', the idea of a hidden path, the enjoyable realization that he is himself on a hidden path, electrify him for a moment.

'Yes, after centuries his poems still have something truly vivacious and fresh.'

He nods. 'He was a kind of priest?'

'Something like that. He was in prison for a while, after a run-in with the Spanish Inquisition, although of course he came out stronger.' For a brief moment her joking eyes catch his. As she talks she continues to look at the screen. 'He does rather tend to go on about how contented he is, away from the commotion. And how he doesn't need applause and how the destructiveness of others can't touch him.'

'You don't believe him?'

She shrugs, realizing that after her lie of the past few days she'd do well not to judge the credibility of sixteenth-century poets or, by extension, him. 'Sometimes these mystics exaggerate. That he wants to be "by himself", fine, but also "freed from love and lust, delivered from hatred and hope, from suspicion and envy". That's a lot! In English *La Vida Retirada* is translated as "The Life Removed", which makes it seem not just as if Luis de León has withdrawn from the commotion to be able to know real life, as it were, but as if life itself has been removed. What's actually left to you if you throw overboard all the things he mentions? Nature?'

Yes, thinks Alphonse, among other things, but he knows what she means and opts for rapprochement. 'Delivered from love, okay, but from lust: I don't buy it.'

He kisses her hesitant smile.

'Are we going for a walk?'

'Now?'

'This might be the last fine day of the year.'

'Nature after all, then.'

Sometimes they'd like to be people who can set off armed for a nature walk at a moment's notice, whose walking shoes aren't wet because they've been left out in the garden for two weeks, who can find the bird book they bought right away, and whose neighbour doesn't knock just as they're about to leave.

'Hey, Willem, we're going for a walk. Coming with us?' says Alphonse at the front door. Willem knows all the trees and birds by name.

Disconcerted by the file under their neighbour's arm, Cat signals 'not now' to Alphonse.

'I walk far too slowly for you,' says their neighbour firmly. Then: 'Later, maybe.' He takes an opened packet of biscuits out of his coat and puts them on the kitchen table, sits down and lets Cat pour him a cup of coffee.

'Do you remember that propaganda picture on the commemorative coin?' Willem asks. '"The Black Shame!"' As he makes inverted commas in the air, his hands shake.

'Vividly,' says Cat. The picture showed a huge erect penis wearing a helmet, a kneeling white woman attached, arms tied behind her back, around the penis, her long hair hanging down over her bowed face. Willem had made a poster-sized copy of the illustration from a book.

'We didn't hang it on the wall,' says Alphonse.

He knows from Cat that some of her friends have questioned her on the subject—is it true?—and that she never dared to get angry. Later they came to visit, all those people with their explicit interest in the size of his sexual organ and their emancipated right to the word 'Negro'. He cooked for them; mostly they seemed quite nice.

Willem understands perfectly well why they didn't put the German propaganda on display, but now he's copied another illustration. He pulls off the elastic holding the file shut, folds back the cardboard flaps and leafs through his documents until he finds what he's looking for. Alphonse knows which newsagent he used to make photocopies. Willem cycled there, the heavy book in a plastic bag tied to the baggage rack of his bicycle. I like this man, thinks Alphonse, but we have to stop him. He looks at the picture held in front of his nose: a gorilla with a French soldier's cap, a rucksack, and bared teeth is dragging a blonde and apparently unconscious woman behind him. '"The Black Terror in German Lands".' Again those trembling commas in the air.

'Jesus, what's happened to her stomach?' says Cat. It looks as if the woman has been torn open from anus to navel.

'The extent to which the *tirailleurs sénégalais*, and other coloured soldiers too, incidentally, were portrayed as a sexual threat is beyond imagining,' Willem begins, unaware that his neighbours are exchanging glances. 'It also reveals the fear of active female sexuality, of course.' For those final words he turns, breezy but uncertain, to Cat, who, to his surprise, winks at him over her cup of tea.

'Come on,' she says. 'We're going for a walk.'

'Good.' Still confused by the wink, he stands up. They follow his lead.

Outside they discuss how long it's going to stay fine and where they'll walk to. Cat deploys her veto against the military cemeteries that Willem wants to include in the route. The neighbour is hurt by the fact that she hates graveyards, and perhaps for that reason starts talking about his research into the *tirailleurs sénégalais* again: 'The American officers in the First World War were the worst when it came to the treatment of black soldiers. That obsession with sex and black men wasn't new for them. Military doctor R.W. Shufeldt had already looked into the possibility of castrating "the entire Negro race" in the United States. But since not even castration, segregation, and lynching would be enough, in his view, to overcome the hypersexuality of the black man, he concluded that the best option was compulsory repatriation to Africa.'

'The things you know, Willem,' says Cat.

'Oh,' Willem clears his throat to counterbalance the

proud but rather sheepish laugh that escapes him.

Suddenly Alphonse grows more irritated than he wants to be, more irritated than the other two expect of him. 'Can we just talk about the trees now?'

The walk continues in silence until interrupted by Willem's knowledge of trees. Cat meekly allows him to lay leaves in her hand and Alphonse names them: 'Elm. American oak. Poplar. Willow. Ash.' Strange that no one ever taught him these names, when he knows everything about paint and strings and can name all the parts of a tea service. Out of the chicken coop at an isolated farm, juvenile chickens emerge with unruly feathers, having coarsely outgrown the sweetness of chicks.

Cat puts the leaves in the pocket of his coat. He seems to appreciate that, her beautiful man with his eccentricities. How could she have lied to him?

'Are you working tomorrow?' she asks. They're in bed, back to back.

'Yes.'

She says nothing.

'And after that we really do have to visit your parents.'

'Yes.'

'On Wednesday Amadou and his girlfriend are coming.'

'Shit. I already forgot.'

'I'm working from Wednesday to Friday all the same.'

'What?' She turns to face him, making the sheet strangle him for a moment. 'So I have to take care of them all on my own? I've got work to do too!'

'They're on holiday, so they'll sleep till midday. And they'll keep themselves busy till the evening. Amadou was talking about cycling.'

She sniffs.

'I found out too late. I couldn't cancel my appointments.'

'You could if you wanted to. He's your friend. I barely know him.'

'I'm here at the weekend,' he says curtly.

Is he still angry with me? she asks herself. Will he slowly punish me?

Am I still angry with her? he asks himself. Under the covers sleep grabs their ankles, pulling them with it more quickly than expected.

22

He's got work to do at a writers' residence just over the French border, surrounded by a park where a famous author played as a child. He's never been contacted by the French before, but the staff at the annexe where he reports for duty don't seem to think there's anything strange about it. 'The greener the district, the more porous the border,' one of them says, but also that the Belgians are trying to get rid of the French cross-border workers by withdrawing the beneficial statute that encourages them. Alphonse is the housepainter who lives closest; the reason for asking him is no more exciting than that. He's to paint one of the rooms, as well as the spacious entrance hall and stairway.

'The most important thing is to work in silence,' says one of them, half turned toward him at her desk. 'There's one author and one translator at the moment. They're here for the peace and quiet.'

The room looks out across a domain swelling under oceans of late-summer light. He's walked in this park in spring, amid purple strips of bluebells and the all-pervasive scent of wild garlic. Both have gone now, replaced by a lawn that's ready for leaf mould, fat earthworms, wet feathers. That red of the tree crown there, he ought to put that on the walls. This time, however, no one has asked his opinion. The requirement is white.

He spreads the tarpaulin and starts taping the skirting boards and window frames. Now and then he hears the floor of the adjoining room creak and twice a coffee maker grows agitated, interrupted by a short intermezzo of clinking china. A man coughs, spends a long time coughing and ends each salvo with a series of plaintive, exhausted 'oh's. This could be a day without stories. Alphonse wonders why authors and translators come here. Do they travel from residence to residence, like addicts pursuing a story, or more like refugees, moving away from something? White, then. All the walls. The ceilings too.

He hears footsteps in the corridor and waits with curiosity to see who'll walk past the doorway. It's a woman, over forty, who looks as if she's just escaped from a tiger.

'Been jogging?' he asks.

She stares right through him with the most astounded expression, her thoughts miles away, before recovering her focus. 'Yes,' she says, as she tries to wipe the sweat from her red face with a bare arm. 'Hello. It's been a while. I'll have to give up the fags. And drink. And shower. I mean, I have to drink and shower, now. Water. And stop smoking. Sorry. I can't talk any more. Say what I'm thinking, that is. Not "can't talk to you". I haven't said much here in the past fourteen days. Maybe that's what. Maybe that's it. But now: water. Okay. See you later. I think.'

She disappears in the direction of her studio apartment, the door at the end of the corridor.

'Shit,' he hears her say. Her feet drag her into view again, in profile. She holds her head tight as if it might otherwise fall from her body and stares at the ground.

'What are you looking for?'

'My key.'

He tears off a piece of cling film and wraps the wet paint roller in it. The paint in the tray ran out for the first time a moment ago.

'You don't need to help me,' she says in surprise when he joins her in the corridor. Only now does he notice her embarrassment.

'Are they on a key ring?'

'A round one. Brown.'

They peer along the brown corridor and down the brown stairs, out of the door to the brown path across the grass. After they've searched in silence for several minutes she calls out: 'Ah!'

'Got them?'

'No.' She stares at him with raised eyebrows, her nose and mouth hidden under a roof of hands. 'Sorry! I'm really terrible.'

'You left the door unlocked? The key's in your room?'

She nods.

His tittering chases the birds out of the closest trees. In between apologies she laughs with him. 'A shower, then,' she repeats on the landing.

One wall has received its first coat when she comes in again. She's now a woman in a dress, with make-up and an ironic, rather distracted look on her face. She's brought a thermos flask and a cup.

'Coffee?'

He nods. On the cup a man is being attacked by a wolf.

'Writing going okay?'

She rolls her eyes and slowly shakes her head. 'I'm here too soon. A residency is only useful, I think, if you've been working on a book for a long time and are getting to be disagreeable. Then those around you benefit from it as well.' She stares past him. 'In the first phase too, though, really. Disagreeable. Like now. I'm still nowhere. Nothing. I haven't got an idea. And I'm not going to find it here. I need a city, I think. Or drugs. Ha ha ha.'

'People tell me a lot,' he says. 'My clients. Unbelievable what you hear if you listen. Sometimes I think there's a book in it. But I'm not the one to write it.'

She seems not to have heard, dreamily turning her attention to the ceiling and planting her backside on the edge of the wrapped desk in the middle of the room. Arms crossed, she continues daydreaming.

'So I just drive around a bit. For two weeks I've mainly been driving. Across the fields, from one unknown village to another, along those narrow lanes. And sometimes I drive home, because I miss my husband and he misses me and I don't actually live very far away. It's ridiculous. I even get cooked meals here.'

'How does it usually start?' he asks. 'A book.'

'It has to present itself, then I can take over the job, there's no other way of explaining it. But now I first have to write an erotic story on commission and because I'm all cramped up from waiting for the new book to arrive I can't do that either. Of course it would be better to start with the short story. Then I'd have that out of the way and there'd be room for the bigger stuff. Yes. I'll just have to get it done. I'm going to start now. If you want more coffee, the thermos is here.'

She hurries out of the door, turns and sticks her head back through the doorway. 'Sorry for griping and thanks for listening.' Then she shakes his hand, with her other arm around the door frame as if the rest of her body is trapped behind it, and introduces herself.

By early afternoon he's largely finished the room. He opens the windows a little wider and has the impression the park is calling him. It's bathed in sunlight. The view makes him want to storm downstairs and throw himself into it with a somersault.

He eats his sandwiches on a bench under one of the beech trees. It pleases him to know their names. They have considerably more bulk than the others in the park. When they were younger and slimmer they stood their ground in a blackened plain, two lone survivors in a forest of crudely amputated trunks. That the soughing, scented crowns and the question repeated insistently by a bird create the impression no war ever took place here is perhaps the only victory that matters.

He wants to know the name of this bird too. It doesn't fly down, it falls as if shot, lands on the grass and shows itself to him in both profiles before hopping toward him with inquisitive leaps, three at a time, interrupted by a brief rest. How birds jump. As if the earth pushes them skywards, or the sky keeps sucking them up and spitting them out. This is a fairly inconspicuous specimen, its feathers mostly brown, its belly yellowish and white. On its head it sports a short, flat crest, around its eyes a slightly lighter band, as if it's been sitting in the sun with glasses on. Alphonse doesn't move, doesn't even dare chew the bread in his mouth. He can hardly believe it when the bird comes even closer, right up to his heavy, steel-tipped shoes, then joins him on the bench, only a few centimetres from his fist.

He cautiously looks sideways, his right eye meeting the bird's left. They blink in unison. The only thing he knows for sure is that he mustn't put a finger out to it, that the last thing this creature wants is to be touched. When the wings spread he's startled; for a moment the take-off seems like an attack, the belly and feet turned toward him, the robust beak silent. He resists the defensive move he's inclined to make. The reward is immense. The bird flies in a curve to his shoulder. He feels the firm grip of the bony toes, the barely perceptible pressure of the light little body, then the feathers, the disconcertingly soft feathers pressed voluntarily to his ear, and behind them the thrumming of the bird's heart. He mustn't ridicule the emotion. Just experience what he has. What is given to him.

The bird flies up, singing, but still it's not over. It ascends to a great height and circles there, still singing, spreading its wings, then folding them again, each time for longer than seems possible, singing for longer than anyone would expect.

He looks through the bookshelves with one eye on the news.

'Can't you be quiet,' says Cat. 'What are you looking for anyhow?'

'The bird book. What's it about.'

'Another shooting. I think it's in the bedroom.'

He watches along with her. As usual it's a young shooter and like his predecessors he's described as a quiet boy, perhaps because few people spoke to him. The dead fell in broad daylight in a Western country. This shooter seems to have targeted women. The newsreader suggests problematic maternal ties.

The bird book is not in the bedroom, but he finds it on Cat's desk. He attentively leafs through it, studying all the photos of brown birds. Skylark. That must be it. 'The skylark makes its nest in a small hollow in the ground.' He thought all birds made their nests in trees. How little he knows. 'Migrates en masse in October or November, returning in February or March. A small number of individuals overwinter in northern Europe.' How come? he asks himself. What makes most leave and some not? 'On the endangered list in Flanders and the Netherlands.' Down by the asterisk he sees that the species is 'sensitive' in the Netherlands and 'vulnerable' in Flanders. Its numbers, that is, he assumes, not its character.

'I saw a skylark today,' he tells Cat, who is still watching television, rather more glumly than before.

She says she's trying to watch *The News*. 'Four women have been shot less than a hundred kilometres from here.'

'Terrible.' He means it and decides not to rejoice out loud that she's not one of the four. She'd regard that as heartless.

A psychologist says they'll have to wait for reports to decide whether the culprit can be held responsible for his actions. 'Fuses blow when fuses blow, and at that point all the fuses blow,' Alphonse hears him say. Perhaps he misheard.

He thinks, too, that the strangest thing of all is that it's so rare for someone in peacetime suddenly to go out onto the street and mow people down. There are around six billion people and in each of those six billion heads are some hundred billion brain cells, of which fifty thousand die every day while the rest are connected in all kinds of complex, fallible ways. Most of those six billion people, often with each other's help, go crazy to a greater or lesser extent, or at least become frustrated. There are extremist organizations of various sorts to encourage such an outcome. Furthermore, a lot of people realize sooner or later that they do things purely and simply because they can. Or because they think they're doing what's expected of them. And a lot is expected of them.

And there's a lot they're capable of. Some are happy to use this knowledge to browbeat others, some seek refuge in pharmaceuticals, a few throw themselves into the manufacture of macramé flowerpot holders. But it's rare for someone to take a hunting rifle out onto the street with the intention of killing as many passers-by as possible. All in all, things don't seem too bad, do they?

The News has finished. No Ebola today.

21

Jean-Marc and Constance de Stassart, Cat's parents, are at each other's throats. According to Cat it was never any different and Alphonse, too, who's known the couple even longer than their daughter has, recalls operetta-style scenes in which they attacked each other verbally, on a couple of occasions even physically. Before Cat was born, their diplomatic duties gave them the chance to live for long periods in different countries, even on different continents at one point. When his mother worked for Cat's father in Dakar and Brussels, she taught Alphonse to read the man's behaviour, so that he'd know when it was best to stay out of Jean-Marc's way. A tic that caused the diplomat to give vicious tugs to his—perhaps partly for that reason—rather long nose indicated that he'd spoken to Constance on the phone. When the speed and frequency of the tugs increased and he began to neglect himself, it meant his wife had announced a visit. In the weeks prior to her arrival, the house would echo to the rising and falling scales Jean-Marc hammered out on the grand piano. During the final week they'd mostly see him sitting with his eyes shut on the back seat of the BMW, parked in the carport, nipping from a glass of Cognac Napoléon.

Constance always came on-stage in a garish suit with an absurd amount of luggage. Like a goaded bull she'd circle her husband, and in response he moved like a toreador. She then usually sneered something along the lines of: 'And he's so delighted to see his wife again!' This might be followed by an aggressive kiss or an overblown sigh. Tears or raised voices were never long in coming.

According to Cat, the fact that they stayed together through their childless years had to do with expectations in the families they came from and therefore, fundamentally, with money. Alphonse is inclined to believe his mother's more romantic explanation. She says Constance and Jean-Marc loved each other more passionately than it was possible for people to love; they should have been wind and desert and unleashed an artwork of a sandstorm. In the brief, constricted life to which they were condemned, people like them could only lacerate themselves on each other.

Cat says it's hard for a daughter to interpret stamping on antiques as simply an alternative way of expressing tenderness, or to soothe herself to sleep through mortal screams with the conviction that in essence her parents were made for each other. That's something he can of course understand. He believes, incidentally, that worries about the tempestuous married life of Jean-Marc and Constance contributed to his mother's decision to send him to live with his uncle.

'Oh, I'm dreading this,' says Cat now, beside him in the car.

It's what she says every time they drive to see her parents. There's little point repeating that they're getting older and have both had heart attacks; Cat knows that well enough. The heart attacks came shortly before and after her own malignant diagnosis, and they were the most important reason for the move to the Westhoek. In that period she visited her parents more often than before, to their immense gratitude. For him it had been an entirely new experience during such get-togethers to walk into a room in which Jean-Marc and Constance were chatting quietly with Cat. One time he even found the three of them bent over a board game, a sight so improbable that afterwards he sometimes thought he'd dreamed it.

Meanwhile the calm has in turn given way to a new phase, one that Cat has dubbed 'their Cold War'. Like that period in world history, it involves more than reciprocal coldness. Suddenly, a few months ago, his parents-in-law announced they were getting a divorce and despite the callous battle they'd fought for a lifetime, the news came as a surprise after the short-lived peace. The villa in De Panne where they've been living since retirement is really a kind of summer house, a refuge where both of them—separately, of course—have in the past found repose. That they've shared the same house in recent years is the consequence of a resolve, adhered to with identical stubbornness, to stay put. After argumentatively sharing out the rooms, they each withdrew as far as possible, although they still have a passion for spying on one another.

Cat has said that the fact neither parent was ever seen with any other partner simply illustrated what impossible characters they were. The ways his parents-in-law disparage proven solutions and the trouble they take to make their situation worse have reinforced Alphonse's belief that Jean-Marc and Constance are unable to live without each other. As a consequence they've sabotaged their decision to part after more than forty years of marriage by putting the villa that keeps them together on the market for one billion euro. It is an extremely comfortable villa with four spacious bedrooms and a wonderful view of the dunes, but it's hardly surprising no buyer has come forward.

'How unbelievably childish,' sighs Cat.

At the sight of the 'For Sale' sign in the front garden, Alphonse is unable to suppress a guffaw. The nine zeros have been applied in hot-tempered handwriting, and for lack of space they creep up along the edge.

After graduating from university, Cat never again accepted money from them, although they frequently offered it. Even during her illness and the period of peaceful relations that followed, financial independence enabled her to distance herself from them and all their failures. As if the money might carry germs.

'So they managed to agree on that billion, the idiots. Stop laughing.' She taps him on the hat, laughing.

Cat has a key to the house. Alphonse walks behind her into the high hallway. There's no one in the living room and no one in the conservatory.

'They do know we're coming, don't they?' he asks.

'I spoke to my mother on the phone.'

Their footsteps echo through the empty rooms.

'Strange.'

'Yes.'

Then he catches sight of Constance clambering out from behind a sofa. Unaware that he's watching her, she runs on tiptoe to the front door, which she opens and then shuts. Before she gets a chance to look his way, he turns his back to her, standing in the doorway to another room so that she needn't feel caught out. She comes toward them on stiffer strides.

'Hellooooo!' she says. 'I completely forgot you were coming! Marvellous!' They allow themselves to be clasped in her affectionate arms. Jean-Marc and Constance have never openly disapproved of their daughter taking up with the son of her *m'bindan*. In the first few months they were together, Alphonse caught a conversation between them in which they expressed some dismay at it, blaming each other, naturally. But soon that distress was as nothing to a far more pressing worry, and it wasn't long before the friendliness with which they treated him as a son-in-law began to strike him as sincere. He suspects Cat of being slightly disappointed at the absence of any objection from them, of seeing it as confirmation that what she does could never be more important to them than their own domestic conflict. And he sometimes thinks her parents might have been relieved to see their daughter choose a partner already familiar with the nest of vipers in which she grew up.

'Coffee? I've got petits fours. If your father hasn't eaten them all, at least. That would be all we need, not doing the shopping and then eating someone else's.' The illuminated interior of the fridge calms her. 'Ah, he's lucky.'

'Where is Dad?'

'I don't know, Catherine. On the bottle, no doubt.'

Cat drops despondently into a sofa. He gently squeezes her knee.

'How's it going?' he asks Constance.

'Old,' she says, gloomily.

She had a birthday last month. Seventy-two. She's lost her ballerina body and the thick bun at the back of her head. She seems to have slowly shifted from a primary colour to a pastel. None of this has negated her beauty, only made her more fragile.

'You're sure to reach a hundred,' he soothes.

'Another three decades to complain about your age,' Cat offers. 'And you've been at it so long already.'

'We'll talk about that in twenty years from now,' says

Constance, her mouth small. 'If I'm still alive, that is.' She means to go on, but spots something and falls silent. Her grey eyes peer, twinkling, at the window. She rushes over with a pointing finger, virtually tugs the curtains off their rails and bangs loudly and threateningly on the glass with a ring. From the bottom left-hand corner of the window, an apparition vanishes. Constance turns to face them, continuing to point at the spot with a sharp nail.

'Look! Come and look!'

Alphonse and Cat do not stir.

'That was Dad. He was peering in. That's what he gets up to these days, spying on his wife. And you wait, now he'll come in through the front door with some excuse or other.'

They do indeed hear the scraping sound of the front door opening, followed by footsteps. Jean-Marc storms into the room, his forehead sweaty. As his frantic gaze flaps across his daughter and her partner, he develops laughter lines for a moment, which immediately disappear when he turns to his wife. 'I almost died of fright, woman!'

'I didn't. I'm no longer surprised when my husband spies on me. Pay no attention, I tell myself. He's mad.'

'I was doing some weeding!' He shows her his muddy hands as if stigmata were at issue. 'Someone has to do it! Hello, girl. Hi, Alphonse.'

'Hi Dad,' says Cat.

'Hey, Jean-Marc.' Alphonse has a feeling the man has quickly rubbed his hands in the dirt.

'Weeding!' Constance laughs derisively, then screeches, and for several minutes pretends to be unable to free herself of the giggles.

'Cow,' says Jean-Marc, with sincerity and resignation.

Constance's laughter turns to sobbing. Her fingers assist her make-up in swimming relays across her face.

'My latest tests were good,' says Cat. 'I'm officially cured.'

Her words have the desired effect. Alphonse makes room on the sofa so that the dramatis personae of a moment ago can come and sit next to their daughter like fragile elderly people, one on either side, with identical trembling smiles on their faces. They kiss Cat on her cheeks and her hair, then look sweetly round at him.

'I'll go and fetch some more petits fours,' says Constance. She heads off girlishly to the kitchen with the empty plate. On the way she stops at a mirror to wipe the black smears from her face.

'I had every confidence,' says Jean-Marc. 'But the fear is always there, all the same.'

Alphonse allows his father-in-law to slap him woodenly on the shoulders and looks at Cat's smile, which has been slightly twisted by the poignancy of her parents' reaction. It's no doubt the memory of her lie that makes her want to change the subject.

'Now we can start thinking about children again, too,' he hears himself say. He has no idea where that bomb came from and why it had to roll out of his mouth right here. Constance barely manages to ensure all the petits fours that are sliding about on the plate come to rest on the coffee table. Jean-Marc stands up, spends several seconds strenuously straightening his trouser leg, then sits down again.

'We can talk about that somewhere else.' The face Cat has turned toward him gives the impression she's delivered a very different message. When she's angry she looks like both her mother and her father, whereas otherwise he can detect no trace of either.

It has indeed been a long time since they talked about

possible offspring. The closest they came to a conclusion was to decide the subject wasn't open for discussion for a while, and needn't necessarily be so after that, either. Just as long as she got better. The favourable test results of a few months ago did nothing to alter that tacit agreement.

'Sorry,' he says. But there's no way back now.

Jean-Marc clears his throat. 'There's a Jewish saying: life begins when the children have moved out and the dog's buried.'

'Next to your wife, no doubt?' Constance sniffs.

'Yes, in my case that too.'

Alphonse can hear thunderclaps in Cat's insides as she looks at her sniggering father. Constance calls her husband a bastard.

Jean-Marc turns to his daughter again. 'Your life's over as soon as a child arrives, my sweet. And your relationship ruined.'

Constance nods. Cat clenches her fists. That they have the nerve to connect their own quarrels with parenthood troubles Alphonse as well.

'Don't do it, Catherine. A child makes everything far more difficult. You try and try, but it all turns out wrong and ultimately you get the blame.'

'Yes, your mother's right about that. I'm glad she thinks the same way on the subject.'

Her parents' harmonious nod seems to send an electric shock through Cat's limbs. She stands up and walks away from them before Alphonse can grab her hand. A few seconds later they hear the front door slam.

'What's the matter with her?' her father asks.

'Still so quick to take offence,' Constance pouts.

'Women!'

'Oh, right, it's the women now!' Constance feigns a fresh giggle.

'Excuse me,' says Alphonse. 'I've got the car keys.'

'And it's raining,' says Jean-Marc.

'Just you go,' Constance adds. 'I know her. She's too stubborn to come back.'

He leaves without any exchange of parting kisses. From the corner of his eye he can see the effect on their faces. When he raises his hand they follow his cue, a picture of awkwardness and wordless regret.

He's already apologized twice for the poor choice of a change of subject and she's limited herself to agreeing, tersely, that his intervention was less than clever.

'There's still plenty of time,' he says.

She shifts her position with a sigh and looks fixedly out through the car window. A great many cows stare back in identical ways. He thinks of the cow in the fog, the morning after their last argument. She's only twenty-eight. He refrains from repeating the fact.

'And that's what you want? You want a child?' She's still not looking at him.

'I think I do, yes.' If she does too. If they're both able to be happy about it. He can of course imagine disaster scenarios.

'And you're going to spend just as much time as you do now in the houses of strangers while I sit at home with a baby and never get another translation finished? And I can't even go anywhere because there's nothing to do around here!'

The disaster scenarios push themselves into the foreground, forcing him into silence. There's no point reviving the dispute about where they live. They both thought this was a good idea, at first.

'Shall we eat there?' He nods at a sign saying Sally's Farm. She does now glance over to see where he's looking, then says 'No', surprised at having to articulate such an obvious answer. They stopped there once before, in the spring, out of anthropological curiosity. In the driveway car park in front of the farmhouse, which has been done out as a dance hall, next to the adjoining beet field, is a Statue of Liberty in camouflage colours. There's also an Expo 58 train and a glass case in which visitors can read *The Sally's Gazette*, a curious document in which reference is made to a menu as well as Elvis Presley's life story and that of the owner. Cat laughed at the spelling errors in *The Sally's Gazette*, but objected when he labelled the combination of all these elements (replica Statue of Liberty, hop poles, Elvis Presley, farmhouse, man named Sally) 'Belgian-style weirdness'.

Now she protests because he's on his way up the long drive despite all that. In the rain the craziness makes a drearier impression than it did six months ago.

'Come on.' He's standing next to the car door on her side with an unfurled umbrella.

'We're going to regret this,' she says. They hurry across the puddles.

The walls of the farmhouse are incapable of containing the wild piano music.

'Look at those flags,' Cat points through the windows. The walls and wooden beams of the adjoining barn are draped with the Confederate flag. 'I really don't think this is something for us.'

Alphonse has his doubts now too. Before he can make a decision, a man walks up to them with a disembowelled pig on one shoulder. The hand that isn't carrying the meat hangs limply at his side, and the dragging leg likewise suggests a survived stroke.

'Good evening.' The man has a calm, engaging look.

'We haven't booked,' says Cat.

'There's still room.'

'Are you Sally?' asks Alphonse. The man nods.

'There sure is a remarkable combination of stuff here,' Cat giggles as Sally pushes the door open for them. He turns patiently to face them and says: 'I'm Sally and Sally does whatever he feels like.' Then he leaves them a little lost, possibly slightly hypnotized, and carries the blood-smeared animal away. In the banqueting hall are a good hundred people, most of them looking in their direction, some with a degree of hostility. They include elderly couples with tears in their eyes and girls with a devotion to Elvis that may or may not be ironical in intent—the girls themselves no longer know. Some of the flags show a Red Indian standing in front of the Southern Cross.

Alphonse and Cat hesitantly pay a woman at a cash till near the door. They're told the payment entitles them to a piano battle, a gospel performance by Sally, and three portions of spare ribs.

They survey the entire scene from the table allocated to them. So he's not dead. He stares at them from photos, drawings, and polyester statuettes, from T-shirts stretched across the rotund bellies of residents of these borderlands, most of them French-speaking. His voice blares from the speakers. 'He knew suffering and he cared for the poor of Memphis,' intones a pastor who seems to be saying Mass for him in between two performances. He repeats everything in French. 'We're being swallowed up in a cloud that bears too much rain, but there is hope.' Then Sally sings: 'Take your troubles to the chapel / Get down on your knees and pray' and during Communion he adds an all-too-impassioned 'I believe'.

'Oh,' says Cat when he sings very flat.

Alphonse puts his arm around her shoulders and

pulls her to him. There's nothing more they can hope for now than that the singer will find the right note.

After the song, Sally announces the piano battle with easy-going flair. The priest goes out to bless three Harleys. Alphonse has learned there's a kind of extremism that belongs in remote villages, and it's not a matter of whether you like it but of whether you're able to abandon yourself to it.

The man sitting at the table in front of them turns round. 'My brother-in-law always cries when he hears Elvis,' he says, in French. The rotund grey man at the head of the table nods at them, his eyebrows a roof. Then the first man wants to know if they agree that the new Elvis T-shirt he's bought is a bit smelly. To a frenzied series of arpeggios, Cat and Alphonse lean across the table. They could hardly have picked a better moment to sniff at a man together.

20

He's draping the art deco staircase with plastic sheeting when a pale, slightly older man opens the front door. When Alphonse greets him he stands nailed to the spot, before hurrying upstairs with an apologetic cough.

An hour later the author appears on the landing. She looks cheerful.

'Plenty of writing done?' he asks.

'Yes! My story's coming along and I was bombarded all night by ideas for the novel.' At a cautious trot, she thumps down the wrapped stairs.

During his lunch break he waits in vain for the skylark. For a moment he thinks he can hear it, but he never actually gets to see the bird. There are insects that look like walking pine nuts and sunflower seeds, and a brown-haired caterpillar he keeps moving further away along the bench, where it immediately resumes its journey toward his knee. If he puts it down facing in the opposite direction, it first slowly turns round. The next time the caterpillar climbs diagonally across a fold in his trousers, he picks up the coiling little body. He can't be certain it's the eyes he's looking at, nor how many of them there are. The tips of his thumb and index finger have started to itch. When he puts it down on the ground it immediately sets off for his shoe.

The translator walks out through the front door, coughing. He seems about to break into a run as Alphonse walks toward him. The caterpillar clings resolutely to Alphonse's foot.

'Bonjour.'

'Hi there,' says the man, in English, and he adds that he's just out for some fresh air and is very busy.

'Where are you from?'

'That's not important, I think,' he says, not unfriendly but nervous. Now that Alphonse has asked the question himself for a change, it's waved aside. These days people usually add the word 'originally': 'Where are you from, originally?' Also quite common is a 'really': 'But where are you really from?'

Persevering somewhat sardonically in his attempt to make conversation, Alphonse asks the man how long he's been staying at the writers' residence and whether he's getting plenty of work done. He adds something about the area, something about the weather. Although he understands Alphonse's French, the man continues to answer in English. His accent is impossible to place.

When he sees the caterpillar on the shoe, it's as if his head has been blasted full of sunlight. His pale, bulbous jaws take on a pink glow, his dull hair suddenly inclines toward red. He falls to his knees. Before Alphonse can start to feel uneasy, the translator takes out his phone and captures the creature in his virtual butterfly net.

'Every kind of butterfly has its own caterpillar. This one's going to be a moth, in fact. No other creature is known to grow so quickly. During their lives they burst out of their skins four or five times. Do you know how they breathe?'

'Through their mouths?' It pleases him to find himself in a quiz.

'No! Of course not!' the man exclaims, instantly convincing Alphonse that he'd punch anyone who angered him. 'Through little tubes that come out at their sides!' Calmer, he goes on: 'This species doesn't eat at all as an adult. So the caterpillar needs to build up sufficient reserves.'

Alphonse now looks with some admiration at the small animal on his shoe.

'They're full of protein. Birds love them and parasitic wasps lay eggs in them. The larvae then eat the caterpillars from the inside out. If ants get hold of one, they slowly cut it to pieces.' The man smiles dreamily, showing two yellowed canines. Then he hurries inside without a parting word. Alphonse can hear him climbing the stairs.

By early evening one half of the spacious entrance hall is finished. He meets the author on her way to the dining room. She stops to ask him whether she can ask him something, which enables the coughing lepidopterist to catch up with her, nodding vaguely in Alphonse's direction, with a fleeting glance at his shoe.

'Would you read my story?' she asks. 'There are no other Dutch speakers here.'

'I'm dyslexic,' he says. 'It might take a while.'

Must be difficult, she mumbles, a thing like that. It's only when she's going back up the stairs that he notices she's holding several sheets of paper. She probably wanted to give him her story and took what he said as a refusal. Beyond the window, dancing lime trees distract him with thousands of little yellow-green fans. He watches a hare run a path through the grass.

'You could take a few days off, couldn't you?' says Cat. 'At least the day after tomorrow, when they get here.'

'I want to have the job finished. Amadou understands.'

'But I don't.'

They're both too tired to argue and too tired to cook. Cat tries to order a pizza by phone and relays the message from the man who answers, seeking Alphonse's reaction: 'Too far.'

He sinks into the sofa with a sigh, cracks his neck and turns on the television.

'Cold by the time he gets here, of course. Fair enough. It's not exactly round the corner.'

Haven't they ordered pizza before? Why is it impossible now? Is she lying? Is she just pretending to phone? Is she lying again? Will he ask himself that regularly now?

She shuts off the call without saying anything more and stares with him at a documentary about tropical fish: yellow, orange, blue. Until she gets up, opens and shuts the fridge, throws food onto the counter and starts energetically peeling carrots.

'How do you want them?' he asks flatly, coming to sit opposite her.

'Slices,' she says.

'What kind of slices?' It's competitive toneless speaking.

'Half.'

He knows she'll fall out of her role, as will he.

'Half-slices?'

'Yes.'

First there's her irritated laugh, and when it lasts longer than intended he joins in. Until she manages to control herself and the room falls quieter than they'd like.

'Don't you have to go to yoga?'

'I'm stopping that for a while.'

'Why?'

'I've already told you. Don't you have to play kora?'

'Yes.'

It seems she wasn't expecting that answer. Next to the cooking pots she ducks behind her smartphone.

One floor up, he leans on the windowsill and the long strings tell her everything he thinks she should know. At first it sounds like a reprimand, then, increasingly, like a thin, agile dancer, tirelessly turning on his own axis.

19

The corridor between the studios needs painting too. Alphonse is alone there with the translator's cosy cough. The whisper of the tape he's applying to protect the skirting board brings the author out. They greet each other.

'I'm waiting for a journalist who was supposed to be here at 9.30 and it's ten o'clock now. Will you send him my way if you see him?'

'Sure. Is it for a newspaper?'

'I can't remember. Annoyingly. I've forgotten his name, too. And I've lost his emails. In my diary it just says "9.30: interview".'

Fifteen minutes later, Alphonse hears a fanfare of loud sighs and dragging footsteps ascending the stairs. The anger emanating from the lean thirty-something can't be the consequence of a bad night's sleep or a missed train; it's a life's work. In response to a hello he merely looks over the top of Alphonse's head. The author appears in her doorway and invites him in.

'Was it easy to find?'

'Not particularly.'

'Coffee? Or tea?' She hasn't shut the door behind him. Perhaps she wants Alphonse to listen in.

'Coffee,' the journalist sighs. 'Black. If it's strong. But I don't have much time.'

'I'm sorry, but for which ... ' the author begins. He interrupts her:

'Your books are all about weak, disturbed young women who try to assert themselves but can't. Do you think you'll ever move away from that as your subject matter?'

The author is silent for a moment.

'I don't think that is my subject matter, actually. I use men as much as women in my work. I don't think most of them are actually disturbed. Young? Often they're not, actually.' All those actuallys. She's in a panic. 'In my last book the youngest character was five and the oldest eighty.'

'Shhh! Shhh! Not so loud!' the journalist shouts. The masking tape in Alphonse's fingers tangles. Inside he can hear tinkling porcelain; perhaps the author has dropped a cup. Or did the visitor throw something? Shouldn't he take a quick peek?

'Let's agree not to keep going on the defensive all the time!' the journalist says, furious.

'But I do have to answer,' the author squeaks.

'Please! I know that's the type of person you are, but try, just for once, not to let your negative attitude get the upper hand! This! Is! Not! An! Attack! Re! Lax! Otherwise this interview is even more pointless than I thought. I'm not here for my own entertainment!' After a slurping noise he adds: 'Sorry, but this really is the most disgusting coffee I've ever tasted.' Another slurp.

'Would you like tea?'

'I'm not chancing it. Right ... ' Rustling. 'So, what else can I ask about your work? It's always about love.'

'Er. Really?'

'Er. Really?' He imitates her, a retarded version of her. Alphonse stands up. It's not his world, but this conversation hardly seems routine.

'Love.' He hears her swallow. 'In a certain way perhaps. Usually not so much about romantic love, then, actually, but in the sense that everything is in a way about love?'

'Come on, don't give me that fuzzy shit, okay? "In a way everything is about love." For God's sake! Keep that inane babble for your women's magazines!' He whistles between his teeth, then makes his voice sound as exhausted as possible: 'Tell me something about the main character in your latest book.'

'It was a short-story collection,' the author whispers.

His sigh goes on for a long time before surrendering to a passionate yawn.

'Do you want me to pick out one of the characters?'

'Don't bother. How much do you earn from your writing?'

'Oh, that's really not very interesting and anyhow it varies a lot. One year ... '

'Do you think you're attractive?'

'No, not very. I'm not completely dissatisfied either. But what does that actually have to do with ... '

'Well, let's say it's good there's not a photographer here. What is it like to be forced to abandon your desire for children?'

'I've never really had ... '

'Yes, yes. Whatever. Who are your epigones?'

'My epigones?'

'Ah, right, that'll be a difficult word. E-pi-gones. Ex-am-ples. Ma-jor art-ists from the past, people you look up to because you can't do what they do.'

'I'm sorry, but that's not quite correct. Epigones are followers, imitators who don't add anything new. As far as I know I don't have any epigones. Do you want to know who I model myself on?' For the first time since the angry man walked into her room, Alphonse hears something other than polite despair in the author's voice. She manages to restrain the triumphant breeze blowing between her words only when a chair or some other heavy object falls over. Alphonse takes a step in the direction of the room. He decides to wait for her to call out. She knows he's here.

'Pass me a dictionary!' the man spits.

A heavy book slams down on the table. More rustling. Then a sound he can't place.

'What are you doing? Hey! Stop that!'

The author bumps into him as Alphonse storms into the room. Horrified, she points to the red-faced, crouching man who, foam on his lips, is relieving himself on the parquet.

'Ohlalalalalalaaa!' The cry is new to Alphonse, but then so is the situation.

'Not my Van Dale!' the author shouts. But the man has already filled his right hand with a thick wad of torn-out dictionary pages and is wiping his bottom, staring demonically at the two of them as he does so.

'You can't do this, man,' Alphonse begins.

'Is that Negro yours?' the man asks, fastening his trousers. His smell rises from the floor, spreading to all four corners of the room.

'You're going to clean that up!' Alphonse makes himself into the biggest and broadest man he has in him, repeats his order, then follows up with swear words and reproaches in Wolof, a language he doesn't speak faultlessly but finds best for issuing curses.

The author stands looking at him aghast. The journalist, his face utterly untroubled, tries to walk past him to the door but Alphonse blocks his way and slams the door shut with his fist. Then he takes the man's head in his hands and turns it in the direction of the turd.

The head he's holding begins to shout. 'I'm not going to eat it! No way! I'm not going to eat it!'

'No one's asking you to,' says the author, who has now subsided into a state of resigned solemnity. She hands him a plastic bag. 'Pick it up with this.'

'Do as she says.' Alphonse folds his arms in front of his chest.

The man hurries, rinsing the sponge in the bucket the author has filled for him, scrubbing and wiping until nothing is left of the stain. 'I'm Belgian! I have rights!' he's shouting now.

Alphonse steps to one side so the journalist can run out of the door with the filled bag. Through the window they watch him leave the grounds.

'What a to-do.' The author tries to smile at him. 'I'm sorry you had to get involved. And thanks.'

'Not every interview is like that, right?'

'No, no. Sometimes they're nice. Sometimes you even have a conversation.'

He lets her pour him a cup of coffee. They sit across from each other in silence, their attention captivated by the wet patch between them. It still smells bad.

'I need something stronger now,' says the author. She fetches a bottle of rum from the bedside cabinet. He fends off a glass and sits in silence while she drinks.

The translator, who must surely have heard the commotion in the neighbouring room, sticks his head out into the corridor just once. Although he stares at Alphonse with suspicion, he nevertheless thrusts under his nose a few photos of butterflies he's made on his smartphone. He stays out of sight after that.

During a late lunch on the bench, his eyes on the sky above the beech trees, waiting for the skylark, Alphonse sees the author coming toward him. She smiles broadly and waves. Waving back, he realizes she's drunk.

'Sorry, I'm a bit pickled,' she confirms. She comes to sit next to him and smiles sweetly, slightly mischievous. One of her eyes drifts a little under the influence, it seems. He doesn't know which of them to look into. 'Thank you. I just wanted to say that.'

'You already did. You're welcome. Do you think the interview will be published somewhere?'

'I still don't know where it was for. You were really impressive.'

They laugh a little. He searches for something to say. She's probably doing the same.

'Impressive is a strange word, since everything makes an impression,' she remarks with great diligence.

'That's true.'

For a moment he thinks he can hear the skylark. She listens along with him. 'No, that's not it,' he says. 'There's a bird here that let me listen to his heart. But I haven't seen him since then.'

She rests her head on his shoulder and prints a pointed kiss on his sweater around where his heart must be. 'People like you are thin on the ground,' she murmurs.

He doesn't really dare to touch her, then does so all the same, a few gentle slaps on the back, as with a baby after a feed. The head against his shoulder grows heavy, her breathing louder. While a trickle of rum-scented saliva flows out of her mouth onto his sweater, he eats his last sandwich. The skylark isn't coming today. He wakes her up. She apologizes effusively and hurries inside. She doesn't show herself for the rest of the day.

He finds the story after he's back at work and can't understand how she could have slipped the pages into his hip pocket without him noticing. He reads the title: 'The Dietician and the Plasterer'. At the wheel of the parked van he wrestles with the letters. Curiosity wins out over frustration.

As of next month the dietician will no longer be available exclusively through the hospital. For two days and every evening of the working week she'll be in a position to receive patients in part of the converted ground floor of her house. Some dieticians call their patients 'clients', but she doesn't. The high-ceilinged room is beginning to look like a proper consulting room. All that's needed now is some filling of holes and a little light plastering. The dietician has opted for stucco, which she thinks looks nicer than paint.

'All self-employed tradesmen are thieves,' her husband says, before leaving to run his company. 'Just you keep an eye on him.'

He quite often speaks to her in a tone that suggests he regards the dietician as a danger to herself.

'I can't just hang around the man while he's working,' she objects, but it seems her husband is no longer listening. The front door closes behind him. A little later she hears his car drive away.

Since there's not yet any furniture in the consulting room, the dietician has installed herself at the dining table with a laptop and a filled notebook. She doesn't need to go to the hospital today and she's determined to make good use of her time. She has only to recast a few scrawls into Word documents, and there are some patients who haven't yet been filed away in the right places. Today she'll sort them out. Children. Professional sport. Morbid obesity. Categorization is something the dietician enjoys.

She's just immersed herself in her notes about a nine-year-old she's been trying for a while to convert to a three-

hundred-calorie breakfast when the doorbell rings.

'Good morning,' says the plasterer politely in the doorway, with a bronze voice and an accent.

The dietician has no difficulty admitting to herself that she finds the plasterer attractive. It surprises her, though, because for years she's paid hardly any attention to masculine beauty. The plasterer is not particularly young, the same height as she is, thinner than slim and, all right, black—or at least very dark brown. He's wearing jeans and a blue shirt with white smears of plaster. In one hand he holds a bucket of tools, in the other a sports bag.

The dietician feels her face break open in a broad smile.

'Good morning,' she says. 'I'll show you the consulting room right away, or at least, the consulting room to be.' Her voice bounces stridently off the walls. Her laugh, too. She really did say that: 'the consulting room to be'.

'Thank you.' The plasterer walks in behind her. He stalks along the walls, skimming them with an enormous hand. 'Today the filler,' he says. 'I'll go and fetch my ladder.'

When he returns with a ladder and starts mixing filler, the dietician remains motionless. Except for her eyes. She finds the spot where his hairline gives way to his neck particularly successful, almost moving. She's gripped by an insane desire to lay her hand on his head and press down gently, to test the buoyancy of his tight curls. His shoulders are broad and bony, his back straight, his hips narrow. The dietician recalls that she prefers men's backs, even those of men with beautiful faces like this one. His small, round bottom fascinates her the most. Hypnotizes her, as it were.

When she finally manages to wrench her eyes away from it, she sees that he's staring at her over his shoulder. A tiny bit fearful, perhaps, but expectant more than anything. She doesn't know for how long already.

'Coffee?' asks the dietician.

'Yes,' says the plasterer, without looking away. 'Thank you.'

The coffee maker gurgles while the dietician walks back and forth across the kitchen. She arranges several bran biscuits in a glass dish, then eats, one by one, all that are left in the packet. Next she fries two eggs, which she consumes over the pan.

She walks into the room, tray in her hands, to find him three rungs up on the stepladder, filling a high hole. The plasterer's buttocks are at eye level and they move a little as he shifts his weight from one leg to the other.

'I'll put the coffee here,' says the dietician. 'On the floor. Or shall I fetch a little side table? I can fetch a table if you like.'

'Thank you,' says the plasterer, too intent on what he's doing to turn round.

The dietician briskly walks over to him. When she gets close, the buttocks hold still. Arms around him, she unbuttons his trousers, pulls them down with a powerful tug and plants her teeth in one buttock.

The plasterer shrieks but the dietician doesn't let go. She can't help the fact that this has happened and she doesn't want to stop.

'It's weird!' the plasterer shouts. 'Please! It's too weird!'

The dietician looks at his skin, which is without blemish, apart from the imprint of her teeth. She wonders whether the bruise will show. With the side of her index finger she strokes his tight scrotum and from there moves slowly along the full length. She can't see his prick, but by the time she reaches the glans it is indisputably erect. Then she hurries out of the room.

It's taken him fifteen minutes to decipher the first few pages. Darkness is falling. Cat is waiting for him. Amadou is coming tomorrow. He turns on the light in the car roof and focuses on the letters once more.

Gone mad, thinks the dietician. Nothing to be done, it was bound to happen. And she's happy as well, overjoyed, to a frightening extent. Is this a light shining inside me, she wonders, or an all-consuming fire?

It's a question he's sometimes asked himself when, as happens regularly now, he suddenly floods with happiness for no reason. He thinks a light.

She walks into the garden, takes off her shoes, then her leggings and knickers. The sunlight flows like honey between the branches of the young apple trees, between her fingers and legs. There's a gusty wind; she can feel it brush her blonde cunt under the smooth dress. Short and fresh, the grass pricks the soles of her feet. It invites her to lie down. Come here, she thinks.

He doesn't come. She refuses to wonder what's got into her, whether it has to do with a lack of vitamin B, or iron. She kneels down, then lies on her stomach. The earth presses heavily against her hips and breasts, against her left cheek. Come! she thinks. Flies land in the dietician's field of vision and copulate on the grass.

The sound of her phone makes her stand up, startled. She brushes grass from her legs and walks into the kitchen, then marches out again with it pressed to her ear. It's her husband.

'Debentures hard core catalytic converter Scheveningen exactitude,' he says. 'Cyberbullying polemical parking ticket —worth mentioning, naturally!'

'Naturally,' the dietician echoes.

'Based on increased expenditure, dense undergrowth, penitentiary pogo in spite of chassis a hundred and eighty?' her husband verifies, irritated.

'Could be,' says the dietician, with some caution. 'But I'm busy with something here at the moment.' The plasterer has

appeared in the doorway. He sucks at his full lower lip and steers his focus to the edge of her skirt. She lifts it. A little. To get a better feel of the wind. His eyes drill deep into all that she shows him.

'Okay,' says her husband. 'Floodline cultural policy amphetamine.'

'Okay,' says the dietician, before letting go of her skirt and turning off the phone. She tosses it from one hand to the other, then into the grass.

The plasterer looks at her naked legs, her feet with impeccably painted nails in the grass, before meeting her gaze. His failure to return her smile makes her nervous. She stands still as he walks toward her, convinced now that there's no more beautiful man in the world.

For several seconds the dietician's imagination explodes in all possible directions—rope, pee, groups—but she wasn't expecting a kiss. It's a long, caring kiss, with tender lips and a tongue as pink as her nipples. He holds her face in warm hands. For a moment the dietician thinks she's about to howl like a wolf or lose consciousness, until everything is swept away by a new, even more bountiful dose of happiness. Then a strange kind of calm comes over her. The immense sky resting on her small body is the perfect temperature.

He removes his face from hers and looks into her eyes. She lays her chin on his shoulder and he does the same to her. They stand like that, breathing, waiting. He smells of earth, of tree trunks. Also of mangos, perhaps, or rather berries, raspberries. Being the same height is a big advantage, thinks the dietician. She could be content like this for hours, but she still wants all kinds of things, so she says: 'Are we just going to stand here like this?'

'Like giraffes,' he grins.

His giggle hops through her, transfers itself to her, then they sigh in unison. The dietician could fall deeply in love with this man, may even have done so already.

'What must I do with you?' he asks.

'Whatever you like,' she says.

He unbuttons his shirt, his fingertips flat and soft on the white buttons. She pulls her dress over her head, lets her bra slip from her arms. His eyes crawl attentively all over her body.

'You're beautiful,' he says.

The dietician has never believed otherwise, but it pleases her to hear it from someone else. From that voice. He must talk, too.

He takes her arm, kisses the inside of it. She stretches the other arm out toward his back and shoulders.

'Your skin,' he says, 'is very soft.'

She thinks the same of his.

'Cream,' he says.

Above them flies a large, colourful bird, one she's never seen before. What a day, thinks the dietician. Perhaps I'll die soon and this is what's granted to me in my final moments— I couldn't have imagined anything better.

She helps him out of his trousers, holding his heavy but elegant prick in her hand. He is circumcised. A Muslim, perhaps, thinks the dietician. Her other hand slides over his buttocks, which she kneads and pushes slightly apart.

'Hm,' he says.

'Hm?' she asks.

'Hm!' He looks happy too.

He bends his knees slightly, so that his member can lie along the split, damp underside of her triangle. She slides along it, holds onto this thin dark tree, sits on a branch and moves back and forth.

When he grasps her bottom she wraps her legs around him, so she can feel him along her arse as well. He bends her backward, holding her tight and laying her carefully on the grass.

She pulls him down next to her and kneels beside him. His calves are narrow and long, his thighs muscular. She licks and fondles his beautiful prick, puts her lips around it, strokes the plasterer from buttocks to balls.

'Wait!' he says.

She kisses his belly, his dizzyingly lovely nipples. The muscles move beneath his skin as he raises his head. They find each other's mouths. He kneels in front of her and leans forward.

'Jaguar,' she says.

He thinks for a moment and answers: 'Fox.'

Now he descends, kissing, licking, a cushion of flesh pressed firmly upon her, the softest mouth her clitoris has ever encountered, the most purposeful tongue. His hand takes over, grasping the swollen bud between thumb and index finger and pulling gently, stroking as if it's a small prick, which increases the swelling. Don't stop, she thinks. He goes on. When she shuts her eyes she's sucked into a bright red light. Mars, the sun, the interior of the earth. Once again she looks at what he's doing; she's glistening, as smooth and pink as his tongue. She moans, presses herself to his palm, which now completely covers her cunt with one finger extended between her buttocks, a thumb along her clit.

'I'm going to fuck you,' he says.

'Yes,' she says. 'And I you.'

She presses him down onto the grass, turns her back to him and sits across him with her legs spread, sliding his prick inside her with a groan. She can feel him perfectly, hard as a slippery rock, thrusting slowly, deeply, while her hips describe prostrate figures of eight. Several times she glances over her shoulder, sees him looking, his neck raised, his mouth open, desire and wild astonishment on his face. It's at one such moment that she's hit by a first wave. Teeth clamped together, their faces briefly averted, they sink into themselves, sucking in the spring air, tasting the scent of washing on the line, and sweat, grass, young trees, prick and cunt, sweet and sharp and everywhere. The weight of his hands slides from her hips to her buttocks, which he gently opens to get a better view of her filling herself with him and then letting go. He moans, straightens up. One hand climbs to the other side of her hip, strokes her labia, draws a trail on them with her moistures, along the insides of her thighs. Then he taps her cunt with the flat of his hand, faster and faster. Continuing to take her, he scrabbles upright, kneeling behind her on the grass. A second, higher wave reaches her. This is for her alone and it floors her; she bends forward while long sounds roll out of her mouth. He's put his arm around her waist and is pressing her trembling body firmly into his lap.

For a moment she's rudderless, unable to tell where his voice is coming from.

'I want to see your face,' he says. 'And your breasts.'

In a single move their positions change completely, she on her side, his arm in the fold of her knee. She sees that it won't take much more now, that the flood is creeping toward him too, to carry him off. He looks at her, helpless and slightly insane. She carries on moving her hips, making his prick glisten until just short of the top before swallowing him up again. She repeats the move inexorably, looks at her nipple against the tip of his tongue, which grows bigger, longer, a wider mouth, his soft lips. It inflames her. She wants him to fill her completely, then gets what she wants and wants even more.

'Nice,' he says. 'So nice.'

His voice gives the word a whole new charge. She strokes the tender curve at the base of his spine, feels the glow pass through her belly again. She's now lying on her back, her legs as wide as she can get them. He grabs one breast, nibbles at it until his face contorts. She pushes her pelvis up, his buttocks down, holds him tight like that, comes. All the muscles of his belly tense. Deep inside her his prick jolts.

Beneath them the dead perish and everything that crawls and multiplies is in the thin crust separating them from a core that never shows itself, from thousands of kilometres of pouring, vibrating heat waiting for the next way out, the next grab at the clouds.

That's what the dietician and the plasterer are looking at now, the clouds, lying on their backs side by side, still naked and throbbing but no longer entwined. His hand gropes across the grass between them in search of hers. It's the first time anyone has done that, the dietician realizes with emotion, search for my hand while lying down. It's beyond pleasurable. United. Goodness me, she thinks next. I never really noticed before that the top floor of that block of flats looks out over the garden— ah well, it's too late now.

'Thank you,' says the plasterer.

'And you,' says the dietician. 'Thanks.'

Then it's not clear where the laughter starts, but after they look at each other sidelong, with triangular mouths and teeth that suddenly seem much wider, it judders unstoppably through their bodies. They screech and hiccup, gasping for air, daren't meet each other's eyes because it would only intensify the pain in their sides.

From this too they need to come round. Time is still flowing onward without them. They still haven't let go of each other's hands.

'I do need to get some work done,' says the plasterer eventually. 'I haven't even finished filling holes yet.'

'Yes,' says the dietician. 'I still have to do some categorization. But perhaps a toasted sandwich first?'

He'd like that. She makes one for herself as well. They pull on their clothes and eat side by side on the patio, slightly shy.

'I'll fetch some coffee,' she says.

'Yes,' he says.

He presses a childlike kiss to her cheek, stands up and walks to the consulting room, out of sight. She switches on the coffee maker, turns on the tap, hesitates, turns it off again. When she comes into the room and puts the fresh cup on the tray, he's filling another hole, with a serious look, not on the ladder this time.

'Thanks,' says the plasterer.

'If you need anything, I'm just in there,' says the dietician.

She wakes the laptop screen and sets to work, enthusiastic and focused. In the neighbouring room he studies the walls attentively, filling any holes he finds.

What neither knows about the other is the intermission, the unwashed hand they each independently bring to their noses, press to their lips, drugged by each other's scent, the flash of lightning that passes through their limbs.

When he's finished, half an hour before her husband is due to return, he knocks softly on the living-room door.

'I'm done.' He smiles. 'For today at least. Now it needs to dry, to set a little.'

'When will you be back?' she asks.

'In three days,' he says. 'Then I can start the plastering.'

She accompanies him to the door but doesn't open it yet. They turn to face each other, grinning, then circumspect, two quintessential idiots, who fall lovingly into each other's arms.

It's nine o'clock by the time Alphonse folds up the pages and puts them back in his coat pocket. He knows his increased heart rate isn't merely a result of the effort of reading them. As far as he's aware he's never before been a character on paper. It's a dubious honour. He feels himself distilled into pure body and he has a hard-on. He starts the engine.

As anticipated, Cat is angry. She rang him and he didn't answer. She demands he's there when his friend arrives tomorrow. He promises to do his best, tells her about the insane journalist, managing to divert her anger that way. He says nothing about the story he's just read. Later, he thinks, without completely believing it.

18

For the time being it's his last day at the big house in the park. After they've gone he'll come back to do the rooms where the writer and the translator are staying.

They seem to have left already. Neither of them walks in or out of the house and there's no sound from behind their doors. He suspects the author is deliberately avoiding him. The last of the walls quickly grows whiter; he'll definitely be home by the time Amadou and his girlfriend arrive. Mitsy is her name.

The bench under the beech trees is wet from the rain, so he eats surrounded by his painting materials. He's just taken the first bite of an apple when the author sticks her head into the corridor. She first looks in the other direction. Her eyes are startled when they meet his.

He swallows with difficulty and grins. 'Hi.'

They giggle a little like slow-witted children, she leaning on the door frame, he with his apple.

'Thanks for your story,' he says.

'Ah yes,' she replies, helpless. 'Did you enjoy reading it?'

'Yes,' he says. 'Although it's strange to be playing a role.'

Her smile freezes and disappears.

'It's fiction.'

'Yes. Of course. Sorry.'

'That's not you.'

'Okay.'

'Jesus,' she mumbles. Before he can say anything more, she's turned away from him and firmly shut her door.

He decides it would be better not to knock and apologize, which he doesn't feel like doing anyhow. He feels silly, awkward, and a bit cross. He longs for his bass.

It doesn't diminish his keenness to work. By a little after three he's finished and glad to be going home.

She knocks on the ground-floor window as he strides away from it. They exchange lopsided smiles that for a moment flash with glee, then embarrassment takes over and, from their own sides of the glass, they part with a fleeting wave.

The translator is waiting for him at his car. He shows Alphonse a photo on his smartphone of an immense, colourful butterfly. How the frilly edges of the black-and-red wings mirror each other perfectly.

'Kenya,' he says.

'Beautiful.' Alphonse stares distractedly at it. Kenya. That's a place he'd like to visit.

'Are you on Facebook?'

Alphonse shakes his head. After a despairing nod, the translator hurries off.

Above the narrow roads hangs a ponderous, elongated stratocumulus. There seems to be no escaping it, until the dark underside is drawn upward before him like a heavy theatre curtain. He's a character driving into an unexpected decor, with charming clouds like lambs frolicking in a blue meadow. Suddenly he's looking forward intensely to the reunion and can understand nothing of his reticence of past weeks. It's the twelve-year-old version of Amadou that comes to mind now: a young Senegalese Fula with a skinny little body, sticking-out ears, and round cheeks that later caved inwards, the first contemporary to speak Wolof with him in Belgium and for years the only person with whom he kept up the language. They lived in the same street and later went to the same high school. Amadou became a walking database of colonial history and was often subject to other odd impulses. He grew obsessed by the idea that the Atomium in Brussels should be renovated. He circulated a petition that interested no one, apart from a peculiar girl who consequently became his girlfriend for a time. Alphonse could also remember in great detail a sweatshirt with Bob Marley on it that Amadou wore almost every day at one stage. Through excessive exposure to washing powder and the weather, Bob soon became alarmingly white, then ancient. When his face mutated into a cracked monstrosity that began to flake off, so that it seemed to have delicate, curly tentacles growing out of it, Amadou abandoned the sweatshirt and took to wearing self-knotted red, yellow, and green dreadlocks. On his first appearance with them he was laughed at by the entire school but he persisted for several months nonetheless. They reached to the folds of his knees. Thinking about that hair and that stubbornness, Alphonse feels increasingly cheerful. The pubescent chickens spring to mind, the ones he saw coming out of a chicken coop on their walk a few days ago. What a strange phase to go through. Tenderness refashioned by a benevolent brute. The rites of passage that people invent for themselves often demand the exaggeration of their own ridiculousness.

Are there always so many flowers in September? They burst luxuriantly out of front gardens and paths laid next to drives. Yes, yes, say their colourfully swollen sepals and erect pistils, yes, yes, people have sex here too.

At the end of his street the boy is in the front garden again. On crutches and with a plaster on his leg, but he's back. Alphonse lowers the window and sticks out his hand. Just as on all previous occasions, the boy shouts back: 'Hi, scallywag!'

They're already here. To get in, Alphonse has to clamber over their travel bags. Talk leaks out of the living room.

So this is how he is now, Alphonse. A man of forty, broader than he was ten years ago, otherwise unchanged. The overalls are a joke. His eyes are still the same: eyes that seek you first and leave you first. Amadou remembers that look, both roguish and protective below the surface, and suddenly he recognizes what he sometimes seemed forced to do battle with on less harmonious days: the elusiveness of his friend, the wall of independence that surrounded Alphonse, and that unbearable feeling it aroused in him of needing to gain the man's approval. He feels pleased that he never confessed this nonsense to his friend. Because now he sees straight away: there is no wall. It's good that he's here.

'Gorgui!' shouts Amadou. Old man. He jumps over the coffee table, wiry as ever, no different, aside from a few wrinkles and some fine grey threads at the temples, the rest of his hair concealed by a black Borsalino. His presence seems both unreal and familiar, Alphonse holds onto him, looking at him and slapping him on the back, for longer perhaps than he has ever done. 'Good that you're here,' he says. To stand like that, with eyes squeezed to half-moons, and to give a throaty laugh, to fall silent, to laugh, another handshake, a friend still alive.

He sees Cat watching their reunion with glad amazement. She met Amadou once about ten years ago, when she and Alphonse hadn't been together long. Shortly after that Amadou disappeared from his life, in pursuit of a Rotterdammer who was carrying his child.

'Mitsy,' says the blonde woman standing next to Cat, a beautiful woman of his age—not the mother of the child, he recalls from a phone conversation. He leans down to kiss her on the cheek. 'Three,' she says, and he complies.

They switch from Wolof to French, then from French to Dutch, for their loved ones, from Ebola and family to the dead. Alphonse and the women drink. Amadou spends hours over a glass of juice, passing up the local beers. He seems to have become a more compliant Muslim than he was. Alphonse recalls the remarks he often used to make about the drinking behaviour of Catholics, the kitchen's worth of gilded pots, jugs, and beakers they cram their altars with; he was hilarious at imitating preachers. Alphonse's mother has always creatively mixed Catholicism with an animistic faith. Ever since his childhood in Dakar, religion has seemed to him above all a convenient way of needlessly complicating human interactions. He jumped over the waves at the beach with young Muslims, but sometimes he suddenly wasn't allowed to go with them or wasn't welcome. The Catholics for their part seemed to distrust him because his father was a Muslim, and left, and because his mother adhered to her own version of their faith. On his last visit to his native country he was immensely irritated by the muezzins who tried, far more loudly and frequently than in the past, to shout each other down from strategically placed minarets, time and again making any conversation in nearby rooms, streets, and offices impossible for the length of a prayer. The guilt you were made to feel if you expressed any displeasure at it did nothing to temper his resentment.

'You still smoke dope sometimes?' asks Amadou from beside the stereo. He's loaded a CD by Alpha Blondy and is turning up the volume.

Alphonse shakes his head. It must be about two years now. He was expecting Amadou to have supplies with him, religious or not. His love for the marijuana plant seemed in those days to be an additional motivation for following his pregnant ex to the Netherlands. Years before, just turned twenty, they travelled together for three months through Senegal, Gambia, and Mali, with a reggae band, standing in for the guitarist and the bass player, both of whom had become psychotic. In their rehearsal room in Cambérène, at the home of the remaining drummer, they sat on cloth sacks filled with weed. They thought that was great and were continually in a panic. Every night Amadou dreamed of filthy prisons. The drummer, Momar, started to behave more and more strangely. During performances he sometimes stopped drumming altogether and stared vacantly into space, until their shouting reached him and he began faultlessly thrashing away again. According to Amadou he was using something else too, it couldn't possibly be just the weed, but Alphonse wasn't so sure. Somewhere in the middle of those three months he ran helter-skelter between the stalls of Marché Kermel, powered by a belief in the Devil, who was intent on killing him, Alphonse Badji, by some horrific means. He stood shouting next to an old market trader's cooking pot, convinced the carrots boiling in it were goldfish. It's just about his only clear memory of that period; the rest has degenerated into a slush made up of snippets of conversation and angles of light. Plus the fact that they cut a record then, which became a modest success but earned them nothing—he still remembers that.

The friends tell these stories to their willing listeners but above all back and forth, so that they know who they are for each other. Cat and Mitsy have heard most of them before, only not in this order. Now and then they follow up on something. Mitsy recognizes the encounter with the Devil.

'What on earth are you doing in this hole?' Amadou suddenly asks. 'There's nothing here.'

'I like living here.'

'He wants to stay,' says Cat. There's too much detachment in her voice for it to sound supportive.

'I've never said that. I don't want to leave yet, which is a different thing.'

'But I don't understand why,' Amadou takes over again. 'You've lived all your life in cities. You move around freely there, get the best out of them, know masses of people. You're not the African spied at from behind the curtains, for God's sake.'

'It's not that bad. I enjoy my work. People expect something concrete from me, something I can offer them. I can help them.' Seeing that Cat is about to reproach him in some way he goes on, mainly to her: 'It makes me happy.'

'I understand completely,' says Mitsy. 'It's good to have a job where you can help people to move forward.'

'Mitsy helps people too. But only if they're fat.'

'Not all of them are fat!' Laughing, she hits Amadou on the shoulder with a clenched fist. 'I'm a dietician,' she explains.

'But what makes you so happy here?' Amadou wants to know.

It's a moment before Alphonse can shift his focus away from Mitsy's job.

'It's precisely because there are no distractions that you can look at what there is. It demands your attention. It takes on a glow.'

'A glow?' Cat frowns at the ceiling, pained. 'This is the region of mass graves and unexploded munitions, abandoned border posts, defunct cafés, and the elderly.'

Their guests' eyes jump from her to him and back again.

'And blossom, salamanders, flocks of wild geese,' he says.

'And pumpkin-shooting, of course,' Cat adds.

'Pumpkin-shooting?' Amadou sits up straight. 'Cool.' He grins.

'Nature interests me too, these days,' Mitsy begins.

Cat doesn't let go. 'Oh yes, nature. That's why people shut themselves up in their houses here for three seasons a year.'

'That's Belgium,' says Amadou resignedly. 'The Netherlands too, for that matter. Rain. Hail. Fog. Snow! But what was that about shooting pumpkins?'

Alphonse and Cat seem not to have heard.

'People do live here, you know.'

'Old people. All the heavy labourers have retired, if they're not already dead. There are no new gold mines being dug here. Of all the Belgian provinces, West Flanders has become the least enterprising. And it has the most suicides.'

'There's such a lot that lives here.'

'The only thing kept alive here is death.'

'By you, right?' The thought of her lie stops him from

regretting it immediately. The injured cast to her mouth changes that a little.

Mitsy coughs and Amadou observes that it was quite a long drive, that they really ought to be getting to bed. Alphonse helps them to carry their suitcases upstairs. They'll be sleeping between the instruments and the mixing console. It seems Cat has had the presence of mind to unfold the sofa bed and provide it with bedding. She thinks of that kind of thing. He does too, but usually only at the last moment. He must say sorry. But he was right. The fact that he's made her look a fool in the presence of guests, given them a glimpse of her lie, will be what she resents most. But she started it. Alcohol sometimes makes her spiteful. He shows the guests where to find the bathroom, the towels. He must say sorry.

'Sorry,' he says, downstairs again.

She walks past him in silence with hands like spiders that have stepped into empty glasses.

He follows her to the sink, empty bottles at the ends of his dangling arms. He puts them off to one side, nestles up to her, feels her stiffen.

'If you say a thing like that, how can other people see how we are?' she asks.

'I know.' He doesn't add that he doesn't care what other people think of them, because that's not true, not in all cases. 'Come on,' he says, and he leads her by a less and less defiant hand into the garden, in the hope that stars will be hanging over the fields, that one will fall.

Sure enough. A great abundance. Before they came to live here he had no idea you could see such a thing in this country.

She stands next to him looking at the sky and says: 'Most have died, light years ago.'

Is she determined to keep this up?

'August is more the month for falling stars isn't it?'

'There!' he says.

A quick white fish below the surface of a muddy lake.

'I saw it!' She grins at the enthusiasm she's caught herself feeling. 'I even made a wish.'

He did too. That everything will stay the way it is now. Perhaps he means: that I'll stay the way I am now.

17

He hears Amadou and Mitsy through the ventilation grille in the bathroom as he's brushing his teeth. Cat has remarked in the past that it's as if he's playing bass right in her ear when she sits on the toilet here. He didn't realize she meant it so literally. First he hears their panting and moaning. It makes him think of Tonton Jah, all the times he treated him to his sex noises. It sometimes drove Alphonse to outright fury, tormented as he was by a confusing mixture of titillation, sleep deprivation, and puberty, and one time, when he was about seventeen and the cotton wool in his ears proved insufficient, he shouted: 'Go fuck somewhere else!' Seconds later his uncle was standing next to his bed, with the cold response that from now on he was to keep such outbursts to himself or he'd be the one having to look for a bed elsewhere. The next day Tonton was all smiles and mischief again. Shortly after that Alphonse found a place of his own.

Under the shower, even closer to the ventilation grille, he hears Amadou and Mitsy start a conversation in hushed tones, unaware that every word is being broadcast to him.

The first thing he notices, more so than yesterday, is how they speak. He finds Mitsy's Dutch funny. Sometimes he tries to mimic the northern accent, although

Cat keeps pointing out that he comes nowhere close. Yesterday Mitsy asked whether it was Spanish or Portuguese that she translated into Flemish, and Cat reluctantly explained that Flemish isn't a language, not a separate language anyway, that her language is Dutch. He's always found the weariness that sometimes overcomes Flemings in the presence of their northern neighbours entertaining.

Then he suddenly realizes who they're talking about.

'I can't believe he's happy,' says Amadou.

'He doesn't look depressed.'

'All the same.'

'Well, I do believe he likes his job.'

'But he was a night person, know what I mean? He liked dancing, for instance. Where does he do that now? In a forest?'

'How often do we go out dancing these days?'

'And he's a great musician! Maybe he's just let himself get discouraged by a couple of fuckwits, but that doesn't seem like him either. He had at least ten basses. Where have they all gone?'

'That's not the point, surely. Maybe he's realized he only needs one. You could give that some thought too.'

'He plays "for himself". Isn't that what he said? He doesn't seem to have any plans at all.'

'You play for yourself too, don't you?'

'Yes, but that's just how things turned out, as you know. It's not as if I wanted to work at C&A all my life. He didn't have any of that stuff with a baby and so forth. And he's better, if you really want to know. He was always a better musician than me, more dedicated.'

'You brought it up. Maybe that's just how things turned out with him, too. How would you know?'

'He had individuality. His own path.'

'Maybe he's got a project going that he doesn't tell any-one about. Or wants to learn new things. He never used to play the kora, you said?'

'His uncle played kora. A Jola who plays kora!'

Alphonse can tell from Mitsy's reaction that she fails to see what's so astonishing about that. He carefully soaps himself.

'His uncle wasn't a Saussai,' Amadou explains. 'They're Jola.'

'So?'

'Saussai. Mandinka? The kora is their instrument. But Tonton Jah was in the Keur Moussa monastery in Sebiko-tane. The white priests there played the kora, along with black priests from other ethnic groups. That alone seemed strange, to us.'

Us, thinks Alphonse. He feels a fondness for Amadou and that 'us', even though it usually leaves him wonder-ing what to make of it. His thoughts drift to Tonton Jah's time in the monastery, which he knows almost nothing about except that he fled, and that his flight had to do with a woman. He kept running, across seven national borders, until he arrived in Brussels in the mid-1970s and settled in the Kuregem district of Anderlecht, one of the few Senegalese there at the time. Alphonse has always imagined that flight from the monastery as a cartoon: his uncle, pulling his braces over his bare shoulders as he runs, his kora tied to his back, sprinting to the horizon with a furious cheated husband at his heels. He never completely turned his back on his reli-gion. Sometimes he used to demand that Alphonse do Bible study.

Amadou hasn't finished.

'When I first saw him again I thought: he hasn't changed at all. But if I think about it ... I don't know, it's more as if he's given something up, a form of protection or something, and I don't know whether that's good for him. Whether that can be good for anyone.'

'Was he ever with anyone for long, before he was with Cat?'

'Never for long. He was always careless with women. Lots of love affairs and love trouble, but never anything that really seemed more important to him than music.'

'This isn't the right one for him either, I'm afraid.'

'You've only just met her. She's likeable enough, isn't she?'

'She's not the one for him.'

They say good morning and join him at the breakfast table.

'Coffee?' Alphonse holds the thermos over the cups he's put ready for them.

'Nice,' says Mitsy.

'You don't know that yet,' he laughs. Cat's right. Dutch people don't say 'Yes, please' when you offer them something, they assume it'll be nice.

'I have to go. I can't be with you all day till the weekend.'

'That's fine. You told us that on the phone.' Amadou stirs three lumps of sugar into his coffee.

'And Cat never gets out of bed before eight. Not even when we have visitors. Not even for the apocalypse.'

'Sleep is healthy.' Amadou nods wisely. '*Wach lo kham, def lo mane, so tede nelew.*' Alphonse grins. It's a long time since he's heard that. He translates for Mitsy: 'Say what you know, do what you can, and when you lie down you'll sleep well.'

'She doesn't need to make allowances for us, of course she doesn't.' Mitsy feigns consternation. 'We're the last to judge. This morning we were awake unusually early. We'll see both of you this evening, right?'

Of course you don't judge, thinks Alphonse as he closes the front door behind him. People have given up judging. All they do now is gossip. The west wind strokes his hair and takes the insight with it.

A little over eighty-four hours ago, Marco Springels, after a relationship lasting almost fifteen years, was walked out on by Peter Van Renterghem. For Marco the break came like snow in July, exceeded in its unpredictability only by the fact that the new love of Peter's life was until recently Marco's employer, Mr 'Just call me Ronny' Van Den Abeele.

The name sounds familiar to Alphonse, but he's not good with names.

Marco took—naturally, he believes—the honourable way out and resigned immediately, after deleting a number of important computer files. All he wants to concentrate on for the next few weeks is new wallpaper.

'And I know what you're thinking,' he snorts at Alphonse, upset, 'but I'm not usually the least bit interested in interiors. It was Peter you spoke to on the phone—when was it? A month or so ago? He brought you here. Apparently he still wanted to resolve his need for a revamp in some way.' He breathes slowly in and out. 'But I'm glad you're here. It's simply ... It all simply has to be different now. All out!'

'That's okay,' Alphonse nods. 'I am interested in interiors.'

Leafing through a catalogue full of wallpaper samples, Marco calms down a little. What Alphonse suggests is entirely to his taste. They come to a decision: the ground floor in a soft khaki, broken by a wall that will have a climber with luxuriant flowers running across it. Upstairs: chick-down yellow as a jumping-off point.

'And don't let me just hang around here while you work: tell me what to do.'

Alphonse has only once allowed a client to help—a man who thought he knew better in every respect. It was an exercise in Zen meditation, the outcome complete havoc. 'I usually work alone,' he says.

'Don't do this to me,' Marco implores him. 'Tell me how I can help, that's all I ask.'

Alphonse hesitates. If it's what his client needs, then perhaps there's no avoiding it. In any case, he's willing to bet that after a morning of scraping old wallpaper Marco will have had enough.

'I can do it, you know. And if you're afraid I'll steal too many of your hours, we'll put everything down on paper before we start. Or not, whatever you like.'

Alphonse agrees to the proposal before Marco's tetchiness can drift into something more venomous. He orders the necessary rolls of paper.

'Where are you from?' Marco asks as they're moving a table with a heavy slate top. 'Originally? No, wait. Let me guess. Zimbabwe.'

'Senegal,' says Alphonse. How could anyone think he was Zimbabwean?

'In a previous life I had a thing with a boy from Mali.' Marco subsides into memories. 'That was a right old farce, I can tell you. And quite a relief when he was thrown out of the country, to be honest.' He chuckles. 'Sorry, that's really wrong of me. But it's true! He was a thoroughly naughty boy. Really disturbed. Every time he had a shower, he stood on my balcony to dry himself. I lived in Kortrijk then, on the Grote Markt. He stood there naked, arms and legs spread apart, drying himself, because—well, why? It shows how little you really know! Because he was completely mad, I suppose? And he wheedled money out of me, in that respect he was cunning, and I was naive. So his mother could have surgery, I thought, but it went straight to some kind of shaman.'

'A marabout, probably.'

'That was it.'

'Some are charlatans.'

On nights out in Brussels and Ghent, Alphonse has crossed paths with men who were in five relationships at once and hauling in the loot left, right, and centre, for a marabout who was waiting for it. He also knows a Nigerian who managed to gain asylum by pretending to be a persecuted homosexual and then didn't dare to be seen with a woman for fear of being found out, never came out of his house and sank into a deep depression. He knew a gay Jamaican who was sent back and murdered.

'I wish him all the best,' says Marco. 'It's years ago now. I have different problems these days.'

'You're quick!' Alphonse calls out to the man prodding strips of paper loose beside him.

Marco looks him belligerently in the eye. He's working with such a passion that Alphonse can barely keep up. His helpful client possesses self-knowledge: the work seems to be doing him good. As soon as Marco throws himself at the wallpaper, his manic torrent of words dries up. When he goes to make tea his broken heart and vocal cords are automatically reactivated.

'And I cooked for him as well! The time I spent on that, you don't want to know! And the amount it cost!'

'For the Malian?'

'No. For Ronny. And you know who else? For his wife!'

Suddenly he knows which Ronny. 'Sieglinde?' It slips out.

'Yes.'

Under Marco's dumbfounded gaze, Alphonse rolls his tongue up into his mouth. That he knows who this is prompts an interrogation. It takes quite some effort to flounder through it, slaloming. He doesn't know anything about them, has simply painted their walls.

In the end Marco gives up. 'I understand. You have a deontological code,' he says, disgruntled but not disapproving.

Just as Alphonse is wondering whether Ronny's new life will mark an end to the complex relationships he and Sieglinde have entered into with Els and Dieter, Marco starts talking about his own neighbour, Gewijde, with whom he grew up and whom he's watched go off the rails. There's a great deal that aggravates him—he tells of the 'irritating little noises' the man makes and leads Alphonse to the guest room on the first floor so that he can see the junk in Gewijde's garden—but he also continually calls him 'poor soul' and says he's 'no dunce; he speaks six languages'.

Most noticeable in the heap of rubbish in the garden are the seven rusting barbecues.

'That's right, several times a year he wants a barbecue so he buys a new one forgetting he already has one. It's the same with the things he says. He often rings my doorbell to reveal to me something he told me earlier in the week. You'll see that again today.'

After about an hour, Marco is holding open a rubbish bag for Alphonse so that he can get rid of the first load of stiff paper scraps when, sure enough, the neighbour calls him to the front door with a persistent ding-dong.

'Gewijde, I can't let you in, we're stripping wallpaper, it's a war zone in here,' Alphonse hears him say, a rejection that Gewijde ignores. Seconds later a spectral man is gaping at him as if at a ghost.

'This is Alphonse. He's come to revamp my interior.'

'I thought you were being held hostage!' Gewijde exclaims. The sucking noise made by the tip of his tongue against the back of his front teeth is indeed annoying.

'Held hostage? Alphonse speaks Dutch. He can understand what you're saying.'

'I thought he was your hostage,' says Gewijde, this time in English, exceedingly amused at himself. Receiving no answer from Alphonse, he begins telling a story, interrupted by a complex range of mouth noises, about welfare payments, from which it's possible to divine that there's something he won't agree to. While talking he goes to sit on a chair in the middle of the room, a position that allows him to survey the progress of the other two. It's not just his breath that's putting out that volatile stench of alcohol, all his pores seem to be collaborating to exude it. Marco's lips press together more firmly as his irritation increases. A couple of times they let slip a 'You've said that already.'

For a long time it seems that only the sternest of commands might persuade the neighbour to go back to his own house, but in the end it's he who apologizes: he's got such a lot to do that he urgently has to leave.

'Korsakoff's syndrome,' says Marco when he's gone. 'I just tell myself that it's worse for him. You might ask yourself whose fault it is, too, his or that priest's. You know what I mean.' He sighs. 'Something a small country's big in. Although it doesn't only happen here. Did you see that documentary recently about an Irish boarding school?' Sidelong he watches Alphonse shake his head. 'With Gewijde it was from the age of about twelve, maybe earlier. Pure evil exists, Alphonse, that's one thing the bastard taught me. Father Piper we called him. Everyone knew about it and no one did anything. Including me. If I'd done something then, I wouldn't be stuck with this now, I sometimes think. Gewijde barging in here all the time, I mean. For a long time I had the stupid idea that he hadn't been affected by it, by what was done to him. That he could cope with it. Really, that's what I thought! He was top of the class for years and he was good at sports. I envied him. When he was about seventeen he started to hear the voice of Pan, the god of the forest and animal instincts or what have you. Anyhow, Pan didn't seem to have any better intentions with him than Piper. He says the voice only goes away when he drinks. No doubt that's true. There was a woman who put up with him for quite a while, an angel, but in the end she only made matters worse, because when she left he naturally had to drink twice as much to forget that he'd botched his chance at happiness.'

'One of those stories,' says Alphonse.

'One of those stories,' Marco agrees. 'He's able to forget if he comes here to grouch about his welfare payments or all kinds of other things that aren't his real problem. All I can do is listen, I think.'

'I think so too,' says Alphonse.

At home Willem is visiting. With some relief Alphonse establishes that his tears are the fault of the onion on the wooden plank he's stooping over. Across from him, at the kitchen table, Amadou is sunk in fierce concentration peeling potatoes. Cat and Mitsy greet him from the sink.

'Hi, man,' says Cat. She seems happy today. He kisses her neck.

'I was just telling them about my friend Pierre,' says Willem. 'The one who accidentally flew over Russian territory in his jet in the middle of the Cold War. He found the Russians very polite and they didn't hold him for long. But when they asked him if he wanted to spy for them he said: "Over my dead body."' He thinks for a moment. 'That won't have been how he put it, but that's what it amounted to.'

'No *tirailleurs* today?' Alphonse checks.

He catches Amadou's eye. Don't encourage him, signals his friend.

'We went to look at the commando bunker on the Kemmelberg,' Mitsy explains. 'It was actually rather interesting. I hadn't thought about the Iron Curtain for a long time. The term, I mean.'

'I painted it,' says Alphonse. 'For the wall near the entrance they wanted a chamois leather technique with two kinds of red. Apart from that all they asked me to do was to paint the heating pipes dark-green, the pipes that run through all the underground passageways. They didn't yet have permission to do the other walls, or anything else.' Dark red, ochre, and various shades of green: he's connected those colours with the Cold War ever since. And a ceiling full of asbestos.

Amadou looks at him with undisguised pity.

'The building itself is great, isn't it? On the outside it looks like a little farmhouse. And then all those manual control rooms, telex machines, radio equipment and encoders, and an automatic telephone exchange as big as a room.'

'The idea was to make it into an international air defence post, but the building wasn't nuclear-proof. It was obsolete before it was finished,' Willem has taken over from Alphonse.

'Yes, we read that,' says Amadou.

'So exercises were staged there,' Willem continues unperturbed. 'They never called the enemy from the East "the Soviet Union" or "the Warsaw Pact", did you read that too?'

It troubles Alphonse that Willem and Amadou have started to act like a canny schoolteacher and his rebellious pupil.

'Orange, the enemy was called,' Willem goes on without waiting for an answer.

'Really?' says Mitsy, startled. 'Why Orange?'

'No one knows,' Willem grins. 'I really don't think it had anything to do with the Netherlands. Maybe just because orange is close to red. Pink probably wasn't an option.'

'Lots of mountain bikers on the Kemmelberg,' says Amadou. 'It wasn't a race, they were going in all directions.'

'Can we rent bikes somewhere around here?' Mitsy asks.

Cat remembers that their bicycles have been at the repair shop for more than three weeks and Alphonse promises to pick them up on Saturday. Willem suggests that the other two use his till then. They'll have to be careful with them, especially Marie-Jeanne's; he cherishes everything of hers he has left.

'We'll wait till Saturday,' says Amadou.

They eat together and sit drinking for hours in a cloud of cigarette smoke. Apart from Willem they all smoke, even though they say they've stopped. The conversation jumps from sightseeing in French Flanders to Senegalese politics and back again. Willem manages to weave the post-war fate of the *tirailleurs sénégalais* through it; the tour of military graves he proposes meets with polite approbation.

The conversation tumbles into their childhoods. It's Willem who starts talking about his earliest memory, the pink chrysanthemums his weeping mother flung down furiously on the grave of a dead soldier in 1941, a young man with a hat and a dark-blond moustache. The hand that clutched his was damp, as if it were crying too. The fear of those days. Much later he found out she'd had a relationship with the man. It was impossible to keep a secret like that in these parts. He never confronted her with it, and later he could never find the grave again.

Mitsy remembers a misunderstanding, a psychologist who visited her nursery school and was furious with her because he thought she'd tried to steal something from his backpack, whereas her four-year-old self thought she'd been asked to take an egg out of it.

Alphonse wonders what Cat will talk about. It's strange that they've never had this conversation before. She shrugs and then says, reticently: 'My parents arguing. They always did that in French and I've always connected that language with their quarrels, even though *M'bindan* spoke much gentler French with me. In my earliest memory my mother pummels her fists on my father's chest. "*Une avalanche!*" she shouts. "*T'es une avalanche.*" I imagine she must mean he's an item of clothing, a long colourful jacket. I tell *M'bindan* about it. "No," she says, her cheek against mine. "It's snow. But don't you go worrying about that."'

Cat and Alphonse laugh out loud, with a mixture of anxiety and affection at the thought of his mother's role in her life.

Amadou breaks in on the moment. 'With me it's something spectacular. The first thing I remember is walking with my mother across a vacant plot of land in Dakar. She's pulling my little brother on a cart behind her. Then there's a terrible racket above our heads. We duck, my mother pushes us to the ground—for a Frenchman in a private plane, an aviator skimming over us, just missing us. For fun. But I must have told you about that before.'

'It's a long time since I heard it,' says Alphonse.

'And you?' Mitsy asks.

'Yes, now you,' says Willem.

'My first memory isn't a story. And according to my mother I was too young to have remembered it. A bird on the beach. That's all. A pelican with a string around its leg and a man trying to sell it. The only time I've ever seen anyone do that on a beach. I look at the bird. The white feathers are a bit ruffled. The huge beak looks like a boat. The bird stares back, one eye drilling into mine so hard that it unnerves me, but I'm not afraid. The man takes my hand and when I touch the pelican I can no longer tell where I end and it begins.'

Alphonse yawns. Sleepiness lies like a blanket of moss around his shoulders. Amadou is looking at him with silent curiosity, he notices.

'I listened to that last album of Fabrice's,' says Amadou. 'By chance. That number. What did you think of it? You must have been furious.'

'I don't want to talk about that,' says Alphonse, so calmly and simply that no one could possibly think of contradicting him.

He'd like to play his kora now, without an audience. Cat's fingers slide in between his. Cat. He feels his hand come alive, enclosing hers within it. The others do their best to combat the silence, because they don't understand how peaceful it is, as long as Cat holds him like that.

16

Under the blankets, sleep pulls his lover's hand out of his, leaving him there alone with his thoughts.

He's managed to keep memories of Fabrice Mlapa at bay for a long time, but tonight all resistance will be in vain. Amadou has roused them and they seep into the bedroom through gaps and cracks.

It was during the period when Amadou threw in the towel as a musician that Fabrice and Alphonse wandered into each other's lives. They knew the same people and played different instruments in the same small world of jazz clubs and African music festivals. Both of them hated the term 'world music'; what they made was music. Like Amadou, Fabrice played guitar. Amadou didn't like him. Alphonse did. A friendship developed. Fabrice often voiced respect for Alphonse and several times even called him 'my rock'. Quite why was never entirely clear to Alphonse, although he did put Fabrice's name forward in preference to other musicians when producers or festival organizers asked him for a guitarist. Some people got the two of them mixed up: two muscled black men of the same age, equally single-minded. Others warned Alphonse about what they called Fabrice's unhealthy competitiveness, his tendency to manipulate—warnings Alphonse never took seriously. He felt the cause of Fabrice's bad reputation had to do with the fact that he liked to announce that his father was the Ambassador of Togo and his American mother was allowed to address Oprah Winfrey as 'Baby-O'. Things like that created ill feeling in an environment where so many were yearning for a residence permit and hardly anyone had the resources that make for true independence and real prospects. Alphonse took no notice of opinions and bad tidings, even Cat's. Never had shaky concepts like reputation and intuition stood in the way of a friendship.

At one of the first performances he helped to set up, Fabrice's sister was waiting for him. 'He's massively insecure,' she said. 'Almost pathologically so. He'll never tell you how grateful he is for what you do for him, but he is, all the same. I thought you should know that.' Alphonse made himself scarce with an 'Okay' and never saw her again. He found it odd that the sister assumed he was expecting Fabrice's gratitude like some kind of overdue payment. They were friends, weren't they?

Fabrice found it hard to enjoy his successes discreetly. From the moment someone in the audience whistled encouragement, he strode through backstage rooms like a golden god looking down on other musicians from on high. Alphonse found it amusing rather than unforgivable.

During one of the many breaks in the exhausting love life that Alphonse and Cat shared at the time—one of the occasions on which she left him—his friend rang. He loudly tried to convince Alphonse of the similarities between him, Fabrice, and the woman who had walked out on him.

'Don't you see what he's doing?' Cat asked when he mentioned the call after their reconciliation. 'Did it reassure you?' He didn't know what she was getting at and imagined she was telling him—as she had done before—that Fabrice had tried to seduce her several times. He'd said that the way she tried to make him jealous was typical of a woman and that he disapproved of her persistent contempt for his friend. She told him he hadn't understood her point at all. They argued about it, and then they argued about the argument. The next time they broke it off, he was the one racing for the emergency exit.

Then there were Fabrice's recording contracts and the songs Alphonse wrote for the debut album. Feeling rather lost, he wandered around the studio, having come to record the bass line. The producer—a woman of a certain age, famous for her sharp mind and a list of awards impressive by Belgian standards—followed Fabrice everywhere during the sessions like a poodle on heat and was encouraged by him in doing so. She complimented Alphonse on his contributions without ever looking him in the eye.

When the album came out and there was no trace of his name on it, Alphonse understood that they'd erased him even as he watched. He rang the producer, unable to bear the way Cat nodded at him, unable to bear being used, perhaps right from the beginning of what he'd taken to be a friendship. According to her voicemail, she wasn't there. As soon as he put the phone down, Fabrice rang him. When attempts to remind Alphonse of never-made agreements about credits got him nowhere, Fabrice suddenly begged: 'I want you to be angry with me. Now you have to be angry with me.' Alphonse looked at the hairs on his arm when he said that, how they were standing on end. 'He's not your friend,' Cat summed it all up, and he was grateful she left it at a simple conclusion that evening.

From then on he stayed away from Fabrice, who initially pretended not to understand why but soon began to emulate his evasions. When they were forced to meet, Alphonse did his best to steer the lack of interest he now felt in the man's presence in the direction of politeness. When the producer crossed his path by chance and he greeted her, she pounced on his hand, which she shook and shook, nodding, until he carefully pulled it free. He started to believe that most people are a good deal weaker than they seem, but he also believed in courtesy, and lapses, and the right to make mistakes. He wanted to start a conversation with Fabrice, to make things easier. Except that no matter how hard he tried, he couldn't imagine what they might talk about. He thought it had all gone too far and tried once again to see Fabrice as someone with whom he'd shared an idea for a song, a joint, and a laugh. Sometimes he forgot about him for weeks. Fabrice had become a blind spot. 'I wonder whether he'll punish you for not paying him any attention,' Cat said one evening under an umbrella, next to him in a cinema queue. He knew immediately who she was talking about, even though they hadn't mentioned Fabrice for ages, even though the possibility she was raising had never occurred to him.

Fabrice made his existence felt with an album on which there was a track about a character who revealed himself to be the son of a marginal warlock, an unsavoury womanizer, smelly sluggard, hypocritical thief, amoral addict, and sure-fire loser. In the final verse Fabrice himself appeared as 'Diamond Bullet Mlapa', who killed the baddie and then died by his own hand. He reached a far larger audience with that album than with the previous one. It was also issued on vinyl.

For the psychoanalyst in Cat, a lot became clear.

Alphonse didn't have one of those in him. He'd never have recognized himself in the song if it hadn't been given his name. 'The Assassination of Alphonse Badjie', it was called. The extra 'e' was probably there for legal reasons.

The contempt and obsession manifested by the attack were grotesque, but no longer comical. He turned to Cat. Why did Fabrice do that? Yet again. Why all that time and energy? Why him? What had he ever done to the guy?

'He thinks you're fighting him, because he's fighting you,' said Cat. 'He interprets the help you've given him as a stratagem, because to him help can only be a stratagem.'

'But what does he think we're after?' Alphonse replied, distraught. 'A world sausage-grilling record? To see who can stack the most beer mats between their teeth? Table football? What does he want, a gold medal? We make music. It's not a contest, all you can do is get better. That's precisely the point: you don't have to attack anyone, you get a chance to rise above all that nonsense. I thought he understood. I thought he was cleverer than that.' What a great shame it all was, if Cat had read Fabrice correctly— as she'd done unfailingly up to now. What a shame that Fabrice wanted to reduce the two of them to rivals, cocks crowing for the entertainment of a crowd that was after clichés. Alphonse hadn't seen this coming because he'd refused to believe it.

Cat paced up and down with him through the small kitchen of their flat, unable to bring him to a halt with her touch. 'I don't think it has anything to do with intelligence. Some people are like that. You know they are, don't you, Alphonse? Why do you always put so much effort into tracking down goodness in people when they show so few traces of it? You're probably right to say there's always more than one story to be told, but when someone repeatedly shows that they haven't got your best interests at heart, you no longer have to do your best for them. It's okay to turn your back on them then.'

He thought of what his mother used to say: 'Everyone you'll meet is a child. Those who're aware of it are the nicest people. All the rest are the sort who take all their impulses seriously and grab every chance they get to use them against others. There are two kinds of people, those who deliberately harm others and those who don't. With the first group it's simple: keep out of their way.' Should he have known? Do you have to be permanently on guard in case someone, based on hazy delusions, wants to set fire to your life? And if he hadn't expected it, did that mean he deserved it?

He put that question to Cat, quietly. 'Did I deserve it, then?'

She looked at him in disbelief and threw her arms around him, roughly, almost. 'No, of course not, Alphonse, of course not, my sweet.'

Her love for him then, his love for her, they both poured through him, they were still there. At the same time he felt a complete idiot. It was the first time he'd cried in her presence, his head on her stomach. 'I don't want to be a victim,' he sobbed. 'And I don't want a fight, either. Not that kind of a fight.'

'You'll never be a victim for long, and you'll never become an aggressor, because you're a hero,' she consoled him.

She advised him not to confront Fabrice, nor to talk to anyone else about it, because most people are all too fond of other people's quarrels—and Fabrice was too fond of attention of any kind.

Alphonse withdrew, although not all at once. He

began to see music as something intimate, something he wanted to keep away from stages and other arenas. And after that Cat got sick, and he willingly allowed himself to be led by life to other places, other goals. The contempt had hit home, the obsessive nature of it appalled him, but he hadn't grown fearful, hadn't gone down. Fabrice's attacks led him to the unpleasant conclusion that he must be more careful with people, with friendship. It was an impediment he deplored, refused to accommodate, and that he hoped wouldn't turn out to be an insight. He decided Fabrice had simply asked him a question to which he had no answer.

Outside the sun is rising. The world is turning. Alphonse has lain down and breathed calmly, even if he hasn't slept. Cat is warm.

Marco hasn't slept a wink either. When he opens the door to Alphonse he looks years older than the day before. His white scalp shows between the tangled hairs on the top of his head. 'You're early,' he says. 'Gewijde came round again last night, with a special whisky. I had a few things about the place myself. Haven't drunk like that for a while.' He points with his thumb behind his back at the kitchen counter, at the bottles in a row, each a little emptier than the last, as if someone intended to play a tune on them.

'Go and lie down again for a bit,' Alphonse suggests.

'No, that's the problem. When I drink I sleep like a log, but two hours later I'm wide awake.'

Marco's hangover does little to slow his working pace and by about midday they've stripped the upstairs as well. He does swear more.

During their shared lunch he starts talking about the neighbour again. 'The great thing about Gewijde is that he never says anything behind people's backs, or has opinions about them. What others do or don't do escapes his attention completely. I'm sure he hasn't noticed Peter's gone. Actually that's rather comforting. Not having to talk about it.'

The wallpaper arrives. Cheered by the perfect timing, Alphonse holds an unrolled strip against the wall.

'Beautiful.' Halfway through expressing his approval, Marco loses his voice. The hangover flares up. After a glass of water and much hesitation he's persuaded to take himself off to bed, just for a while.

The pasting table, the frogspawn-like glue: Alphonse has come to be good at this, a fact that elicits in him a sober pride. He hums 'Waliyou' (Messiah), a number from the latest album by Seydina Insa Wade, which Amadou played for him yesterday, fuming slightly on realizing he didn't already know it. Now that he's dead, he's regarded as the most important Senegalese musician ever. Absurd consolation for anyone longing for due recognition: when you're dead you'll finally have a chance. The track includes a bit of text, in Wolof, that seems too quick for Seydina's mouth, too quick for the listener's ears. Although he doesn't understand what he's singing, Alphonse can't shake off the impression that the singer is holding a conversation with approaching death. When he tried to explain that to Amadou yesterday, his friend thought it a strange suggestion. Now he thinks so himself.

He's just about to stick a glued length of wallpaper on the wall when his phone rings. He carefully lays the paper down again.

'I'll come straight to the point because this is a really expensive call, but we've got second prize!' a euphoric voice reverberates.

'Congratulations!'

'Thanks! Japan is fantastic. Including the food. I hadn't expected that. Speak to you soon!'

Shaka Duran: big in Japan. Alphonse is happy for him.

Marco is profoundly impressed by the wall that Alphonse has already papered. Arms crossed in front of a clean shirt, he stands staring at it for a long time, his head tilted slightly to one side. Then he makes coffee and scours the cupboards 'for something greasy to eat'. When the doorbell rings, he drags himself reluctantly to the front door.

Predictably, it's Gewijde. He's in a state of inebriation, having started again already, or not having stopped since the night before. And this time he seems to be on a mission. Glassy but serious, his eyes bore into Marco's. Not a single annoying sound escapes him. As if about to commence a solemn ritual, he grasps his neighbour's shoulders. 'What's this I hear?' he whispers.

'What is it you hear, Gewijde?'

'Has Peter left?'

'Yes. Several days ago.'

Alphonse turns his attention to a new mix of glue so as to look as little as possible like an audience.

'What a donkey!' the neighbour shouts. His lips and tongue let out a long wet fart.

Marco looks apologetically at Alphonse. 'Uh-huh.'

'I always thought you were the likeable one! You are at least ... likeable. He's ... He's just a ... I always thought he was actually very ... not likeable!'

'Okay.'

'You're sociable, too, you are!'

'Thanks.'

'And I'm going to say it like it is: you look a lot better

than he does. Can I say that, man to man, without meaning anything by it?'

'It's fine, Gewijde.'

'And you on TV and everything!'

'I'm not on TV.'

'No? Didn't you have a talk show?'

'No.'

Gewijde has to think about that. He decides: 'Well, he'll be sorry yet. And you know, it happened to me too and with me everything turned out all right.' Invigorated by those final words, he administers a slap to Marco's cheek, rather a hard one as it turns out.

It's only then that he notices Alphonse. Again that sucking sound with tongue tip and teeth. 'Who are you?' he asks in English, like a British policeman of the shrewder variety. Before anyone can answer, inspiration strikes. 'Sorry. It's none of my business,' he says to Marco. With his hand pressed to his chest he turns to face Alphonse again. 'I didn't realize you were a prostitute.'

'He's hanging wallpaper! And he speaks Dutch! He was here yesterday too!'

'Never mind,' Alphonse soothes.

'*Mi scusi tanto!*' Gewijde shakes both their hands before heading home.

'And soon he'll have forgotten all that as well,' says Marco.

Without explaining, he empties the bottles one by one down the plughole.

In the evening they take their guests with them to Rijsel. Amadou in particular seems to like the town. 'Good that you're close to Lille, anyhow,' he says several times.

They've missed the market in Les Halles de Wazemmes, but there's still a smell of fish in the Rue Gambetta. In the middle of a bar, a woman sobs loudly as she throws herself into the comforting arms of a man. Both then calmly go to sit and drink at the tables outside.

They walk past a memorial plaque for men killed in Indochina and North Africa; the general astride a horse a little further on is Louis Faidherbe.

'Ah, who have we here?' says Amadou.

'The man of the bridge to Saint Louis,' says Cat.

Amadou sniffs, then plays guide, lips pursed, speaking dulcet, humming French. 'When he'd killed enough Serer and Toucouleur, and burnt villages to the ground because in his dreams they'd once belonged to France, the highly esteemed General thought: I'm going to get those Negroes to fight instead of us; then French soldiers will no longer have to suffer malaria and diarrhoea. So he bought some slaves and put some tribal leaders in charge of them in exchange for false promises. When the Europeans began fighting each other, those powerless musclemen were invited to come and have their feet frozen off under a French flag. And as soon as it was over, they were ordered to bugger off again.'

'Yes,' says Alphonse. It's the first reminder since he arrived of Amadou's interest in colonial history. His vocabulary always gets larger and his tone more bitter when he engages in outbursts like this.

'Your neighbour probably has a poster of Faidherbe above his bed,' Amadou adds, in a failed attempt at light-heartedness.

'Willem's okay,' says Alphonse.

Amadou's eyes narrow. He falls silent, one corner of his mouth and one eyebrow raised, as if a puppeteer is gently pulling a thread attached to that side of his face.

They eat at a Japanese restaurant, where Alphonse tells them about Duran's silver medal, until he notices that Cat is saying nothing—she's probably thinking of the ice figurine that disappeared from the freezer—and the others don't understand what he's talking about.

The town shines and flickers, bass tones and girls in towering heels stumble into the streets. North Africans in fast cars. Asian shops, which remind Cat of the 1990s. A squall of rain chases them back under cover. Below an awning, Mitsy shares her tobacco with Alphonse. They talk about giving up smoking and starting again and not giving a damn, about having to die somehow and only living once, doing as you feel. They laugh. The puddles turn white, pink, green.

'Naice 'et,' says a passer-by with a nod to his hat.

'*Merci*,' Alphonse answers.

In a bar their colour stands out, for the club they wander into they're too old, but then they find a place where no one notices them until they dance. He likes dancing, Alphonse, and when he dances he likes best of all the continent on which he was born, what the body can do there, how it's allowed to be both powerful and seductive at the same time, and to laugh at itself. Many Europeans don't understand the humour behind those moves, or think the dances are funny only to them. He likes seeing Cat dance; she's capable of letting her body be taken over by the rhythm, it's just that she doesn't much feel like it tonight.

Talk doesn't come easily to her either. On the way to the car Alphonse looks over his shoulder several times to check that the women are following. Mitsy is speaking and when she's finished Cat stays silent. She doesn't just look tired, there's something else, and because he becomes more convinced every time he looks round that there's too often something, and because he doesn't want to feel guilty about going on ahead with Amadou, he stops worrying and turns all his attention to the conversation with his friend. They're talking about music, walking the way they used to.

An older man who seems out of place against this nocturnal backdrop attracts their attention. He's furious. *'Sales pédés,'* he flings at them as they pass. When they stop in amazement he breaks into a run.

Alphonse and Amadou search each other's disbelieving faces, their suits, scarves, and hats. Simultaneously they discharge loud bursts of laughter into the black sky. Few people see any problem with referring to them as 'blacks', even 'Negroes', and they've been called 'monkeys' often enough. 'Dirty faggots' is a new one. Who knows, perhaps that's progress.

15

They were late to bed and up earlier than they wanted to be. There are sporting resolutions waiting to be fulfilled. Amadou is in the shower and Mitsy has asked whether Alphonse would play the kora for her; she's never heard the instrument live. He plays sitting on a kitchen chair.

'Gorgeous,' she sighs a number of times.

'We still have to fetch our bicycles,' Cat says. Since only the strings answer, she grabs the car keys from the table. 'I'll do it. Have you got the ticket?'

Alphonse shakes his head in time to the music. The memorably unfriendly wife of the bicycle mechanic insisted they mustn't lose the ticket, a plastic-coated piece of paper with a number on it and on the back the message BICYCLES LEFT HERE FOR MORE THAN A MONTH WILL BE SOLD OR REDUCED TO SCRAP METAL!!! Cat and he had laughed at that. 'You've got it, I think. Can you wait a minute? I'll go with you.'

'Must surely be possible without it.' Her attention is drawn to Mitsy, who is now listening to the sounds of the kora with her eyes closed. 'Have fun,' she says drily, to him.

Shortly after the front door shuts behind her, Amadou joins them in the kitchen. He too stops to listen.

Mitsy presses both hands to her breast. 'Incredibly beautiful.'

'Yes,' says Amadou and then, without disapproval: 'A Jola who plays kora.'

Alphonse smiles at him.

'That peace can sweep you away like that,' Mitsy coos.

Alphonse plays a little more, then takes leave of the improvised melody and puts the instrument aside. 'Breakfast.'

He can tell immediately that Cat is in a stinking mood when she storms into the kitchen half an hour later.

'What a nightmare! Not having that stupid ticket with me was the worst thing I could do to those people, apparently. Unadulterated panic!'

'Shit,' says Alphonse. 'Could have predicted that.'

'Yes, you might have tried to find it. Then I wouldn't have been accused of attempted theft. They both kept saying I was lying, the repair man and his wife, that I was trying to steal bicycles. They both stood there pointing at me and bellowing that they'd call the police and there I was, shouting back: "Go on then! Go on then!"'

Alphonse laughs. Not the right reaction, clearly.

'In the end they found a note stuck in the rack at the back that had my name on it. They were still suspicious, but they couldn't really do anything except give the bikes back and let me pay for the repairs. It was still a whole carry-on getting them into the car on my own. No one came over to help, of course. My legs are still shaking. Totally absurd!'

'I think it was your skin colour,' says Amadou.

'What?' The thunder cloud surrounding Cat dissolves.

'They don't like blacks around here.'

Surprised, she laughs dimples into her red cheeks. The others join in. 'It might actually have been my accent,' she adds, serious now. 'Wrong province. Tribal country.'

Amadou finds that very amusing.

Even after cycling for an hour, neither the guests nor Cat feel any urge to wax lyrical about the landscape. They concentrate on climbs and descents and how their muscles are responding to them. They barely notice even the most charming things around them: the timeless decor of sparse houses and windmills in slopes of lush grass, beneath ever-changing clouds, dragons, teapots. He wouldn't have been surprised by a trail of breadcrumbs leading to an elf who invited him to make a wish. 'To speak all languages' is what he'd wish for.

Several times they pass signs saying 'Belgium' or 'France', signs ignored by the landscape with boundless indifference. They have a drink with a manager of fishponds who tries to convince them on this sun-drenched September day that it's beautiful here in winter. He fetches several dozen underexposed photos of snow and ice to prove his point. Afterwards Amadou claims the man 'looked sadistically at him' as he did so. He says several times that it wouldn't suit him at all, this part of the world.

Although Alphonse is astonished by his friend's desire to visit a windmill, he takes him up on it. He leads them to George, the owner of the last stone mill in the region, whom he met when he applied roughcast to the back wall of his house, one of the few times he's allowed himself to be tempted to work on an exterior.

George, a Frenchman who speaks the local Flemish dialect, switches back into French. Amadou, utterly captivated, doesn't move a metre from his side. Mitsy learns something new about her boyfriend. The sails turn. Between the huge basal structure and the ancient ingenuity of felled tree trunks and gouged millstones they climb in single file up narrow stairs to the top floor.

Ecstatic, Amadou shares an insight: 'Now I finally

understand what the problem is with the sleeping miller's mill that turns too fast!' And because Mitsy is now staring at him with concern, he sings: '*Meunier tu dors, ton moulin va trop vite!* Didn't you understand what he said? That fire will break out if two wooden surfaces rub against each other too fast. Of course!'

'Honey. Chill.'

He pays no attention, charmed by an old photo of the mill with broken sails. 'Various kinds of flour are still milled here today for educational purposes,' they read in a folder pinned to the wall. George, a fifth-generation miller, talks in despondent tones about the coming of the steam engine, which over time distilled the rationale for the windmill into purely its idyllic nature. Given that the introduction of electricity put paid to his craft, it sounds like a confession when he says he used to work for an electricity company and took over the milling business only when his father retired. His son is interested in becoming the sixth generation, but it'll be another twenty years before he draws his pension and who knows what might happen in that time? The economic crisis has radically reduced interest in windmills; even the schoolchildren have stopped coming. Amadou listens, nodding, touched by the injustice of it.

'I'm genuinely quite worried about him,' Mitsy tells Alphonse in hushed tones. They're the last to descend the stairs, backward. 'It's not as if we don't have windmills back home. I've never heard him talk about anything with such enthusiasm, not even his little boy. It couldn't be a brain tumour, could it?'

Alphonse smokes a cigarette with her on the stretch of land between the mill and the agricultural museum, where the other three have gone in ahead of them.

'He often used to have sudden whims like this. They

pass.' Despite his passionate defence of the Atomium, when it was at last fully renovated a few years later it left Amadou cold.

'You coming?' Cat calls from the door.

'Yes, yes, we're coming,' says Mitsy. There's a hint of perverse pleasure in her voice that he doesn't like, and neither does Cat, he can tell from her lower lip.

In the agricultural museum, an overfilled barn, a radiant George shows them his latest acquisition: two life-sized dolls representing his father and mother. They're sitting at a table. The mother doll is stabbing a needle through some knitting, while the father doll mechanically runs his fingers through a pile of beans, battling Parkinson's disease by the look of it, his face turned to the far side of the room. George presses a button in the back of the father doll and a grating voice echoes around the space, while hinges move its chin up and down with noisy jerks. They don't know what to say, and as a result the miller seems suddenly to have doubts about his pride in all this. To distract attention he tells them about the olden days. Tobacconists near the border posts handed out free cigarettes to him and his friends. Once addicted, they were good customers. He switches unannounced to a story about South Africa, an abandoned emigration. The company he worked for wanted to send him there and he'd have been happy to go.

'Regrets?' asks Alphonse.

George, dreamy, says nothing, then: 'The children didn't like the idea.'

In the toilets Alphonse finds a shiny card in his coat pocket. BICYCLES LEFT HERE FOR MORE THAN A MONTH WILL BE SOLD OR REDUCED TO SCRAP METAL!!! he reads, before putting it back.

Lashing bags of pancake flour to their bicycle racks, they say goodbye to the miller. After the first bend he sees tears in Cat's eyes. 'Those dolls,' she says. He understands. Folklore and polyester have had this effect on her before. The image of the father's flapping mouth has stayed with him, too. He cycles beside her. The others are several metres behind and to judge from Mitsy's contorted riding posture Amadou is once again losing himself in a digression on the subject of windmills.

'If it's what you want, we'll move back to the city.' Alphonse hasn't given this very much thought.

'Do you want to?'

'I want you to be happy.'

'But do you want to leave this place, yourself?'

'No. Not yet.'

'Ah.'

Don't ask then, he thinks, if you don't want to know.

Alphonse Skypes his mother, who is happy to see Amadou sitting between him and Cat, looking at the eye of the camera. An outburst of joyful cries and compliments. Those two have always liked each other. His sister is there as well. As ever, she and Alphonse manage to do little more than smile intently. He doesn't know her very well. Aline is ten years older, the child of an earlier vanished father; they don't resemble each other at all and have lived apart since he was eight. Her mother would have liked her to move to Brussels with them but she refused, preferring to stay where she was. The memories featuring her are affectionate: she blows across his sweat through a small gap between her lips, sings a song with a slow, deep voice, giggles behind her hand as she shows him her ingenious hairdo, her party dress—he sees that she's a beautiful woman now, an adult, and that she sees with pride what he's thinking. Now they can only smile and say 'ça va?' 'ça va'. Most of the conversation is between his mother and Amadou.

After the phone call his friend fills the room with Bob Marley and starts talking about Tonton Jah—whose real name was Lassana—his women, his mysterious death and whether the two were connected in any way.

'There was never an autopsy. As you know, I always insisted there should be one.'

'If you'd been white, they'd have listened.'

Alphonse feels an aftershock of the fury the thought aroused in him at the time. He says a culprit and a punishment would have changed little, but when he was nineteen and went to identify his uncle's body, he thought differently. Such a bitter twist to his mouth. Tonton Jah had been all kinds of things, but never bitter. And he'd never injected. The fatal shot must have been his first; he drank.

'But what do you think yourself?'

During his short life Tonton Jah energetically explored his predilection for married women. For reasons known only to him, they were mainly Congolese married women. Alphonse had joked before his death about a 'Missing' photo of his guardian that they could stick up all over the Matonge quarter of Brussels.

'Alphonse? What do you think?'

'That he's no longer with us.'

Amadou nods, realizes he mustn't insist.

'What kind of a person was he?' asks Mitsy. 'Apart from being a fan of Bob?'

'That's hard to explain,' Alphonse smiles.

A washer-up who talked about 'his' restaurant. A man with taste and style and debts. Someone who slept it off in the morning on the floor next to your bed and the following night took you to the early market in Laken to buy ten kilos of prime rib for you and flowers for nine women.

'Alphonse and his uncle had a neighbour who couldn't stand music. At the very first note he'd start kicking the wall. I heard it. It was as if a wounded rhinoceros was trapped in the adjoining room.'

Alphonse grins. Monsieur Banane they called him, because he often shouted 'Go eat a banana, macaca!' when his uncle played the kora. If they saw him outside he'd scurry off. Alphonse has forgotten his real name.

'And Tonton Jah would pluck away for longer and with more harmonies than he'd been planning to do and call back in the seductive French of his mistresses: "You live in my heart, my love! You give colour to my days, my ray of sunshine!"'

Cat and Mitsy laugh.

'It drove Monsieur Banane crazy, literally.'

'Bananas,' says Cat.

'One day I saw him hanging around at North Station in his pyjamas. He didn't know who I was but he let me take him home. A few weeks later his apartment was up for rent.'

'Suicide?' asks Mitsy.

'An institution, I think.'

Amadou's hand flutters through the air. 'That was nothing to do with your uncle. Monsieur Banane was mad already.'

'Also possible.'

Yet every single memory of his uncle is ambiguous. There was always light, always shadow. 'We'll be forever loving Jah,' he sings along with Marley. With a heavy heart, rather drunk, he dances over to the stove to make pancakes.

'She likes you,' whispers Cat, next to him in bed.

'I like you,' he says. His prick lies stiff against her bottom.

'What do you think of her? Of Mitsy?'

'I don't know her.' He kisses her back. She straightens up, tilting her head so that he can reach her neck, then turns to face him.

It seems many couples give up kissing after a while. They haven't. They love the smooth embrace of tongues and lips in a rhythm all their own. They carry on kissing when he slips inside her, when she sits on him.

'Yes,' she says, afterwards, in his ear.

'You,' he says, before sleep comes to fetch him.

14

The light that infused recent days with colour is absent today. They drive through a cheerless landscape. The windscreen wipers wearily deal with the rain; farmers and cows walk with a stoop. Wet, the soldiers' graves seem more present, sharply outlined against the white sky.

Cassel is Cat's idea. She's at the wheel. They drive past an abandoned customs post with a petrol station and tobacconists, then, after a long, boring road, climb modest hairpin bends to the northern French town. Arriving in a fresh squall of rain, they immediately dash into the Musée de Flandre. There's an exhibition about the Flemish Mannerists, mostly anonymous painters from the first half of the sixteenth century. Mitsy puts on an interested mask. Alphonse likes this stuff. As a sixteen-year-old, his nagging hunger for discovery given extra impetus by an urge to distinguish himself, he saw, after a long, aimless walk through Brussels, an exhibition of Flemish Primitives in the Museum of Fine Arts. When he came out he felt enriched and grown up. That unexpected love has remained. Cat is the only one he can share it with; it's not their first visit to this museum. 'The Mannerists came after the Flemish Primitives,' she tells their friends.

Slowly they walk past the paintings of elongated bodies in contorted poses, mostly in religious and nocturnal scenes. A golden angel leaps from his plinth. Lower legs sail independently in little boats. Bodiless *putti* fly through the clouds, their wings on the sides of their heads. Out of the head of a deer grows a crucifix. A bagpipe monster plays itself. A crablike man with a fish in his mouth hastens to the corner of a canvas. Twelve dogs, some transparent, jump over blue-green rocks. A man with a bear's head runs away from a boat, followed by a chicken-slug-man. Amadou and Mitsy look and point. Cat seems content.

Alphonse stops for a long time at a painting that also struck him the last time he was here. 'Portrait de fou regardant à travers ses doigts'. On the label under the laughing fool it says MAÎTRE DE 1537. It's true, he thinks. You must spare them, the people. The eyes of the fool express something other than gaiety. He can't quite decide what it is and he goes after the others.

In the church a sacristan is practising. In a side room, its door open, the priest is choosing a new cassock, helped by two stout women and a thin man. They're engaged in a debate, but not a fierce one.

Behind the church the landscape stretches away. Despite the drizzle they can see for miles, as in a sixteenth-century painting.

'What are the French doing with all these Flemish flags?' Amadou and Mitsy stare at the front wall of 'Radio Uylenspiegel', which sports the text FRENCH FLEMING, ALSO FLEMING. Across from Taverne de Vlaming is the Hôtel de Ville. The words LIBERTÉ, EGALITÉ, FRATERNITÉ on the front wall are accompanied by a message in the window: FLEMISH WAFFLES!

'In Antwerp it would make me nervous,' says Alphonse. 'But here, aside from being understandable historically, it's more bizarre than anything.'

Mitsy looks around in amazement. 'Exuberant, too.'

'Remember when Momar came to visit? He thought the Lion of Flanders was the Lion of Judah,' says Amadou. 'So many Rastafarians in Flanders, he couldn't fathom it.'

Their laughter ceases when they walk into an old corner bar, forced into silence by the hush on the other side of the door. It seems their arrival has struck the elderly couple as very odd indeed and they greet with friendly amazement the time travellers who have landed in the past they secretly inhabit. She wears her long grey hair in a high bun; he sits bent over his newspaper. There are no other customers. Yes, yes, they're open, and they have coffee, certainly. On the bar behind them are two stickers with lions. On one is the slogan, in Dutch, WELCOME AMONG THE FLEMISH, on the other, in the local Flemish dialect, FLEMISH AND PROUD OF IT.

'All those flags,' Amadou hazards tentatively. 'Do you really still feel Flemish?'

The man and woman don't respond straight away. They look from each other to their guests, then demonstrate laboriously but obligingly, by turns, their ability to pronounce the sentence: *'Ik kan een beetje Vlaams.'* I can speak a little Flemish.

The man turns his attention back to his paper, to an article about the clearance of an improvised refugee camp in Calais. Alphonse has never seen a camp like that first-hand.

Together they listen to the coffee maker beneath the dried hops.

He looks just like him, he thinks, that one. He watches the four of them in the doorway, folded newspaper under his arm. The big black man who picked him up when he was eight and ran away with him, as he tried to hit him in the face with his little fists and kept shouting sale bête, and that he didn't want to go there, that he didn't live there. And then, through the windows of equally frightened, equally destitute people, he noticed that outside, above the back of the black man, the sky was darkening, the whistle of a bomb, of destruction, of Second World War, which for him was the first, the one that endured; deaf on one side all his life and never a chance to say thank you.

They're sitting in a Cassel restaurant eating lunch when Madeleine Claeys rings him.

'I know it's impossible, but he's here.'

'Who?'

'My brother. He's in my bed and he's shouting again.'

'That can't be, Mrs Claeys. He's not real.'

His companions stop chewing and their eyes turn to him.

'I told you I know that. I don't believe in ghosts either. But I keep seeing him. And hearing!' There's a moment's silence which, suddenly hesitant, she fills by saying: 'Just call me Madeleine.'

'You have to convince yourself of what you know. That what you're seeing is impossible. Or call a doctor.'

'The doctor was here yesterday. All he could do was prescribe sleeping pills. My brother's been here for three days now!'

'Sleep seems to me a good start.'

'How can I sleep with all that screaming?'

'Madeleine.' He lets his eyes rest on Cat, on the tiny scar on one of her cheekbones, which seems redder than usual. 'What do you want me to do?' The scar turns away.

'You could chase him out. I know you could.'

'Why would I be able to?'

He can hear her breathing. Calmly, given the circumstances. 'I feel it. I've felt it, when you were here. There are things you can do.'

'What kind of things?'

'Help. Healing.' Her voice turns to a whine: 'Come here, please! I know I'm hallucinating but I can't stand it any more.'

'Right,' he says. 'I'm coming.' He turns to the questioning faces around the table. 'An emergency. But first carry on eating.'

'Oh, thanks.' Cat gives him a hard stare.

'Was it a client?' Mitsy wants to know. 'Someone where you were wallpapering?'

'Painting,' he says. 'But now I have to go and chase a hallucination away. I think it's pretty strange myself.'

Mitsy is the only one who laughs.

'It's abnormal,' says Cat. 'And typical.'

'His mother's in touch with the Bois Sacré,' says Amadou. 'And he's got that too.'

'The Bois Sacré?' asks Mitsy.

Just carry on eating, thinks Alphonse.

Cat parks next to the little front garden with the windmill, hydrangea, and low holly hedge. Along with the others she tries to catch a glimpse of the thickset woman who opens the door to Alphonse.

'Your friends must think I'm crazy!' Madeleine Claeys exclaims. 'I am crazy, of course. Right now at least.'

She's talking loudly to make herself heard above the imaginary screams of her brother, Alphonse realizes. Hallucinations are immune, it seems, to vocal cord surgery. He can't think of much else to do than sigh at her with his hands on his hips.

'I think you'll only have to do this once,' she calls out

reassuringly, ahead of him on the narrow staircase. 'He's up here.' She seems plumper than last time. Her bedroom has the impersonal look of a hotel room, but one from several decades ago.

'So, there he is.' She makes a quick gesture toward the smooth sheets. Then she presses her hands to her ears.

So, there he is, thinks Alphonse. He also thinks: this is going too far. Then: I might as well try.

'What's his name?' he asks. Even while burning the letters she didn't tell him that.

'Alphonse,' she says, quieter now. 'Fonske, we called him.'

'He has the same name as me?'

'Yes.'

Ah well, he thinks, it doesn't make the situation all that much more insane. Yet saying his own name does increase his discomfort. He sits on the edge of the bed, losing himself amid the fine floral pattern on the pillow.

'Alphonse,' he says. 'You have to go.'

He tries to imagine the handicapped Alphonse, a great shapeless child with dribble running down his swollen shaving rash, a person made up entirely of cramp. I need to get out of here, he thinks.

'Your sister didn't drop you deliberately,' he says. 'She's visited you every day. Now you're dead and you must leave her in peace.'

Madeleine watches in anticipation, hands still over her ears. When he gives her a questioning nod, she shakes her head.

'He can't walk!' she shouts. 'He probably can't leave all that easily!'

I've tried, he thinks. And again: this is going too far. Then: I need to tell her that.

He goes to stand in front of Madeleine. She frees one ear.

'I'm not a guru,' he says. 'Not a magician. I don't even believe in that kind of magic.'

She nods. 'Yes you do.'

'No, listen to me, Madeleine. You mustn't expect miracles from me. I can come and paint your other rooms and listen to you, but I can't help you with this.'

'We needn't call it magic,' she says.

He wonders what she's about to do with his hands. She lays them on her head and keeps hold of them. Her hair is soft like a baby's. 'Madeleine,' he says. 'This is going too far. The others are waiting in the car. I have to go.'

He feels her nod and removes his hands. She looks so torn, ashamed, and violated that he can't stand the sight and turns away. It's weakness, he thinks for the first time, the way I want to be good, need to be good, nothing but a weakness. It doesn't feel like his own thought; he doesn't succeed in believing it.

Halfway down the stairs he has an idea. He runs back to the bedroom, finds her on an antique chair in the corner, hands over her ears, tearful eyes wide open.

'How about I take him with me,' he says. 'Might that work?'

She nods, laughs, tears skipping over her cheeks.

He goes to stand next to the bed, legs slightly parted, and bends his knees. Then he carefully slides his arms, palms upward, under the invisible burden on the bed. 'Have I got him?' he asks.

She continues nodding and laughing, the tears pouring with increasing abandonment into the depths.

He staggers, jolts the heavy, imaginary body higher in his arms until the rump rests on his shoulder. He looks at her over the place where the buttocks must obscure his view.

She keeps on slapping her hand rapidly to her bosom, as if trying to dribble a ball, her face showing nothing but love. 'He's not shouting any more,' she sobs.

'Can you open the door a bit wider for us?' he asks, his voice distorted by effort. She hurries over to it, follows him down the stairs and outside. In her front garden she stops. She and the astonished faces in the car watch one Alphonse carry the other with slow steps and full arms all the way to the road, then order his friend to open the car door and move further inside. 'Shove up, someone else needs to get in.' As he lowers her brother into the back seat, he covers his head with a protective hand.

The sky has cleared. Through the blue between the little high clouds flies a bird. He suspects it's a skylark. That skylark. He tries to track it, his head almost touching the steering wheel, until the bird disappears via the top left corner of the front windscreen. He lowers a side window slightly, in the hope of hearing it. There is only wind.

'What are you looking at?' asks Cat. It's the first time any of them have spoken since they drove away from Madeleine's house.

'A bird,' he says.

In the rear-view mirror he sees that Amadou and Mitsy are still sitting close together, leaving room for the hallucination.

'You can take the whole back seat now,' he chuckles.

A little hesitantly, Amadou slides along. 'Do things like this happen often?' he asks.

Alphonse says they don't.

Their guests leave for home. On Monday a new working week begins. They enjoyed it, must do this more often, not wait so long. And then, during the embraces, close to his ear, the saved-up, more intimate messages.

'You're special,' says Mitsy, rosy, purring.

'I've missed you,' says Amadou, casually, in Wolof.

Alphonse waves them off, feels his heart in his chest, misses his friend too, suddenly, already; they ought to have played music together, here. He waves and waves.

Cat went indoors halfway through the waving, and now she's sitting at the table with several crookedly folded sheets of paper in her hand.

'Is this by her?' she asks him. 'Did she write this for you?'

Alphonse knows what she's talking about an instant before he recognizes the paper.

'Is this by Mitsy?' she asks.

'No, no,' he says. 'That's by an author.'

'An author?'

'A woman at a writers' residence I painted last week. Just over the French border.'

'And her characters are in your line of work and Mitsy's? That's a coincidence?'

'I'm not a plasterer.'

'What's the author's name?'

'I've forgotten her name.'

'And can you remember whether you fucked her or not?'

'Come on, Cat!'

He knows this dialogue. It's a long time since they performed it, but they've practised it so often in the past that he has no trouble getting the lines in the right order.

'What am I supposed to think, then? You'd have to admit you've been given a racy role in her story!'

'It's fiction,' he says. 'To think that you go through my coat pockets.'

'I didn't.'

Now he's supposed to add sourly that she could simply trust him. Then she'll be able to start on the itemizing, the suppositions, and the shouting. He refuses.

'She made very clear that it wasn't about me. That woman.'

'You asked her?'

'No.'

'But you did read it? Ten pages?'

'I can read.'

'I know.'

He leaves the room. Sometimes, angry, he wishes he could play the trumpet. The bass remains indifferent to his anger, the kora is above it, an instrument that ignores any tendency to exaggerate, compels reflection. Is that why he took it up? To curb his anger? Is there an anger in him that he knows nothing about? Who is it he hates? His father? At one point he got together with his Saudi half-brother and agreed on a place and time to meet their begetter: the De Brouckèreplein in Brussels, at the height of the evening rush hour. He watched him looking around, a huge man, his skin far lighter in colour than his own, for whom someone parked illegally and opened a Bentley door; the gold chain on his glasses, the impatient way he closed the strap of his Rolex. Their looks crossed just once and Alphonse turned round and walked into the metro station. His father didn't follow, didn't recognize him, had never recognized him. There was aversion then, but no hatred. It was over. 'Who is it you hate?' he lets the kora ask again. 'Could it be Fabrice?' The music compels him into a clearer train of thought: 'There is above all regret for which I'm not responsible.' Cautiously the kora probes the distrust of a moment ago: 'And your wife? And your wife?' The kora never shouts, it reiterates. 'I love her!' the strings answer, then again, then more, then again.

No, he thinks, swimming in the sounds, to this instrument hatred is a trifling thing.

13

Again a horrible dream. A walk through a bare wood with hanged people. He doesn't see their faces, only their bodies, some already motionless, others still fighting, convulsing. The legs of a child running wildly through the air. Her small coat, knee socks of dark-green wool, buckles on her little shoes. It's not as if the image, once he's awake, leaves him unmoved, but it's relief that dominates, as after vomiting. The dreams aren't mine, he thinks with great clarity; it's the world that pours its iniquities into me and then I dream them away.

He's struck by the absurdity of the thought.

Cat is not at his side, even though it's only six-thirty. He finds her in the bathroom. She looks askance at him as she flushes the toilet.

'Started yoga again?' he asks.

'Running,' she says.

How she engages in a brief daily battle with her bra, each time managing to overpower it. He knows this only from her and he still enjoys watching as she fastens the catch under her breasts, then moves the back part from forward to rear and puts her arms through the straps.

While he makes coffee, she fetches the paper. 'Jesus,' she growls. 'Isn't there anything worth writing about Syria or Ukraine? A butterfly thief, photofit and all.'

'Show me!'

She shows him the front page. 'He stole them from a butterfly garden, somewhere in France.'

'I know him.'

'You know him?'

'He was in that big house across the border. A translator.'

'The place with the author who writes porn about you?'

They look at each other. Their mouths are straight lines.

'I thought he just caught butterflies with his smartphone. I never went into his room. Does it say where he kept them?'

Cat's eyes move across the paper. She shakes her head. 'They were rare butterflies, though, some of them virtually extinct. Go and take a look in that house, maybe they're still there.'

Mouths as straight lines.

'Have your run,' he says. 'And kiss me.'

They kiss.

Hungry seagulls skim over a field. The sun bathes in the fog, a ripe apricot in custard. That was the first thing that struck him about Belgium, all those years ago, when he first arrived. How low the sun was over Brussels, the city that suddenly lay at their feet as they drove away from the airport. And in the evenings, how long that low sun left the light on. He wondered whether the country lacked conviction: the sun came up, but not completely; it never got completely dark.

In Marco's house the work is moving along. Although his client keeps up a hectic pace as his assistant, the start of a recovery seems to have settled into him. Their collaboration is harmonious. They unroll the strips of wallpaper, glue them, and hang them up as if they've been working as a team all their lives. Now and then one of them takes a few steps back to look at the result from different angles, in different casts of light. Daylight. Artificial light. Standard lamps on and off. Walking in through the door. Lying on the floor.

'Beautiful,' says Marco. 'Thanks. It's totally different yet it seems familiar. Just exactly right.'

'We made good progress this way. Maybe you should consider a new career.'

Marco makes a defensive gesture. 'I'm a bookkeeper. Even now that I don't have a job.'

He insists Alphonse get stuck into one of the filled rolls he's bought, even urging him to eat up what he leaves of a baguette with brie and honey. Alphonse feels his paunch, which Cat calls a phantom paunch. He's always found his body attractive, and now, with the threat of a stubborn band of fat, more so than ever. The hard muscles and firm bones under his supple skin, his build, his strength, his prick—he's lucky. He wants to retain this admiration for his body and thinks self-love healthy, when there's no audience.

The telephone cuts through the silence.

'Hello?' A brusque female voice. 'Are you the person from Rainbow House?'

Alphonse concurs. In the background he hears a man prompting her.

'We didn't know you were from over there,' says the woman. 'We couldn't have known. Rainbow House. Doesn't say a thing. You didn't tell us your name, but we found it out.'

Alphonse realizes that he feels calmer than is possible, that the anger has yet to come. He waits and says nothing. Again he hears the man mumble.

'But we don't go along with all that "multiculti clap-trap" as my husband calls it. We once rented out our apartment to Bosnians and were forced to conclude that Bosnians are apes. We don't like to be made fools of. We didn't know you weren't from here. So we don't want you in our house tomorrow.'

He hangs up.

'What is it?' asks Marco.

'Someone cancelling an appointment because I'm black.' He hates having to confess this to a client, that an idiot has succeeded in upsetting everything.

'Racists!' Marco exclaims. 'Does this happen often?'

Alphonse shakes his head, his face hardening around the jaws with anger. Racism. He's developed such an aversion to the word, the staleness of it, the repeated arguments that go on above his head, and how it can still find its mark, even though he's happy now, and strong, and shining too brightly to be touched by it. The muscles in his upper arms tense, his eyes are slits, his nostrils wide. Why did he involve his client in this? He ought to have kept his mouth shut.

'Flanders is really backward, you know, in that sense,' says Marco, conspiratorially.

'Actually it's not bad at all. Most people are fine.'

A wave of doubt in Marco's lower lip.

'It's much the same everywhere, I think, the general distribution of idiots.' Alphonse wishes his voice would sound normal again. 'My first job here, in Zoetemore, was great. The mayor—he lives in my street—got me to paint the statue of the virgin. I was just standing there brushing it down when cars began stopping. People came to stand around me. Someone eventually had the courage to ask what I was planning to do. I said I was going to paint her black and went on brushing. They turned silent as mice and one by one they drifted away. In the evening the mayor rang. He'd had to reassure thirty worried callers by telling them that Africans can have a sense of humour.'

His laugh turns into a cough. Marco moans through it. 'Gewijde was great, too. "I didn't realize you were a prostitute."' Then, seriously: 'I'm worried about him. More than usual. He hasn't shown his face since Friday.'

'Oh?'

'And I didn't want to go and knock on his door because it's not as if I need to see him every day necessarily.'

'We can both go.'

Marco nods. The looks they exchange confirm the sudden urgency, so that without a word they stand up, put on their coats, and go outside.

The bell seems to make no sound, and no one opens the door. Gewijde's house holds its breath. It's always chaos that takes over, thinks Alphonse, as they're clambering across wobbly hills of rusting barbecues to the back door. Life is a glorious dance partner, if you follow her rhythm, if you immediately manage to scrabble to your feet each time she trips you up. Turn your back on her for a moment, or try to steer her steps, and one time she'll applaud you, another time her animosity will transform you into the floor on which she's dancing the tarantella in stilettos. Or she sweeps you high into the air and doesn't catch you, whines that she doesn't know why: perhaps it's you, perhaps you're too nice. As he pulls his fingers up into the sleeves of his coat to help Marco wrench a pile of scrap away from the back door, Alphonse feels a storm of invincibility rise in him, the same as the wave that earlier swept the horrific dream away with it. He wants to go inside to find this unfortunate man, to comfort him and care for him, and not because that unhappiness makes him feel better, because it leaves him cold or because he needs it, but because it's something he can do, help, because it's what he does. Because he's strong. He manages to get the door open and feels a roll of drums in his chest, a glow behind his eyes. All you can do now is murder me, he sings to his unpredictable dance partner in his thoughts, and even then I'll love you unconditionally, because as long as I live, I can't be floored any more.

He hears the skylark, hears it even though the white sky shows only geese. After the V has disappeared behind the roof he steps into the house.

They find him in his bedroom, amid the stench and the filthy splotches and empty bottles they were expecting. What they weren't counting on was the injury to his wrist, the pool of blood. 'It's not what you think,' Gewijde assures them, shockingly chirpy. He was trying to push a reluctant cork back into a wine bottle when the broken neck pierced his flesh. At that point he curled up in his lair like a sick animal, the night before last. He hums, smacks his lips.

'Poor boy,' Marco keeps saying, until he replaces that mantra with: 'You need to go to hospital' and 'I can't really handle this.' He goes ahead of Alphonse and Gewijde down the stairs. As soon as his neighbour is sitting on a kitchen chair, he leans over the sink and retches, vomiting into the green hairdos of mouldy food. 'I can't really handle this,' he repeats. 'I'm sorry.'

The neighbour has turned his sheet-white face away from him with a scornful smile. Alphonse sees his embarrassment. The ugly wound on the forearm.

'I'll take you to casualty,' he says.

Marco nods, bent forward.

'Thank you very much,' says Gewijde, in English.

That African looks familiar to her, but she's probably confusing him with someone else. You see so many of them these days. It's getting out of hand; the dykes are breaking. On the news just this week, those pictures; it wasn't on Lampedusa. One of the Canary Islands perhaps, where they washed up in their hundreds, climbed over fences, rejoiced at being on European soil. And close by here, in Calais, that failed storming of a ship. They were still talking about it, she and her husband, how it'll get worse yet, and then what? He resents them for it, her husband does.

Alphonse recognizes the doctor immediately: the passion, the flaming hair, the difficulty with the letter 'r'. She takes her time, interrupting the inspection of the wound on Gewijde's arm with meditative looks at his face. Gewijde makes that clacking noise with his tongue, no doubt unconsciously.

'Weren't you here before?' she asks Alphonse after a while, frowning.

'With Duran,' he says. 'The young man who accidentally hacked off his finger. You were glad it wasn't frozen. About two weeks ago.'

'Aha! I knew it. Well? Did it heal properly?' she asks, before immediately answering herself: 'Must have done!'

'Yes, yes. He's back at work. He's won a prize.'

'With his finger?'

'No, with something else.'

'And this gentleman?' She abruptly turns to Gewijde as if he's a young child, or hard of hearing. 'If he wants to win any prizes then he'll have to stop drinking first, eh?'

Although her patient continues to stare at her in disbelief, she turns to Alphonse again, unperturbed: 'What do you do, actually, for work? Here to deliver an injured man twice in a row … You don't mutilate them yourself, I hope?'

'No,' Alphonse laughs. 'It's a coincidence. With Duran I'd gone to buy a shawarma. Gewijde lives next door to a house where I did the wallpapering.'

'Aha! And sanding parquet? Do you do that too?'

Alphonse nods.

'So when could you come round? There's a lot of sanding to be done in my house.'

'Tomorrow, actually,' says Alphonse. 'An appointment just fell through.'

'Well, come then, okay? I don't know what it is with tradesmen these days; I make appointments and no one shows up. They don't want any additional income, I reckon; they've got too much black money. We're spoilt in this country, don't you think?' That last question, in the voice of a nursery school teacher, is directed at her patient.

'I'm thirsty,' says the patient.

In the car, Marco's neighbour stares at the bandages, as if he can see through them to the wrist and the stitches. He trembles.

'Does it hurt?' asks Alphonse.

'No more than everything else.'

Alphonse has never known the dishevelled man to be so quiet. He's also stopped speaking English to him and is more sober than usual. On the back of his head his greasy hair is still standing on end. His chin is littered with irregularly distributed stubble.

Alphonse slides 'Águas de Março' into the CD player. He can't think of any better number to greet a wounded alcoholic. How tragic that Elis Regina didn't manage to use it to save herself.

Does he see the trees scatter birds from hundreds of arms? Does he see their circles, arrowheads, exclamation marks in the sky? He's certainly looking, Gewijde, but Alphonse can't see his eyes, until he straightens his shoulders and stares upward. Now little knives gleam in the irises. They turn with the house they're passing.

'He lives there.'

It's a well-maintained 1970s house. The thatched roof is being replaced. Father Piper, Alphonse guesses.

'Would new thatch burn better than old?'

Alphonse doesn't think he's expected to answer, and he asks a question himself. 'Didn't anyone ever press charges?'

'It's outside the statute of limitations.' He doesn't seem surprised that Alphonse knows about his trauma. 'And I don't believe in hell. Not after death, anyhow. Hear that? Open the window.'

Alphonse does as he's asked and turns the music down. Geese gaggling as when danger looms. An ecstatic wind.

'That,' says Gewijde, full of awe, 'is Pan.' He hums briskly. 'If you read Plutarch you'll be told he's dead. Hundreds of years before, in the time of Emperor Tiberius, a ship's captain called out to the quayside: "Pan is dead!" Everyone was broken-hearted, but I know Plutarch was wrong. Can we park up for a moment? I'll show you how he reveals himself.'

Alphonse parks in the verge. They get out. Beyond the fields the hills fraternally celebrate their timelessness.

'Here,' says Gewijde. He points to the slope. 'Here,'—to the waving branches, to the sunlight and quick sky they're letting through. 'Here,' he points to himself, his narrow face with the swollen nose and yellowish eyes, laughing aloud, moved. The knives in his irises have turned to liquid; he dabs them away with the back of his hand, the one with the uninjured arm. 'Here. Listen.' Wind through the branches, hesitant rustling, an approaching car, then a bird flying across. Alphonse looks up. A raptor, in a lazy, wide spiral. Gewijde follows it, head back, resigned, as if he knew this particular bird would appear. Then he turns to Alphonse. He seems a younger man, one Alphonse briefly recognizes. 'Are we off?' Alphonse nods, squeezing his passenger's shoulder for a second before he gets in.

They drive on. 'And Pan says: new thatch burns better than old.' Gewijde grins like a cartoon villain.

'Go to sleep for a bit maybe. Shouldn't you eat something healthy?'

'Eat something healthy,' Gewijde mimics him. A little later, however, back in a built-up area, he says: 'All right. Stop at that shop there. I'll stock up on some liquid food.'

'You're not to destroy yourself with it any longer. Because of what happened. Because of him.' That the conviction drains from his words as he speaks them does not escape Gewijde. He bangs on his chest with his fist. 'I'm going to destroy myself!'

Drinking as self-determination, thinks Alphonse. Would Tonton Jah have seen it that way? He parks in front of a small supermarket and goes inside, along with Gewijde.

Searching for stock cubes, he walks past an aisle of toiletries and catches a glimpse of Mila and Lana. It seems to be a day for bumping into acquaintances. Or simply a sparsely populated area. The girls are stealing mascara.

'Hi,' he says.

'Hi,' they say, in unison, hands in the pockets of their almost identical lilac anoraks. How long have you been standing there? they want to ask him.

He has shoplifted himself, when he was their age, for the sake of experience.

'How are things at home?' he wants to know.

'My father's moved out,' says Lana.

'And my mother's smashed everything smashable because my father now wants to move out too, with her mother.'

'But he'll probably stay with her mother, says my mother. So she's pretty unbearable as well.'

'*Merde*,' says Alphonse, a word that elicits a teenage giggle from them, then helpless laughter, braces bared. When they've finished, he nods discreetly at the round mirror on the rack behind them, the look of the woman at the cold meats counter reflected in it, worthy of Interpol, her light-blue apron like a uniform waiting for a medal.

'Walk to a different aisle and leave everything you've taken there,' he says.

They nod, horrified, and immediately do as he's asked. The woman at cold meats bends down to the edge of the round mirror.

He shuffles up behind Gewijde at the checkout, buys peppermints, forgets the stock cubes.

'I'd burn well too, don't you think?' Gewijde is frolicsome. 'Explode, perhaps.' He holds the plastic bag of whisky and beer in his arms like an infant. One can is empty by the time he gets into the car. He's still trembling.

'Do you think there comes a point where there's no way back? Do you think some people are lost?'

He's found Cat behind a book in the garden, next to the walnut tree, among the burst husks, in a trapezium of autumn sunlight. 'Of course,' she says. She turns her face, eyes closed, to the warmth. 'Are you talking about us?'

'No!' How could she think that?

He cooks angrily. He's stirring the soup when she slips her arms around him. She presses her head to his back.

'You've no idea how often I lose you, in dreams, in what I hear and read. What I want most of all is to be your friend, but I'm too scared to be. Loving you makes me lonely.'

He's turned round and is holding her face in his hands. Why are her lips trembling?

'What did you say? What was that you said?' he asks.

'You're too big for me. Too great.'

'No,' he says. 'I'm not. We're together.'

'But I disappear. I turn into a rotten kind of desire.'

'But that's not what I want. I need you!'

'Don't!' She'd turn away from him if he wasn't holding her wrists. He ought to have said something else, something more obvious, but he can't think what.

'Let me go!'

He obeys her order, wondering how they got to this point, all this gravity suddenly, all these thorns. After she's withdrawn to her study with a plate of food, he becomes a squirrel on opium, sluggishly collecting waste paper, tying string around it, piling up the bundles. Then he goes out to saw a fallen branch without knowing why. Conclusions fail to come.

In bed he seeks her hand. She gives it to him and squeezes back.

'Sorry,' she says. 'An exaggeration, it seems to me now, what I said. Really. Exaggerated.'

'But is there something to exaggerate?'

'Now and then.'

'Now and then you're unhappy with me?'

'Yes.'

'That's terrible.'

'It's over already.'

And she's laid her fingers on his prick. This is how we do it, he thinks. 'We'll fuck it away,' he says. 'You and me, and not for the first time.' His prick is hard.

'What do you want then?' she asks, so carefree, so gentle. 'Talk? Now?'

He says nothing, lets her come to him.

12

'Five years ago we liked the look of it, white-painted parquet, but now we miss the wood. Silly, but it's that simple. There are machines for it, aren't there?'

'Yes,' says Alphonse. It's a big living room, boring work.

'You miss it precisely because you've covered it up, I sometimes think.'

He waits, but she's impossible to read.

A chubby boy comes into the room in a dressing gown, his wet hair combed back. He greets Alphonse like someone much older than eight, or a child from a different era.

'It'll need varnish of course,' the doctor goes on. 'But colourless, and preferably something matt.'

In the open kitchen the boy stirs cocoa into a cup of milk. He puts it in the microwave, which he turns on. For a moment he leans on the draining board, arms crossed, before moving toward them again.

He crouches down on the white parquet. Then he chants: '*Ka mate! Ka mate! Ka ora! Ka ora!*' He beats himself on the chest, on the thighs, sticks out his tongue till it touches the underside of his chin. '*Tenei te tangata puhuru huru!*' Alphonse knows this, hasn't thought about Maori for ages. He's good at it, this boy. '*Nana nei i tiki mai!*'

'Hadrianus, I'm busy with this gentleman!' his mother shouts above him. 'And if you're ill, you should stay in bed. Being ill and hakas don't go together.'

'*Whakawhiti te ra! A upa ... ne!*' He hauls a force down out of the sky, rams it into his thorax. '*Ka upa ... ne! A upane kaupane whiti te ra! Hi!*'

He remains motionless, wide-open eyes looking straight ahead, until the bell of the microwave steers him back to the kitchen. He walks past them with his cup. Together they listen to his footsteps ascending the stairs.

'It's a syndrome,' his mother explains. 'In the summer holidays we were in New Zealand, *et voilà*. If we travel somewhere else it'll be some other thing. He's very, very suggestible, especially in a geographical sense. In his mind he's usually on another continent. Not exactly a boon to his school career. According to his psychologist he'll have to work on it for himself. Psychologists have it easy. I ought to say that to my patients—"Patch it up for yourself!"'

'But he does it extremely well,' says Alphonse. 'That haka.'

'When you see it for the first time, it's amusing,' says the doctor dejectedly. 'Okay then, I'm off.'

Is there anyone to look after Hadrianus?

She reads his thoughts. From the hall her heels hammer back in his direction. 'You're here alone with him,' she says. 'There was no other way. My husband sleeps at the office when he's got a big project on, so that he can work eighteen hours a day instead of sixteen. And I have to go off and do my little hobby for a bit, ha ha ha.' She speaks her laugh. 'We're still looking for a new baby-sitter, the last one stole my night lotion.'

'I don't have much experience with children,' he begins.

'You've got my number, haven't you?' She seems unable to fathom how any problem could arise. 'Aside from a few hakas you won't have any trouble from him. The fact that he's gifted doesn't mean he can't be pleasant. And his syndrome doesn't affect his self-reliance.' She strides away from him in a huff.

There are bigger machines for this kind of work that allow you to stand upright. But he'd prefer not to rent anything. Mainly, he has to admit, because it would feel like disloyalty to his own Metabo SRE 4350 Turbotec. He had the same thing as a child with the nine toy cars he owned: each of them had a soul, so it was his responsibility to divide the time he devoted to them equitably. The Metabo SRE 4350 Turbotec would suffer terribly from his rejection. I'm crazy, he thinks.

Hadrianus is a source of concern, so although Alphonse doesn't want to subject him to too much control, his hearing becomes more acute. He hears brief footfall in the room above his head, then a sound on the stairs. He's already looked over his shoulder at the empty doorway a number of times. When the child is suddenly there in plain sight he's so startled that the sanding machine slips out of his hand and describes a growling circle on its own initiative. He looks possessed, Hadrianus; he has a weightless way of standing that seems at odds with his round little body, as if he's floating. In Senegal he might be a devotee of the water spirit Mami Wata, if a very young one.

'Everything okay?' asks Alphonse. 'No temperature or anything?'

There follows another haka, performed with no less conviction than the previous one. Alphonse stays sitting on the ground to watch, arms around his pulled-up knees. 'What do they mean?' he asks the child's face, which is motionless, under extreme tension. 'The words.'

The face relaxes. He looks forthrightly down at Alphonse and answers in affected tones: 'Well now, no one's ever asked me that before.'

Hadrianus' canines have only recently started pushing out through his gums, Alphonse notices.

'I can die! I can die! I can live! I can live! This is the hairy man who brought the sun and made it shine. A step upward! Another step upward! A step upward! Another step upward! The sun is rising!'

Alphonse can't help it. The tears come before he has time to admonish himself for his sensitivity. The boy was very convincing. The sun shone right through him.

'Sorry,' says Alphonse. 'I found it really beautiful.'

'It's a moving text,' Hadrianus soothes conceitedly. 'The hairy man, that's probably a reference to someone who hid a Maori tribal leader when enemies were searching for him. Someone who saved his life. Or in any case a helper.'

Canine shoots.

'What on earth's wrong with me?' Alphonse sniffles. Maybe it's the first sign of a midlife crisis. A time full of animated happiness and surges of emotion.

'I'll get you a glass of water.'

Hadrianus needs the kitchen steps to reach the cupboard with the glasses. From the tap a powerful jet squirts over the rim. Alphonse bashfully takes the wet glass from him. While he's drinking the boy asks: 'Shall I teach it to you?'

'First I need to sand this floor,' says Alphonse. 'And you need to rest. What's wrong with you, actually? Why aren't you at school?'

'Gastritis.'

'At your age!'

'I get too worried about things. It all ought to slide off me like from oilskins, but it doesn't.'

'You come across as very self-confident, all the same.'

'Thank you,' says Hadrianus. 'Hakas help.'

'This afternoon? Before I leave?'

He nods like a waiter who knows a diner's wishes. For the next three hours he doesn't make a sound. Now and then Alphonse checks round behind him all the same.

When he looks up from the planks and the sander, the African masks on one of the walls catch his eye. Authenticity for tourists; they could be from almost anywhere.

Then he notices Hadrianus watching him from the doorway.

'Haka?' he asks, suddenly very young and shy.

Alphonse stands up and nods.

He delves into his memories, but he can't think of any previous occasion on which a child has taught him something. Except when he was a child himself. Awa, a girl from the neighbourhood who sang a song to him; Jimbo, with his knowledge of insects.

Not having heard the front door, he's standing with eyes wide and tongue sticking out at Hadrianus' mother when she comes in. She's unsurprised.

'Fun, apparently.'

He gives a little chuckle. She turns her delighted attention to the floor. 'You've done a lot already!' Then, to her son, switching abruptly to disapproval: 'Hakas and being ill, they don't go together!'

Hadrianus slinks away, pouting.

'I was wondering, have you ever been to Africa?' He nods at the masks.

'Yes,' she says. Caught out, he thinks.

Her mouth works against itself. The teeth part behind the closed lips. The lips stand firm.

A secret lurks in her eyes.

'Long ago,' she says, as airily as possible. 'On our honeymoon. Madagascar. Will you be back tomorrow?'

He'll be back tomorrow.

'*A upa … ne!*' he chants at the wheel, out across the fields, at the last days of summer. '*Ka upa … ne!*'

He winds down the window and waves to the boy in the front garden on the corner of his street. 'Hi, scallywag!' is the response.

'*A upane kaupane whiti te ra! Hi!*' Crows gather in a large flock and throw themselves cawing to earth.

On his arrival home a strange scene awaits him, introduced by barking. Before he can see who Cat is talking to, an enthusiastic dog runs into the hall. He recognizes the animal: it's Björn, Els and Dieter's dog. He strokes its head, which twists in all directions in an effort to lick his hand.

His master leaps to his feet when Alphonse comes into the kitchen. Behind him is Cat, sitting at the table, joyful and alarmed.

'Fonzy!' says Dieter. 'Good to see you, man.'

'Hello,' says Alphonse. 'How you doing?' Will he meanwhile have opted for his wife or his lover?

'In the eye of the storm,' says Dieter. 'That's where I live now. And so does Björn. Eh, Björn?'

Björn continues to look expectantly at Alphonse while his owner strokes him.

'Els and I can't guarantee the safety of our pet any longer. Sieglinde shot at him. Not with a poisoned dart but with a double-barrelled shotgun!' He holds up his hand. 'This time it was definitely her. We caught her red-handed.'

Does he know she's pregnant, Alphonse wonders. That she's carrying his child? Is that actually true? What a tangle, these neighbours, how light and carefree his own life.

'Would Björn be able to stay here for a bit? Sorry to spring this on you, but needs must. Where could he go? we asked ourselves, Els and Mila and me. We thought of you immediately.'

Alphonse looks the animal in the eye. With frantic enthusiasm, Björn's tail thumps the wooden floor, as if counting down to his consent.

'Why here?' asks Alphonse, before Cat can.

'Björn's chosen you, in a way, remember? He really likes you. After you left he sat at the window for days waiting to see if you'd come back.'

'Why not?' says Cat, before Alphonse can. 'He looks nice. Doesn't he?'

Björn follows the conversation attentively. In response to Cat's compliment he almost bursts with eagerness. Fuelled by their laughter he plunks, skips, and slithers across the parquet. He licks Cat's jeans, snuffles at a head of garlic in a kitchen rack, backs off in horror, then stretches out yawning with his paws on Alphonse's toes.

'He seems to like the idea,' says Dieter, in truth a little disappointed. He scratches his armpit thoughtfully.

'Then that's arranged,' says Alphonse. 'Do you know roughly how long he'll be here?'

'No,' says Dieter, still dreamy. 'No clue how long this will last.'

'What kind of dog is it, actually?' Cat asks.

'A Portuguese Water Dog,' says Dieter.

'Oh,' says Cat. 'Like Obama's dog.'

'Yes,' grunts Dieter. 'Okay then, I'm off.'

His departure leaves Björn cold. Head held high, the dog looks in Alphonse's direction, deeply in love.

He taps Sieglinde's number. Cat feels he's crossing a boundary by doing so: not only does he keep allowing himself to be bothered by clients in need of help, he's now started ringing the ones who don't make contact of their own accord.

'Shooting at an animal is pretty extreme,' says Alphonse.

She's no longer listening. She's making the dog happy. Björn likes her, although clearly this is a more free-and-easy kind of love than the passion he displays for Alphonse. He meekly allows himself to be fed by Cat, performs a trick she teaches him. He steps up his wagging as her enthusiasm at his cooperation increases and waits patiently until she's finished stroking his belly. When she moves to replace his head on her lap with a laptop, he makes no objection. He climbs the stairs to Alphonse, who is phoning Sieglinde from the top step.

'Does he know it's his child?' he hears himself ask.

'He doesn't even know I'm pregnant,' says Sieglinde. 'You still can't tell. I'm glad you rang, by the way. Thanks.'

That's pretty strange, thinks Alphonse. Five months— and a half by now. He peers into the mouth of the dog, which is breathing at his face from very close by.

'I decided to let whether or not to tell him depend on the choice he made. And he didn't choose me. There's too much riding on it, he said. Nice. As if I don't add up to enough in the end, or something.'

'I don't know what to say,' Alphonse admits. He has the impression he's said that a number of times recently.

'Doesn't matter,' says Sieglinde. 'I'm enormously grateful you phoned me. Do you have a cold?'

'No. The panting?'

'Yes.'

'That's the dog. Björn's here.'

Silence at the other end of the line.

'You have to be there for everyone.' She says it in a neutral tone, as if it's a fact known to all.

'Shooting a pet is not a solution,' he says.

'It would give me a certain satisfaction now.'

'The dog can't do anything about it.'

'That's true,' she says. 'Just bring him back.'

Björn lets out a fart of terror.

'I'll keep him here for a while,' he says. 'Until everyone has calmed down a bit.'

'Whatever you like.'

'How's Lana doing?'

'Oh! She's at her music lesson. I've forgotten to fetch her!'

'You'd better be quick then.'

'Yes. Thanks!'

'Is he still watching?' Cat asks. They've pulled the down quilt over them. Alphonse's prick grows softer between their bodies. Still entwined, they stretch their necks to see where he is. He's still watching, is Björn. He's laid his head on the mattress and he's staring, motionless, at their spasm of laughter. Then his tail joins in.

They give up.

'Can anyone be five months pregnant without it starting to show?' he asks, and he tells her about Sieglinde.

Cat says something about a panda in a Chinese zoo

that had a phantom pregnancy. It was said to have staged the pretence for treats and attention. How anyone discovered those motives, she doesn't know.

11

The horrific dreams stay away. He wonders where they came from; there was no apparent reason for them. Was it really the world vomiting through him or were they his own demons, put to flight? Of the night just past he can recall only that he found himself in a warm, glowing cosiness, like a chick incubator.

Cat is awake too. As are the birds outside. They fill the early morning with pleasant chatter. It's Cat who asks: 'Don't you get the feeling that in each language "God" is a different kind of guy? In Slavic languages he's called Bog. You'd expect someone like that to punish you instantly.'

'And not always justifiably,' says Alphonse.

'Exactly. Dios sometimes throws a party. And Dieu is more the type to pomade his moustache with feigned indifference and think: go right ahead; just you wait.'

'God is an awkward softy with a tendency to overreact.'

'Allah is a bit of a bellyacher.'

'Jalla is good at something odd, which wins him respect, but people steer clear of him all the same.'

When she laughs like that he can only join in.

They don't know what to make of Atemit, the God of the Jola. His name suggests intelligence, but also a habit of never ending an argument until he's won.

Cat has an appointment in Brussels for a translation job and she'll spend the night with a friend. She's been looking forward to seeing her city again, but now they have a dog. She considers taking Björn along and rings the friend to ask if that's a possibility. It's not. Should she cancel?

'I'll take him with me,' says Alphonse.

The words 'with me' have a vitalizing effect on the dog.

Björn's black hair has been trimmed. Without regular trimming it would hang in front of his eyes like a curtain, making less noticeable the fact that they're continually fixed upon Alphonse from the passenger seat. On getting in he ordered Björn to sit under the dashboard. 'This is the place for feet and dogs,' he heard himself claim as he did so. Björn looked at him pityingly with a 'You know better' and Alphonse left it at that. The bag with the kora is in the back between the pots of paint. He can play something for Hadrianus today.

He doesn't know how the doctor will react to the dog. He hasn't warned her in advance. When she opens the front door he tells her straight away about his travelling companion and adds, with little conviction, that the dog can stay in the car. Endearment rips itself loose from the doctor's otherwise stern face. Arms wide, she walks over to the van. Björn responds to her enthusiasm with a polite wagging of the tail, walks obediently behind her and allows himself to be served dry sausage cut into tiny pieces in the kitchen. Hadrianus, who was sitting in front of the television, follows his mother's example. They take turns throwing crumbs of sausage into Björn's mouth.

'Going back to school today?' he asks, because the boy

has exchanged his dressing gown for trousers and a jumper.

'No, he still needs to rest for a bit,' his mother answers.

Hadrianus has found a tennis ball and to Björn's delight he throws it through the house.

'Do that in the garden.' After her son has taken her advice, she turns to Alphonse: 'What part of Africa are you from?'

'The West. Senegal.'

'I've been to Madagascar. The other side.'

'On your honeymoon.'

The doctor laughs, caught out again. 'As a doctor, too, in a way, but that wasn't the intention. A safari. That was the idea. And just to relax.'

He waits.

'My husband likes to play golf. I don't, and because of that I met a man, on the street, in Antananarivo. He was sorting rubbish. Between us someone slipped off a kerb. I examined his ankle. The man sorting rubbish buttonholed me. "*Docteur?*" he asked. It turned out to be more or less the only French word he knew. I followed him. In my head I could hear a choir, led by my husband, strike up a resounding "Don't go!" But the whole time I was completely convinced I wasn't in any danger. He led me into a shack made of corrugated iron and scrap timber and there, in the dark, lay his daughter. About six years old.'

She follows the arc of a tennis ball thrown the length of the garden by Hadrianus. 'Over here you could have done something. An infection. Not life-threatening as such. I tried. Administered injections. I couldn't find all the drugs I needed. I went back every day, but I ought to have done more, ought to have taken her to a hospital, even though it seemed the father didn't want that. My husband said it was a fact of life that on some continents more children die than on others, that otherwise over-population would be even worse and that a doctor can't save everyone. My husband is very good at putting things into perspective. He likes to argue, too. He said I was ruining our honeymoon, told me he usually found my stubbornness charming but not in this case. He said precisely the same before and after she died. It's twenty years ago—twenty years! A snap of the fingers!—and my husband with his golf, how ridiculous, how idiotic life is, and how fleeting. I don't say it's his fault, that he forced me toward a certain insight. I know well enough that I belong here, and I enjoy my possessions, it would be stupid not to, wouldn't it? I've adapted to my environment, become completely absorbed by it. I am, I believe, a success.'

She looks at him angrily. He says nothing.

'Rindra, she was called. We couldn't talk but she watched me all the time with those huge eyes and the day before she died she pointed to herself and said "*docteur*" and her father repeated it, he pointed to her and said "*docteur*". I think she wanted to be one. She'd be about twenty-six now. She didn't have a birth certificate. Officially she never existed.'

She's talking loudly and rapidly, as if she's about to attack him.

'Say it!' she says. 'Say it. What should I have done? What should I do now?'

'You have to do what you can.'

'But I can do far more, it's just that I've chosen a safe path.'

'You have to do whatever you're happy to do.'

'Really? Do you know what everyone's "happy" to do on a safari like that? People come with lists of the animals they want to see killed by other animals. They want to see lions kill fleeing antelope, and crocodiles kill passing gnus, otherwise the holiday is a failure. What if you're happy racing through a village at two hundred an hour, or torturing people?'

'That's got nothing to do with you. Don't believe people who try to convince you that getting involved is a weakness, that you're mistaken or lying if that's your way of loving.'

Her uncertainty takes the form of fury and she hits the marble worktop. 'How can you know what you want? Happiness is far more complicated than what you're talking about!' Another thump.

'But you told me what you want,' he says.

She stares at him. He can hear her breathing. Then she nods until the nodding seems to wake her up. The luminous mist between them becomes air again. The smell of autumn wafts in as Hadrianus slides open the door, a cheerful Björn behind him.

'A really clever dog,' the boy says.

'Coffee?' the doctor asks Alphonse. 'Tea?'

'I've got something with me,' he says.

Again the sound of the sliding door, the clink of china, footsteps that know where they're going, and a dog being patted as it passes.

Hadrianus stays upstairs playing with Björn. They dash back and forth across the ceiling while Alphonse moves the sanding machine in small circles. He's piled up the furniture in the tiled area. He uses a finer grain this time, stroking the soft planks that he leaves as he goes. Like that, defenceless, wood is at its most beautiful. It's as if he can hear it sigh as they part. The chances of it remaining undamaged with nothing to protect it are slight. He vacuums, mops, strokes it once more, on his knees.

Near the front door, he goes to sit in a garden chair. He fills a glass and a bowl with water, for the child and for the dog, then takes his kora out of the back of the van. He plays something he knows, floats away from it, rises with it, becomes the wind through the branches, leaves about to drop. A blackbird that keeps announcing rain suddenly falls silent and listens, its head to one side; the rain doesn't come. As Alphonse expected, the music draws the dog and the child outside. They move rather awkwardly around him, bobbing about in the sounds, then go and sit on the doorstep. Which is where the doctor finds them. She leans against her letterbox and listens.

Before he drives away, she shares her name with him, Brigitte Dubois. He needs to know it, after all, for the invoice.

Alphonse orders Björn to wait in the car while he goes into Pita Merci.

Duran fills the bread with falafel and asks: 'No chicken, then?'

'How's your finger?' asks Alphonse.

'Good.' Duran moves his right ring finger as if wanting to check straight away how it's doing. 'It feels different, but it doesn't hurt at all.'

'Didn't you get some kind of trophy in Japan?'

'Yes, but the Argentines took it with them. I was in their group. I've got photos of our work, though. In the freezer. Go and take a look, you know where it is.'

The drawer that held the ice figurines is empty, apart from a brown envelope.

'I'll make another Shaka Duran for you. I let everything melt, in Japan. It cost enough just to get it all there. The photos are in the envelope.'

'Why do you keep them in the freezer? You could stick them up on the walls here.'

'I like to keep things separate. When I'm here, my art is in there.' The pita bread points to the counter and freezer in turn before he lays it on a paper plate.

Alphonse slides the photos out of the envelope. They're in A4 format and they show a colourfully illuminated nightscape full of palaces, bridges, and figures in snow and ice. There are several images of an impressive tree, sparkling-white, with a crown of huge leaves. This must be the Argentine contribution.

'They're walking past it,' says Duran.

Now Alphonse sees them, a row of Durans like an ant colony against the tree trunk. Close-ups show that they're climbing it. A line of them is emerging from an igloo the size of a hedgehog, next to the tree. 'Beautiful!'

'Merci.'

'Is everything okay?' asks Alphonse.

'Well, you know.' Duran has been waiting for this question. 'My father is right when he says I can't go on making Durans in ice for the rest of my life. I have to think of something new. And at the same time I wonder why I'd make anything any more. Why would I do it for an audience? Is the idea that everyone says every time: "Bravo, Duran, great job"?'

Alphonse has just taken a large bite of his falafel, so he chews and swallows before saying that Duran is trying to tell people something, isn't he? Trying to touch or connect with them. He thinks about his kora among the pots of paint, his bass in the empty house.

'Yes, something like that.' Duran plays with the salt cellar. 'It was really great when people leaned over to get a better look at my figures. So it's not just that they respect my work, and therefore me. It's not just that. It has to do with something they don't completely understand, and neither do I. It's the fact that they want it, for a moment at least, they want to understand. They asked questions, the people. It made them more animated.'

'That's great, isn't it?'

'Yes, but not all of them were like that of course, and there was a prize to be won, and I thought it was fantastic when we won it, the second prize, but some of the Argentines were annoyed because they thought the Canadians didn't deserve first prize and then the South Koreans suddenly started protesting. So spiteful. They asked what a Turkish Belgian was doing on the Argentine team. What they'd created was beautiful too, in a different way. I don't understand how you can make a comparison, how a jury can choose. And what I found worst of all, and this is ridiculous of me, I know, but what made me so unbelievably sad was that everything melted. I'd seen it coming of course, but still. Everything that was there melted, and then it was gone.'

His hands have meanwhile let go of the salt cellar. He stands staring as if it too might melt at any moment.

'But you were there and you saw it,' says Alphonse.

'Yes, and I'm very glad I did.'

'You even made a contribution.'

'Yes.' Duran shrugs, smiling. 'That's true.'

The arrival of another customer brings the sound of the radio into the foreground again. Alphonse pays and Duran insists on stamping a loyalty card for him.

'Had dinner yet?' asks Willem. He's come to stand in the doorway on hearing Alphonse park his van.

'Yes, I've just eaten.'

'I've made soup.'

This is new, Willem making soup. He promises to

come round after he's had a shower. Björn can come with him.

It's usually Willem who visits him. Mainly because Willem, with Marie-Jeanne's absence hard at his heels, wants to flee his house. But Alphonse also has a horror of the dark living room with its worn carpet and dusty masks and especially the grandfather clock that dominates Willem's entire home. The thing doesn't escape attention for a second, wanting to make time heard and seen, determined to strike every hour. How can an old man bear to have time counted down so obtrusively? It drives Björn crazy too at first. He snaps and barks at it before at last haughtily turning away.

Alphonse compliments Willem on his paprika soup. 'I miss my car,' Willem confesses. 'I should never have got rid of it.'

'Buy a new one then,' says Alphonse.

A dismissive gesture. 'I'm nearly eighty; how long could I go on driving it?'

'Does that matter?'

There's a silence.

'I've got a day off tomorrow,' says Alphonse. 'A client cancelled and where I'm working instead I'd like to let the floor breathe for a day. Shall we drive somewhere together? Go looking for tirailleurs sénégalais or something?'

It's as if he's proposed a trip to a theme park to a disadvantaged child. Willem even claps his hands. They make a date for the following morning.

In his underwear he stretches out on the sofa. He plays a lazy tune on his bass, puts it down on the coffee table, turns on the television—the man from Guinea in Dakar has recovered from Ebola and been sent home cured—

and then off again. Björn yawns on the rug next to him, stretches, then saunters to his feeding bowl. Everything's fine with Cat, Brussels has missed her, is happy she's there; she's staying an extra day, he doesn't mind does he? Alphonse remains lying there after the call, his hand on his abdomen, around his prick, which slackens when Björn tries to get a close look. He wonders whether the animal will remain an obstacle to all forms of eroticism. An SMS from Aline: could he get on Skype? Unusual, for his sister—something wrong with Mother? He's sitting up straight now, but Aline has only a dream to report. She dreamed he was in danger. And when she woke she heard the same voice again, saying the same thing: that he was in danger. She knows what he thinks about that voice, but is he feeling okay? Are people being nice to him? His sister is named after Aline Sitoe Diatta, who heard a voice telling her to liberate the Jola, and after them all the Senegalese, from the colonialists. She became Queen of Casamance, performed miracles and saved people, before dying in prison. His sister takes the voice very seriously. He doesn't think any of her premonitions or predictions have had real consequences. The one time he tried to speak to her about schizophrenia she brushed him off almost as if she pitied him. Now he says soothingly that dreams are dreams, the voice isn't real, he's doing well. And how is she doing?

10

Willem wanted to set out at half past six. Arguing they wouldn't be able to do much at a cemetery before sunrise Alphonse got him to agree to 7.30. He wants to walk Björn first, so he still has to be up by six. The prospect of turd-smeared gravestones and excavated ribcages initially persuaded him he should leave the dog at home, but Björn's dramatic reaction to his departure and the possibility of a wrecked house dispelled his reservations.

'Okay, he can come too.' Joyous frenzy.

Cat went by train yesterday, so he takes her car. While driving he tries to read the document Willem is holding out in front of him. The font is too small. The names of the dead and the numbers of their graves are barely legible, the text accompanying the list has been cut short with three-quarters missing. He manages to decipher the key to causes of death: succumbed to wounds, died of illness, killed by enemy fire.

The darkness gives way to a wet glass curtain. 'Sun,' Willem predicts, but the trees look more lacklustre and bare than yesterday. Alphonse drives past distant woods, past farm supplies wrapped in white plastic and scattered with car tyres. Willem creates an impression, larded with figures, military terminology, and personal enthusiasm, of how the lads from Senegal, Guinea, Mali, and Benin arrived in November 1914 in ridiculous uniforms of blue jackets and plus-fours that they'd been kitted out with back in Algeria, most wearing a red fez on their heads, some carrying a *coupe-coupe*. He tells how the survivors scrabbled to their feet not long afterwards from among shell casings made with Congolese copper and stumbled through the streets on balled feet, crying, dragging friends along with them. In Diksmuide, according to notes made by a French officer, they sang to a rhythmic beat as they attacked the Germans. The response was a burst of machine-gun fire.

As predicted, at this hour they're the only visitors to the French cemetery, Saint-Charles de Potyze. The Muslim graves stand out immediately among the crosses. 'Most are Algerian or Tunisian *tirailleurs*, Moroccans, and Zouaves,' says Willem at the entrance. 'Officially sixteen of the graves are of *tirailleurs sénégalais*, but I reckon there are more, some were put in the wrong category. You'll have to point out the West African names to me. We're going to go through my list and add to it where necessary.'

Alphonse looks out across the cemetery. Every grave has a number. There are so many.

'Almost all of them died on 10 November 1914, in Diksmuide. And a few in the second batch of conscripts, brought here when the war was almost over.' He points to the grave on the far side of a field full of crosses. 'There must be some over there as well. It's a mass grave with more than six hundred bodies. At first all the dead who weren't officers were thrown into large pits. Until the men started burying their friends themselves.'

Many of the crosses are marked INCONNU. 'More than thirteen hundred of the bodies here are unknown, which usually meant "unrecognizable".' Slowly and solemnly, Willem marches between the graves, deter-mined to find everyone on his list. Dew soaks through their shoes. Alphonse keeps Björn on a short lead, doing his best to avoid tripping over him.

'There must be a point when mutilation makes it impossible to tell even your skin colour.' He's thinking aloud, but Willem nods furiously.

'Look,' he says. 'Babakar Lo.'

No circumflex on the 'o', Alphonse notices. Someone has tied a red-and-pink ribbon around the gravestone.

A little further on they find Maalick So. He has a cross instead of a stone.

'That must be Sow,' says Alphonse. 'With a 'w'.'

'Are you sure about that?'

'Sow. A Fula.'

'A Fula?'

Alphonse nods.

'I don't think so. I haven't read anything about Fula at the front.'

'That's a Fula.'

Their feet wet, they continue to search.

One family name touches him. Not painfully, more in a whimsical, even mildly thrilling way. Badji. He points to it. 'My name.' His mother's name.

The inscription doesn't say a great deal: MATRICULE 9344. MORT POUR LA FRANCE EN 1914–1918. Willem reads the name out loud: 'Mamadou Badji'. He carefully searches his list. 'Do I have to add his name or not? Do all the Badjis come from West Africa?'

'I think so.'

Willem scribbles something, using a pencil. The point breaks off. 'Have you got anything to write with?'

'No.'

Willem puts the list away and starts on the next row.

Beside Mamadou Badji are Goujot Georges and Corbel Fernand. In contrast to the soldiers from the colonies, their surnames are given first. As if the men came from worlds that were mirror images of each other. Next to Goujot and Corbel lies Farajonbonon. 'He could be from Benin,' says Alphonse. He tugs at the lead when Björn, intrigued by a scent, begins to scratch at the soil.

The boggy earth and the lush grass conspire to hide almost instantly the footprints they leave between the crosses. 'Galo-Sall,' Alphonse reads. 'That must be Gallo Sall, without a hyphen and with one more 'l'. And I don't understand why he's been given a cross. That's a Toucouleur. The Toucouleur are Muslims.'

Is he annoying Willem with his corrections? 'Something wrong?' he asks.

Willem shakes his head without looking at him and walks on. He's shivering.

Moro-Sidibe between Boisnault René and Guieu Adrien. Moussa Kone next to Mousette Lucien. Mouchet Alphonse beside Mohamed Okkat. A Jewish stone for Levy Leon. Bala. Jacques. Boubou. Julien.

'M'diagomdir,' Alphonse reads. He keeps to himself the fact that it ought to be M'diagom N'dir. There's a white rose next to the grave.

'Not on the list,' says Willem, his nose right up to the paper.

'It says "*tirailleur sénégalais*" on his stone but he didn't die until 8 January 1915, look.'

'I'll add him at home.' His neighbour now sounds distinctly terse. 'So you really don't have anything to write with? What about in the car?'

They search the car in vain.

'Now isn't that simply ridiculous!'

In silence they work through the rest of the list. The

furrow in Willem's forehead deepens. The war tourists they pass at the gate look at him with concern. They don't have a pen to lend him either.

They're going to visit another cemetery, on the French side of the border, but Alphonse suggests a cup of coffee first. Two roundabouts further on, they find a new-looking tavern.

'Is the dog allowed in?' asks Willem.

'Nyuh,' says the proprietor to Alphonse's hat.

On the far side of the room a man is reading a paper and eating a chicken curry roll. Close to the window two elderly ladies squeeze lemons over their prawn croquettes. Willem answers their subdued greeting with a brief nod. A commercial radio channel is playing at high volume: a local bigwig of the largest political party is loudly praising himself for his courage.

'What is it, Willem?'

Willem hesitates, focuses on his coffee, asks the waiter for a pen and scribbles something on the list. 'Is that how you write it?' He turns the page to Alphonse, who merely carries on looking at him.

'The fact that they died for France doesn't mean the French can just spell their names however they like,' says Alphonse. A rocket is lit in the back of his head.

'You're not easily satisfied, either, you people,' Willem bursts out. He knows those final two words will sting.

'We people?' Alphonse continues to look at him.

'To that friend of yours I was just a silly old man. Think I didn't notice?'

The women near the window look up from their plates with curiosity.

Fingers trembling, Willem plucks the capsule of milk from his saucer. He opens it and pours it into the cup.

After stirring for a long time he lays down the spoon and looks at Alphonse. The angry furrow has gone. 'Sorry,' he says. 'I apologize.'

'Ça va.'

'No, it isn't all right,' says Willem, suddenly firm. 'That's old age. And having too much time. And spending whole days thinking about who's no longer around and who said something wrong. And burying yourself for months in the *tirailleurs sénégalais* and then forgetting to bring a spare pencil. No longer being the best at anything. Walking slowly and feeling cold straight away. And getting sleepy at the wrong moments, never in bed.'

'You're healthy and in your right mind,' Alphonse begins. This outpouring will lead back to Marie-Jeanne, he'll sob inconsolably again, his neighbour—that phase of mourning isn't over yet, how could it be?

'And not to be forgotten,' says Willem, now with something roguish about his mouth. 'Griping! How old men can gripe!' His laughter is the louder of the two. At the window the women stare meaningfully at each other. One of them makes a discreet drinking gesture with thumb and forefinger. Alphonse squeezes his old friend's shoulder and Willem does the same to him, still hiccupping a little, no less nervous than relieved.

They're about to drive up to the former French customs post when he recognizes the woman at the wheel of a light-grey Renault Mégane. The author! They're close by the time she starts waving in surprise. He slows down and sees her brake lights, but when the car behind her sounds its horn she drives on. He too presses the accelerator.

'Another time,' he tells himself.

Willem asks no questions.

The border post isn't exactly deserted. French traffic police have taken over part of the building, their white vans doing their best to reflect the weak sunlight. The tobacconists are still there, flowers and petrol are still thought cheaper on the Belgian side.

The landscape wards off the traffic with its spaciousness and sparse buildings. Shoulders swathed in dark trees, it shrugs at past wars.

Björn barks enviously at a little dog in a passing car that has stuck its white head through an open window. The dog ignores him.

'Watch out!' Willem shouts.

Alphonse brakes for a young man who has appeared right in front of them like a ghost. The car's nose comes to a halt just short of his legs.

With throbbing temples and a sense that his hair has shot several centimetres out of his head, Alphonse stares through the windscreen at the beaten face. It looks back, unblinking. Björn sniffs and then nestles into the back seat that he tumbled off. He growls.

'Where did he come from all of a sudden?' Willem is startled when Alphonse opens the door on the driver's side and all the other doors unlock with a click.

He's standing on one leg, the young man, the other leg hanging limp, in trousers smeared with dark fluid. Is that blood? Alphonse looks at the face again, which turns away, glancing back at the bushes it must have crawled out of.

'We didn't hit him,' says Willem.

'He needs help.'

Alphonse shuts the car door behind him. He greets the young man in French and is interrupted by a proud and urgent 'Can you give me a ride?'

English, but he can't place the accent. He nods. 'What happened?'

'In the car,' the young man says, looking round again, then limping toward one of the back doors. 'Please. The dog.'

Alphonse urges Björn to go and sit in the front with Willem, addressing him with such seriousness that the dog immediately obeys. Then he helps the young man onto the back seat. Through a tear in the trouser leg at the level of the right shin he catches a glimpse of an ugly wound.

'To the hospital?' Alphonse asks.

'Of course,' says Willem.

The man refuses, saying he'll show them where he wants to go. Alphonse starts the engine.

'Police did this,' they hear from the back seat. And that it's the third time they've beaten him up, and that if they don't beat you they bully you, forcing you into a combi-van and dropping you thirty kilometres away so that you have to walk back, because you haven't got the money for a bus. There's a telephone number people can use to inform on you if you're living in an empty building somewhere.

'We don't know if that's true,' Willem says.

They overtake a giant of a farmer's son; the tractor underneath him looks like a toy. He gives them a surly look through their windows. A kilometre further on the wounded man points to a country road and tells them to take it. Alphonse immediately does as he's asked.

'Turn the car round next to that open spot and drive backward across the field. Then we can leave quickly if we need to.' Willem has a point. He asks the young man where he's from.

'Paktika Province,' he says. 'Gomal District.' Do they

know which country he's talking about? While turning the car, Alphonse sees the ridicule in his eyes through the rear-view mirror. Willem doesn't answer either.

'Durand Line?' The question continues to float about in the car. 'You watch the news? You don't care? I saw your number plate, you live in Belgium. Not a good country any more. War with Pakistan? US drones? Still no idea?'

'Afghanistan,' says Willem.

The response is brief applause. 'You can stop here.'

Alphonse removes the car keys. They're standing next to a stretch of pastureland, with a few trees, a ditch, then the barbed wire of another field.

'I don't like this,' says Willem.

'Thank you for bringing me here,' says their passenger. 'The others can take me downstairs. You can go now.'

'What do you mean?' Alphonse asks. 'The others?'

'Want to see?' the young Afghan asks. He can barely part his teeth as he talks.

'He's in serious pain,' says Alphonse, in Dutch.

Willem nods.

Now that he's out of the car, Alphonse can see smoke rising above the ditch. Björn's panicky barking comes out muffled through the closed car doors. Between wooden beams embedded in the mud they go down. Alphonse supports the young man. Willem stands undecided on the top step, then dutifully follows, his frightened hands searching for something to grip. Only now do they see the tents of ragged tarpaulin and dirty blankets, men around a fire. The rags above their heads have large holes burnt in them and scorched patches. There's a smell of smoke and ash. The inhabitants stare with curiosity at their guests and at their friend's wounds, but there's no tone of surprise in the words they exchange in their own language.

Alphonse and Willem look around. A short distance away a boy is sitting cross-legged between the improvised tents, motionless, with a blissful smile on his face. Along the flanks of the ditch, boxes have been nailed together for shoes, and others for firewood. Their eyes meet, wide open. 'A trench,' Willem whispers. Alphonse nods. When the wind turns, the smoke makes them cough.

Only two of the men look older than thirty. They're all from Afghanistan, says one of the more talkative English speakers among them. He's been in other camps in northern France, with Somalis and Iranians and goodness knows what else. This is better.

Moaning, the wounded man lets the others tear open his trouser leg. Once again Willem insists he needs a hospital.

'He wants to go tonight,' one of the Afghans explains.

'To the hospital?'

'No. He wants to try tonight. He's tried four times before.' He tells them the trucks carrying chemicals aren't so carefully checked.

They've seen the pictures, the photos in the paper, the dismantled camps, the tightened controls. I LOVE YOU ENGLAND, Alphonse reads on the side of one tent, behind the broadly smiling boy sitting cross-legged, who now scrabbles to his feet. The smile remains. He walks among the blankets and tarpaulins with a smile, sits by the fire with a smile, accepts friendly slaps on the back with a smile.

Alphonse asks how the wounded man could get treatment. Someone says something about Doctors of the World, but they've just been through and won't be back till next week. 'I know a doctor,' he says. He's got their attention. They agree to let him bring his doctor here.

As they're clambering out of the ditch, Alphonse sees the grinning boy sitting on a log. He's plaiting the tassels of his scarf, deathly fear in his eyes.

'What do we do if she doesn't want to come?' asks Willem. He's staring at the large detached house through the window on the passenger side.

'She'll come.' Alphonse gets out.

Alphonse has never said anything about his work except that his customer database is growing fast. Strange. It's how he spends most of his days yet he, his neighbour and friend, has never asked about it. Do his clients trust him blindly like this woman, who listens, hurries indoors to get something and is now coming out with a fat child and a small leather case, ready to go? Is he sleeping with her? Might that be it? He did it himself once, Willem, a long time ago: extra French lessons for a child who turned out to be at a scout meeting. A mother with a plan and a teacher with surprisingly weak flesh. He never told anyone about it, better that way, and he's not proud of it. It was very exciting, certainly. Wild. And agile! That's why he associates something like that with Alphonse. Because he's done it himself. His suspicions have nothing to do with Alphonse's origins, of course. Do they? No.

The woman greets Willem as he gets out of the car. He insists she sit in the front. He slides onto the back seat, next to the child, who shakes his hand with a formal 'A pleasure' and then, along with the mother, throws himself affectionately at Björn.

'I first need to fetch a few things from the hospital,' says the doctor. 'No one else must know.'

'Wait here with Björn and the elderly gentleman,' she says to her son, after they've driven backward onto the grassy field.

Alphonse has to smile at Willem's aggrieved expression. Then he goes down the improvised steps with Brigitte Dubois. She can't believe her eyes. The patient pulls himself upright against one of the wooden poles supporting the burnt tarp. It's started to rain softly. There's more mud than before.

'I have to get this done before it's completely dark,' she says. 'Electricity?'

'No.'

'Water?'

'Not running.'

'Bloody hell.'

'Can't you do it then?'

'Oh I can. It's just: bloody hell.'

'Yes.'

She applies herself to her task. She's good at this; he sees the exhilaration in her face. 'Nothing's broken,' she says.

Is that disapproval in the incomprehensible words the Afghans are exchanging? Were they expecting a male doctor? She numbs the leg and the conversations fall silent.

Along with one of the camp dwellers, Alphonse collects candles to combat the falling darkness. Surrounded by a respectful silence, Brigitte Dubois stitches the wound. Every time she looks up at the green-brown eyes of her patient, which are continually fixed on her face, he says 'thank you' and she briefly shakes her glowing head.

'*Ka mate! Ka mate! Ka ora! Ka ora!*' Willem chants from the back seat as Alphonse drives them home. Björn looks anxiously out through the window. '*Tenei te tangata euh ...*'

'*Puhuru huru,*' Hadrianus mouths soundlessly.

Willem looks attentively at his lips. 'I don't know. Just say it.'

'*Puhuru huru! Nana nei i tiki mai!*'

Together they go on: '*Whakawhiti te ra! A upa ... ne!*' Willem rams a force into his thorax. '*Ka upa ... ne!*' Brigitte and Alphonse bellow out the last line along with them: '*A upane kaupane whiti te ra! Hi!*'

9

The sweater he puts on in the morning still has a burnt smell about it from the Afghans' camp. It reminds him of a Christmas dinner when he was still living with his mother and Jean-Marc on the Waversesteenweg. He must have been nine or ten. Jean-Marc had invited his brother and sister-in-law—Constance, who wouldn't become pregnant for several years yet, was safely on another continent—and asked his housekeeper and her son to join them, it was Christmas, after all. Although they had plans of their own, his mother thought it would be impolite to refuse. In the middle of the festively laid table, the fondue set suddenly caught fire. The spiky, rapidly multiplying flames hurried onto the table cloth. In complete contrast to their swiftness, delay took hold of Alphonse, then utter passivity, a paralysing kind of fascination. He watched. His mother's reflexes were working normally. With her bare hands she picked the thing up and put it outside, on the patio of blue stone, close to a garden bed. Then she doused the hissing table. As if by a miracle, she suffered no burns. They all watched through the window to see if the fondue set would explode. It didn't. It burned for a long time, though. A fallen star at Christmas. He freezes in the proximity of flames, hasn't trusted himself near them since. He's learned the word for fire in various languages, in case it should ever be needed. In Russian it's 'Požar!' and in Greek 'Fotyá!' Both people and animals have a fight or flight reaction to danger. The freeze response is less common, he once heard in a nature documentary. Animals are subject to it when doubt takes hold, in the hope of being absorbed into an environment that's deaf to their wish to dissolve boundaries.

He takes the sweater off again.

'This evening I'm going to go and check that young man's injury. It's hard to imagine he made it to Britain last night.' That's all Brigitte says the next day. Alphonse limits himself to 'I'll go too.' Then there are the fingers she lays on his shoulder, the brief moment that his palm covers them.

Hadrianus has chosen this Friday as the occasion on which to show his face at school again after ten days at home; he'll have the weekend to recover. Alphonse wishes him luck and doesn't say he's no idea what to do with Björn. He could take him home. He rings Cat, who says she won't be back until late afternoon. He'll put colourless varnish on the soft planks.

For the first few hours Björn manages to entertain himself in the garden. He chases late-summer insects, snapping at them cross-eyed, missing, even though they make it easy for him with their slow, fat bodies, until he gives up and chews to bits some of the first fallen walnuts, then squirms from side to side on his back, with regular, motionless, dreamy pauses. Meanwhile Alphonse varnishes his way toward the tiled kitchen island where the stacked furniture waits, plank after plank pushing him back. At one point he has to stand up and go to the end of the garden to reprimand Björn, pointing to the hole he's dug between the hollyhocks. He flattens the soil with his hands and washes them amid the furniture pile. The next time the dog goes to the flower bed it's enough to bang on the glass, project an angry stare and a cautionary finger into the garden and wait until Björn goes to lie down in the middle of the lawn with a guilty sigh, head on his front paws.

How odd that he's discovered only now, at forty, what it's like to have a dog. He never wanted one, always thought dogs were dirty and demanding. Slavish. How little he's been confronted with non-human lives. The dog's expressions surprise him, illustrating how feelings precede thoughts, how feelings are thoughts in their primal form. Those eyes, the white margin to the dark brown—he understands the attraction now: it's not the obedience, it's the open book. When after three long lengths he looks toward the window again, Björn is sitting on the other side of the glass, so close that his breath leaves a tiny ring of moisture at the level of his nose. He hopes they'll be able to keep him.

Oh, this person. Oh, this good, strong master. Master! Master! Master! Master! Master! Oh, master, oh, sweet person, oh! To be with you, master! Something to eat, master! Good food, oh! With you, master! Master! To be indoors with you and eat something good together, master! Master! Master!

The dog wants to come in, and he's making that clear by tapping on the glass twenty times a minute with the claws of his front right paw.

'Wait a bit,' says Alphonse. Then: 'Be good and wait.' And then: 'Be nice and quiet.' Nothing for several minutes until he shouts in a tone that strikes him as offensively angry, 'Björn, *s'il vous plaît!*' He has no idea why he shouted it in French. It occurs to him this must be what it's like to have young children: tenderness and admiration alternating with irritation and tedium. And that the tenderness prevails for most people, that it would for him, too.

After the seven-thousandth tap on the window he stands up. He opens the sliding door and looks at the dog. 'You've got just one chance,' he says.

Björn's tail is paralysed by disbelief for a moment, but then starts to wag energetically. He has a shrewd idea of the seriousness of the situation, though, and meekly follows instructions. He drinks from the bowl of water Alphonse puts in front of him and eats a dog biscuit. Then he goes to lie down with his head on his front paws on a part of the floor that hasn't yet been varnished. When Alphonse approaches him several lengths later, he sits up and, to the command 'Backward', does as he's asked, if with a melancholy sigh.

The hours glide casually past. Alphonse forgets each thought immediately, following the gleaming trail left by the brush. Until the harmony is disturbed. Björn sets up an angry barking, bumps into the pot of varnish and forces him to brush open a lump immediately and paint over the paw prints. He didn't hear the man in the doorway approaching.

'Well, well,' says the man, of the rather mature type featured in wristwatch advertisements. 'Is this normal?'

From the floor Alphonse turns toward him, smiling. The question 'Is this normal?' always has that effect on him. The man turns away. Alphonse stands up, opens the sliding door and drags the growling Björn to the other side of the glass by his collar. Sticking out one hand, he introduces himself.

'My roses will be up the spout if he pees on them,' the man mumbles. 'Go home and leave the dog there in future.'

Alphonse lets his hand drop. 'I'm almost finished,' he says.

The man stares at the parquet behind him. 'No idea why this was necessary. Have you?' Although expecting a reply, he still doesn't look at Alphonse. Then he answers himself: 'It must be the menopause. Upstairs you'll leave me in peace, I hope?'

'Yes,' says Alphonse, at which the man hurries off.

Before Brigitte and Hadrianus return, and without saying goodbye to the husband, he leaves the house. His work is done.

At the wheel he notices the clouds becoming excited, planning to release their rain only when they've saved up enough for a flood. The agitation that's pacing back and forth from one chamber of his heart to the other is an old acquaintance. It's been some time since the question arose in him: was the man so unfriendly because he's unfriendly or did his humiliating tone have to do with how he, Alphonse, looks? And if the effect is the same either way, does it make any difference whether or not this guy who is so completely unimportant to him behaves like that to everyone? Yes. It makes a world of difference.

Tiredness creeps over him. Björn licks the fist around the gear stick until Alphonse opens it and walks his fingernails over the dog's head. He wants to abandon his thoughts and he starts a frantic search for a CD by Toumani and Sidiki Diabaté while allowing an agricultural vehicle to pass. He looks at the sombre, self-absorbed face of the farmer. They're having a hard time, the farmers. They sell their produce at a loss, squeezed by supermarket chains. There's a lot of unshared sorrow.

To the kora, sorrow never seems like a complaint,

passion never like hysteria, and vulnerability never melts into defeat. This music makes him feel like driving, experiencing how the faces behind other wheels turn in on themselves, how the traffic increases and then thins again, how the landscape changes colour and the sun sparkles through the tops of the trees.

As a young child he answered 'griot' when asked what he wanted to be, indifferent to the laughter that followed, deaf to the assertion that only the griots can be griots, that you have to be born into a lineage that's upheld the tradition for hundreds of years. He wanted to become a griot, he'd seen them at work, heard his mother say that if West Africa was a person, the griots were its blood, and he wanted to be blood and to flow and to keep something alive.

He hasn't thought about that for a long time, he's never thought about it in the way he does now, and he sees himself playing kora for Brigitte and Hadrianus. It surprises him that he actually did it, that he took the instrument with him and played it for them, that they sat and listened without asking questions. He could do it more often, play for clients. Maybe he's become a griot without even noticing. Then it strikes him that all that time, through all those living rooms, bedrooms, bathrooms, he's listened rather than spoken. He thinks of everything he's been told between the naked walls and bare floors, the stories he's collected, as a griot in reverse, and what they've shown him, the people.

He stops driving, not even parking at the side of the road, ignoring the expectant thumping of Björn's tail. What he feels is confusing. In his mind's eye he's dancing, as a child, while the kora fills the car, the plucking faster and faster. He sees himself growing and as he grows he multiplies, becoming the floral pattern in a kaleidoscope, becoming everyone he has been until he can no longer see the unity of it all. The splintering frightens him and steadily distances him from the old griot dream. Then the expanding floral pattern turns out to be a core, there's a body around it and that body is his; it contains all the stories he's heard, and the senses that want even more. If I were to play the kora right now, he thinks, if I could feel the twenty-one strings under my fingers right now, then I'd be able to tell all the stories I've been saving up, all of them at once. He presses the accelerator.

Followed by Björn, who thinks it's a race, he runs to the front door and impatiently puts his key in the lock. Cat sticks her head into the hallway. He refuses to guess her frame of mind.

'Ah, you're back,' he says. 'Sorry.' He kisses her mouth, her temple, runs up the stairs, Björn racing after him again. 'Inspiration.' Foolish and inadequate word, he thinks, something to squeeze onto a cream cake in light-green lettering, but he mustn't think these things now, he must press his glowing fingertips to the strings.

The kora likes movement. Even immobile, sitting down, the sounds refuse to be static. Alphonse feels gravity lessening slightly. He stands up, even though he knows he's still seated. Is this music mine? he wonders, or do I merely have the honour of passing it on? His toes cautiously let go of the floor. He lies on the air, and slowly the sounds turn him round and round on his axis. The kora doesn't mind a bit of hypnosis. He mustn't see this as ridiculous, this realization that he just might be allowed to touch the essence. No doubts now, he thinks, no embarrassment. He plays himself toward it. It's not like an orgasm, even though it comes suddenly and overwhelms him. It's a tenderness filling the room, not concentrated at one point but a light-emitting mist, and he knows, knows already, that he'll soon lose it again; he feels regret at its approaching loss, but now it's still here, now he can still see it, see that beauty reigns, see that he's never stopped dancing and see what the music confides in him, him and anyone who wants to hear it, always ending with the same promise: with you, everything will be all right.

When he opens his eyes, Cat is standing in front of him. She looks angry, gesticulating and moving her lips. She's talking. He stops playing to listen.

'Hello! She's waiting for you. Says you and she have an appointment.'

Her words continue to exist in their own right for a moment, without evoking any images.

'A woman. She's waiting in the kitchen.'

'A woman?' he can only repeat it.

'Getting on for fifty. Stern-looking. Impressive hairdo.'

'Brigitte.' He's no idea how much time has passed since the kora crept onto his lap. 'I agreed to go to the trench with her. To the Afghans.'

Cat stares at him, first with pity, then incredulity.

'What do you mean by that? Afghans in a trench?'

'What I mean is: Afghans in a trench. Come with us!'

'Why not! Can I put the shopping away first?'

'Bring it along.'

'Naturally.'

Brigitte drives. Cat sits on the leather back seat of the Alfa Romeo in which the woman picked them up. She's introduced herself as 'Dr Dubois'. Just once Cat interrupts the conversation about Hadrianus' relationship with the teaching staff in order—persisting in her ironic compliance—to ask whether she might be allowed something from the shopping she's bought, something small, a biscuit perhaps, just to stop her from fainting with hunger. In response Alphonse merely looks at her. Brigitte absent-mindedly informs her that she too has brought some shopping, to which Cat responds, with emphatic relief, hand spread across her chest, 'Thank goodness!'—but only Alphonse notices.

He's confident her attitude will change when they drive backward into the field, and it does. After two hundred metres in reverse her uncertain eyes catch his.

He takes her hand in his as they make their way down the steps, the plastic bag of shopping in his other hand. Brigitte Dubois walks behind them.

There are diffident greetings. The young man with the injured leg is nowhere to be seen.

'He's gone,' say two other youngsters before they reach the campfire.

'So he's in England?' asks Brigitte.

'Possibly.'

'In a truck?' Cat speaks to the grinning boy. She wants to see that mouth do something else, Alphonse realizes, to see it speak, pout in a moment of hesitation, something other than smile. The sight of a woman with a sleeping child on her arm worries him. She seems so absent, the child so quiet.

Someone else explains to Cat that the checking is getting increasingly tough—cargo spaces are scanned, the British government insists on it—but the customs men sometimes let you through because it takes time to detain you, and any loss of time entails an economic loss for the companies the truckers are working for.

'Still, most of the time they get you,' someone else says.

'We should try swimming.'

'Please don't,' says Cat.

'We are not idiots,' is the rapid reply.

'Of course not.'

Brigitte goes to sit next to the woman, introduces herself as a doctor, asks whether she speaks English, how she's feeling, whether she'd let her take a look at the child. The woman returns her gaze but remains distant. She does allow the doctor to touch the child's forehead, and her own.

Alphonse feels a few drops and looks up at the murky sky. Beneath his feet, the mud made by the last shower of rain has not yet dried. He goes to sit with the others by the fire. Soon the skin of his cheekbones, nose, and forehead is on the point of cracking. He slides further away, but then his back gets wet. Someone throws a log on the fire. For a moment the flames climb to the roof of the tarp and Alphonse stiffens.

Slowly and with dignity the young men pass the bags of shopping from hand to hand. Each of them gives the other time to take something out and examine it more closely, then put it back, while elsewhere in the circle, at the increasing pace of the raindrops beside the tent, words of gratitude fall.

Cat stares at a beautiful man in his early twenties. He lowers his head, with its thick black hair, over a bottle of shower gel, flips back the top and sniffs, slowly and warily. When he looks up at her they exchange a timid smile.

On the way back nothing is said for a long time, until Brigitte asks: 'Did you actually meet my husband, or had you finished varnishing by the time he got home?'

'I saw him,' says Alphonse.

'How was he?'

Alphonse hesitates. 'A bit tense, I think.'

'He can be really terrible,' says Brigitte. 'But he has his good sides. We're all many people at the same time.' The resignation in her defence requires endorsement.

'That's true,' says Cat.

Everyone is a pageant, thinks Alphonse, and there's a leader, perhaps always a different one, depending on the situation or who happens to be sharing a space with you. There were times when he had the rather unhealthy tendency to pose as more stupid than he was, curious about the kind of leaders to be found in another person's parade. On rare occasions you have to turn your back on what they show you.

'Anyhow, he thinks the parquet looks beautiful,' says Brigitte.

Alphonse is distracted by a man some distance away who, on his own, is washing a bus. They passed him on the way here, when he'd just started. Now he seems to have finished. He takes the sponge off its long stick and wrings it out in the middle of a short sweeping motion. That's what Alphonse likes so much about this part of the world: because so little happens, what does happen acquires a miraculous aura, demands sharper attention. To his astonishment the man looks him right in the eye as they approach. He holds up his hand and it's a moment before the three of them realize he's not waving, he's ordering them to stop. Brigitte complies. He's a skinny man in his forties with short strawberry-blond hair, greying at the temples. His hooked hand accompanies the window on the passenger side as Alphonse lowers it.

'Bonjour,' he says.

They all greet him in return.

'What have you been up to back there?' he asks, with a

nod in the direction from which they've come.

All three remain silent like children caught red-handed, waiting for the man to reprimand them—why?

'Stay away from those people. They're destroying this area. They don't belong here. They shouldn't be given food, or whatever it is you're offering them so you can feel like good people. What they need is eradication.'

He returns to his bus, leaving them behind in the cold bath the car has become. Brigitte's hoarse 'Don't agree at all' bounces off him. He climbs into the bus and starts it, turning onto the road a short way ahead of them.

'Just drive,' says Cat.

'We're not going to take it to heart,' Brigitte decides, with little conviction, as she drops Alphonse and Cat at their door.

In the hallway they stroke Björn, who is overjoyed they've come back and walks around them in worried circles for as long as they say nothing.

'Have you had your hair cut?'

'Yes.'

'Looks great.'

'Thanks.'

'Are you hungry?'

'We need to eat something.'

They hurl themselves up against each other like waves, undercurrents, covering each other's faces with kisses.

8

In his dream he re-experiences several events of his childhood. It's as if someone, in a voice he doesn't know, is telling him about his time at primary school, his first few years in this country, his high school days, his mother far away. When he landed up in a class with Amadou, he was the only other black child out of twenty-eight in that year. In French-language education in Brussels it would have been different, even in the 1980s, but his mother, under the influence of Cat's father, her as yet childless employer, decided that speaking Dutch at school would be to his benefit. There were Moroccan twins, a Chinese boy, and a girl from Chile in the same class, but they didn't stick out from a distance.

There was no physical harassment, only words, although they were often spoken from far too close. He put up with it because there was no alternative. He didn't understand what a teacher meant when she praised him for his courage. Alphonse put a stop to it all in a full classroom. The commotion in anticipation of the teacher's arrival was silenced when he turned to face Matthieu de Schaepmeester—he can now clearly see the boy in front of him, the weakest of the attacking group—and said: 'Matthieu, you're going to bully me? You've got no friends here and you're going to bully me? You think they care a damn about you? You've got nobody. If you had friends, someone would say something now.' It was a gamble, but there was total silence. The boy broke. Not a pleasant sight. A few weeks later Matthieu changed schools. Alphonse's performance was judged a success. After that no one dared torment him. He felt sick at himself and knew what he never again wanted to be: a victim turned perpetrator, a common predator.

He opens his eyes and focuses them on Cat's white shoulder, which is poking up above the duvet, while the events of the previous day—especially the man with the bus—come to mind again. That he actually used that word: eradication.

No Saturday work today. He has to do some shopping, for them and for the Afghans. A refugee camp an arrow's flight from his bed. He could go and play for them. He begins by kissing that warm shoulder. She turns her head toward him, eyes still shut, a flush to her cheeks that seems painted on.

Recently he's sometimes felt he was looking through the eyes of an extraterrestrial, absorbing everything individually as if seeing it for the first time. He looks at himself in the mirror that covers one of the sliding doors of the wardrobe. He's sitting upright, one leg beneath him, his sex leaning against it in an undecided state. The pale soles of his feet are visible. His hair needs trimming; he doesn't like it when it starts to look like a helmet. Out of nowhere it occurs to him that the plasterer in the author's story was described as 'thinner than slim'. She was right: it's not him. He draws his belly in, tenses his arm muscles.

'No, you're not fat,' Cat mumbles.

He chuckles. There have been years in which she wanted to hear that from him over and over. He can't remember when the role became his.

'Where's Björn?'

'Downstairs. The door's shut.'

She sits up too, presses her soft breasts to his back and puts her arms around him. 'I think we're at our most beautiful now,' she says, her chin on his shoulder. Their reflection smiles bravely. 'It's not going to get any better than this.' They laugh and at the same time they're struck by a flash in which they really are more beautiful than they knew.

'No!' he hears her shout a little later, above the noise of the trimmers. Then, next to him in the bathroom, disappointed: 'Oh.' Björn licks at the shorn hair on the floor, then makes smacking noises as he tries to get it off his tongue.

'It'll grow back.'

Walking at his side through the supermarket, she's still looking above his eyes. Below one corner of her mouth curls a small 's' for 'shame'. 'We've become the sort of people who shop on Saturdays for the whole week,' she says to his shorn scalp.

'Yes, but we also buy food for Afghan refugees. Is that out-of-the-ordinary enough?'

They choose the till with the shortest queue, a fact apparently unconnected with the speed of the employee assigned to it, a boy with a very pointed Adam's apple who stares at the bottom of a jar of preserves as if reading a death threat targeted at him personally.

'How are you doing?' the boy asks the woman shuffling forward in front of them. He has an unsteady voice with a West Flanders accent.

'Just get on with it,' she says wearily.

His Adam's apple bouncing up and down and red

patches creeping from his neck to his forehead like the leaves of a climbing plant, the boy reaches with trembling fingers for what are described on the packaging as party sauces. 'Card payment?' The woman nods and pays.

'How are you doing?' His desperate eyes float from Cat to Alphonse.

'Good,' says Cat obligingly.

'Fine,' says Alphonse. 'And you?'

Behind his glasses the boy's eyes grow damp. 'But how are you *really* doing?' he adds hoarsely.

Cat and Alphonse search each other's surprised faces for an answer, then turn back to the boy: 'Fine.'

His next outward breath turns into sobbing that soon grows wet. The customers who have joined the queue after them move to other checkouts. An elderly man who has just placed a sack of cat litter behind the 'next customer' bar picks it up again with a struggle and looks indecisively this way and that.

Cat opens the packaging of some paper tissues they're about to buy and pulls one out for the boy. They don't even need to ask for an explanation; it gushes over his lips with question marks attached: 'And why do students with holiday jobs have to join the campaign? Am I expected to have the answer? Is it my fault there are so many suicides around here? Am I supposed to solve that? Me?'

Alphonse knows what this is about. The Westhoek was recently found to have one of the highest suicide rates in Europe and the provincial government has started a campaign aimed at tackling the supposed surliness of the population by getting people to speak about their feelings in public.

'Isn't it enough that I have to come and work here so I

can pay my own college fees from October onward?'

The customers at other tills study the shopping in their trolleys. More and more smartphones are zipped into view. The cashiers shift back and forth in their chairs. One of them stands up.

'And why didn't I pass? Isn't that a good question? Might it be because of my mother? Doesn't she talk far too *much* about her feelings? Might that not affect me? Who do they think I am? Superman?'

'No, no,' Cat hushes, coaxing another tissue out of the packet. 'No one thinks that.'

The boy pushes his glasses straight. The eyes between the wet eyelashes take on a hostile gleam for a moment.

'Nobody expects that of you,' says Alphonse.

'Liam.'

The cashier who stood up is now at their side.

'Liam.'

'What?'

'I'll take your place for a bit. Go back there and have a breather.'

'Ah! Ah! So people aren't allowed to see my distress?'

The only sound is the muffled voice of someone making a call in one of the aisles and the bleeps from the one till where work is continuing undisturbed.

'That's not distress, Liam. That's being infantile.'

Liam climbs onto the conveyor belt. He's going to undo his trousers and urinate on us with a lilac-coloured member, thinks Alphonse. The journalist and the dictionary come to mind. He swiftly sticks his hand out to Liam, who fails to respond to the invitation.

With a brusque thrust of her foot, the cashier uses the pedal of the till as a kick-start and the conveyor belt jerkily begins to move. Liam loses his balance and with an awkward twist ends up in Alphonse's arms. Astonished at how light he is, he holds onto him longer than is wanted.

'You can put me down now,' the boy says. His beaming smile makes Alphonse shiver. The cashier is grinning too. Her colleagues stand up and applaud. Several customers join in, even though they have no idea why.

'Wave to the camera,' says the cashier. 'You're going to be on regional TV.' She cheerfully waves at a spot above their heads. Alphonse and Cat can't immediately see the camera. Liam tells them they reacted with empathy and must therefore be rewarded with a thirty-euro voucher. Although urged to treat themselves immediately in this very supermarket, they want to get out as fast as they can.

'So meta it's beyond comprehension,' says Cat as she drives them past an industrial zone. 'Good thing the boy isn't really that unhappy, of course.'

'That's true.'

'Talented actor.'

'Yes.'

'They couldn't run a campaign like that in Brussels, could they.'

'I don't think so, no.'

'Alphonse?'

'Cat?'

'What are you thinking about?'

He starts a list: the journalist's excrement, Sieglinde's pregnancy test, Gewijde's barbecues, his connection with Pan. He fills the entire trip home with it.

'That was all this month?'

He nods.

'We have to get out of here.'

'It's not the fault of this place.'

'Everyone wants to confide in you about their secret madness, I've known that for a while, but it wasn't ever as bad as this, was it? Then that whole song and dance just now. I reckon people around here have gone collectively insane out of boredom.'

'Come on, Cat. You've lived in enough places in the world to know there's no such thing as "people around here". They're always just people.'

He doesn't feel like arguing. What she's said has made him uneasy. He really doesn't believe it's the fault of the place they're in, and he'd like to stand by his conviction that very few people go out on the street and fire hunting rifles, that things aren't too bad generally speaking. Yet he sometimes thinks he's witnessing a mass loss of control, a growing wish to tear each other apart, the swelling thunder of a war of all against all. He presses his head to the headrest. Their street strikes him as more dismal than usual.

'That's my father's car,' says Cat.

She's referring to the Audi in front of their house. On the back seat, Jean-Marc is sipping from a glass.

'Another lunatic,' she says.

She knocks hard on the window near her father's ear. He spills his drink on his loosened tie. 'Childproof lock,' she hears him call out in a muffled voice.

'Why is there a childproof lock on that door?' Cat releases him.

'I don't know.' Head back, Jean-Marc shakes the last drop from the glass, which he then puts down with a bang on the car roof. 'She's left,' he says.

'Mum?'

He nods, staring at her, lost. 'I don't know where she's gone. She's taken half her clothes. And pulled all the houseplants out of their pots. Not to take them with her.

Divorce, all well and good, but the way that she ... '

Behind the windows in the street, Alphonse sees curtains move here and there, several fingers, an eye. He proposes they go inside and the other two meekly follow.

'So what happened?' Cat asks angrily, after the door has shut behind them. 'Where did she go?'

'I don't know where she is. She's turned off her phone.'

'How long ago?' asks Alphonse.

'Two days.'

'But why?'

'Oh it probably has something to do with my new girlfriend.'

Cat stares at him in amazement. 'A girlfriend? A new girlfriend? You have girlfriends? It's quite possible, yes, that that has something to do with it.'

'God, Catherine, of course I do. What do you expect?' Jean-Marc answers his daughter's dismay with sombre impatience.

'I thought cheating was the one thing you didn't do to each other.'

Alphonse fills two glasses with water from the tap and puts them down on the coffee table between father and daughter. Cat and Jean-Marc look at them as if he's trying to play a trick.

'Cheating! Cheating!' with limp hands Jean-Marc depicts untidy clouds. 'Don't go dreaming up all kinds of things.'

'Then how am I supposed to imagine it?'

'Well, there's some degree of affection involved. But it's usually just a matter of lying naked against one another.'

Cat has put her hands over her ears.

Jean-Marc concentrates on the glass of water, although

without actually drinking from it.

'I thought you and Mum still slept together, in spite of everything. That you stayed together because there was still that.'

Alphonse refrains from saying he thought so too. Jean-Marc now seems softened by sympathy for his daughter.

'That used to be the case, yes. In spite of everything. But not for the past fifteen years.'

There's a silence. Alphonse strokes Cat's back, which seems to reanimate her. 'And does she have boyfriends?'

'No idea. I don't think so.'

'But she knows about your girlfriends.'

'Mmm.'

'Mmm?'

'Yes, she knew a bit about some of them. And she didn't really have a problem with it.'

'That seems very unlikely to me!'

'No, it meant I was out of the house a bit more often and she was comfortable with that. She has a problem with this one because she's fat.'

'Excuse me?'

'Because she's fat?' Alphonse repeats.

'Yes, she finds that a let-down, that people—don't ask me which people, we no longer have any friends—that people are going to see me with a fat woman. That's a let-down for her.' Then, with his hands half a metre from his hips and a smile at Alphonse: 'She sure is fat all right.' Because his daughter and son-in-law continue to stare at him, he adds a conclusion: 'But I can actually talk to her. Your mother doesn't understand that either. That I simply like to have a good conversation with a woman sometimes. Without all-out war. From time to time I need that.'

Alphonse imagines Jean-Marc chattering away in the lap of a huge, naked, listening woman. In the toilet he's able to grin at the image without restraint. He hopes Constance has someone like that too.

Back in the living room he sees that the glasses of water have been replaced by vodka.

Cat's father urges her to ring her mother. When she fails to get through he disappears into their sofa behind a newspaper. Alphonse wonders whether Jean-Marc ever made any advances to his own mother in all those years he shared a house with her. He could have found a new housekeeper in each of the major cities he lived in. Why did he take her with him? Because he had a good heart, according to his mother, and because it gave him, Alphonse, the opportunity to study in Europe. Because she was a welcome calming influence, he's always thought. She was a mother to all of them.

On the back of the paper that's hiding Jean-Marc's face is an article about the modern slave trade. Jean-Marc turns a page and reads out something about Ebola in Senegal that says the country has managed to ward off the disease. He smiles at Alphonse with the same benevolence but less detachment than the younger Jean-Marc of his childhood. Then the awkwardness squeezes its fat buttocks between them again. It feels like the time when Jean-Marc put a piece of amethyst into the hands of the nine-year-old Alphonse and tried to tell him something about it, tried to explain why he was giving it to him, because he was a good boy, and Alphonse simply said thank you, although they could read in each other's eyes that they'd rather have been spared this.

Cat decides not to go with him to the refugee camp. After another fruitless attempt to ring her mother and a short-tempered altercation with her father about something trivial, she goes to her study to Skype Alphonse's mother. Alphonse promises to be back soon.

In the camp the mother and child are sleeping on a filthy mattress next to the fire, lying there as if they've collided. Why doesn't she sleep in one of the tents? Does she stand less chance of being assaulted outside?

Some faces have gone, others have joined. Two young men he's seen here before take the food he's brought and put it in a makeshift cupboard. Two others speak about him in vicious tones and for a moment he's the intersection of dangerous looks, a man passed around between sharp tongues in an incomprehensible language. Yet another asks him if he has papers and how long he's been here. His answer is followed by silence. He's been a great help to them, says one of those he knows. The young man nods at him, then nods again, and after that Alphonse says goodbye.

As he's driving home he looks at his hands on the wheel. Are they shaking? They're shaking. There's no need for that. The shaking stops.

The plan was to have a night out in Rijsel, but now that Cat's father is snoring on the sofa and Cat's concern about her still unreachable mother has increased, they decide against it. They fry the fish they bought in the supermarket and leave some for Jean-Marc, who starts eating it while they're watching a TED talk about the oldest living organisms in the world. It's accompanied by pictures that Jean-Marc says are not conducive to a good appetite, which his daughter says means he shouldn't look.

In South Africa there's an underground forest that's existed for thirteen thousand years, a wood that has hidden itself; only the highest leaves stick out above the ground. Humans and animals casually walk above trees that are spared when fire takes hold.

He's making no move to go home, Jean-Marc. Again he's fallen asleep on the longer of the two sofas. From the other Cat keeps turning up the volume of the film they're watching to drown out his snores. Eventually she gives up and disappears to their bedroom. With some reticence, Alphonse removes his father-in-law's shoes, lays his legs next to each other so that his back isn't bent at such an odd angle and covers him up. He exchanges an adult look with Björn, who seems to agree to keep watch over the man.

Contrary to his expectations, Cat is already asleep. He feels his sex swell as he creeps up against her hip, then turns over because she'd be resentful if he woke her now. One hand inside his pyjamas, he's sucked into a dream. He digs a tunnel and under it a cave in which everyone who needs him can rest.

7

The day begins at five in the morning with shouting underneath the parquet. Alphonse has slept deeply. His dream and the direction from which the voices are coming confuse him, and for a moment it occurs to him that up and down are illusions, just like gravity. A split second later he hears the voices of Cat and her mother, like badly tuned violins, her father a worn-out double bass. Then Björn sets up a high-pitched barking as well.

The first person he sees is Constance. On her knees on the carpet, howling, she's tugging her head onto the floor by the hair. A little further away is Jean-Marc, also on the carpet, his cheekbone featuring what could be the bloody tear of a Pierrot, apparently not having originated from his eye but from a small cut just below it. As the tear swells he makes animal noises, sniffing and rasping. What Constance is saying is no less incomprehensible, the syllables are too long. He can understand only Cat, who is standing between them like a reed after a tornado, forced to survey the destruction. With pale revulsion she shouts that they must get out, now, immediately. What Björn is barking is clear too: 'Don't do that! Don't do that!'

'Throw them out!' Cat has now turned to face him, mouth deliriously wide. 'How could you sleep through this?'

'What's happened?' he asks.

'Can't you see?! It's not enough that they smash each other's heads in, now they have to do it in our house! Throw them out, right now!'

He doesn't know how to respond to that order. Her parents alone react to it. With renewed energy they squirm across the carpet, crying and sniffing. To anyone willing to hear they also say 'sorry'. Does he really have to drag them out onto the pavement one by one and push the door shut? Would they just lie there, or haul themselves off in different directions like lame caterpillars? He must prevent them from getting behind the wheel.

'Do we have to call the police?!' he asks Jean-Marc and Constance threateningly, hands on hips. This is weird.

'Go right ahead!' Constance shouts.

He proposes that Cat and he should each drive one parent home. Cat can take her own car and he'll drive Jean-Marc's.

'And we just drop them both at their house?'

'Yes. They'll calm down a bit on the way.'

'I wouldn't bank on it.' Just like the blue hour outside that's eating up the landscape, the pain has overpowered her. He can feel the damp edges of it, pulls her to him. He rubs her head.

'Can they both go with you?' she asks.

They drive coastward, he first, in Jean-Marc's car, the man himself unconscious on the back seat, his wife sobbing in the seat next to Alphonse. Cat follows in her own car. Somewhere around halfway, in a district that seems abandoned apart from one confused bird, Constance tugs at the wheel. Since Alphonse is not driving fast and is stronger than she is, he manages to avoid the line of young trees along the verge. The beam of the headlights slides across their thin trunks in a sea of time. There's the startled squeal of brakes, the blow from Jean-Marc, Constance's return blow, her words: 'I didn't mean to do that!' The flashing of the lights of Cat's car in the rear-view mirror. His heart in his throat.

Then the monotone hum of the tarmac resumes and no one says anything further. At their house they both meekly get out. Without looking round, Constance disappears deeper into her coat, Jean-Marc turns the key in the lock, pushes open their front door and goes inside.

Alphonse parks the Audi, runs down the drive and gets into the passenger seat next to Cat. She doesn't take her eyes off the road. He strokes her short hair, the thin muscles of her neck, climbs with his index finger along the tendons in her throat, strokes the pouch under her right eye with his little finger, her ear with his thumb, her hair with his whole hand.

'You know what I want?' she asks. His hand is resting on her knee again.

To not love her mother and father perhaps, for them not to be there any longer, so her love can be free again at last. She once said something like that.

'What do you want?'

'I want to move to a big city and adopt a child together.'

It's an unexpected answer, a wish of which he had no knowledge, and it makes his head light. 'Then that's what we'll do,' he says.

Something between a laugh and a sigh escapes her. Outside the sky grows a lighter and lighter blue.

So the day bursts in: a new, honey-coloured room that is slid slowly over their bedroom until all the walls shine. Her thin, tough ribs under the supple, warm skin, the descent of her belly, her mound of Venus a bulwark. She comes to sit across him, squeezing his prick between her legs, almost the way a child is held to the shoulder to let out a burp, the way a friend is comforted. He pulls her closer, his hand around her shoulder, around the back of her head, her short hair, her tongue familiar, her green eyes near. He wants this so much.

'My woman,' he says. '*Ma femme. Sama diabar.*'

She has to laugh at that and it's as if the laugh goes on bubbling through them while they imprint each other, turn, rend, before it flows out of them in a gentle chuckle as their cooling, softened limbs entangle in their sleep.

His bladder wakes him from that sleep at a later stage than usual. He's reluctant to climb up out of the abyss, to remove his cheek from her shoulder, his arm from her hip, to break off one of the rare times when the prolonged fusion of two bodies is not just desired but comfortable.

The quarrel of the previous night has left its mark on Björn. Dispirited, he turns away from the cheese rinds they hold out to him during breakfast. He goes to sit on a chair by the window on the street side and stares as if traumatized at the wall opposite. The trumpeting farts that escape him, which usually make him leap in wild circles, leave him cold. Since they feel guilty about having shut him out of their presence for half a day in that state, they promise him a long walk. It disturbs them that, for the first time, the word 'walk' has no apparent effect on him.

Willem comes round with a cake—the first one he's made himself—and a distressed 'Everything okay?'

'That was my parents,' says Cat. 'Not us.'

The neighbour exhausts himself with apologetic reassurances: of course that wasn't them, he saw an un-familiar car in the street and noticed that a taxi stopped there later in the night, not that he pays attention to such things. All the same, a thing like that can't be easy for her, they're still her parents, Marie-Jeanne often used to say as much, she could tell Cat had lacked something as a child. But he realizes that what he's saying is getting on her nerves and that they're not planning to reveal anything about the events of the night just past, so he turns his attention to Björn.

'What's wrong with him?'

'He's a bit shocked, we think,' says Alphonse.

'Björn, come here.' Willem's authoritarian tone im-presses the dog. He nervously walks over to Willem, lin-gering next to his legs. When Willem orders him to sit, he does as he's told; even his head tends toward the floor.

'Björn, this is the region of courageous dogs. In the mid-nineteenth century there must have been around six-ty thou-sand smuggler dogs operating along the French–Belgian border.' He peers at his neighbours for a moment, restrains his laughter and gives his words extra force with a didactic finger, which makes Björn bow his head a little lower still. 'Many were shot by cus-toms men, or got into bloody battles with customs dogs. The dog that belonged to Marguerite Yourcenar's father, called Red, was shot by an overzealous customs agent on the road between Ieper and Zwarteberg, and the writer Maxence Van der Meersch wrote from the perspective of the strong dog Tom who, during his long trek over dunes and beaches with eighteen kilos of tobacco on his back, managed to evade a customs dog. You must model your-self on them!'

Björn starts shaking from nose to tail, stopping only when his owners both shout at once that their neighbour is joking and Willem strokes his head with a laugh. 'Good dog,' he says. 'Ever read anything by him? Maxence Van der Meersch?' he asks Cat and Alphonse. 'Fantastic stuff. He writes about the peat bogs, the desolate dunes, the wide sky, and about the hutments at the border, smuggler dogs, cockfights, social unrest in Roubaix, Flemish migrants, many bad people at all levels of the population and here and there an angel. Never read anything by him?'

They shake their heads.

'Writers are immortal. That's not normally true, is it?' Willem mumbles. 'Dust and ashes, yes. Like everything.'

Since they don't want to let the silence that follows drag on any longer, Cat asks him whether he's got anything by Van der Meersch. That revives the neighbour. He goes off immediately in search. They can keep the cake.

With Cat at his side and Björn ahead of them, Alphonse walks through the village. They'll be leaving before they've made it their own. He'll work through the clients he's already taken on, cancel the rental contract, respray the address and phone number on his van. Today he's not daunted by new beginnings. They're close together now, this is a good kind of love, and he's the happiest man in the world, the self he loves best, the one that here, between these fields, has taken the lead, the one he wants to be and will still be elsewhere. They'll care for a child that already exists and needs parents. He hopes Cat sticks to that wish, finds it a brilliant plan. They must talk about it, but not here.

In the streets closest to their house he's seen only a few interiors. He greets the people he recognizes, the baker, the mayor, the man whose Jacuzzi he has surrounded with tiles.

'Your hat is very nice,' says an unknown man carrying a sports bag to a front door, in English.

'Thanks,' answers Alphonse, in Dutch.

A child almost cycles into something while turning to look. Björn walks on ahead of them, pulling harder and harder, regaining his strength.

'Did you see how that guy looked at me?' asks Cat. She means the former client with the Jacuzzi. He waits for her answer.

'Slut, he thought. Fucking a Negro.'

'You don't know that.'

'I know that look. If it's not that one, then it's the one in between contempt and compassion: "Didn't find anyone?"'

'You seem very certain about other people's motivations.'

'And you give people an absurd number of chances. Until they attack.'

He sees an elderly lady duck back behind a curtain. He thinks of the woman on the phone who cancelled an appointment, the doctor's husband, the man washing the bus, what he said, and that she, Cat, lied to him. Suddenly he can't stand the fact that she's walking beside him, that she wants to take him away from here. She does this often, breaking through his cocoon with something that could be either a warning or a threat. The latter, he thinks now. And what is this wasp doing here. It's not a month for wasps. He bats it away.

'Sorry,' she says, genuinely shocked at herself, it seems, or at what she's caught of his thoughts. 'That was totally out of order, what I said. I'm sorry.'

The resentment turns over one more time inside him, with blunt spines. Then the scene of the early morning comes to mind, the impact it must have had on her.

There are grounds for clemency.

'Don't be angry.' She kisses his shoulder. 'Björn can't stand it, either.'

Indeed, he can see that Björn has flattened his ears back along his neck and is pulling less hard at the lead.

'We must kidnap him,' he says. 'When we leave here.' Although it hasn't occurred to him until now, he really doesn't think he could bear to give the dog back to Els and Dieter.

'Oh, yes! That has to be the plan!' Cat exclaims.

Their unanimity seems to make Björn relax a little. Further on he barks at a man on a ladder. At the edge of the village he tries to ingratiate himself with some well-wrapped residents who are resolutely holding a barbecue.

They lead him away from there, along narrow concrete paths into a landscape full of bushes and trees that fight the wind and birds that make use of it, nonchalantly landing on deliriously shaking branches. Houses climb up against the hills, stalls vomit cows. There's a pony that gallops toward them from the far side of a sunny meadow and acts as if the grass Cat holds out to him is far nicer than the grass he was eating a short distance away.

Passing a restaurant called Chez Le Voisin they walk into another village, possibly on the French side, even more forgotten by time than their own. 'Those flowers,' says Cat. They're vivid yellow and so oddly big it's as if they've been plucked from a toddlers' television programme. They beam out over the surrounding district, contributing to an atmosphere of unreality. Diagonally across from the little front garden is a corner bar—Alphonse happens to know it's one of the oldest around here—named after St Eloy. The door is open. There's only one client who, like the proprietor, looks astonished at the sight of them.

'*Est-ce qu'on ne dérange pas?*' asks Cat.

'No, not at all, come in. I'm surprised, that's all. Young people never come here any more. They don't even greet me; I'm an old woman.' She says it without rancour.

'And me then?' says the man at the bar. He's Cat's age and they can tell from his joyful posture that he's been waiting for this: a visit from people under fifty.

'You're from here,' the woman says curtly.

Expecting they'll ask, she reveals she's determined to keep her bar open until the end, fully aware that her end will also be the end of the bar, and that it won't be very much longer before those overlapping ends arrive.

Cat and Alphonse explore the small space, careful not to do so too greedily. A poster of a German Shepherd, a carpentry saw with NOT HERE written on it in Dutch, twenty or so sansevierias in the window, chairs upholstered with scuffed red leather. Will they be counted among the customers when it's all over? Today it seems far from unpleasant to be looking at something that's almost gone. It's a privilege.

They ask for coffee. The woman walks, with little steps, to the far corner of the small room, where a half-full jug of coffee is waiting patiently in the coffee maker.

The young drinker is now staring at her lovingly. 'Germaine is eighty-nine,' he says.

It's he who asks questions, Germaine who listens to their answers. When Cat tells them what she does for a living, that she translates from Spanish and Portuguese, the conversation turns to the subject of language. Germaine demonstrates her command of the border dialect, saying she used to be punished at school for speaking Flemish, and that nowadays, when there's little interest in it, it's taught as a subject in schools. Too late. In an attempt to relieve the atmosphere of transience, Cat says she'd like to translate more literature. Initially that stops the conversation altogether.

'I've only read the Bible,' says Germaine after a while.

'The Book of Job.' Tonton Jah, who never usually imposed anything on Alphonse, insisted on it. Year after year he was subjected to that educational extravagance.

'Ah. Job!' Germaine nods at him mysteriously and with some fervour. 'I could tell you a thing or two about that, about Job. Wait, first I'll make some fresh coffee.'

Because his uncle saw immediately that Alphonse, tormented by his dyslexia and the French he wasn't used to reading, was simply looking at each page for an appropriate length of time before turning it, every year there was a period in which he was made to read aloud from Job night after night at the kitchen table. He hated it and never managed to come up with a convincing answer to the question Tonton Jah put to him afterwards: 'What is this about?' At the age of seventeen, in the last year of the incomprehensible trial, he announced that it was about some guy who is rightly furious at God for deliberately taking everything away from him and for behaving like an exhausting child, with his bragging about the dangerous crocodiles he's created. And Job, having insisted for so long that he's not done anything wrong, eventually says God is right, probably in order to have done with him. Tonton Jah threw back his head laughing and for a moment Alphonse thought that was the answer his uncle—who after all had fled from a monastery—had wanted to hear. That was the moment, however, when he decided his nephew was too young for Job. He had a look on his face that Alphonse wanted to interpret as resignation but that might equally well have been disappointment.

'Marcel used to come here often,' Germaine begins as she joins them at their table. 'In my young days we were lovers but I soon realized he wasn't a person to share a home with.'

'Really?' says the regular. 'You and Marcel?'

'Marcel had the misfortune to be born into a working-class family despite having an aristocratic soul. It happens, and if you can't stay off the drink then it always takes you to a bad end. By twenty he was already a serious alcoholic. It's a wonder he lived to be almost seventy. *Enfin.* He worked in a factory in Lille but he read philosophy. He liked to talk about it and got angry with people who wouldn't listen. So he was angry most of the time. If you run a bar you have to listen to people. Especially the ones you've broken off a past relationship with—it made him desperately unhappy—and who are good customers partly for that reason. You may well think: man, shut up. But you can't say that.' She points with her chin to the 'not here' saw on the wall opposite. 'Marcel was obsessed with Job and with what all those philosophers said about him. All those things he started saying about Job actually began to interest me. Because I'd already asked myself: why does this man persist in believing in someone who deliberately takes everything away from him? Don't ask me for the names of all those learned people Marcel talked about, but there was one who said: Job goes on believing because he wants to protect God from himself, doesn't want him to stoop to being an unjust God. Then there was someone else who claimed that the God he accuses is a different God from the one he clings to, and the one he clings to is the Messiah. Then there was yet another—and I regret that I don't remember the name—who said that yes, it was indeed all about two kinds of God and that Job turns away from the one who was a friend of Satan, whereas the faith that remains is a faith in the good God within Job himself, his conscience, in a sense. That he doesn't base his morality on faith but faith on his morality. And that life isn't fair and it's not true that honesty is the best policy, but he remains faithful to the goodness in himself, and that goodness is God, and enough.'

No one is drinking any longer. They're staring at her, Alphonse and Cat sitting down and the regular standing at the bar.

'I've forgotten everything else Marcel came here to talk about, but I've always remembered that. Job says: "Even though he kills me, I'll continue to hope in him. At least I'll be able to argue my case to his face! I have this as my salvation: the godless person won't be appearing before him."'

'Germaine,' says the man at the bar, shaking his head. 'My goodness, Germaine.'

She turns her bosom in his direction. 'But that's beautiful, isn't it?' she says angrily.

Yes, it is, thinks Alphonse. Was that what his uncle meant? Was that the faith he wanted to pass on? Did he in fact do so?

'That's how I'll leave,' says Germaine. 'I'm the old heart of a village where no one comes to live. I'll stop beating and the little I've known that's not yet disappeared will be gone. I can weep and curse as much as I like about that and none of it will change, but I'll be happy in the knowledge that I've done what I could,' she laughs with tears in her eyes. To avoid self-consciousness, she shuffles across to the sink.

Alphonse wants to stand up and squeeze her to him.

'For God's sake, Germaine,' says the drinker. He rubs his face with both hands, stricken.

'What?'

'I don't recognize you any longer.'

'Well, Cédric, that's because I usually listen instead of talking, but I thought: I'm eighty-nine, I'm going to say something for a change.' She polishes a glass with exaggerated thoroughness.

'You're not dying yet, are you?' the man wails.

Germaine sighs. The moment to embrace her has passed.

'Even conscience isn't separate from that unjust, arbitrary world,' says Cat.

'Yes it is,' Germaine snaps at her.

'You're a product of your environment too. You have to be very certain of the rightness of your conscience, convinced of your own innocence and goodness and your own version of the facts if you're to justify everything to your last breath. What makes you so certain you're not the villain yourself?'

Dammit, thinks Alphonse. Good question, wrong moment. Cat searches his face. 'It's not just about conscience or guilt or goodness,' he says. 'It's about something bigger than that, bigger than yourself. Like she says: that's God.' He turns away from Cat's raised eyebrows to face Germaine. For a moment her watery eyes shine, laughing through the sour mask she's put on. The spell is broken, however.

Cédric looks dead tired. He gloomily tells them he has a headache and is going home. Asking for what he owes to be put on the tab and with a half-hearted goodbye, he disappears from their lives.

Germaine having been at it for seventy years already, they manage quite competently to talk about trivialities. At the door Alphonse grasps her hand. The hand is startled at first, but it lingers in his and then squeezes tenderly back.

On the way home, through the dark, it's Cat's hand he holds.

'Might you be having a midlife crisis?' she asks.

'Quite possibly.'

On the Belgian side of the border they pass four noisy young men pushing a fifth in a wheelbarrow. The word 'nigger' skips over the laughter behind their backs. Then it grows even quieter than normal, until a firework goes off several villages away. They have no idea why.

6

The house looks like the head of a maddened robot wearing a sun visor. He wonders whether the structure of blue glass sticking out from below the edge of the roof serves some function or is intended to be decorative, or who knows, even artistic. Where is he supposed to ring the bell? There are just three long, narrow windows: two eyes and a mouth.

'This is the way I bought it.' The man walking toward him is holding one hand up close to his beard by way of greeting. 'That thing up there is going to go.'

'Hello.' Younger than me, thinks Alphonse. That the faces around him are getting hairier makes it hard to estimate ages.

'Réginald de Vis?' The man says it as if he's guessing.

'No, Alphonse Badji. I'm here for your walls.'

'Yes, yes, but I'm Réginald de Vis.'

'Sorry.'

Réginald's face becomes rounder as he laughs. His teeth are small, like a child's.

'This way. The door's at the back.'

Strip lights have been incorporated into the side wall. Réginald notices him looking at them.

'You ain't seen nothing yet,' he says, in a sudden snatch of cowboy English. 'It was empty for three years. No one wanted it. Otherwise I could never have afforded to buy such a spacious house for myself.'

The metal door at the back of the house opens from the bottom up. 'Couldn't be any more inconvenient,' says Réginald, lifting the thing over their heads. 'Go on in. Careful of that handle. The number of times I've bumped my head on it ... I plan to do something about that too, the door. But first things first.' While Alphonse follows him along a snail-shell-shaped corridor, he goes on: 'At first I thought it would be great to have a house unlike anything anyone else has. Up to a point I still do. I'm amazed how you get used to it. At the same time, there are some things I don't want to get used to.'

They arrive in a wide living room.

'Oh,' says Alphonse.

The only wall not interrupted by corners and bends has an enormous mural that is hard to interpret as anything other than the gang rape of a bound girl by four virile extraterrestrials. None of the proportions are right. The heads are triangular, the eyes elongated. The two penises not actively penetrating the girl are shaped like daggers.

Alphonse whistles through his teeth.

'I reckon the world should be punished for not giving whoever was responsible for this due recognition. And take a closer look. It wasn't sufficient to paint it, here and there bits of the plaster have been chiselled out. In an attempt to create a kind of 3D effect, I think.'

Alphonse feels the wall.

'It was only half the starting price,' says Réginald. 'There's double glazing throughout. Solar panels. I thought: I'll have this seen to and forget about it.' He turns hopefully to Alphonse.

'Can be done. I'll have to fill the holes first. I hope I can get it smooth. There's so much damage. Otherwise I'll have to hack it all off and replaster. In that case it'd be better to leave it to dry for several months before applying paint. I'm not a plasterer, either. I've done it, but not very often.'

'Several months?'

'Filler will probably be enough. By this evening you won't be able to tell what was on there. Only that something was.'

Réginald nods. 'Go ahead. Will I see you later? I'm back around six.'

'I'll still be here.'

After locating his car keys, he looks up again at the painting. 'A house like this confronts you with the arbitrariness and absurdity of life. There's something to be said for that, I think. It's more honest, or something. Even if that's perhaps not necessarily what you want in a house. Why? I've been thinking that a lot recently: why?' He seems to be startled awake, looks at the clock on his smartphone, then at Alphonse. 'In the end you want a home, right?'

'I'll do my best,' says Alphonse.

Few things fail so wholeheartedly as murals by lesser masters. He recalls the zombie-like children playing sports that were left by a teacher on the fence around his primary school. How often had they featured in his nightmares? Then there was a rehearsal room with a defecating pig, and a café with a portrait of the owner looking down at you from the ceiling as if he wanted to spit in your beer. He's painted over one before: a window with billowing curtains framing a view of a fluorescent tropical beach.

Ugly things expose an abyss. That any white wall can be filled with a scene like this is the tangible, domestic version of the certainty that anything can be ruined. It's one of the reasons he likes this job: the chance to reverse the damage.

He presses the sandpaper to the wall. First he'll free the victim from her suffering. The paint does more than obey, it disappears with alacrity. As the erased area expands, he becomes convinced it's not true that anything can be ruined. No human will ever extinguish the stars. How unutterably tiny the greatest tyrant is. What's now disappearing beneath his moving hand is merely a picture.

Réginald is delighted by the blank wall. It's still damaged, but it has a coat of white primer.

'I haven't got round to the filler yet,' says Alphonse.

'Nice,' says Réginald, in English. 'Super.'

He puts his keys on the counter separating the kitchen from the living room. Without taking off his coat, he pours himself an abbey beer.

'Like one?'

Alphonse nods and carries on clearing up.

'Every evening nowadays I walk straight from the car to the beer. I know that's something you should watch for.' He switches unexpectedly to English again: 'But I need a drink when I get home from work. I really do.'

Not love, then, but work. Is there more to come? Not yet. He explains what he'll do the following day. Réginald nods, frowning, not listening.

The level crossing is open. If the car in front hadn't delayed him, he'd have driven across without looking. Now, just before moving off, he catches sight of two lilac anoraks amid the foliage. Two girls are standing on the grass next to the tracks. He even thinks he might know them. Not until he's on the other side does unease take hold.

As he begins to turn the car, the crossing signal startles him. The flashing red light takes over from the white and the barriers come down. He grips the wheel and slaloms between them as quickly as he can. For a second he has the sense he can feel the train, through the rails, through the tyres, through the accelerator. A train driver once told him that stopping in time is impossible, all you'll achieve is a derailment, braking too hard can even split a train in half. You're too fast and too heavy to save anyone's life.

Alphonse unbuckles his seat belt and dives out of the car. 'Hey!' he shouts. 'Hey! Hey!' In emergency situations you do little more than bark. His voice is inaudible above the train, which thunders past.

They're still there. They're still there. They're not going to jump. They've pulled up their anoraks and are showing their young breasts to the passengers. The wind from the passing train tugs at their hair. Not many people are looking; most are hidden behind screens or newspapers. Of the few faces turned toward the windows, most look disturbed by his presence.

Mila is the first to see him. She yanks her coat down suddenly, followed by Lana. Their hair stops frolicking. The train grows smaller and quieter in the distance.

'What are you doing here?' she shouts, angry.

He too raises his voice. 'What am I doing here? I thought you were going to jump!'

Their nervous giggling calms him a little.

'Did you come by bicycle?'

They nod.

'Then cycle home.' He goes ahead of them, to the road. They don't hesitate. The driver of a passing car lowers his head and shoots a little suspicion their way from the corner of his eye.

'How's it going with Björn?' Mila asks.

'Oh, very well. And at home? How are things there?'

They glance at each other.

'Don't take this the wrong way, but it's not really any of your business,' says Mila.

Lana takes a step backward, all her attention on the road and her shoes.

'Sorry,' he says. 'I was worried. Bye, then.'

From behind the wheel he watches them cycle off. Just as he's about to start the engine, a car stops next to his. It's the author, a tense smile on her lips. She's come from the opposite direction, so they open their windows close to each other. He catches himself thinking they ought to be on horseback. He asks how she's doing.

'As you can see,' she says nervously. 'Not writing.'

'Where are you driving to?'

'No idea. I'm just driving around. Almost every day, really.'

'It'll come.'

'Yes. It will.' She drums on the wheel with two fingers, then abruptly stops. 'And? How about you?'

'Good.' He nods, smiles. 'I'll be off to dinner, then.'

'Yes. Me too. See you.' She says it quickly, then drives away without looking back. He has to turn the car, cross the railway line again. For a while he has no choice but to drive behind her.

He'll be off to dinner, then.

While he's shaking the mussels and she's opening a bottle of wine, he asks Cat: does he interfere too much with people?

'Did someone say that?'

'More or less.'

In her view his way of dealing with people comes down to: they demand his attention, his time, and all the rescuing he can afford and not afford to do, and after they've dumped their crap all over him, once he knows what a plight they're in or how small-minded they are, they call him meddlesome. 'People often confuse the exceptional things in a person's behaviour with their "true nature". If some disgusting member of the human species shows the slightest sign of empathy, most observers will decide that deep down they must have a big heart. But if someone who's spent a lifetime doing their best to help others makes what's taken to be a mistake, then all their virtue and generosity were nothing but a thin civilized layer that we can all enjoy seeing stripped away.'

He's just put the mussels on the table and she's just poured the wine when his telephone hums.

'Don't answer it,' she says. 'Eat.'

'Sorry.' It's a number he doesn't know.

'Hello? Alphonse?' says a little girl's voice.

'Mila?'

'No, Lana. I don't want to disturb you.'

'Tell me.'

Cat uses a mussel shell to empty another with a venomous tug.

'You know my mother a little bit, don't you?' He can tell from her voice that it's taken a lot of courage for her to ring him. Her giggle has nothing to do with pleasure.

'A little bit.'

'Maybe you could call her?' Again that nervous laugh.

'Are you worried about her?'

'Yes. Very.'

'Where are you now?'

'With my father and Peter.'

'Is everything all right there?'

'Yes, it's fine here. But my mother's alone at home and sometimes I think that she—I don't know, she's bought a cot—there's one of those campaign spots on TV about how you have to talk to people about their problems—she sometimes talks to herself, she once said that you listen when she tells you something and I try to listen too, but ... '

'You don't have to do that,' he says. 'Not in that way. Have you spoken to your father about this?'

'No.' She swallows. 'It makes him angry when she acts like that.'

'I'll ring her.'

'Okay, thanks,' she laughs. 'And sorry about what Mila said.'

He can see her braces in front of him. 'That doesn't matter. Bon appétit.'

'Bon appétit?'

'If you're about to have dinner.'

'No.' Another giggle. 'Don't forget to ring my mother, okay?'

'I promise. Bye.'

'Bye.'

'Don't do it,' says Cat.

'What?'

'Phone young girls. Just don't.'

'She rang me. She wants me to ring her mother. She's worried.'

'All very understandable, but a confidential relationship between a child and an unrelated adult—that's been out of bounds for almost twenty years. I'm just telling you how it is. Supposing someone checks her phone and finds your number. It's suspicious.'

'This country isn't that sick yet.'

Cat lets a significant silence fall.

The national trauma that's crept into their conversation is neutralized by a national custom. Have they eaten mussels yet this year? Are they big or small? Tasty or not? They decide with a synchronized grin: 'They're good.'

Sieglinde's voice tells him she's not there at the moment but will ring back as soon as possible. Should he drive to her house? No.

Cat leaves for her yoga class, her aversion to groups having apparently abated. He Skypes his mother. Someone he doesn't know is standing next to her with a baby in her arms. After a while she leaves. His mother talks about distant relatives. Some of the names don't bring any faces to mind. There are problems with the water supply in Dakar, there's Ebola, bowls of diluted bleach. She asks after Cat and her parents, clicks her tongue at his report about Saturday night. Some people don't know how to ask for love, is her conclusion. And Aline, how are things with her? The hesitation that's so unusual in his mother doesn't escape him. She says Aline is fine, but that she sometimes has strange dreams, and so on.

'About me?'

'Yes.'

'There's no need for that.'

'I hope not.'

'And does that voice of hers still have so much to say?'

'Yes.'

'Maybe she ought to talk to someone.'

'She talks to me.'

'A psychiatrist, I mean.'

His mother plays with her rings, frowning. The moment

she looks up at him again the picture freezes; it breaks up into hundreds of tiny squares, so that he can no longer read her face. The sound is distorted as well. 'Aline' he catches, and 'contact'. Then the connection is broken. They both hate it when technological failure determines their final word to each other. He calls her on his mobile. To keep the costs down they don't continue their conversation, just say their goodbyes and see you soons.

He misses her after hanging up, and a drawer is opened inside him in which all the previous times he's missed her lie sleeping. Even if their love always outshone it, the missing was there, and it flies at his throat now because it's been more than two years since he hugged her. When winter takes hold of Europe he'll go, for a fortnight, three weeks. December is close now, he hasn't taken on any work for that period, he must make haste and buy tickets.

On the internet he gets caught up in the latest episode of *Journal Rappé*, the news in rap, every evening after the normal news on Senegalese television. He loves this programme. Senegal has discovered Belgian singer Stromae, it turns out. In a parody of his hit 'Formidable', they make fun of the former president's son. Small world. Björn follows him everywhere he goes, falling exhausted at his feet when he finally sits down. Alphonse leafs through the newspaper, wrestles with the letters until they stay in their places because he wants to read an article about a Chinese man called Chen Si, who has single-handedly prevented two hundred and seventy-eight suicides. He couldn't bear to watch any longer, all those desperate people he saw from his little shop at the foot of the bridge over the Yangtze in Nanjing. Every free weekend he waits on the bridge. He recognizes them instantly and urges them to get on the back of his scooter. The times when he reaches them too late, he looks away. He used to put them up at his house—it drove his wife crazy—but now he rents an apartment and goes there every evening with a meal. He gives them something alcoholic to drink and listens.

Alphonse cuts the article out of the paper and sticks it up on the wall of the room with four bits of Blu-Tack, above the place where the musical instruments laze. He decides he's going to cover a wall with heroes like this one, his heroes. He secures the shoulder strap of his bass and thinks of his mother, and of Chen Si. It's an evening for bass, for the basics.

5

Driving past a row of swaying plane trees, on the way to Réginald's house, he thinks of a passage from Job. Germaine has called back to life those strange intermezzos. In one of his outbursts of anger, Job is unable to understand how an almighty God could have it in for something as vulnerable as a human being, who, his life already fleeting as a shadow, withers as quickly as a flower. Then he says by way of contrast something crazy about trees, something along the lines of 'there is hope for a tree'; a tree can still sprout when it's old, rotten and cut down; it's never too late for twigs, for leaves. Alphonse remembers his impatient teenage protest: that wasn't even true! As if there were no dead trees, no parquet floors, tables, and chairs. He's changed his mind since then. In Senegal centuries-old baobabs have looked down on him patiently, and with Cat five years ago—after months of disagreement about a travel destination and a blind finger on a map of the world—he visited the primal forest of Białowieża, the oldest lowland forest in Europe, largely inaccessible, which straddles the border between Poland and White Russia. With no trouble at all, they made him aware of his insignificance, the trees did, every year seeming to die and then regain life. Through their growth rings they showed him how accommodating they are. He's learned to respect wood, the way it smells and feels, the way it takes a nail without splitting, courts the file, settles with a creak.

Before he knows it, his thoughts have leaped from the branches to the street, running into the city and the past, to Evy. Their friendship petered out after she moved to Berlin. With a deadpan look on her face, his blonde, mouse-like companion expressed concern about her new girlfriend, a woman who hugged trees without even being discreet about it. It was a serialized story that culminated in Evy ending the affair when her lover started knitting sweaters for the tree trunks. The yarnbombing tree hugger kept coming up in their conversations. He smiles dreamily again at today. As long as he doesn't feel the urge to clothe them, he'll give his love of trees free rein. He'd like to see her again, Evy. All those people who disappear before they die.

He sees a sign at the side of the road and stops to read the painted words. OPT FOR A QUICK, REALISTIC PATH it says, with 'realistic' in frivolous handwriting. There must be a context.

'That's the one,' says Réginald, in another brief snatch of English. 'A company in Chicago paid five million euro for it.'

They both look out through a window that gives onto a mown field. In the distance is a tall mast with several satellite dishes attached. Still higher and further off a cloud is evaporating.

'And those dishes send microwaves that regulate data transmission for stock markets in Frankfurt and London. Computers deal in shares between themselves now, so it's all about fractions of a second and I can talk about it but frankly I don't understand it, do you?'

Alphonse shakes his head. 'My microwave's staying

right out of all that for the time being.'

Réginald laughs in surprise. 'My grandmother took hers to a recycling centre. She's ninety-five and she doesn't have dementia or anything, she simply never trusted the thing and she thinks the mast has proven her right. The rest of the family just more or less ignore it.'

This is a cheerful man, thinks Alphonse. The dip he came home with yesterday was nothing more than fleeting tiredness and stress.

'In that sense she has form. For years she used to answer the phone in a deep male voice. She said it was to scare away a "whisperer". She claimed that was something like a heavy breather. He was stalking her. In the end it turned out that someone had been trying to send her a fax.' They laugh together and can't immediately seem to stop. Giggling, Réginald leaves for work.

Alphonse stands staring at the mast. You don't need to be a centenarian to feel distrustful of it. He once saw an interview in which a stockbroker admitted he'd left his job when he realized his colleagues had no better idea than he did what the numbers actually meant that they saw on their screens every morning. It seems to him perfectly possible that everything has speeded up so much that no one any longer knows what's going on. They're just keeping up the pretence. Seeing an American company buy a rusting television mast in the Westhoek to serve a runaway computer programme is not reassuring.

Several layers of filler will be required. He fills the first hole with the first of them, scraping it off a broad knife with a narrower blade and smearing it over the hole with a firm hand. He's put the radio on and, fifteen fillings further, defying the drizzle that's soaking the stubble outside in mud, defying the hundreds of tiny tears that run down the window and the chill between the walls of this inhospitable house, Billy Stewart's 'Summertime' pours in. It's the best version of Gershwin's number, the best of many. Not quite thirty-three, Billy was, when he died in an accident, plunging into a river with several members of his band, and even before that the wrong image: grossly overweight and too many gold teeth. But this is him. As soon as he hears the brrrruck-chuck-chucka-chuck-chuck at the start, Alphonse lays his filling knife on a sheet of newspaper and turns the radio up. Huh! His head nods with conviction, his hips insist. He doesn't try to stop them, knowing it would be senseless with this number, which is coming on racing thunderclouds. The drums and trumpets challenge him to spread his arms, to extend. Show how far, they say, show how many. His chest catches a ball in slow motion. 'Until that morning, there's nothing gonna harm you,' the singer hushes, not wishing it but knowing for sure. Alphonse rocks now, his knees rocking him from the floor to the ceiling. He glides around his axis, legs ahead of him, taking him out in front, stamping on the spot. He dances close to the ground, the way the Jola who begot him dance, then with arms and legs at the same time, as he would to Mbalakh, as if trying to throw his limbs from his body. The sky belongs to him, he belongs to the sky, they pull and push and cut each other into strips that immediately grow together again and carry on moving. And just as he's danced himself warm: that feigned manoeuvre, that unashamed, theatrical slowing, the long hush, pretty baby with raised eyebrows, rising to a new frowned brr-chuck-chuck and the thunder bursting at full force, Billy Stewart, who goes crazy without missing a beat, inviting you to roar inaudibly along with him, below the lightning, between the tornados. Alphonse turns round and round, the muscles in his arms demand it; he does a handstand, comes down into a bridge position, jumps up with burning feet. 'Huh! Little darling do not let a tear fall-e from-e your eye,' Billy Stewart finishes, with an Italian accent for the sake of the rhythm, and the bow of a conjurer before disappearing in a puff of smoke.

He turns off the radio to keep hold of the feeling, breathing with a quick heart. He's hurt his back a little. He growls and laughs at himself, amplified by the silence. Does everyone dance like that sometimes, breaking loose in complete solitude? Even the most fearful, the most bitter? It would be an enjoyable secret. With the sleeve of his overalls he wipes the sweat from his face. Right, then. Filler.

Again Réginald looks whacked out when he gets home, and again Alphonse allows himself to be poured a strong beer. He explains what he's done with the wall and what he's planning to do, but clearly his client isn't listening. The taste of the beer must surely escape him as well: something is going on in his head that demands his attention. Alphonse doesn't want to interfere without being asked. The lighted fog always comes by itself. The other will speak.

'Do you have a few minutes?' Réginald asks.

Alphonse nods and then says 'Yes' out loud, because Réginald isn't looking.

'A few years ago something strange happened to me,' his client begins. 'I'd been through a difficult time. The love of my life had left me and people in my family kept dying. I reached stages of grief I'd known little about up to then. Foetal position. Snot and tears. Too much drink. The world seemed to be turning against me, intent only on damaging me even more deeply, and the past too appeared in a different, unpleasant light. All the grief I'd ever felt turned out to be unprocessed and did hellish things to me. There was only one possible conclusion: my life was a failure. I told myself I must stay alive because I couldn't end it and put my parents through that. So with a huge effort I threw myself into sport and fresh vegetables. Sometimes I forced myself to sing. Help me, I kept thinking. A year later it happened, totally unexpectedly. It was a moment of complete bliss, one morning, walking past the snow-covered fields under a clear blue winter sky. There was no apparent reason why happiness should come over me with full intensity at that moment, but suddenly I had the unmistakable feeling that I'd survived something. It was accompanied by a great sense of satisfaction with myself, almost like falling in love, a love for myself that convinced me it would be there for good. I did wonder whether it might have something to do with loneliness after all, the fact that I suddenly loved myself so much, whether I really was the one for me.' He laughs. 'But since then, something essential has changed. I think. Everything that was to happen from now on was okay. I put my hand on my heart and knew: with me everything will be all right.'

After he casts a sidelong glance at Alphonse, his smile takes on an apologetic look.

'I'll get to the point,' he says.

'Tell the whole story.'

'So I thought ... or rather I think I've been happy since then. Not that I'm never sad or angry any longer, but fundamentally everything's been good, since that time. And it's not just self-love, it's love for everything and everyone. Anyway. I've simply become glad to be alive, I think. But there are people ... There's someone, a colleague at work, a relative, too, a cousin who—I don't know how to put it, it sounds really idiotic—who deliberately gets in my way. More than that. For a long time I thought: okay, so he's not on my side, you probably can't expect everyone to be. But he has it in for me. He bullies me in fact. That's what it comes down to. And the others at work and in our family don't see it. My father doesn't like him, I believe, but I don't think anyone sees what I see: that he's driven, a leader, but also a wimp. Although that's a word I apply to it in retrospect, I'd once have said vulnerable. He's my cousin, understand? My own flesh and blood. That means nothing, apparently. I've always noticed his destructiveness and for a long time I thought it hurt him more than anyone. I think that's why I wanted to protect him, or why I nevertheless ... made myself available to him. And I liked him, I thought we had something in common, something besides work and family. Is that what made him so furious with me, the fact that I saw what was wrong with him and still wanted to be his friend? Or have I really done something that I've no idea of? In any case, I've never deliberately harmed him or got in his way. Quite the opposite. And now he keeps acting as if nothing's wrong but, well, he bullies me. Here and there he puts lies about, spreads stories about me, I get to hear about them in dribs and drabs. At work he makes sure the most important jobs are never passed on to me. This isn't paranoia; I don't talk to anyone about it because it might look like that, like paranoia. Maybe you think ... '

'I believe you,' says Alphonse. He knows this story.

Réginald nods, grateful. 'There's more. There are things I won't even tell you because I'm embarrassed, which is ridiculous in itself. If someone keeps attacking you head-on for no reason and spares no time or effort in doing so, then—basically happy or not, that's the worst of it!—you start to think that maybe there's something about you that makes another person want to knock the living daylights out of you, something you yourself can't see. I've never said I'm perfect or always do the right thing, or always know what it is, the right thing. I've never said that or tried to believe it.'

'How does it go from here?' asks Alphonse. The brightening fog seems to force its way into his head. He doesn't know if that's what he wants, but it makes him curious.

'What do you mean?' Réginald has lost track for a moment.

'What have you done about it? What are you going to do about it?'

'I don't know! That's precisely it. I've no idea what to do. How to stop this. I just want it to stop. I told myself for a long time that none of this could harm me because I'm strong enough. But there's no such thing as strong enough. There's no correct approach, no question of ignoring or accepting the fact that someone's out to get you, because it doesn't depend on you. So what's left? Passively waiting in the hope he'll get sick of it? Hoping he's not replaced by someone who has equally bad intentions? Because it's not just about him, it's the idea that you might become someone's prey at any moment, that your mental and physical powers can do very little about it.'

'No.' Alphonse says resolutely. He can see that the man is hanging on his every word and he's confident of his answer. 'You mustn't wait. You have to get as far away from him as possible. Take a new job. Move house if need be.' That's what he's done. That's one reason why he's living among these open fields. Cat wants to leave, she's healthy now and her parents can grow old by themselves as far as she's concerned. But here he is free.

Réginald's disappointment is impossible to ignore. 'That's what you advise me to do? Flee? Let myself be chased away?'

'You mustn't see it like that,' says Alphonse. 'You must choose happiness. You can have that somewhere else.'

'I've got a great job that I worked hard to get. I've just bought a house. An ugly house, true, but it's mine. I'm not going to give all that up because somebody wants me to.'

'What he wants you to do is to stick around.'

'You think so?'

'Yes.'

The bright mist has become more fluid. Waves have developed. This is doubt, Alphonse realizes, and not just Réginald's. Yet he thinks he knows what he's talking about. 'He needs you. Not in a way that's good for you in any sense, not at all. That's why you have to leave.'

'But it's not just that I don't want to leave, I can't. This isn't the time anyhow, with the crisis.'

'Go self-employed,' says Alphonse, with little conviction. He knows this isn't a good time to set up a business; it's a wonder he's managed it.

'I don't feel like doing that at all.'

'Okay.' Even though this is a familiar situation, Réginald is a different person from him, he mustn't forget that. There's a place on his back he can't reach that's itching more and more intrusively. He no longer knows what to advise. So he says so.

'I think I'll have to stand up to him,' says Réginald. 'Confront him with what he's doing. Tell him what I think of him and not spare him when I do.'

'No.' Matthieu de Schaepmeester looms up before Alphonse. The glistening nostrils of his classmate, the pain that descended like the dust descending over the children as they watched. The common predator that he, Alphonse Badji, has never been since. 'Don't do it,' he says. 'Don't avenge an attack with an attack. It'll never stop.'

'It's not as simple as you seem to think,' says Réginald angrily. 'If I don't, it'll never stop either.'

'But at least you won't have become a perpetrator. You mustn't let him turn you into one. You mustn't stoop so low. It would be a defeat. For you.'

Réginald folds his arms across his chest and looks him straight in the eye. Alphonse doesn't look away, aware that his truth needs to make an effort to stand firm. Minutes seem to pass before anyone speaks.

'I recently heard a historian on the radio,' Réginald says, much calmer now. 'She was talking about the First World War, which is often described as a senseless war, an opinion that she, from the Belgian perspective, refused to endorse. She asked a question. If you decide to stay neutral, and the aggressor tramples on you as a result—not just a little, but with the greatest brutality imaginable—what do you do? Watch your loved ones being slaughtered? Die a pacifist? Isn't there anything to be said for self-preservation?'

'Yes. But you can leave. Many people flee wars for that reason. And you're not in a war.' His thoughts flutter restlessly over the *tirailleurs sénégalais* and what the senselessness meant for them. Afterwards the *tirailleurs* weren't given what was promised. The war nourished an emancipation movement. The Afghans. What day is it today? Tuesday. He agreed with Brigitte to go on Wednesday, tomorrow. What time is it now? He must listen to this no matter what.

'I can keep deciding to ignore it, because you're often told, aren't you, that it's your attention people like that want and that's what you need to deny them. Which is why you say nothing, because of course the people who like you and the value that's placed on your work more than make up for it all. You even keep quiet out of sympathy, because you can also hear the sadness of your attacker, because loneliness creates a bond. You keep quiet because it's obvious that you love life more than the aggressor does, because you're glad you're not him. But you also stay silent the way raped little boys do, or women with broken jaws who've fallen down those treacherous stairs for the thirtieth time. And you wonder, too, whether you're the only one who provokes such attacks, whether there's something in you that makes people think: I'm going to hit this. I have to tell you that even without your approval I won't keep silent any more, and that I'll stay right where I am,' says Réginald, no longer angry. 'Because not everyone can flee and no one can every time.'

Alphonse rubs crumbs of filler off his fingers. 'That's true,' he says. 'So you do know what you have to do.'

'Seems so!' Réginald exclaims, moved.

He likes this man, continues to like him. 'Do you play an instrument?' The question slips out.

Réginald laughs in confusion. 'No. Why?'

'Nothing. I thought for a moment: we'll start a band.' They're laughing together now. Astonishing that he said that. 'I'll see you tomorrow?'

'Yes.'

'For the finishing touches I'll need another half-day.'

He takes more with him than usual after closing the front door. Why did he start talking about a band? Is that what he wants? To play with other people again? Further questions potter around him. If he hadn't turned against the unfortunate Matthieu de Schaepmeester more than a quarter of a century ago, would the torment have continued? For how long? Did he successfully opt for self-preservation, preventing anything worse? The mast and its microwaves don't know either.

Apart from the confusion, he feels content. The voices on the radio fail to reach him. Strange that it's still so light outside. Réginald must have come home earlier than expected and Alphonse stopped working sooner as a result. The sun breaks through the clouds; the sky under the clouds turns a dull gold, turbid. Desert sand?

He slows down at a junction, not immediately sure of the way. The radio gets through to him with a song that opens a calyx in his chest. 'Crazy Love, Vol. II', from Paul Simon's *Graceland*, the first record he ever bought, a purchase that caused a big row with Amadou, who thought Paul Simon ought to have respected the boycott against South Africa. Alphonse always defended the album just as fiercely, saying it showed that music transcends politics, something that he thinks has been proven true. Although their argument was sincere, they both enjoyed fighting out their difference of opinion in public, in Dutch, simmering in their supposed superiority, surrounded by thirteen-year-old classmates who acted as if they weren't listening because they couldn't join in.

Only now does he realize that the track is also about him and Fabrice. About the ever-present possibility that someone will walk into the room to say that your life is on fire. He sees the passion behind the damage, the hunger behind the hatred, the feeble-minded demand for love. He did well to stay out of Fabrice's way, he's certain of that now. He's succeeded in escaping him. But Cat's right: it's time to move somewhere else. It's over.

The track is over too. He's just turned off the radio and started the engine when something falls out of the sky. It comes straight toward him. In an attempt to evade it he decides to take a left turn, but it's already there. With a dull thud it lands on the bonnet, a ball of rumpled brown feathers that scrabbles upright, a small black eye turned toward him. The skylark. The same one, Alphonse believes.

Not wanting to frighten it away, he stays sitting there. He's taken his foot off the accelerator. The bird hops across the bonnet, forward, backward, backward, right, left, right. Almost October. If this isn't one that over-winters here, he'll leave in a few days. Has he come to say goodbye?

It's a fairly inconspicuous, beautiful bird. His quiff and the marks around his eyes make him look a bit like a thief in a cartoon film. Alphonse sees that he's singing and only then hears the song, muffled by the windscreen. It no longer sounds spiritedly joyful, more hounded, desperate. Or no, it still has the old vibrancy: small bird full of life. The bird flies off and Alphonse starts the car immediately, driving away without looking back.

Amadou rings him in the evening. After some vague grousing about relationships, the word 'sick' follows, then 'space', 'distance', and 'time', until Alphonse realizes what he's saying and proposes he spend a few days with them on his own. His friend says he'll think about it; Saturday evening perhaps. Alphonse knows he'll be there, on Saturday, and tells him to bring his guitar. When Björn barks, Amadou asks: 'A dog?'

'No,' says Alphonse. 'That was Cat.' Otherwise he won't dare come; his friend is afraid of dogs.

He lies with his arms folded under his head, staring at the ceiling. The haloes from the bedside lamps form two circles on it, and a Venn diagram. Cat's head creeps along his bicep to his cheek. She barks in his ear like a chihuahua until he turns to face her.

'What are you thinking about?'

'I don't know.' It's true. He seemed to be on the track of something today, but now he's lost the thread. Cat doesn't persist in asking. Only when he hears her snoring gently does he realize she's asleep. The circles and their Venn diagram remain empty.

4

'What's this?' he hears Cat ask from his music room.

Although Björn is slinking guiltily away, her ironic indignation has nothing to do with him. Hand on hip, she's reading the article about Chen Si.

'Why did you put this up here?'

'I'm making a wall of heroes. I've got one so far.' He buttons his overalls.

Laughing, she touches his forehead, cheeks, neck: a quick and peculiar gesture. 'Why?'

'I just am.'

She reads on, then says, her eyes still on the article: 'No doubt he meant well, but those people don't want to be saved, do they. He's turning them into the ultimate failures. Not even able to kill themselves!'

'Most people who survive a suicide attempt are glad they did.'

'Says who?'

'That's what I read, in the paper.'

'I don't believe it. That they're glad of it, I mean. Newspaper articles like that are just propaganda for life.'

'Propaganda for life! Listen to what you're saying!'

She looks at him, hurt. 'Newspapers aren't allowed to write about how bad things are. They're not allowed to publish statistics about how many people jump in front of trains every year because then there'd be even more successes of that kind. And I reckon the total number of suicides is higher than we're told.'

'That doesn't have anything to do with him.'

From behind his sunglasses, Chen Si stares out of the photograph. On the bridge over the Yangtze, cars race past. He sports a white cap on his round head. The shoulder strap of his bag crosses his plump body, which is clad in a red jersey. In his right hand he holds what might be a bunch of keys.

'Yes it does. The article is about how he's had less work in recent years. "Less despair, more good people than you think." That ought to be the headline. That's the message.'

'And it's not true, you say?'

'Of course not. More violence gets suppressed than in previous centuries, but it hasn't gone away. In fact with population growth the quantity has increased enormously. That's how things are. I'm being realistic.'

The casual way pessimists claim exclusive rights to reality annoys him. In a sudden flash, though, the way she's standing there seizes all his attention, as if he can see more air around her than usual. Her separateness from the room forces itself into his consciousness. For too long he's failed to notice how often she's alone here. It strikes him now. He squeezes her to him. 'We're leaving this place,' he says. 'We're going wherever you like. I forget your loneliness sometimes.'

She pushes him away. 'Don't patronize me! This isn't about my loneliness. For God's sake.' She steps away and goes downstairs.

'What?' He follows her, his hands spread out before him. 'I love you, that's what I mean!'

'Then just say so. Loneliness! Terrible! You think you're immune to it?'

They stride across the kitchen, where Björn, disturbed by their argument, almost trips each of them up in turn. Cat whips round to face Alphonse. 'Don't confuse me with your clients! You're not an angel. You're not Jesus! Jesus probably never had an affair! And I don't think porn ever got written for him either, nor that he hid it from his wife.'

He throws back his head, roaring with laughter; he can't help it. An image of Jesus as a secret sex addict looms before him.

They go back upstairs—she takes something from the bathroom, doesn't smile—and then down again.

'You're my man. And I admire you for the zest for life that's given you that glow you've been walking around with, for reasons that completely escape me, for the past year, I think I even love you all the more for it, but what I say isn't any less valid. I'm not any less valid!'

'I never said you were.' It's as if he's trying to worm his feet into shoes that are too small.

'You need me just like I need you.'

'I know that.'

He pulls the door shut behind him so hard that the glass in the little windows rattles. Two houses away a curtain moves. He starts the car with a pang in his chest. At the end of the street he turns round. To the disabled boy in the front garden it's all one and the same. 'Hi scallywag!' he sees him call.

She's sitting on the doorstep. She knew he'd come back.

He removes the key from the ignition and gets out. 'This is ridiculous. I just wanted to hug you and say that I love you.' Now she'll stand there and sulk and tell him to go ahead, then. The whole idea of a relationship suddenly exhausts him immensely. Quarrels and divorces are something for an earlier generation, however, for their parents, something they'll rise above—it's a rule they've thought up together, which they've never put into words. And he knows he can't escape her. What Réginald said comes to mind. Not everyone can flee and no one can every time. She already has him in her arms. She him. He relaxes.

Réginald has considered asking this rainbow man, this Alphonse, to do more work in the house, but the expense deters him. He's got his phone number, of course, but who calls a handyman for a conversation? Would that ever have happened to Alphonse? If he played a musical instrument, the painter and decorator could have become a friend rather than disappearing from his life after this wall. Now all he's got is a chance to leave a good impression, not to say anything about the dream he's just had in which, in front of a classroom full of colleagues and relatives, he wrote a text on the blackboard that screamed out his emotions, his refusal to be a victim. He'll say nothing about his sense of being liberated in the dream or about how, when he woke, to bolster that sense of freedom, he poured the text into an email and sent it to everyone, at four in the morning, and was then immediately cast into a chasm of regret. He mustn't talk about that, because this man, this Alphonse, won't stick around to protect him, the mist he spreads is there for only a short time. Réginald must look after himself, restore the love that he felt for himself for so long. He wants to hold on to the respect the man showed him. He must say nothing about what's tearing him apart and stop coming up with words and phrases in English, too, which is just silly.

'I did something stupid,' says Réginald, in English.

Alphonse puts down the bucket he's lugged in and looks at his client. 'What did you do?'

Although he refuses to show Alphonse the email, he

tells him what was in it, the things that he put rather well and the things that he shouldn't have said. It was in no way relevant, for example, to mention his adversary's tendency to talk too much, nor his appearance, his paunch and moustache. He bares all to Alphonse, the pain of retribution, telling him that's what it was: retribution. He describes what was justified, what unjustified, the doubt that took hold, the fear of moving among those who know, in whose faces he's rubbed his wound, exposing it to their salt.

As is always the case with this kind of listening, there is no Alphonse, he's erased himself, becoming a hand on a back, a grunt of assent, an ear that waits until nothing more comes save a distracted: 'I have to go to work.'

'You can call me,' he says. 'Tonight, or any other time.'

Réginald wipes the moisture from his face and thanks him.

In the afternoon Alphonse crosses the border under lingering clouds. French DIY shops have a broader assortment and the materials are cheaper. He parks his van between other vehicles in the large car park outside the Leroy Merlin in Villeneuve d'Ascq. The doors have just slid open in front of him when he hears his phone. On the way to the *Peinture et Droguerie* department, he puts it to his ear.

Lana, in a barrage of fragmented reproaches and acute panic. 'She's breathing,' he catches and he turns on his heels and dashes back out through the door. In the car park a woman with a handbag clamped under one arm runs away from him between the cars. He powers out of the parking spot in reverse, dragging disapproving looks behind him like tin cans behind a newly-weds' car. He races along the roads, narrower and narrower lanes with more and more bends. He calls Lana, tells her to stay on the line, to talk to him, can't understand what she's saying. He didn't ring Sieglinde again after that failed attempt, even though her daughter asked him so insistently. He's fallen short. He must get there in time.

The district is daydreaming, has no idea. His car rips the peace apart. A raised head over a fence, someone with a wheelbarrow on a drive who takes a step back, the right house. He rings the bell and sees a light on next door in what must, he thinks, be Dieter's study. Then Lana is standing in front of him, with a face that, swollen by tears, seems far too big for her slight body. 'This way!'

The first thing he notices is the smell of faeces, the dark puddle. All he can think is that this is something that must not happen, certainly not with a child around. The little dog Happy whines behind a door.

'Have you called an ambulance?' The firmness of his voice surprises him.

She shakes her head and goes on shaking it. 'I haven't even rung Mila,' she says. 'Not even my father. I didn't want them to see her like this. She must have taken something; there's no blood.'

He's already sitting next to the body. He feels Sieglinde's throat, her wrist, there's a heartbeat but it's clear that she's further away than a dream. She's not wearing her glasses. The flashing lights have swivelled round to the inside of her head. He parts her lips, wrenches her teeth wide, ignores the 'What are you doing? What are you doing?' from the girl, puts his fingers as deep into her throat as he can. There's no spasm, no wave of vomit.

On the fridge is a Post-It with 'Sorry Lana.' She points it out to him, bawling, a suggestion of negligence in the absence of any further elucidation. He imagines an ambulance winding along the narrow lanes to get here.

'Come on,' he says. 'We're going to save her.'

He picks up Sieglinde and wraps her in a blanket he finds on the sofa. By issuing precise orders he manages to stir Lana's courage and determination. The closing front door silences Happy's high barking. Alphonse lays the woman on his own blankets in the back of the van. The girl takes a seat next to him in the front. This mustn't go wrong.

'Call your father,' he instructs her.

'Who's driving you?' he hears the man ask several times with rising unease.

'Alphonse,' she keeps replying. Followed by: 'The man who did our decorating?' Then, still capable of embarrassment: 'The black guy?'

'He's coming,' she says as she puts her phone away. Then she sits staring straight ahead, lips pressed together.

The turning leaves in the crowns of the trees beside the road are sharply outlined against a bright white sky. It's probably asking too much for a foetus to survive a suicide attempt, thinks Alphonse. If it's true. He can't talk to the girl about that. What should he do? Keep her talking?

'How are you feeling?' he asks.

'How do you think?' Her cheeks and forehead go red, a reproach catches in her throat.

On a long, straight road she asks him, snivelling, for a tissue. He curses himself for not having one on him.

At last they arrive at the hospital's casualty department, for the third time this month in his case. He climbs into the back of the van to pull Sieglinde onto his lap, then carefully shuffles out with her and carries her to the entrance. He follows people who stand up, arms that point the way, answering questions with 'I don't know,' laying Sieglinde on the bed that's been rolled toward him, then following the bed, making sure Lana is following too. He'd like to bump into Brigitte and he asks a nurse for her.

He holds the girl's arm tight. The bed is rolled away from them and they take their places on a plastic bench, waiting for her father. The stupefying heat that hangs in the corridor, along with a smell of canteen, the squeak of training shoes and the castors of drip stands on linoleum, laughter-sprinkled voices from an office—it's barely enough to drown out their silence.

At last Ronny arrives, sweating, big-eyed, with an insulted twist to his mouth. They stand up. 'Why didn't you ring me straight away?' he asks his daughter. She doesn't answer, just stares at his shoes until her father presses her nose to his shoulder in a clumsy gesture of consolation. Her sobbing seems to take him by surprise.

'I'll leave you,' says Alphonse and, at the panic in Lana's eyes: 'You can always ring me, even tonight or whenever.'

She nods. 'Thanks.'

He wants to say it'll be all right. Except that he's not at all sure it will be.

After phoning Brigitte he finds her between two patients in the foyer on the ground floor. She enquires of colleagues about Sieglinde's condition and tells him her stomach is now being pumped. She promises to try to find out whether Sieglinde was pregnant. Walking backward, she wants to know whether they're going to the camp later. Alphonse thinks so.

Shouldn't he stay? Would the girl want that? Surely she'd ring him if she did. He calls her. 'I'll come back this evening to see how your mother's doing,' he says.

'Okay,' she says.

After a bit of hissing and crackling, Ronny's voice takes over, his pent-up anger: 'I'd rather you didn't.' After which he shuts off the call.

'What's happening?' he asks Cat when he gets home. 'What's happening to people?' She doesn't know the answer, strokes his neck, says he's done what he could and should try to get some sleep this afternoon.

Two restless hours later he asks the question again, this time of Brigitte's fearful eyes, and because this time he's not the one who knows the answer, he repeats it, wording it differently: 'What's going on?' The last stretch of road to the Afghan camp is barricaded with unmanned farm vehicles. There's no way through.

He turns off the engine. Through the front windscreen they stare at the tractors, he leaning over the wheel, she sitting upright, against the headrest. Fortunately Brigitte's husband was home to look after Hadrianus. If they had a child with them they'd have to turn back immediately.

'Come on,' he says. 'Bring your things. We're going to walk.'

She opens the car door with a brave nod. They take the medicine bag and the box of food from the back of the van and start walking, surveying the empty fields, the shut houses.

'Can you manage, in those shoes?'

'Yes, fine.' The doctor's wide heels tap on the tarmac. There's also the sound of wind through maize, the bottom of Alphonse's coat shaken by it. Wild geese fly over, loudly admiring each other's strength.

'That woman,' Brigitte says. 'You were right, she was pregnant. This afternoon she lost the child.'

True, then. He stops in the middle of the road. In his chest an immense sympathy rises.

Descending into the pit, they notice the change immediately. On the outer flank, separated from the rest as far as possible, are three tents made of tarpaulin and plastic. Next to them, unguarded and unsheltered, a second fire is burning.

Only a few familiar faces. They say hello. Two older men have joined them, but still most of the residents are in their twenties, some even younger. The boy with the smile has gone. Is he now grinning at the Thames?

'Where are the woman and the baby?' asks Brigitte.

There's an exchange of looks, a word is spoken, perhaps it's her name.

'Paris,' answers one of those they know, crossing the 'Calais' of someone else. 'She's in Paris with her family,' the first says again.

Someone shows the doctor an injured foot with crumbling toenails. She switches on her head torch and cups the heel in her plastic glove.

'We have problems here now.' Alphonse recognizes the man who says it, his eyes. With his chin he points to the separated tents. 'Syrians.' He explains that until recently this camp was the only one where Afghans could be with their own kind, but that's changed. There's been a quarrel with the new residents. For the time being they respect a boundary, but if the Syrians were to leave it would be better for everyone.

Alphonse mentions the barricade. Do they know about it?

'They try to stop the Doctors of the World. They try to stop you. They don't think we deserve any care.'

'Who?'

He laughs bitterly. 'Many, many people. You should stay home.'

'I will not be chased away,' says Alphonse.

At that moment three of the newcomers crawl out from under the tarpaulins at the other end of the trench. They settle down around their own fire, a corpulent older man with a black eye and two beautiful, hopeless young men, one a head taller than the other. Alphonse goes over to them with the box of food. Behind him the conversations in Dari fall silent. Each of the Syrians shakes his hand in turn. Only the tallest and youngest speaks English. He translates for the smaller man, who wants to tell his story and shows two photos on the screen of his smartphone. His brother-in-law. Alive. Dead. 'Bashar al-Assad.' The smaller man makes his hand into a pistol and fires it, then goes to sit on a brick next to the fire, one arm around his head, his horror still focused on the pictures.

He's known the other two only a few months, the taller one goes on. He's been on the run for a year already himself. 'Maybe this is my life?'

'I hope not,' says Alphonse. His responses are bound to be inadequate. There's only the box of food to unpack. He wishes they wouldn't thank him so profusely.

He drops Brigitte at her car in the hospital car park, then goes inside again himself. The word 'coma' didn't occur to him when he brought Sieglinde here. Only family members are allowed into the intensive care department.

Cat says he must ease off a bit. Too many emotions for one man in one day. They let Björn scrabble at the bathroom door and after a very long time he gives up. Naked, they sit next to each other on the edge of the bath, she with her feet in the water. She speaks softly to him, her skin covering his, and kisses his temples, neck, and shoulders, before sliding down through the warm steam into the heat. He follows.

I love him. She doesn't think it; it floods over her. It's a waterfall that grows wider with the years.

3

He has an appointment at a terraced house in the centre of a village. The street is busier than those of the quiet neighbourhoods he's usually called to. Children look at him from back seats and bike carriers.

He rings the doorbell twice and still no one comes. Inside none of the lights are on. He closes his eyes, which doesn't help: the image of Sieglinde's lifeless body is now projected on the inside of his eyelids, it plays wildly with his brain, making him fear that behind this front wall a family tragedy has occurred. He takes a deep breath in and out.

A sound from the other side of the street makes him turn round. He just catches sight of a gold-coloured aluminium front door falling shut. He waits. There's no further sign of life, and the same applies to his clients' house, where he's now rung the bell for the third time. He leaves a voicemail message, crosses the road, and rings at the door he saw close. Nothing. Only when he's almost at his van does the neighbour across the street open up, a pixie-like character who shouts something at him hysterically. Alphonse doesn't catch what; a scooter goes past and the man makes no effort to moderate his dialect.

'I'm sorry, but what did you say?' he asks. 'Do you know where your neighbours over there have got to?' He's walking toward the man as he speaks, so the door closes again, except for a crack. And again most of what's roared at him escapes Alphonse. 'You won't get away with it,' he does catch.

Fury slides into him like icicles pushed up his nostrils then pressed around his head in a tightening ring. He controls himself, doesn't go any closer. 'I'm not trying to break in. I have an appointment with your neighbours to paint their living room. Do you know where they are?'

'You won't get away with it,' he hears again, before the door slams shut.

Lana texts him that her mother has woken up from her coma and so far it seems there's no lasting damage. She may be moved to another ward this evening, where he'll be able to visit her.

At home he says nothing about what happened with the neighbour. He won't let an angry stranger take over Cat's day, nor his own, even though he knows the latter can be demanded point blank from him, anytime.

He rebukes himself when he realizes that if only he read his emails more often he could have saved himself this. There are two from the woman who took him on for the job. In the first she reveals, in gushing prose, that she's decided after all to put off the annual family holiday—just Provence this time—until late September, since it's the last chance to take advantage of the children not having reached school age yet; hotels and airline tickets are so much cheaper out of season. Which means to say, unfortunately, with immense apologies and an army of emoticons in the most diverse moods, that she'll have to postpone the appointment she's made with him. In the second email she expresses her concern at the lack of any response from him and hopes he's not standing at her door in vain as she writes this. Underneath she's pasted a sunny beach photo of a family made up of two adults and two toddlers, all of them red-haired, sun-reddened, and happy as pie.

He laughs about it with Cat, who has come to sit on his lap.

He doesn't want to be disturbed by the cast to her mouth when she sees the newspaper article he's stuck up next to the one about Chen Si. An extremely rich Maltese couple have invested twenty-one million euro in a ship to rescue capsized refugees from the waters of the Mediterranean. He doesn't feel like arguing about whether or not wealth and virtue are mutually exclusive, believes in the potential of individuals, kisses the back of the individual in his lap, and announces that today he'd like to cycle around the locale a bit. Does she want to come with him? No, she has a crumb-sweeper instruction booklet to translate and she's already suffering from an overdose of locale.

Because Björn frantically announces his candidacy as a companion on the outing, and anyhow it's starting to rain, Alphonse abandons the bicycle in favour of the van. On a whim he takes his kora with him.

First they stop at the deserted border post he's driven past so often, with its shops, petrol pumps, hotel, and restaurant. English Spoken Here! *Prix Belges!* shout the tobacconists and off-licenses. On a trailer, amid Eastern European trucks, rests a streamlined new yacht, packed in tight, gleaming plastic. The spotlessness of the freight is further enhanced by hasty scrawls in marker pen: 'Anvers/Baltimore, USA. Dufour 45, North Point Atlantic Compass'. This is a region of puzzling hints and huge sacks of potatoes, lost war tourists, men dressed up as moustachioed customs officials of times past, firewood, the Peace of Utrecht, chocolates sold singly, a clergyman clarinet smuggler, mud and floods, every imaginable kind of loss, the last generation of cross-frontier workers to enjoy advantageous statutes, borders belonging to open air museums, and increasingly grim boundaries between land and sea. He can scarcely believe the sky that's clearing for him today.

Drivers stare at them from the cabs of their trucks, most with Romanian or Polish number plates. A pair standing in the open air interrupt their conversation to observe the African and the dog. It's as if they're expecting a conjuring trick. The tiled buildings recently taken over by the French border police have not yet been fully renovated. THE IMPORTATION OF UNDECLARED ANIMALS MAY ATTRACT A HEFTY FINE warns a yellowed poster in a dirty window. Björn remains unmoved.

In the café, mild disapproval awaits, from several tables, soon replaced by indifference. Four elderly men are sitting at the bar, three of them drinking rosé. They're speaking a rapid, indistinct form of French. They've made purchases that were ill advised. The prices of houses and land are too high. The expression 'casser les couilles' (break their balls) is heard a number of times, and one of the three drops a 'godverdomme' (goddammit), with a French accent instead of West Flemish. If anyone asks Alphonse what he's doing here, he'll say he's watching over them. The prospect makes him pleasantly nervous. No one wants to know, however. On the radio a Dutch-speaking newsreader talks about the disasters loosed upon the world, then introduces someone from Doctors Without Borders. Her rapid, seething cry for help involves no raising of the voice but is impossible to interrupt. The woman deplores the absence of any sizeable response from the international community and describes streets in Sierra Leone and Liberia scattered with corpses, people bleeding from their eyes. Cat and he have donated money and had anxious conversations with his mother. Worse than the sickness itself, the woman goes on, is the isolation, the casual way that West Africa is being left to its fate. Infrastructure is needed, trained staff. He's overcome with emotion before he realizes it. To hide his tears from the men at the bar, he bends deeper over his coffee, then over Björn, stroking his side. Should he go out there? No doubt Cat meant something rather different with her desire to be in a city among people. After the news it's the turn of the Beach Boys: Aruba, Jamaica, Bermuda, Bahama, Key Largo, Montego; the list of destinations, like the appeal that preceded it, is probably unconnected with the fact that two of the men, with an 'Au revoir, everybody,' slip down from their bar stools and out through the door.

Alphonse eats in a restaurant a short distance away, recently taken over by a top sommelier, whose parents used to run it. It's a place where businessmen in suits settle down to a three-course lunch next to labourers in overalls, the convivial and time-consuming food culture that the Senegalese adopted from the French. He recognizes the owner from a photo in the newspaper. Now he's standing next to a table of emptied plates, talking and slowly nodding. Someone says that people used to make a living from the border, that the area died when the barriers were removed. Another argues that unification has destroyed the cultural diversity you saw here in the past. A daughter-in-law from elsewhere in the county is told how you could once tell from the type of truck driver what his load was: 'The simplest of people drove vegetables. There were distinguished-looking Danish flower carriers, and rough livestock traders with one foot in the hormone mafia but often with a sort of moral code as well. Now they're all overworked Eastern Europeans who don't have any money to spend here, nor any interest in us.' The sommelier interrupts the nostalgia, a heroic echo to his voice: 'Tourism,' he says. 'That's the future. This will be the Tuscany of the North.' Then, more doubtful: 'But this clay. It permits the crops so little refinement.' He's worked in the most prestigious restaurants of Monaco, Paris, Brussels, New York, and L.A., Alphonse has heard. He doesn't seem unhappy.

The hills and the winding roads bring him a growing contentment. The hops have been picked. He feels grateful for the way the wide landscape has never ceased to embrace him over the months. Björn too seems to be smiling more than usual. They cut through a village out of a snow globe, glowing after a peaceful night's sleep. Most of its life is concentrated in and around a care home. The front gardens are freshly trimmed, the paint on the doors and window frames might still be wet. Out in front of the home sits an elderly man with his eyes closed, slumped at his steering wheel, the radio blaring. To check he's still alive, Alphonse parks behind the car until he sits up.

After several kilometres he gets out at a Portuguese military cemetery. It's close to the Indian Memorial to the Missing and opposite a neat chapel for Our Lady of Fátima. The Portuguese resting place is immaculately tended, but with its dark graves it's reminiscent of the austere, intensely sorrowful German military cemeteries. He pushes Björn firmly back into the car after he starts to dig a hole between the stones where young, unidentifiable men rot. Time is relentlessly erasing the chiselled names of those who did get a stone. All of a sudden, Alphonse is moved by the way the dead are categorized. Even if they died alongside others from a different country, at their burial the boundaries generally remained in force. Practical and absurd.

For the occasion he believes in Portuguese ghosts, improvising a song for them on the kora, less sombre than fado but they understand all the same.

He drives past the slag heaps and through Lens, not stopping at the little Louvre of Japanese design—he was there recently—and on beyond the Bollaert stadium, where the reputation of the area was summed up damningly on a banner a few years ago by supporters of Paris Saint-Germain: PÉDOPHILES, CHÔMEURS, CONSANGUINS: BIENVENUE CHEZ LES CH'TIS. Frenchman to Frenchman. Human to human.

From Lens he drives in a semicircle to Hazebroek, a little town he's never visited before. 'Caravan' on the radio. Didn't he hear that same jazz standard recently, just as coincidentally, wasn't that in the car too? This is the version by Duke Ellington, with Charles Mingus, he believes, and Max Roach. The low piano keys give French Flanders a completely different cachet; this environment demands his whole being. His heart fills with it.

Are the bin lorries really drawn by carthorses here? Yes. The bin lorries are drawn by carthorses, followed by a long line of cars at walking pace with annoyed-looking drivers and a delivery van with a dark-skinned man who thinks it's all quite fantastic. Alphonse parks, puts Björn on the lead, and sets off.

There's a remarkable number of hairdressers and floristry shops, which contribute considerably to his cheerful mood. There's even a salon for dogs. Björn snuffles about attentively but can't see in through the window. Alphonse can: a fat poodle is hanging in a harness, looking resigned, while a woman shaves its legs.

Le Coq Flamand. Le Panier Flamand. The chicory, the gingerbread of a brand unknown in Belgium called Red Riding Hood, and potted meats in the windows. Then again St Eloy, patron saint of this region and of twenty-three trades, protector against seven diseases, and central character in a supposedly humorous story about wife-beating.

More than a thousand servicemen were buried in this little town. Not far from St Eloy's church a sundial is attached to a wall with above it the words ORTA EST LUX IN REGIONE UMBRAE MORTIS. He memorizes them.

She looks younger than before, Sieglinde, without her glasses, in pyjamas, having just escaped death. He's her only visitor. Instead of a melancholic he finds a quiet, wide-awake little person and a prevailing smell of old-fashioned soap. Now he dares to ask her.

'Are you glad you're still alive?'

She nods. 'And I didn't find it at all peaceful.'

'What?'

'The near-death experience. I've been reading about it for years, it's a bit of a hobby. Witnesses almost always talk about feelings of bliss and light and so on. Zilch, in my case. A concentrated depression, yes. Not exactly something I'm keen to experience again.'

'Good,' is all he says.

'Depression *ristretto*.'

He laughs with her a little.

'I do think it's terrible for Lana,' she goes on, serious.

'She saved you,' he says.

'I know. I'm the worst mother in the world.'

'She wouldn't have saved you if you were, I think.' He's not at all sure about that.

'In any case I'm the worst mother I know.'

He watches a recalcitrant drop of fluid fall into the reservoir under the drip and follows the tube that ends at the needle in her arm. The pills she took must have dried her out.

'The baby ... ' He doesn't know how to introduce this.

She stares at him without blinking. 'It's better this way.'

'Okay.'

His feet trapped under Björn's sleeping body, he types into Google the Latin text from above the sundial. There's something like it in the Old Testament Book of Isaiah. '*Habitantibus in regione umbrae mortis lux orta est eis.*' 'For those who dwell in the land of the shadow of death, a light has arisen.' May peace prevail in the land of florists and dog salons, he thinks, and he makes a prayer of it, which he tells no one.

2

Cat makes coffee noisily. Björn barked them out of a passionate embrace when Willem knocked and Alphonse ignored her order not to answer the door. When the coffee is ready she withdraws to the living room with a cup and a book.

'Am I intruding?' Willem asks.

'Never,' says Alphonse.

The neighbour tells him a former colleague died in a fire in a nearby village last night. 'Arson. It's not yet clear who did it.'

Although the skill of starting and controlling fire was perhaps the most important advance in all of civilization, humans still haven't managed to prevent it turning against them from time to time, thinks Alphonse. As if it lets itself get brandished around, complacently succumbs to domestication, until suddenly it's had enough and, certain of victory, brings to bear its unparalleled aptitude for chaos and destruction.

'Honestly, I didn't know what he was up to. I didn't have very much contact with him. Although I did have some. We occasionally organized a cultural outing together. I've sat at the table in that house. I didn't find him all that likeable, he was too inscrutable for that, but I think I admired him. I admired him, darn it. He was an erudite man. I didn't know, I swear I didn't.'

'What didn't you know?'

'Let's just say that over the years he made a lot of enemies in the college, among the children, the boys, who are adults now. There are plenty who might be expected to take revenge. Know what I mean?'

Alphonse nods. An insight begins to march around the kitchen table, its face still hidden, in clothing that's slipped indoors from a harsh winter.

Willem opens his arms. 'He couldn't keep his hands to himself. His trousers buttoned. His force under control.'

'I understand,' says Alphonse. What was it that Gewijde said? Something about how well thatch burns? Was he imagining that now?

'What is it?'

'No, no. I was just thinking ... I was wondering whether, in that case, it's a good thing he's dead.'

Willem is about to say something but restrains himself. Lips pursed, he brushes a few crumbs from the table into his hand. 'Not everyone will be sorry, that's for sure.' He stands up, looks around, until Alphonse points him to the bin and he scatters the crumbs in it. 'But that "dead" is in this case burnt alive,' he says. 'They found him by the back door.'

Alphonse nods.

'And he was old. Older than me. Perhaps he was sorry for what he'd done. Living with regret might have been a worse punishment than this. Right?'

Suspicions are all he has. He doesn't even know for certain whether the dead man is Father Piper. Cat comes in at the perfect moment.

'I'm going to read something out to you,' she says. 'And you have to say where it's about?' Her finger is the bookmark for a thin book, the cover of which she keeps hidden. 'The writer says it's dirtier, of course, than where he comes from, people are affected by grief and corruption, but there's so much more zest for life, even if it may actually be a kind of spirited resignation. "It is,"' she's reading now, '"the realm where mysterious and unpredictable events occur, usually of an unpleasant nature. It seems to thrive on death. A benighted world, truly, which in moments of lassitude we permit ourselves to sink down into and indulge the senses."' Grinning, she looks up. 'Which continent is he writing about?'

'Africa,' say Alphonse and Willem in chorus, but neither with much conviction; this series of stereotypes must refer to somewhere else, or why would she ask?

'It's from Henry Miller, in 1947, and he's writing about Western Europe.'

'He wrote beautifully about France,' Willem defends.

'His adulation of everything French knows no bounds. It makes him ridiculous.'

Alphonse notices that Willem is struggling not to see this as a personal attack. Is that what Cat is after?

'He was mainly sick of the United States,' Cat decides. 'But we love France too, you know. And the French, apart from that extreme right-wing twenty-five per cent. We were planning to go to Rijsel again today.'

'There's a hop festival in Poperinge,' says Willem. 'But I know you aren't really beer drinkers. With Marie-Jeanne I went every year. *Bon.*' He slaps his thigh and stands up. 'The old man's going home at last.'

With their protests and their always-welcomes they manage to elicit a boyish smile from him.

As soon as they're alone, Alphonse tells Cat of his suspicions. He thinks it's odd that he doesn't mention Gewijde's name, is nevertheless certain of her answer to the question of what he should do. 'Good riddance,' she'll say. He's heard her use that expression regularly over the past six months. But she says: 'You first need to find out whether he really is the arsonist. If he is, you'll have to report him.'

'Are you serious?'

For a moment they don't know who they're staring at.

'You've never seen him, the possible arsonist,' Alphonse protests. 'He doesn't need a cell, he's been punished enough.'

'No one forced him to drink.'

'No. And no one forces war victims to flee. In what sense would it help him or anyone to lock him up?'

'He's sure to get out early. Mitigating circumstances.'

'Maybe he can make a new start now. Do some good.'

'He's killed someone, Alphonse. Someone has been burnt alive.'

'If it was him! And if he was intending to kill the man. Maybe the victim was somebody else after all. I'll have to ring my client,' he says. 'I only met him a couple of times. Maybe I'm just imagining it.'

He knows he's not imagining it, and he immediately hears confirmation in Marco's tone of voice. 'Funny, I was expecting you to call.'

'That fire. Is the victim the priest you were talking about?'

'Yep.'

He can hear a cock crowing in Marco's background.

'And do you think ...?'

'We're not going to say that. I haven't heard him yet, but I'm standing here watching him through the guest room window. He's cooking herring on the barbecue. He looks good. Sober. I hope he's not in for delirium tremens.'

He himself would be drinking if he'd killed a man last

night. 'What are you going to do?'

'I'm going to eat fish. Sure does stink, herring.'

'This is difficult.'

Marco sniffs. 'Believe me, there's nothing difficult about it. It isn't just his own revenge. Before him there was someone like him, and after him, and before that and after that. All with impunity. If you're hungry, you know where to find us.'

He's not hungry. He's unfamiliar with this uncertainty. It's not up to me, he tells himself, but the mantra acquires two meanings that swap places. A few centimetres in front of his face a film is projected over and over of a burning old man stumbling toward a burning door, sinking to the floor just before reaching it and thrashing as he roars his way to his end. The film alternates with images of a thin, naked boy who would roar too if his lips weren't being pressed to the floor tiles by a hairy hand until they bleed like his anus. What use is a prison to that beautiful child, whether or not possessed by Pan? No. Alphonse has made his decision, Gewijde will be spared. It was his right. It wasn't his right. Through the head of the burning old man, once more on his way to the burning door, flashes an image of a boy with his bleeding mouth against the floor tiles and that boy is himself, seventy years earlier, his thrashing death throes lasting even longer than the previous time. And the thin boy glides past him, growing older, collapsing time and again, no longer beautiful, shuffling in a square along shower walls, awaited in each corner by tattooed paunches, his lips already bleeding.

It's not up to me, I don't know anything, Alphonse tries to ease himself out of the noose, I'll let that age-old curse pass me by. He'll wait for the details of the investigation. It'll turn out that the unknown arsonist thought the victim was out of the house. The victim first took himself to a place of safety before, consumed by his own guilt, deliberately going back inside to a willing death. It wasn't Gewijde. He never goes anywhere. And if it was, he'd better fry fish. He opts for the one who is still alive. And you don't snitch, that's an important rule. So.

So.

They don't talk about it as they walk hand in hand through Rijsel. On most of their visits to the town their trail has led automatically, as it does now, to a particular hat shop and, just as on previous occasions, Alphonse goes in to buy a new one, which differs only in detail from the previous model. Working in the small space, cut neatly out of the 1950s, are four members of the same family who already know them, and they know that Cat, after trying many on, will leave without a hat. She wants one, she says, but she doesn't yet dare. He wonders how this strange fear of hats took hold of the world. For a long time everybody wore one. A hat was removed only to wave at a biplane taking off. Since he was twenty-five he's rarely been out of doors without a hat, if you disregard appointments for work. People speak to him about it, longing for times they've never known. White men in particular compliment him on it, often in English, and they do so again each time they meet.

They soon turn for home, since they've left Björn there on his own and the resultant feelings of guilt keep taking over their conversations. On the way back, however, they call in on Duran, who is happy to see Alphonse and greets Cat with curiosity.

'Do you still carve those little ice men?' she asks. It's meant as an overture but it makes Duran blush with unease. He peers at the two occupied tables, where no one is listening. Then he turns up the volume on the stereo and leans over toward them. 'I really do prefer to keep that separate,' he says. 'I want to show you something in a while.'

They eat their shawarmas sitting across from each other at a small table near the door. Duran cleans the hotplate with oil.

'When are you thinking of going to the police?' asks Cat.

'I'll wait till there's more news.'

She looks at him, but leaves it at that.

The sisters or girlfriends at one table deposit their rubbish in Duran's bin and walk outside, soon followed by the quiet couple at the other.

'No,' says Duran. 'No little men. Something else.' Something he's proud of, it would seem.

Alphonse bangs his fist down on the table. 'Show!'

'Not here. I've had to buy a bigger freezer for it. Tax-deductible, fortunately. It's in the garage, we can go that way.' He points to a door marked PRIVATE. 'But I'll go first. I'll shout "ready!" and then you can come. If there are any new customers, just tell them I've gone to the toilet.'

'Won't that look a bit strange?' Cat laughs. 'We say you've gone to the toilet and then you shout "ready!"?'

'That's not good,' Duran agrees. 'If I hear a new customer, I'll simply come back.' After running his watchful eyes across the hotplate and the revolving pillars of meat, he hurries away.

Alphonse and Cat stand waiting for him to call, intrigued. On television is a Turkish crime series, something with wolves in the title.

'Ready!' Duran calls after a while. 'Don't be shocked.'

They run over to him like children, close together, with a light tread.

What it's supposed to be is not immediately clear. Standing there like that, Duran, with his back to them, looks like an enormous ice fungus. Under the ice he is naked. When he solemnly turns to face them, they see he's a Samurai-style warrior, sword at the ready. It's all been executed with fanatical care. Swallows and flowers have been carved into the thin, transparent ice. Where there's no ice there are goosebumps. He can barely move. The most defenceless warrior imaginable.

'Wow!' Cat applauds.

'Thanks. The nudity was unavoidable. Sorry.'

'Yes, definitely unavoidable!' she laughs with him.

'How did you get all that done so quickly?' asks Alphonse. 'Were you already working on it when I was last here?'

'On paper, yes.' Duran's teeth are chattering slightly. 'But when you said what you said, I began. Every moment I wasn't in the shop, I was at work in my garage. It's still not completely finished.'

'So what did he say?' Cat asks. She turns toward Alphonse.

'I can't remember now,' he says, to Duran.

'That in Japan I saw the most beautiful in existence and that I'd made a contribution, and that I must go on with it, because it's something I can do.' He's embarrassed at having to repeat the words, and Alphonse is embarrassed to hear them. Is that really what he said? Cat tickles his neck.

'Now I'm going to have to take it off again,' Duran speaks quickly and urgently. 'Or it'll melt.'

After he's removed the helmet, they help him out of the wide armour. He takes care of the hakama of ice.

Some places on his young, slim body are fiery-red. He quickly pulls on a pair of underpants with a Union Jack pattern. Then he puts everything back in the freezer.

'Are you planning on making more?'

Duran dries his shoulders with a towel and nods mysteriously. 'An army, is the idea. I just need to find storage space, and extras. So ... '

'Oh,' says Alphonse, in response to a roguish look. 'I don't know if that's something for me.'

'In winter he wears two tracksuits under his clothes,' says Cat.

'I'll think about it, okay?'

They drive some distance on a dual carriageway, Cat at the wheel, past an area of light industry and a district where the neighbours have copied each other's solar panels. In front of them a jeep makes vanishing tyre tracks through the rain. On the cover over the spare wheel it says DAKAR.

Cat is about to say something about that when his phone rings. It's Madeleine Claeys.

'Please don't take this the wrong way, but those skirting boards in the room upstairs have come loose again already.'

She's done it herself. She's ruined his work so that he'll come back. 'How is that possible?' he asks.

'I suddenly hear "pang!" and I go and look and all the skirting boards in the room you painted have come loose from the walls.'

'Pang?' He bites his lower lip. Cat continues to stare resignedly at the road.

'Yes,' says Madeleine, slightly bashful.

'I'll come right now.'

'Oh! Thanks.'

He hangs up.

'I'm not saying anything,' says Cat. 'Show me the way.'

'Strange, isn't it?' Madeleine moves her increased weight from one leg to the other. On his knees, Alphonse uses short nails to fix the boards that have been tugged loose. At places where Madeleine has wrenched them from the wall they're slightly damaged.

'Wouldn't your wife like to come in for a moment?' Madeleine asks between two hammering sessions, peeping out through the blinds at the car in front of the house.

'She wanted to read a book in the car. She reads a lot.'

'How did you two get to know each other?'

There's that question again. One that Cat and he are often asked. Sometimes a sly smile comes with it, the external sign of a suspicion that some kind of deal must lie behind their partnership or, if need be, some kind of perversion.

'The usual,' he lies. 'Dancing.' He hammers a nail into the hard wood, leaves no pause before the next, nor the one after that.

'When will you be able to come back for the rest of the house?' she asks, when he stands up.

'I could come on Monday. A bit of time has come free.'

The news pleases her exceedingly. Her fists actually make a jubilant gesture.

'Has your brother shown himself at all?'

She shakes her head. 'But when I'm here alone for a long time, I constantly expect him.'

'When are we moving?' Cat asks. Björn leaps exuberantly through the living room and up against them. He's been delirious with joy for half an hour because they haven't disappeared from the face of the earth, as he'd started to believe with rising desperation.

Alphonse kisses Cat, pats the dog, and goes upstairs.

Because his kiss was not an answer, the kora multiplies the question. When does he want to move house and where to? How should they approach the adoption? How long will they have to wait for a child? Will they be good parents? Will he continue to restore interiors? What about his clients? The refugees? Does he want to make music with other people again? Does he miss the audience? And what about the man who was burnt to death? The kora sends the questions out across the mown fields. They hang beneath the heavy clouds and slowly drift along with them. Then he's alone with the instrument. There's no one in the room, there is no room. The strings run through his fingers, through his veins, beneath his skull. The music saturates him, sucks air into his lungs, every capillary, every cell vibrates with it, everything answers: it's good the way it is.

1

Cat's lips purse every time he touches them with his own, but the rest of her face is still held in a deep sleep. He sits up, strokes her hair, and sets his feet down next to the bed, a development that activates Björn. While he showers and makes coffee the animal is impossible to calm, so he takes him out for a walk even before he's finished his first cup.

Halfway along the street he meets the woman he generally sees only as a fragment, cut off by a curtain. She's attacking the weeds between the paving stones outside her house with a potato knife. When she notices him and the dog approaching, she gets to her feet to collect the grubbed-up plant matter in a bucket. They greet each other.

'How's your family in Congo?' she asks. 'It's quite something there now, with that disease.'

'My mother and sister live in Senegal.' How could anyone think he was Congolese?

Nitpicker, he can see her thinking. 'But they're still healthy, anyhow?'

'Yes. Thank you.'

'That's the main thing.'

He nods. Björn tugs at the lead.

'And that it stays there, of course, the virus. That above all.'

'The dog wants to walk,' he says. 'A good day to you.'

The argument she was hoping to have dissolves in the air between her parted lips. 'Same to you,' she snarls at his back.

Cat, hair wet and wearing a bathrobe, is sitting on the kitchen counter reading the paper, sipping at a cup of coffee. 'Hi, beautiful man,' she says. Under her eyelashes, desire dances.

He gives Björn a biscuit, pats him, washes his hands, feels her mound of Venus press against his buttocks, something she often does, but which now excites him inordinately. He doesn't know why the excitement leads him back to his first orgasms.

'Right at the beginning, when I played with my willie I didn't think about girls but about cycle races and so forth,' he tells her, uninvited, still with his back to her, 'and when I ejaculated I won.'

'And you tell me this now?' she laughs. 'After all these years?'

'I haven't thought about it for a long time,' he chuckles.

Again she pushes her hips forward while pulling his toward her, biting the vertebra at the base of his neck.

'Sometimes I'd like to be able to switch sex organs for a while,' she says. 'And back again, mind you; it's not envy, or dissatisfaction.'

Near what must be the marks of her teeth, the sun begins to shine. Its rays stretch to his toes.

'Or that each of us had both,' he says, close to her cheerful smile; he's turned round to face her. 'If we wanted to.'

'Yes,' she says. Then they fall silent, they feel, stroke, and grope, they ignore Björn, they sweat, jolt, and hold, familiar and necessary as ever, and always new. Then they pant, and they don't say how lucky they are, because they know that.

Although she'd love to go with him, in the end she opts, grouching, for the more immediate obligation, the translation of the dust-buster instructions.

Every product he buys for his own kitchen cupboards, he gets in triplicate for the trench dwellers. At the check-out he piles them high on the conveyor belt. The cashier nods at him, recognizing him from the stunt with the hidden camera. Her older colleague and the depressive boy aren't there any longer, so they must have been actors.

A bottle of olive oil slips out from between two packets of spirelli and smashes on the floor. Coarse shards of glass stick up like shipwrecks above a spreading yellow sea.

'Sorry,' he says. 'I shouldn't have piled my shopping so high.'

'No problem,' says the cashier. Into her microphone she requests reinforcements, which are provided almost immediately in the form of a small, older employee in a green apron. He kneels down next to his bucket with a floor cloth and starts fishing shards out of the oil puddle with his bare hands and collecting them on a piece of cardboard.

'I'm sorry,' says Alphonse. 'I can clear it up myself.'

'Don't worry,' says the man.

'It was my own fault,' he says.

'It can happen to the best of us,' answers the man, who, he now sees, is the spitting image of the painted fool in the museum in Cassel, although the latter was wearing a cap with donkey's ears. How can it be that this supermarket man, like the fool on the canvas, is now looking at him through wide-open fingers, his infectious smile trained on him, if only for a second? Is it a conscious reference? But that face. Slowly and precisely the man picks up more pieces, attention turned to his work again.

'Sir?' The cashier doesn't know where to put a can of peeled tomatoes. He quickly makes space. He loads the shopping for the refugees into a large cardboard box, his own into plastic bags, and pushes it all in a trolley to his van.

What a strange coincidence, he thinks, that fool. How often since he came to live here has the feeling come over him that he's on a voyage of discovery in a mysterious fairy tale? For a moment he's completely alone with the portrait, with the face, of which the lower part, the smile, is fading. And what slips out of the right eyelid and bobs in the iris touches him. He's caught off guard by compassion.

The barricade of farm vehicles has gone, the road is empty. He recognizes the ring of pollarded willows in close consultation, hair standing on end. He reverses into the field. As he has each time before going down, he takes off his hat. He doesn't know quite why he leaves it in the car, a kind of humility, he thinks, a kind of grief. He takes the box out of the back of the van and walks across the grass to the steps. He stops at the top.

The trench is empty, a pit scattered with charred scraps of tarpaulin, blanket, plastic. Several black shoes, the trampled remains of a sweater. Burnt wood. He puts the box down.

The Afghans and Syrians have quarrelled. The fire at which they tried to warm themselves seized its chance.

The thought of the heat makes him shiver. It's cold. He coughs into his hand.

No. They didn't do this themselves.

He picks up the box again and carries it back to the van. Then he retraces his steps, goes down into the trench, wanders about in the rubbish searching for an explanation, a clue, and clambers out again. Peering through the thin trees along the edge of the unsealed track, he walks back to the main road. It's still empty. He hears wind and delirious birdsong, recognizes it and looks up.

The skylark falls at great speed out of the sky, smashing to the ground at his feet. He sees it happen, the consequences for the bird, the broken legs and wings, the snapped neck, the splashes of blood. The impact made the body move, the breeze ruffles the brown feathers. Inside them the bird ceases thrumming.

Alphonse takes a step back, feels the shock pass through his limbs, a magnetically charged bullet of airless fear that understands more than he does.

The van is too far away, he ought to have driven it here. Walking back he looks again at the thin trees and now he sees the men standing between them. To judge by their build they are men—four, or five—five. They've been waiting for him to notice them. They walk toward him and each of their paces covers three paces at the same time. They have rusty metal objects in their hands, cudgels, bent bars, sharpened rods. Woollen hats and gloves conceal their skin colour, their hair.

'Do you speak Dutch?' he asks. '*Parlez-vous Français?*' He'll repeat it in every language. He'll flee. With every step bringing him nearer the van, the figures get much closer. He must hold his hands between his legs, so they can't hit them, better his face than his hands. He needs them for the strings, for Cat's skin, to smooth wallpaper. The fear has got into his sweat. That he stinks of it makes him furious, and with that fury the fear disappears. He'll fight.

He grabs the first rod that swings in his direction and uses the force of the blow to floor the attacker.

'Do you speak English? *Habla español?*' He's shouting now. Someone hits him on the shins. He manages to punch a jaw. He frees his arm from a hold and feels a blow to the back of his head, immediately followed by another that closes his left eye. Then, as he lies on the ground where the county road begins, there's an orgy of feet and raw metal on all parts of his body, a pain unable to match the rage that's taken possession of him. There remains a rhythmic hitting, a bare fist, a dull more, more, more.

'*Požar!*' he shouts. '*Fotyá!*' They're hitting his face again. His tongue. He feels something snap in the neck so recently kissed. Cat! They've finished with him, that's how easily it goes. 'Next spring the daffodils will shoot up out of this soil again!' he'd shout after them if he could. 'Agile men will build houses, walls will shine, not everything can be ruined. Just you try putting out the stars, you puny little men!' His fury runs after the attackers, longs for a weapon—one, two, three, four, five bullets—and leaves him in despair on the hard road. 'Nothing doesn't exist!' The sentence echoes in his head. 'Nor does nowhere!' Perhaps nothing and nowhere are standing impatiently waiting for his gargled breathing to stop. In the distance he hears a car drive off, tyres squealing. He wants only to curse now, curse as has been cursed so often in this place, in this country, on this planet. He wants the mud country that cuts off his breath at every horizon to stand up for him, wants all those who ended here before their time to stir.

Mother. Again a car, a different one, coming from a different direction—he can only listen, can't turn his head. He hears the door slam, then a voice that sounds familiar, a woman: 'No! Oh no! Is that you?' Footfall, knees.

The author is kneeling beside him, her eyes piss-holes in snow. The horror in them. Trembling, her hands hover over his wounds. The question of whether he can stand up is apparently not appropriate. His body is a pool of pain, he can't distinguish his limbs in it, doesn't know which direction they're pointing. He wants to make sure he can hear her. But his tongue. He hears himself moaning, far more quietly than he wants to, feels blood flowing out past the corners of his mouth. His head has filled with it.

Then the author takes over the cursing from him. She curses as has been cursed so often to no avail in this place, in this country, on this planet. She uses words he wouldn't expect from her and fires them between the thin branches, hurls them against the trunks of the weeping willows, skims them across the grass, making all she has left explode in the sky.

The sky! He stares at it through the eye he has left, which stings. A small white cloud has drifted away from the herd. Now it's approaching, surrounded by blue, to slide over him. It's almost here.

Flatly the author answers the questions from the emergency services she's summoned. Then a convulsive sobbing bends her downward, still on her knees, and a long cry joins it, as if she's being wrung out. She has no idea how to deal with this.

Nor does he. But he doesn't have much time. He can think just a couple more things and the first thing he thinks is that he must hold on to that thought as long as possible. They want to fight with you because they don't know how to dance with you, he thinks as hard as he can. The thought coolly evaporates. Some people never get any better than the God that Job hit out against. This too seems inadequate. There is music, it's as if he can hear 'Águas de Março', a distorted version, a thorn, a fish, the end of the road, a body in bed, a little alone. Now, while he still can, he misses the living: mother, Cat, Aline. The voice his sister heard. Amadou, he'd be coming tonight. He already misses his life, being alive—so much, so much he's loved it—and soon that sense of loss, sharp as knives and glowing, will be transferred to others. Even Fabrice announces himself. Alphonse has just one sentence for him: we could have been friends, you idiot. But oh, the scent of Cat. There are thick throngs of people suddenly, he recognizes all of them, his uncle, his exes, his classmates, the musicians he played with, his clients, they're all here. They visit cities they don't know in gleaming cars, after long plane journeys; they run through woods and over dunes and into waves, slip between fresh sheets in search of skin, admire the interiors of each other's houses. The dog called Björn wags his tail as he's stroked. There's more music—of course there's music! He remembers chords, slaps the strings of his bass, feels the calabash of his kora vibrate in his lap. And then there's a very old memory, older even than the one with the man who sold a pelican. He sees the furrows beside his mother's armpit; folded together like that they seem darker than the rest of her skin. He looks at them from her breast, he's six months old, a baby, and she's feeding him. No one can remember this, but now he has access to it. Of all the planets, this must be the richest, he's convinced of that, always more and more and more to be found here.

The cloud has arrived, the silence too. He becomes it, becomes the cloud that has slid over him. How dear to him is the man down there. So dear and so very much too small. How he loves that little body. But he has to look around, too, look one more time at the branches of trees, from the trunk out of the ground into the air, the living birds alongside. See one more time how beautiful it is here. How beautiful it is here now. And then he's gone.

Acknowledgements

Contributions by many people and organizations were essential to me in writing this book. My thanks to all of them, including Ad van den Kieboom and Sander van Vlerken of publishing house De Geus for their editing and their enthusiasm, and Lieven Keymolen, Laurence Van Elegem, David Van Reybrouck, Antje Van Wichelen, and Peter Vermeersch, for reading the manuscript and for their support and comments.

I don't live in the Westhoek or in French Flanders, and aside from a great grandfather who emigrated my origins do not lie there, so I could only grow to love this border area as an outsider. The writing commissions I was given for the project 300jaargrens.eu | 300ansdefrontière.eu were a major contribution in that sense. I would like to thank all the partners in that initiative, the Département du Nord and the Province of West Flanders, and above all Bart Castelein of non-profit organization De Boot and Kristien Hemmerechts, who linked me up with the project.

Then there are the many French Flemings and residents of the Westhoek who, consciously or unconsciously, told me their stories, especially Piet Hardeman, Jeff Markey, and Pieter Verheyde. Every story used here has been fictionalized.

Emmy Deschuttere of Médicins du Monde / Dokters van de Wereld in Brussels and Cécile Bossy, coordinator for Médicins du Monde, Nord-Littoral, in Dunkirk enabled me to spend two days with Médicins du Monde as a volunteer, visiting the improvised refugee camps of northern France along with them. I would like to thank the many refugees who talked with me and wish them all the luck in the world, wherever they are now.

For the passages about the *tirailleurs sénégalais* I drew upon *De zwarte schande. Afrikaanse soldaten in Europa 1914–1922* by Dick van Galen Last (Atlas Contact, 2012) and *Wereldoorlog I. Vijf continenten in Vlaanderen*, compiled by Dominiek Dendooven and Piet Chielens (Lannoo, 2008).

The biblical quotation is from Job 13:15–16. For this English-language edition, use has been made of the International Standard Version.

The quotation from Henry Miller is from his *Remember to Remember*, Volume II of *The Air-Conditioned Nightmare*, first published in 1947 by New Directions, Norfolk, Conn.

My short story 'The Dietician and the Plasterer' was first published (in Dutch) in July 2013 in the magazine *Humo*.

I am grateful to A.S. for his stories and his hospitality.

Above all I want to thank Alou Ka, for his help with this book and for what he has taught me. *Mbe de yid ma. Dama la bëgg.*

On the Design

As book design is an integral part of the reading experience, we would like to acknowledge the work of those who shaped the form in which the story is housed.

Tessa van der Waals (Netherlands) is responsible for the cover design, cover typography and art direction of all World Editions books. She works in the internationally renowned tradition of Dutch Design. Her bright and powerful visual aesthetic maintains a harmony between image and typography and captures the unique atmosphere of each book. She works closely with internationally celebrated photographers, artists, and letter designers. Her work has frequently been awarded prizes for Best Dutch Book Design.

Tomas Adel is a Berlin-based photographer of architecture, food, nature, and people. He took this image while on holiday with a group of fathers and their children in southern Poland, on a wonderful windy summer's day with clear blue skies and many story-telling clouds. This particular cloud suggests the shape of a question mark.

The cover has been edited by lithographer Bert van der Horst of BFC Graphics (Netherlands).

Suzan Beijer (Netherlands) is responsible for the typography and careful interior book design of all World Editions titles.

The text on the inside covers and the press quotes are set in Circular, designed by Laurenz Brunner (Switzerland) and published by Swiss type foundry Lineto.

All World Editions books are set in the typeface Dolly, specifically designed for book typography. Dolly creates a warm page image perfect for an enjoyable reading experience. This typeface is designed by Underware, a European collective formed by Bas Jacobs (Netherlands), Akiem Helmling (Germany), and Sami Kortemäki (Finland). Underware are also the creators of the World Editions logo, which meets the design requirement that 'a strong shape can always be drawn with a toe in the sand.'